LAST TO FALL

Books by Lynn H. Blackburn

Dive Team Investigations

Beneath the Surface

In Too Deep

One Final Breath

Defend and Protect

Unknown Threat

Malicious Intent

Under Fire

Gossamer Falls

Never Fall Again

Break My Fall

Last to Fall

Novellas

Deadly Objective

Downfall

GOSSAMER FALLS · 3

LAST TO FALL

LYNN H. BLACKBURN

a division of Baker Publishing Group
Grand Rapids, Michigan

Published by Revell
a division of Baker Publishing Group
Grand Rapids, Michigan
RevellBooks.com

Printed in the United States of America

Library of Congress Cataloging-in-Publication Data
Names: Blackburn, Lynn Huggins author
Title: Last to fall / Lynn H. Blackburn.
Description: Grand Rapids, Michigan : Revell, a division of Baker Publishing Group, 2026. | Series: Gossamer Falls ; 3
Identifiers: LCCN 2025034335 | ISBN 9780800745387 paperback | ISBN 9780800747817 casebound | ISBN 9781493452644 ebook
Subjects: LCGFT: Romance fiction | Thrillers (Fiction) | Christian fiction | Novels | Fiction
Classification: LCC PS3602.L325285 L37 2026
LC record available at https://lccn.loc.gov/2025034335

This book is a work of fiction. Names, characters, places, and incidents are the product of the author's imagination or are used fictitiously. Any resemblance to actual events, locales, or persons, living or dead, is coincidental.

Cover design by Laura Klynstra

Baker Publishing Group publications use paper produced from sustainable forestry practices and postconsumer waste whenever possible.

26 27 28 29 30 31 32 7 6 5 4 3 2 1

In memory of Donald and Juanita Phipps,
the grandparents I gained at nineteen, when I met my
husband and was immediately "adopted" into their family.
They set the standard for how to love well.
I can only pray to be like them when I grow up.

ONE

PRESENT DAY

Whoever said blood was thicker than water hadn't known about the Pierce family.

Bronwyn Pierce could think of several people she could trust more than her own family, and one of them despised her.

But he was the one she needed now.

He would come. She knew it in a place deep in her core. Despite the pain they'd inflicted on each other for the past seventeen years, he would come.

"This is so messed up." She muttered the words into the silence of her office, then clamped her mouth shut.

For all she knew, someone was listening.

She propped up her elbows on her desk and rested her face in her hands. Her head ached. Her heart was . . . numb. It had been bruised and beaten so often in her almost thirty-four years that even the magnitude of this current betrayal barely registered.

The light tap on her office door jolted her from her musing, and she barely stopped the scream that threatened to erupt from her throat. Who was wandering around The Haven at three in the morning?

She slid open the middle drawer of her desk and rested her left hand on the small gun she kept there. And wasn't that just a kick in the pants? She was the CEO of an exclusive resort. She prided herself on how the staff protected the celebrities, politicians, and uber-wealthy visitors who rested in blissful slumber in the elegant cabins that dotted the property. They knew no paparazzi would approach them and no one would harm them while they were here.

But she couldn't expect the same level of security for herself.

She gripped the gun.

"Ms. Pierce? Are you in there?" The deep voice of Randall, one of the night watchmen, filtered through the thick door.

"Yes. Come in."

He eased the door open and took one step inside. "Ms. Pierce, are you okay?"

She understood the confusion on his face. She put in well over sixty hours a week, sometimes closer to eighty, but even she didn't make a habit of being in her office in the middle of the night.

"I'm fine. Thank you." She didn't owe him an explanation, but she gave one anyway. Or part of it. "I thought of something that needed to be done on this computer."

It was no secret that The Haven computer network carried some of the most advanced security available and that some information couldn't be accessed from remote locations. Not even by her.

"Gotcha." Randall's tense smile sent a chill skittering across her skin. "I guess it's in the air tonight. Mr. Pierce is in his office as well."

The chill turned into an arctic blast. "Which Mr. Pierce?"

"Nathan."

"I see."

Randall regarded her with an expression she couldn't decipher. Was it concern? Distrust?

"If it's all the same to you, ma'am, I'm going to stay in this area for a bit. I'd appreciate it if you'd allow me to escort you back to your home when you're done here."

And that didn't sound ominous. Not at all.

Did he want to see her safely back to her home? Or did he want to take the opportunity to . . . what? What would he do? Surely the situation hadn't devolved to the point where physical violence was on the table.

Her home was tucked away in an unobtrusive corner of The Haven property. Out of sight of the guests and staff, and off-limits to all, but close enough for her to be available in case of emergencies. She'd always appreciated her own private haven at The Haven. But if Randall meant her harm, how long would it be before anyone found her?

She gave herself a mental shake. Randall was good people. He was looking out for her. Nothing more. She hoped.

"Sure. I'll probably be another ten minutes. I need to send a few emails."

Randall lowered his head. "In that case, I'll wait outside."

With that, he stepped back and closed the door.

Now what?

Her cousin Nathan was in his office on the other side of the property doing who knew what at 3:00 a.m. Probably plotting world domination. Or her painful death. Or both.

After she'd run away at sixteen, Nathan became the heir apparent to their family's business. He was the golden child. The future of the family. And then he managed to get himself sideways with a guest and had to hide out in Europe for a while.

While his life was spiraling out of control, Bronwyn's had come together. She finished her degree, worked in the industry in several resorts around the world, and returned to Gossamer Falls, determined to atone for her sins.

Neither she nor Nathan had expected the CEO position to ever be hers, but it was now, and she had no plans to let it go.

Her extended family had never been tight-knit. She'd grown up with competition as the name of the game. She didn't know exactly when it started, but over the past few years, the Pierces had somehow fractured into separate, warring factions. There was no trust. No love. No sense of togetherness.

Lord, how did we get here? And how do I get out of this mess?

She didn't know the answer to the first question, but she knew the answer to the second. Or, at least, she knew the first step on the path.

She twisted back to her computer and typed out an email.

With shaking fingers, she hit send, gathered her things, including her weapon, and walked out to meet Randall.

Even after close to two decades of hostility, she knew that while the one person she needed right now wouldn't speak *to* her, he *would* keep her secrets and do everything he could to keep her safe.

And there was no turning back now. She'd placed the charges and lit the fuse. Her walls were coming down. She had to trust that he'd stand with her when the last one fell.

TWO

TWENTY-EIGHT YEARS EARLIER

"Come inside and find your seats."

Mo listened to the teacher, Mrs. Delaney, and was pleased to see that his seat was beside his sister's. His cousin, Cal, was one row ahead of him.

The noise level grew and then quieted as everyone settled into their assigned spots.

Meredith tapped his desk, and he turned toward her. She widened her eyes and looked at the door.

Mrs. Delaney had stepped outside the classroom but kept the door open. From his seat, Mo could see her and the principal, and he could hear other voices too. When a small girl peeked around the edge of the door and into the classroom, Mo caught her eye and smiled.

She returned the smile and then her gaze flicked around the room.

"You must understand," the principal said, "we have a small school, and this is the only kindergarten class." She pointed to the little girl in the doorway. "If Bronwyn is to attend school here, this is where she'll be."

The voice that spoke next was deep and loud enough that Mo heard part of what was said. "We understand, however . . . expect you to try . . . won't tolerate . . ."

The conversation continued for another minute and then the girl, Bronwyn, was ushered into the room by Mrs. Delaney. The adults who followed—Mo assumed they were her parents—barely said anything, but they glared at Cal. And then at Meredith.

And finally, the mom looked at him.

She glanced down at the name on his desk, then turned to Mrs. Delaney. "Just keep her away from the Quinns."

Mrs. Delaney's mouth got all pinched up, and she said, "My students will be expected to interact with all of their classmates, Mrs. Pierce."

Oh.

Cal turned around in his seat, and the three of them shared a look.

This girl was a *Pierce*.

Mr. and Mrs. Pierce left the room moments later. Mrs. Delaney blew out a breath and closed the door to the classroom. When she turned back to face her students, she had a big smile on her face.

"Okay, everyone! We're going to have a great day. Let's start by getting to know each other. Tell us your name, your birthday, something you did this summer, and then a few of your favorite things."

Mo knew most of his classmates from church and T-ball. He already knew their names and what they'd done this summer. But when Bronwyn introduced herself, he listened.

"Hi. My name is Bronwyn Pierce. My birthday is in October. I went to California this summer, but I didn't get to go to the beach. My favorite color is blue, and my favorite food is shrimp tacos."

A few kids laughed at that. Shrimp tacos? Mo had never had

anything but ground beef on a taco. He liked shrimp though. Maybe it would be good?

Bronwyn froze for a moment before she finished in a rush. "I like to swing and ride my bike, and I think I would like camping, but I've never been."

She sat down, and from Mo's seat behind her, it looked like she was breathing heavily. Cal leaned over to her and whispered, "Good job."

She gave him a weak smile.

Mo spoke up. "Camping is fun. You'd definitely like it."

Bronwyn turned around in her seat and grinned at him. "You think so?"

"I do."

"Do you go camping a lot?"

"No. But we camped by a waterfall in June and roasted marshmallows and hot dogs over a fire."

"Really?" Bronwyn's eyes shone. "That sounds amazing."

Mrs. Delaney cleared her throat, but not the way adults did when they were mad. "Thank you, Bronwyn."

Mrs. Delaney wiped her eye and called on the next student. Mo decided that she looked happy about something, which was weird since she also looked like she was trying not to cry.

Adults made no sense. He didn't think he would like to be one. But he had a long time before he had to worry about that.

THREE

PRESENT DAY

Mo looked up from his computer and glared at the door to his home. "Go away!"

Cal knocked again.

"I said go away."

"You're going to change your tune when I tell you why I'm here." Cal's voice held a challenge.

"Don't hold your breath."

"Are you going to let me in?"

"Let yourself in." Mo went back to work.

The beeping on the keypad told him that Cal messed up the first time he entered the door code but got it on the second.

Mo didn't look up from his screen as Cal entered. "You'd better have a good reason for showing up at five thirty on a Monday morning."

"Why do you care what time it is?" Cal closed the door behind him, then leaned against it.

Mo's tiny house didn't leave much room for guests. Just the way he liked it.

"It's indecent to show up—unannounced, I might add—before eight a.m. on any day of the week. It's obscene on a Monday."

"Says who?" Cal asked.

"Says everybody."

Cal grunted but didn't say anything else.

Mo ignored him and continued to type the report he'd been working on since four. When he finished his thoughts, he hit save and swiveled to face his cousin. "Why are you here?"

"I got an email from Bronwyn this morning."

A pall of tension settled into the small space. Mo fought to keep his voice flat. "Okay."

"Seems she's in need of assistance."

"And that has what to do with me?"

"Everything."

"Explain."

Cal pulled his phone from his pocket and handed it to Mo. "Read it for yourself."

Mo took the phone. The email had been sent from an account that probably would have been caught in a spam filter, except he could tell that Cal had received messages from it before. "What email is this?"

"She uses it when she wants to be sure no one is reading over her shoulder."

Metaphorically or literally? Probably both.

She'd sent the email at 3:15 a.m.

Cal had opened it around five.

Mo looked up. "Why were you awake so early?"

"Landry woke up. The baby is making it hard for her to sleep."

"I hear they do even more of that after they're born. I bet I'll be able to hear her crying from here." Mo's tiny house was only a few hundred yards from the home Cal and Landry shared.

"Quit stalling and read the email."

He took a deep breath although he wasn't sure why. It wasn't like sitting on his rear end and reading an email was physically taxing.

But for some reason, he had to take another deep breath before he focused on the screen.

Cal,

Things aren't good, and I need help. The kind of help that, oh, say, a super trustworthy forensic accountant could provide. If he should be available . . . and willing.

Could you determine the availability and willingness of someone like that?

I'm sorry to put you in the middle again, and I'm sorry to ask for his help, but I genuinely don't know where else to go. If he could give me just a little bit of time and tell me if I'm seeing things, or if it's a real issue, then I'd be happy to hire someone he recommends to finish the job.

I'm planning to swing by your office around 9:00 a.m.

Beep

Mo read it again. Then a third time. Then he forwarded it to his personal email and handed the phone to Cal.

Cal slid the phone into his back pocket. "So, I guess I'll see you at nine, then."

Mo didn't respond immediately. Would he go?

Bronwyn had frozen him out years earlier, and he deserved it. He'd been ready to leave the past behind them and move on for a while. Clearly she wasn't.

But she'd come to him.

Sort of.

"I'll think about it."

Cal opened the door and walked outside. "You're both being idiots."

"What's new?" Mo asked the empty space.

Cal stuck his head back in. "For starters? She asked for your help. That's new."

At 8:55 a.m. Mo walked into Cal's office at SPQ Construction. "Morning, Carla."

Carla Shaw was technically his cousin-in-law, but she was practically the big sister he'd never had and was one of his favorite people.

Carla came around the reception desk. "I'm so glad you're here."

He opened his arms, and she walked into them.

"I've been needing a Mo hug." She squeezed him close before she stepped back. She tilted her head toward the back of the office. "She's already here."

He'd seen Bronwyn's car in the parking lot, but he appreciated the warning. "Thanks."

Carla rose on her tiptoes and pressed a kiss to Mo's cheek. "I have faith that you two will sort yourselves out."

"From your lips to God's ears." The phrase was a common one, but Mo meant every word. He'd been praying all morning, but he would take all the help he could get. So far, all he was sure God was telling him was to show up today. After that? God hadn't seen fit to enlighten him.

Carla patted his arm, and he walked to Cal's office. The door was open. Cal stood at the window. Bronwyn sat at the table Cal used when he needed to go over architectural drawings with clients. Her long dark hair fell halfway down her back in waves of almost black with a hint of red that he knew wasn't natural. The cut was slightly different from the last time he'd seen her, but he liked the new look. It highlighted her sharp cheekbones.

Her dark brown eyes were in sharp contrast to his sister Meredith's bright blue. Meredith sat beside Bronwyn and looked up when Mo entered. "'Bout time you got here."

He glanced at his watch. "I'm early."

"On time is late for you."

Mo ignored that remark. "What are you doing here?"

Meredith shrugged. "Cal called me."

Bronwyn turned a ferocious glare on Cal. "I'm not sure why."

Cal gave her a beatific smile. "Because we're a team. You're in trouble. We're going to help you. End of discussion."

Bronwyn fumed. "Mer's soon-to-be husband is the police chief. Did it not occur to you that perhaps I didn't loop her in for a reason?"

"Beep, we love you. Stop complaining. We're here." Cal took a seat across from her. "What's going on?"

Mo took that as his cue to join them at the table. He slid into the remaining chair and studied the intricate woodburned surface. And then he waited.

Bronwyn hadn't said a word directly to him in years, but they'd gotten pretty good at sharing the same space and participating in the same conversations. Maybe one day she'd mess up and speak to him.

Although he had a feeling that today was not that day.

Bronwyn stared at the top of the table. In her periphery, she could see Mo's hands. His long fingers were clasped together, and every few seconds he tapped his thumbs against each other.

He'd done that a lot when they were younger. It was his "ready for anything" posture.

Meredith bumped her elbow. "Bronwyn?"

How long had she been studying Mo's hands? Her face heated, and she pinched her lips together. "Sorry. I'm not sure where to start."

Cal leaned back in his seat. "Why don't you start with what made you send that email? What triggered that?"

Bronwyn slumped forward until her forehead rested on the table. "I don't know if I can do this." These three people were—or had been at one time, when including Mo—her best friends. They'd been with her through everything. Everything she'd allowed them to, anyway.

Why was this so hard?

"What if we discuss what we already know?" Mo's voice was low and gravelly. "For example, we know that Steven's arrest for drug trafficking—"

"Don't forget murder," Meredith cut in. "Oh, and kidnapping."

Bronwyn lifted her head in time to catch Mo giving his sister a look she'd seen hundreds of times. It was the "you're lucky that I love you so much because I also find you exceptionally annoying" look.

"Yes, Bronwyn's cousin's illegal and immoral actions have brought The Haven under unwanted scrutiny. What else do we know?"

Meredith chimed in again. "Some of Beep's uncles and cousins want to make The Haven a more prominent resort, possibly removing some of the safeguards that have kept it in the 'secret gem' category for so long."

"And those actions would undoubtedly have a negative impact on the residents of Gossamer Falls." Cal drummed his fingers on the table. "The whole Pierce/Quinn feud began over fears of this happening, but Bronwyn has always maintained that growing The Haven that way would be a disaster for both The Haven and the community."

How far would they make it before she had to explain anything?

Mo's low voice filled the space. "My question would be what has changed recently that caused Bronwyn to reach out? What has she seen in the files that makes her think she needs a forensic accountant? And let's not forget that she sent that email in the middle of the night, which would lead one to wonder if something specific happened yesterday or early this morning. That's the real reason we're all sitting around this table and might explain why she has goosebumps on her arms even though it's not cold in this room."

Bronwyn looked at her traitorous appendages. Sure enough, the chill she thought was metaphorical had popped out on her skin.

Meredith leaned against her arm. "Spill. We won't judge."

"I'm . . ." Bronwyn closed her eyes and fought against the moisture building there. "I've had concerns for a while, but last night, I wondered if my own security team would turn on me. The fear . . ." Her mouth went dry at the remembered panic. "I found some things that don't make sense to me in several of our accounts. I'm no slouch when it comes to accounting, but I can't find what's wrong, but something is. I know our business, inside and out. I have an innate sense of how much things cost, where the money goes, et cetera. And something isn't right, but for the life of me, I can't find it. Or why it's happening. What's the end goal? Is someone embezzling funds? That would be bad enough, but it wouldn't be the end of the world. We can find out what's going on, put a stop to it, and move on. But this doesn't look like embezzlement to me. I just can't figure out what it is."

She stopped talking and glanced at the three Quinn cousins who were more family to her than her own flesh and blood. "And you're right. The pressure to grow, expand, and ultimately make more money is intense."

"How intense?" Cal asked.

"The board is looking over my shoulder and questioning every decision. One of my uncles is getting close to the point of micro-managing a few things that he doesn't need to be worried about. You all know that I've sensed an internal movement to force me out of my position for a while. I still can't prove it, and I realize that feelings aren't facts but . . ." She trailed off and wished she'd never sent that email. It sounded so ridiculous when she said everything out loud.

Mo's voice cut through her inner chastisement. "In my experience some people ignore their feelings when they should listen to them. It's true that feelings can't be used in a court of law, but that doesn't mean they don't have value. Sometimes we know things with our feelings before our brain catches up and supplies the facts to explain them."

Bronwyn couldn't make herself look at Mo, but she wished she could throw herself at him and tell him thank you. He'd always understood her better than anyone else. Sometimes better than she understood herself. How was it possible that now, years later, he still had the words to express her emotions?

Meredith nodded in agreement. "Bronwyn has always been the most intuitive of us. I'd forgotten that. But if she's picking up on something hinky, it's there."

"I can't accuse anyone of hinky behavior, Meredith."

"No." Cal narrowed his eyes at her. "You'll need proof. And that's why you need Mo." He turned his attention to Mo. "Can you evaluate her accounts and find what's got her spooked?"

Mo nodded slowly. "The Haven's system is solid. Unless things have changed, the main computers are on a private, hardwired network."

"We've stayed at the forefront of cybersecurity. We've had to." Bronwyn tapped her phone. "We have cell phones, and they have Wi-Fi, but I'm the CEO and even I can't access our records unless I'm in my office or the accounting office. We guard our guests' privacy. Those records include extremely personal data that could, in some cases, ruin careers if they got out."

"So what you're saying is that in order for Mo to check out your system, he'd physically have to be on-site." Cal walked over to his desk and grabbed a thermos. "That might be difficult to explain."

"Not really." Meredith grinned.

"How would you do it?" Mo asked Meredith.

"Simple, really. We all pay Bronwyn a visit. She always comes to us so this time, we go to her. We hang out for a while. And maybe while we're there, she asks Cal to look at something in her office." Meredith grinned at Bronwyn. "Didn't you tell me the other day that you wanted a new desk setup and you were hoping someone would help you with that? Like, someone who does beautiful custom work? A local craftsman?"

Bronwyn hadn't expected to laugh today, but she did now. "Did I say that?" She'd never said anything of the sort.

"Well, you haven't yet. But you will before we leave today. Then we'll all traipse over there. Mo will come along because even though he's always sitting at a computer and needs to be out in the sun more, he does have some woodworking skills. Then we'll all go in your office."

"And while you're there . . ." Bronwyn could see it.

Mo held up a hand. "For the record, the kind of work I do doesn't get done in a few minutes. This isn't TV. Real-life investigations take time. Hours and hours of time."

"But does it take hours and hours to copy a hard drive?" Cal asked.

Mo narrowed his eyes. "No."

"So, we go in, and you duplicate everything on the computer and put it on something portable. You bring it back home and work on it. Problem solved." Cal brushed his nails against his shirt. "That was easy. Why didn't you think of that on your own?"

"Yeah." Meredith grinned. "All these years of supposedly being the smart one on the team and you can't come up with something so elementary. You're slipping, bro."

Mo looked at the sky. Bronwyn could almost hear him thinking, *Lord, grant me patience.*

"Would that work?" Bronwyn asked the question to the group even though she knew Mo was the only one who could answer.

"If we did that, it would still take me several days to go through it. And if I find something"—Mo glanced at Meredith—"hinky, then I would need to access more files. Eventually, I'd need to be on-site again. And I don't think I heard Bronwyn address the issue of her physical safety earlier. Did any of you? Because if she's already concerned about that, having me show up and start poking around is going to throw fuel on the fire."

Three pairs of blue Quinn eyes settled on Bronwyn.

She broke. "I'm so scared. Maybe it's all in my head, but I think someone might try to kill me."

FOUR

TWENTY-FIVE YEARS EARLIER

"Can Bronwyn come?" Eight-year-old Mo Quinn looked at his mom and did his best to be adorable.

His mom's face fell. "Sweetheart, I wish she could, but I don't know . . ."

"Her parents aren't even going to be home."

"Where will they be?"

"New York. They travel a lot."

"Yes, they do." She sounded sad. "I would have her here in a heartbeat, but . . ."

Mo was willing to beg. He wouldn't do it for just anyone, but for Bronwyn, he'd do anything. He wanted her at his birthday party. "Can we at least try?"

"I'll talk to your father."

That was the best he could hope for. "Thank you, Mama."

"You're welcome. Now go find Cal and do something outside."

"Yes, ma'am."

He tried to find his cousin. He ran over to Cal's house and knocked on the door, but no one answered. Meredith was spending the day shadowing the town dentist because she was weird that way.

He rode his bike to Papa and Granny Quinn's house. Granny and Aunt Minnie were getting ready to go into town, so one quick phone call to his mama later, he joined them.

"What's got you so down today?" Granny asked as they made the drive into town.

Mo shrugged.

"That wasn't an answer, young man."

Mo looked out the window. "I want Bronwyn to come to my birthday party."

"I see." Somehow, when Granny said that, Mo believed she really did. Granny was old but smart. And she was nice. But she didn't put up with nonsense.

"Did you send her an invitation?" Granny waved at someone as they drove by.

"Mama said we could, but she said Bronwyn's parents might not let her come."

"Your mama's smart."

"She is."

"Why do you want her to come to your party so much? Are there going to be any other girls there?"

So maybe Granny wasn't quite as smart as Mo had thought. "She's my best friend, Granny. Of course I want her there. And Meredith will be there. Besides, Bronwyn's not like other girls."

"She isn't?"

"No."

"What's different about her?"

Mo stared at Granny for a few seconds. He had to think of how to say it. "She's not annoying. Most girls are."

"I see."

Mo looked at Granny and caught a weird look on her face.

"Well, it's completely understandable why you'd want her at your party," she said. "Maybe her parents will say yes. And if not, I might have to make a phone call or two."

Three days later, Bronwyn ran up to Mo. "My mom and dad said they didn't care if I came to your party, but your mom will have to come pick me up and take me back home since they won't be home. Do you think she would?"

Mo didn't have to think about it. "Yes!"

FIVE

PRESENT DAY

Mo jumped to his feet and paced by the windows lining Cal's office. It was that or he was going to grab Bronwyn, haul her out of here fireman-style, throw her in his Jeep, and drive off with her. He might not stop until they hit Texas.

Where was Maisy when he needed her? Cal had left his golden retriever with Landry today, but Mo wished she were here now.

Meredith had her arm around Bronwyn.

Cal stood as well. He leaned on the table and gave off hurricane vibes. He was the calm center but the storm raged around him. "What exactly happened to make you think that someone's trying to kill you?"

"I don't know!" Bronwyn's breath came in fast, short gasps.

"Back off, Cal. She's going to hyperventilate." Mo's voice was strong. "Meredith, give her some space."

Meredith leaned back and rubbed Bronwyn's back in slow circles. "Breathe. I know you're scared. But you're safe here. No one will touch you."

Bronwyn wiped at her eyes, took a deep breath, and rolled her shoulders a few times. "I'm okay. Sorry. That's the first time I've said it out loud. I've barely even let myself think it."

Mo pressed his head against the window and stared toward the mountains. He saw nothing. His focus was on the words coming from behind him.

"I don't know how to explain it," Bronwyn went on. "Little things have been happening. Strange sounds, shadows. Last week, I was so sure someone was following me home that by the time I got inside and locked the door, it felt like I'd run a marathon. Then a few days ago, I went into the office early and when I walked in, I had the strangest sensation that things were out of place. Nothing I could put my finger on. I dismissed it, but then the same thing happened the next day."

"Did you figure out what was off?" Meredith asked.

"Yes."

Mo turned around at that.

"My office chair had been moved."

"Could it have been the cleaning crew?" Cal asked.

"No. They didn't come in that night. And before you ask, the reason I'm sure is because I intentionally left it in a specific spot. I did it in a way that if someone had snuck a camera in my office, they wouldn't be able to tell what I'd done. But the chair had definitely been moved."

"When was this?" Cal's question had the command of the Marine officer he'd once been. Mo had no doubt Cal's investigative mind was already preparing a strategy.

"Two nights ago."

"Why didn't you call us yesterday?"

Mo turned to watch Bronwyn respond to Meredith's question.

Bronwyn threw up her hands. "And say what, exactly? Someone moved my chair?"

"Yes!" Meredith mimicked Bronwyn's hand motions. "Because no one was supposed to be in your office."

"So what happened last night? Because it sounds to me like

you've been jumping at shadows for at least a few weeks." Cal walked in a circle around the room. "I'm not saying the shadows aren't real. I'm repeating your own words. Things have been weird. You've been stressed. But last night, the wave crested. Why?"

"I saw something I don't think I was supposed to see." Bronwyn dropped her face in her hands. "I'm not even sure it was about me, but in light of everything else, it felt personal."

Mo waited for someone to ask the obvious question, but no one spoke up. They all sat there and waited for Bronwyn to continue.

"I got a text. It was only a few words. It said, 'We might be able to take care of the problem tonight.' I didn't have the number in my contacts, and the person who sent it tried to delete it."

Cal looked confused. "What?"

"You know how you can delete a text but only if the person didn't already see it?"

"Yeah."

"Well, I had my phone in my hand. I saw it. Then I saw that the person had unsent it." She tapped the screen. "But, again, all of this could have a perfectly reasonable explanation. It might be nothing. It could be paranoia on my part. But I couldn't get it out of my head. I worked super late, and normally, I'd be there alone. But Nathan was working in his office too. Randall came by on his rounds, and at first, I thought he might be there to harm me. I really did. But when I settled down and thought about our conversation, I realized that he didn't think it was safe for me to go back to my place alone. I think he wanted to protect me from my own cousin."

First on Mo's mental checklist: Find out who Randall was and whether he was trustworthy.

"Okay. But why would you think someone in your family wanted to come after you in the first place?" Cal asked the question in a quiet voice.

"I can't explain it. I think they're watching me. I've been wondering if they might have bugged my office."

Second on Mo's mental checklist: Scan Bronwyn's office for bugs.

"Who has access to your office?" Meredith asked.

"Too many people." Bronwyn ticked them off on her fingers. "My assistant. The cleaning crew. Nathan has a master key. A few others do as well. No one should be entering, and there's video surveillance that would be triggered if they did. But if someone wanted to plant a bug, it wouldn't be that hard to do. It would be even easier to bug the conference room."

Meredith grimaced. "That's a lot of people, but why would any of them bug your office?"

"I don't know. To follow up on me? To see if they can catch me doing something they don't think I should do? To find out if I'm planning to oust a few board members?"

"Are you?" Cal asked.

"Am I what? Doing stuff I shouldn't do?"

Cal grimaced. "I doubt they think they could catch you doing something inappropriate. What I was asking was if you're planning to get rid of a few board members."

"Yes. Steven's mother is on the board. His. Mother." Bronwyn's frustration was palpable. "She's refused to acknowledge her son's crimes and refuses to step down. We have a pretty weird setup when it comes to our board, but there are guidelines and requirements of which she's in breach."

"What are the requirements?" Meredith asked.

"You have to be family by blood or marriage. Multiple family members can work in the business at different levels, but no more than one member of an immediate family group can be on the board at any one time. So going back to Steven—his dad served for several years, but then he rotated off and his wife filled his spot."

"Okay. But what about business requirements, financial skills, that kind of thing?"

Bronwyn gave Meredith a flat look.

"Oh."

"Yeah, oh. There are no requirements beyond faithfully attending the board meetings. This means they roll up in there with random and ludicrous requests that are beyond the scope of their responsibility or authority. Sometimes they make no sense at all. Once in a while, there's good, solid discussion, but usually, it's a disaster."

"So they have to be family, and they have to show up. What else?" Cal asked.

"There's a morality clause. My grandfather put it in, and no one ever bothered to take it out. If I can prove"—Bronwyn tapped the table with her finger—"and I mean beyond a shadow of a doubt that a member of the immediate family group has committed a crime, I can oust them. And Steven is guilty of kidnapping, drug trafficking, and attempted murder. Everyone knows he's guilty as sin. But there's that pesky 'innocent until proven guilty' aspect of the case that's been keeping me in check. The minute he's found guilty in a court of law, his mother is off the board. And if I can figure out how to do it before then, I will. They know that."

"So you can't get rid of them unless they're convicted of a crime in a court of law?" Meredith shook her head. "I'm sorry, but that's not much of a morality clause. There's plenty of stuff a person could do that is immoral that would never get them convicted of a crime."

Bronwyn glanced at Mo for the briefest moment before she fixed her gaze on a point somewhere behind Cal. "I can also oust them for any involvement with a guest that is not of a"—she made air quotes—"professional nature. And yes, since that's the elephant in the room, that clause was put in because of me. My father had it added. Basically, if anyone in the family has a tryst with a guest, they and their family unit lose their spot on the board. They don't lose their job, but they don't get to be part of the decision-making process."

Mo tried not to react, but heat flared down his spine. "Does anyone else think Bronwyn's dad is a real piece of work?"

Meredith and Cal raised their hands. Bronwyn huffed and raised her hand as well.

"Just checking." Mo had never liked Bronwyn's dad. He would never like him, but he did seem to have some kind of control over Bronwyn that made Mo's skin crawl. At least she acknowledged that the man was a jerk.

"Was your father putting that clause in some kind of power play?" Cal asked.

"I think he did it to embarrass me. He's never taken any responsibility for what happened. Don't get me wrong. I did it. It's on me. I'm the one who ran off with an older man."

"Excuse me." Meredith reached over and grabbed Bronwyn's hand. "As previously discussed, you were sixteen, and he was a predator."

"As previously discussed, I was sixteen, not six. I'm not free of culpability here. He turned my head. I let him turn it."

Mo wasn't sure how long he could stay in this room and listen to them talk about this. It was a raw, open wound, and he wasn't sure it would ever heal. He caught Cal's eye and saw the understanding there.

Cal cleared his throat. "How does the part where Steven sold drugs to guests not count as involvement with a guest?"

Bronwyn waved her hand back and forth. "It's a gray area. But he isn't the one on the board. And his mother is dug in and has some supporters who think that she shouldn't be booted out because of her son's actions. My father thinks she should be kicked to the curb. That is one subject where we're in full agreement, and I have no doubt I have his support. He wants her gone."

"Does he want you gone as well?" Cal looked as confused as Mo felt.

"No. Well, I don't think so. My father is a complicated man. He doesn't want to be on the board, but he would never give up our family's place on it. He doesn't want me ever to stop paying for the shame I brought to our family, but he wants to tell everyone how proud he is of his phenomenal daughter who has"—here she put on a lofty tone with a horrible British accent—"taken The Haven to new heights." She dropped the tone. "Every now and then, he mentions that he'd appreciate it if I married and provided him with grandchildren." Mo clenched his jaw. "But he doesn't want me to be a stay-at-home mom."

Mo tried to ignore the image that sprang into his mind—Bronwyn holding a little boy with her brown skin and dark hair and big blue eyes and . . .

This was not going to work. He couldn't stand to be around her and not . . . not . . . he didn't know what. But until she was willing to forgive him and move on . . .

He needed to leave. Soon. He didn't want to be a jerk. He'd spent a lot of time in prayer and counseling so that he wouldn't react badly in situations like this, but he wasn't sure how much longer he could hang on.

"My dad is a conundrum, but I don't think he wants me to step down. And he wouldn't condone anyone harming me physically."

Mo wasn't sure he agreed with Bronwyn's assessment of her father, but he kept his mouth shut.

"Unfortunately, I suspect Nathan has violated the morality clause in every imaginable way. I can't prove it yet, but I'm trying and I think he's on to me. He has a mean streak, and he wants my job. I wouldn't put anything past him."

Bronwyn looked at her watch. "I can't stay any longer. I'll be missed and I—"

"Tonight." Mo looked at Cal, then Meredith, then made eye contact with her. There was something in his eyes that sent a shiver down her spine. And it wasn't in fear.

Meredith jumped in. "Tonight works. Bronwyn, thank you for inviting us over!"

Bronwyn looked between the three people who'd had her back for almost thirty years and who, even now, stood with her. They'd been friends so long that it took her only a second to catch on. "Tonight works. Say six o'clock?"

"Perfect." Cal walked to his desk. "Landry will be thrilled that we have dinner plans."

Meredith leaned toward her. "We're going to work this out, but you have to tell us if it gets dangerous for you. We'll get you out of there."

Mo left the room without a word to anyone.

When he was gone, Bronwyn let her head fall back and she stared at the ceiling. The words came out without her permission.

"He hates me."

The silence that followed her admission could have shattered eardrums and was broken only when Cal stepped closer and leaned until his face filled her vision. "He doesn't hate you. He told you he'd never speak to you again. He's keeping his word." Cal put his phone to his ear and stepped out of the office.

Bronwyn straightened in her seat and caught Meredith holding her hands in a distinctive way. "Do you want to strangle me?"

Meredith didn't back down. "Not really. I love you, but I'm starting to feel some intense emotions because of you. When are you going to get over yourself about Mo?"

"I think I have."

"Then why won't you talk to him?"

"What would I say?"

Meredith stared at her, incredulity written across her face. "You could start with 'Good morning, Mo.' Or 'Hi, Mo.' Or even, 'Mo, I think you're hot, and we should date.'"

Cal had taken one step into the room, but at Meredith's last remark, he turned around. "I'll be back when y'all are done."

"Get in here!" Meredith called after him.

Cal returned, with Mo on his heels and Carla right behind them.

"What's going on?" Bronwyn looked at the three who'd blown back into the office like someone was chasing them.

"Your mother." Carla's eyes were huge.

"My . . . what?"

"I saw your mother on the security cameras." A chime announced her entrance into the front office. "She's here." Carla looked at Cal. "What do I do?"

"Welcome her in and ask her what she wants." Cal opened the outside door to his office, which exited into a fenced-in area behind the building. "Meredith, you and Bronwyn come out here. Mo"—he tossed a set of keys to him—"go into Connor's office and open his exterior door."

"Got it."

"I'll call you." Cal all but shoved them outside. The door closed behind them.

A moment later, a different door opened, and Mo waved them in. Bronwyn followed Meredith into Connor Shaw's office and when she did, she understood Cal's plan. Connor's office had three doors. One to the exterior, one to the interior hall, and one that must lead back to the reception area. From here, they could escape the building without her mother seeing them.

"Once we find out what she wants, we'll sneak you out."

Meredith leaned a hip against Connor's desk. "Let's head to Mountain Brew. We'll grab a latte. If your mom asks, we'll say we met here and walked to town."

Bronwyn had a moment of clarity. "Wait a minute. Meredith! What are you doing here? Why aren't you seeing patients?" If Meredith had cancelled appointments to come . . .

"I don't have any patients until ten thirty. You're good."

"I thought you had something planned with Gray this morning." Mo gave Meredith a pointed look.

"I did. But Gray wanted me to come to the aid of my oldest and dearest friend. We'll do it again another day."

Bronwyn shared a look with Mo. They still hadn't spoken directly to each other, but sometimes, words weren't necessary.

"Would you two stop already?" Meredith asked. "We were going to talk to Cal about house plans this morning. It's not like we can't talk to him any day that ends in *y*. The land is mine. It isn't going anywhere. Cal is obligated by blood and friendship to build us our house, and we aren't in a hurry. Gray's house is adorable, and I'll be perfectly happy to move in there after the wedding. I'm not rushing this. Besides"—Meredith leaned against Mo—"there was no way I was going to leave the two of you to stare at each other and try to communicate without speaking. Full disclosure, I'm done with both of you. Get yourselves sorted." She pinched Mo's arm. Based on the way he jumped, it hadn't been gentle.

Mo grabbed Meredith's hand when she went to pinch him again, and for a brief moment, they were all ten again. Mo and Meredith were squabbling over something while Bronwyn and Cal looked on and waited for them to work it out.

And like they had as children, they resolved the fight almost as soon as it began. Mo pulled Meredith into him and hugged her close. He whispered something that sounded like, "You need to back off."

Meredith replied, "Not until you two are married."

Bronwyn choked on air. She tried not to make any noise as she coughed and attempted to regain her composure.

Married? To Mo? What was Meredith thinking? Maybe that had been their future at one time.

Not anymore.

The door to Connor's office opened, and Carla stepped in. "Your mother is in Cal's office. She declined to tell me why she wanted to speak with him. He'll text later. Go!"

Mo handed the office keys to Carla and led the way. Bronwyn followed him out into the reception area. A few minutes later, she and Meredith were seated in Mountain Brew, Gossamer Falls' best and only coffee spot. Mo was at the counter.

"It's going to look weird if we don't have any coffee," Bronwyn pointed out to Meredith.

"Mo will get us some. Sit tight and act like you've been here for hours. Breathe in the aroma of dark roast. Inhale the doughy scents of freshly made pastries. Savor the unique energy of a room full of people in varying degrees of caffeination who should be drinking water and going for long walks in the woods. But are they? No. They're here. Filling their bodies with stimulants and hoping that helps."

"You can't be serious." Bronwyn pointed to the seat Meredith occupied. "You're here so much, you have your own chair. I tried to sit in it one time and one of the baristas told me that if you came in, I would have to move."

"What can I say? I'm a woman of the people." Meredith tossed her hair and looked around the room. "Also, why were you here without me? Friends don't drink coffee alone. They call their besties and say, 'Hey, I'm in town. Want to meet me for coffee?'"

"I did call you. And you were up to your elbows in a root canal."

Meredith grimaced. "Okay. You're forgiven."

"Forgiven for what?" Mo set a large iced coffee with some kind of cream in it in front of Meredith. And then he set a medium hot coffee in front of Bronwyn.

Meredith eyed it. "Ooh, what did you order for Beep?"

"A mocha. Extra shot. Two pumps. No whip."

Bronwyn's heart nearly flatlined, then raced for the fences. Was that vein in her neck pulsing as fast as she thought it was? Could anyone see it? She managed to pick up the cup and take a tiny sip. "It's perfect. Th—"

"Bronwyn?" Her mother's voice had a unique pitch. Some people said it was soft and girlish. Others said it was like nails on a chalkboard. Regardless, she'd silenced the entire room with one word.

A sip for luck. "Mother. Good morning. What brings you into town?" Another sip because it was delicious, because it was warm, and because Mo had remembered her favorite.

"I would like to have a word." How many times had Bronwyn heard that phrase from her mother?

"Good morning, Mrs. Pierce." Mo extended his hand, and Bronwyn's heart launched back into a chaotic rhythm that couldn't possibly be healthy. "Good to see you. It's been too long."

Her mother looked at Mo's outstretched hand and then took it for the shortest handshake in human history. "Montgomery." She said Mo's name like someone might say "pond scum" or "phlegm," and if Mo hadn't bought the coffee for her, Bronwyn would have spilled it on her mother's new pumps. Accidentally, of course.

Meredith grabbed her iced coffee and took a long sip. Then another. Bronwyn knew that maneuver. Meredith would either burst out in laughter or say something she shouldn't, so she shut herself up.

Unfortunately, that wasn't an option for Bronwyn.

"Mother, please join us. We were catching up." Mo sat in the chair beside her, and she was sure she imagined it, but for a second, she thought he might be leaning toward her. He was definitely giving off a "touch her and die" vibe.

Maybe it was time for her to stop reading romance novels.

"Yes, Mrs. Pierce. Sit." Meredith had recovered and now flashed her trademark smile. "It's been ages. How are you?"

Bronwyn enjoyed the long moment it took for her mother to devise a graceful way to extract herself from the situation. Quinns being friendly to a Pierce! Perish the thought. But for a Pierce to act out in public? That couldn't be borne. Pierces were better than everyone else, of course. And that included in their manners and decorum.

How many times had she heard that?

Her mom pasted on a smile only the people at the table would know was fake. "Darling, I hate to disturb your social time with work matters. Why don't you step outside with me for a moment?"

It had been fun while it lasted, but her mother had boxed her in. Bronwyn stood. "Of course." She took the coffee with her. It was still hot, and she wouldn't let it get cold while her mother berated her for some perceived slight.

They stepped outside and took a few steps down the sidewalk before her mother turned. "Bronwyn Elena Elizabeth Pierce." She'd been full-named. It was on. "Why are you not in your office?"

Bronwyn could remind her mother that she was the one who worked far more than full-time hours. She could have pointed out that it was rich being taken to task for her work ethic by a woman who had never worked a day in her life. Or she could have asked her why *she* was slumming it in town when The Haven currently hosted this year's Oscar winners in both best actor and best director categories.

But her mother didn't give her time to do any of that.

"I came to see you during normal business hours," she continued, "and you were not there."

"Clearly."

"Do not sass me, young lady."

"Mother, if you could get to the point of why you've chased me down, that would be great. I'm enjoying coffee with friends this morning, but I do have appointments that I need to return for."

"I received a phone call that you were seen walking into SPQ Construction this morning at 8:45. Why were you there?"

Bronwyn took a sip of her coffee. A tiny rebellion that only worked because her mother would rather hike naked than cause a scene. "I was there to meet with Cal, Meredith, and Mo." Truth was always the best policy.

"Why?"

Another sip. Her mother had no right to any of this information. "Why not? Cal couldn't join us for coffee. It's easy to park in his lot. Meredith doesn't have patients until ten thirty. I got to see Carla. It was a win-win."

"But why are you in town at all?"

"Mother, this is ridiculous. Did you really drive into town because you think I'm hobnobbing with the lower classes again?"

Her mother's eyes widened. If she'd been wearing pearls, she would have clutched them. "Of course not. I came to tell you that your grandmother is sick."

This wasn't news. Her grandmother had been near death for the past decade.

"The doctor called this morning. The scans show that her cancer has spread. It's everywhere. There's nothing they can do. The hospice nurses are coming this afternoon."

That was new.

SIX

TWENTY-TWO YEARS EARLIER

Bronwyn sat at the large dining room table with her hands in her lap. Her ankles were crossed. Her shoulders were back.

Grandmother Pierce eyed her with approval. "Excellent. Now what do you do when the server brings the salad?"

The etiquette lessons had been going on for a year, and Bronwyn rarely misstepped. She knew how to handle every piece of silverware, understood which glasses went with which beverages, and knew where to put her napkin if she needed to leave the table midmeal.

Today's lesson ended with a divine chocolate mousse that came in a tiny cup because Grandmother said girls had to be careful to never overindulge.

Bronwyn rose to tell Grandmother goodbye but resumed her seat when Grandmother gestured for her to stay.

"You've been hanging around with the Quinn children." Grandmother raised an eyebrow and her lips pinched, transforming her face into an imperious expression that frightened many. But not Bronwyn.

For all her formalities, Grandmother Pierce liked her. She wasn't like Granny Quinn. She wasn't affectionate or warm, and Bronwyn didn't think her grandmother even loved her. But she didn't despise her, and that was saying something because Bronwyn was certain her grandmother couldn't stand most of the Pierces.

"Yes, Grandmother. They're my best friends."

"Do they still drag you all over the forest and bring you home with dirty clothes and twigs in your hair?"

"Sometimes. We went camping last weekend. It was awesome. We played in the water at the base of the falls, and we roasted hot dogs over a fire, and we—"

"Yes, yes. I know. It was a delight. I'm glad you enjoyed it. But you're old enough to understand something."

Bronwyn waited.

"You can be friends but nothing more."

Bronwyn had learned never to say "Huh?" or "What?" around her grandmother, but she was confused. "Ma'am?"

"Those boys, Cal and Mo, they can be your friends. But nothing else."

"Yes, ma'am."

"Do you like them? As more than friends?"

"No, ma'am. We've been friends for years. But they're boys. They do gross things and make loud noises, and the things they think are funny are . . . not."

Grandmother sighed. "Yes. Boys this age are often like that. But they grow up."

"Well, we aren't going to grow up until we have to." She'd heard Mo say that, and she wholeheartedly agreed.

"Good plan, child."

SEVEN

PRESENT DAY

Mo sat by Meredith and they shamelessly watched Bronwyn interact with her mom.

Meredith spoke around her straw. "That woman has always hated us."

"Not always. She liked us fine when we were small and kept Bronwyn out from under her feet so she could entertain the starlets."

"True. But then we grew up." Meredith leaned her head on Mo's shoulder.

"Yeah. What were we thinking?"

"Worst move ever."

"I don't know. Your happily ever after is looking pretty good right now," he said. "You'll marry Gray and start giving me nieces and nephews. I'll be the coolest uncle ever since I'll take them to do all the fun things that their worn-out parents won't want to do."

"And what about your happily ever after?" She nodded toward the window.

"Meredith, my happily ever after ran away, and when she returned,

I treated her like trash. I made my bed. I get to lie in it. But do me a favor?"

"What?"

"Never bring up that pervert in my presence." Mo could hear the bitterness and anger in his voice, and he tried to smile through it. "Please."

"I'm so sorry, Mo. I won't."

Mo didn't want to get into it, so he turned his gaze back to the window. Bronwyn's expression had shifted from one of thinly veiled frustration to one of dismay. Something had happened. He couldn't look away as her mother walked by and Bronwyn returned to her seat in the coffee shop. She clutched at her coffee.

"What's the matter?" Meredith had obviously seen the same shift in Bronwyn's demeanor that he had.

"My grandmother is dying."

"Oh, Bronwyn. I'm so sorry." Meredith wrapped an arm around her.

Mo ran a fingertip along the rim of his mug as Bronwyn filled them in.

"Will this change anything for tonight?" Meredith asked the question Mo needed to have answered.

"No." Bronwyn's voice was firm. "I'll go see her this afternoon, but I'll be home by six."

Mo stayed put as Bronwyn and Meredith made small talk for another ten minutes. Then he stood. "I have to go. There are a few things I need to pick up before tonight. I'll see you later." He nodded in the general direction of both women and escaped outside.

He walked to Cal's office. Carla was on the phone when he entered, and she waved him back. When he got to the office, he filled Cal in on what had happened. "Could you have Landry call Bronwyn? Her relationship with her grandmother has always been unique. She was staying strong, but I'm sure she's reeling."

Cal called Landry immediately. Mo flopped down into a chair as they talked.

"Okay, baby, thanks. I love you. Yes. You're the best. Kiss Eliza for me. Yeah. I love you." A low chuckle. Another. Then, "Landry, Mo's sitting here waiting for me. Okay. Tonight."

He ended the call, and Mo did his best not to vomit all over the rug. "You're disgusting."

"What?"

"The mushiness. It's intense, man."

"I love my wife and our girls."

"I know you do, but I don't need to hear it."

"Hear what?"

"I can read between the lines. That chuckle? Please."

"I'm a married man."

"And we're all thankful. But keep your pillow talk away from me."

Cal threw a pen at his head. "You're jealous."

He was so jealous, it was a miracle his skin didn't have a green tint. But he didn't want to talk about it.

When he didn't respond to Cal's teasing, Cal sobered quickly. "Sorry. How can I help?"

"You're already helping. Keep making it possible for me to be in the same space with her. I don't know how to do this without the buffer of someone else around to keep the conversation going."

"I can do that. I'll tell Landry. She'll help."

"Thanks."

The silence stretched.

"Landry's been talking to Bronwyn. Encouraging her to open up. She's . . ."

"Stubborn?"

"Well, yes. But it's more than that. Landry thinks she's

embarrassed. It's one of those things she got herself into but doesn't know how to get out of."

"I think y'all are seeing what you want to see. Bronwyn needs my help. She knows I'm trustworthy. That's one thing she knows about me. *I* have never lied to her. I won't start now. She doesn't have to like me, forgive me, or even be friends with me. She's a great businesswoman. She's in a situation, and she's going to use whatever means she has available to her. I'm the means."

"You'd never let any harm come to her."

"Never. I owe her that much. She's changed. I can see that. Everyone can see that. She messed up. She paid for it. She's still paying for it. But forgiveness is a two-way street. And trust once it's broken? Sometimes it can't be restored. We're not like that Japanese pottery they break and glue back together with gold. We're more like recycled tires. We've been chopped up and while we can still do some good in the world, we won't ever be a tire again."

Cal rubbed his eyes. "Did you just describe yourself as playground mulch?"

"If the shoe fits."

"That shoe doesn't fit. I don't even know what kind of metaphor that was. No, I take it back. I do know. It was stupid. Why can't you be Japanese pottery?"

"Cal, we weren't broken in pieces. We were crushed. We're lucky to be what we are. But we won't ever be what we were."

"You're wrong." Cal's face was set in a stubborn line.

"And you're delusional. But you're allowed to be. Life kicked you in the teeth and then brought you more beauty than any of us could have imagined. I'm happy for you. Ecstatic. And I'm glad I get to enjoy some of the spillover. When Eliza runs over to see me in the morning before school, she melts me every time."

Cal's voice was rough when he said, "You spoil her."

"Sure do. Gonna keep doing it. She deserves all the spoiling she can get. So will her sister. I've accepted my fate, Cal. I really have. I don't know why God gave me this road. All I can do is make the best of it."

Mo could see Cal thinking through multiple arguments, but he didn't share them today. Instead, he asked, "What do you need for tonight?"

"I should have what I need at home. If I think of anything else, I'll pick it up and bring it with me."

"Want to ride together?"

"Nah. I'll see you there." Mo walked out of Cal's office a few minutes later.

When he got home, he spent two hours on his current projects. Then he went to his storage building. By the end of the night they'd know if Bronwyn had been bugged or was being tracked, and he'd have access to her entire system.

Then the real work would begin.

EIGHT

TWENTY YEARS EARLIER

Thirteen-year-old Mo waited by the side of the school building. Bronwyn climbed out from the limo.

They'd sent her to school in a limo. The driver was probably headed to Asheville to pick up a guest for The Haven and Bronwyn's trip to school was tacked on to the route.

Even though he was out of her line of sight, Bronwyn came straight to him.

"Hey." Her voice was tight, but her smile was real.

"Hey." He rolled his eyes in an exaggerated fashion. "Nice wheels."

She groaned, and they fell into step beside each other. "Mother saw no reason whatsoever to miss her Pilates class this morning. There's another one in an hour. She could have taken me and gone to that one. But no. A future senator and his wife are attending the eight thirty class, and she wants to make a good impression."

Mo bumped her arm with his. "Sorry." She hated coming to school in the limo. The last time it happened, some girls had made fun of her in the bathroom. Meredith had been in there with her. That time. It made him wonder how much teasing she endured.

"My parents shouldn't have had a child. They have no clue what to do with one."

Mo didn't have words for his reaction to her words. Anger? Frustration? Fear? Horror? "I'm glad they had you, even if they're clueless."

"Yeah. I matter to six people. And none of them are my parents. Not sure what that says about me."

"It says you don't understand how many people care about you."

He guessed she was counting Meredith, Cal, and of course him in that number, but who were the other three? His parents maybe. And his grandparents. And Cal's parents. See. He'd come up with more than six without even trying.

"They're sending me to a camp this summer," she said suddenly.

"What? No!"

Her eyes glistened. "I don't want to talk about it now. Later?"

He nodded. "After school. How are you getting home?"

She shrugged.

"Come home with me. We'll go for a hike."

She looked down at herself. Her clothes were too nice for hiking.

"You can wear some of Meredith's stuff."

"We aren't the same size, Mo."

"We'll figure it out. Say yes?"

It took her longer to reply than he would have liked, but she said, "Sure. Why not. It's better than going home."

"Great." He paused at the door to her first class. "Bronwyn?"

"Yeah?"

"I really am sorry."

"I know. Thanks."

Mo walked four doors down to his next class. He liked school. But today, all he wanted to do was escape and get into the forest. Bronwyn was sad, and he wanted to show her something that would make her happy. He wouldn't be inviting Meredith or Cal.

Not that either of them could come, anyway. Cal had work and Meredith had play practice. But even if they could, he didn't want them there. Not today.

The school day dragged worse than ever before. When the final bell rang, Mo met Bronwyn in the carpool line. When his mom paused at the curb, he opened the door, and Bronwyn climbed in first. "Hey, Mrs. Quinn."

"Bronwyn, hello! How are you?"

"I'm fine. You?"

"Lovely." She turned her attention to Mo, and he understood the question in her gaze.

"I want to take Bronwyn hiking this afternoon. Can you take her home when you pick up Meredith from practice?"

"Of course, but does she have permission?"

"Yes, ma'am," Bronwyn piped up. "I called home at lunch. My parents won't be home this afternoon, anyway. They don't care. Mother said I should be home by nine. She has one of the staff ready to sit with me."

Mo's mom's face pinched, but her words were welcoming. "Then that works out beautifully. I'm coming back to pick Meredith up around eight thirty. We'll grab her and run you home."

"Thank you, Mrs. Quinn."

"You're welcome, sweetheart."

They rode the rest of the way in silence, and as soon as they were home, Mo dashed inside, found clothes for Bronwyn, changed his own clothes, and met his mom in the kitchen.

"Mom?"

She looked up from the soup she was stirring on the stove. "Yes?"

"I thought we'd go to the falls."

"I figured as much."

"I was going to show her that trail Dad showed me. And I was going to tell her she could go there. You know, if she wanted to. From her place. Without asking."

"Do you think that's safe?"

"She's not as good as Meredith, but she knows how to hike, Mom."

"Fair enough. Of course it's fine." His mom set the spoon across the pot, then walked over to where he stood. She put her arm around him and whispered, "She's special to you, isn't she?"

Mo shrugged. "She's Bronwyn."

"Yes, she is. And I adore her. But you need to be careful and respectful of her emotions. Do you like her? As more than a friend?"

Mo squirmed away. "I don't know. Maybe. She's Bronwyn." Did he need to say more than that?

His mom's sigh was cut off by Bronwyn's entrance into the kitchen. "I'm ready."

Bronwyn had braided her long hair into a single strand down her back. Meredith's clothes were a little baggy on Bronwyn's leaner frame, but she looked comfortable. And excited.

"Let's go."

They took the four-wheelers to the trailhead. Then they hiked for thirty minutes to Catherine's Falls, kicked off their boots, and walked around in the river at the base. Eventually Bronwyn climbed up on a large stone at the edge and lay down. Mo joined her. The rock was warm against his back, and they lay there, eyes closed for a while.

Mo had the weirdest urge to touch her. To reach out and hold her hand. What was with him? She wouldn't want to—

Her hand slid into his.

His heart exploded. He laced their fingers together and held on.

NINE

PRESENT DAY

Bronwyn stood by her door and welcomed Cal, Landry, and Eliza into her home. Meredith and Mo were a few steps behind them.

At the first opportunity, she slipped into the kitchen and ran her hands down the towel hanging from her dishwasher. What was wrong with her? Why was she so sweaty? And nervous? She hadn't felt like this since . . .

She froze. Thoughts of waterfalls and small hands reaching across the bond of friendship to become something more crashed through her. She forced the memories from her mind. She couldn't go there. Not tonight.

But she watched Mo out of the corner of her eye. He took in every detail of her home, and she saw the moment he spotted the tiny rock on the shelf. A rock she'd found the first time they held hands. It was heavily lined with orange veins, and she'd carried it with her everywhere she'd gone since.

His gaze met hers, and the turmoil she saw there nearly melted her on the spot. Was he angry? Hurt? Both? She didn't know. But he definitely wasn't apathetic.

Eliza rushed in. "Aunt Bronwyn?"

"Yes, darling?"

"Did you ask Aunt Cassie to make the chocolate cookies for me like you had last time?"

"You know it."

"Thank you!" Eliza threw her arms around Bronwyn's waist. "You're the best."

Mo gasped in faux outrage. "I thought I was the best?"

Eliza released Bronwyn and ran straight to Mo, but instead of hugging him, she jumped and he caught her.

She giggled and whispered something in his ear.

Mo's face was usually all sharp lines and angles, but in the presence of Eliza, it softened into something so beautiful that Bronwyn had to stifle a gasp. A wicked light filled his eyes, and he spun Eliza upside down. She screamed in delight. He pulled her back up and said, "Just for that, I'm going to eat all the cookies."

Eliza squealed with glee as he tickled her.

"We've covered this, young lady," he said. "I'm your favorite. Got it?"

"Yes, Uncle Mo! You're my favorite." Her giggles only eased after he stopped tickling her, and then she said, "But Aunt Bronwyn's tied for first."

Okay, now she really was going to melt.

Mo narrowed his eyes and pressed a kiss to Eliza's forehead before he returned her to her feet. "I'd say you chose your favorites well, so I can live with that."

Bronwyn all but ran from the kitchen and collided with Cal. "Whoa! What's lit your shorts on fire?"

"Nothing. I'll be right back." She slipped past him and went to her room, closed the door, and leaned against it, gasping for air. What was happening? What was wrong with her?

She'd spent years building up her defenses against Mo. For a time after his last betrayal, she went full no contact. It had been tricky, but she rebuilt her relationship with Cal and Meredith while avoiding anything that would put her in the same space as Mo.

Then Landry's stalker situation forced her to figure out how to live *without* avoiding Mo, and for the past year or so, they'd existed in a messed-up but manageable détente.

She'd forgiven him. Mostly.

She just didn't think she could have him in her life.

Or she hadn't thought she could.

Bronwyn sat on the edge of her bed and tried to process what was happening with her emotions. This squishy feeling when Mo was around? She'd experienced this before. And she had to stay far, far away from it, not just for her own sake but for his and for their friends and family.

The knock on the door was her only warning. The door opened, and Meredith's voice preceded her. "Beep?"

Landry followed close on her heels. "Bronwyn?"

"I'm here. I'm fine. What's wrong with you two? Since when do you barge into people's bedrooms?"

"I beg your pardon." Meredith's tone was hoity-toity. "I would never barge in. I knocked first."

"You didn't wait for a response."

"Didn't I?" Meredith looked at Landry. "Huh."

Landry and Meredith stood by the bed. "It's like she's trying to get away from us."

"Us?"

"Well, somebody. It couldn't be us. We're awesome." Landry delivered the line while staring at Bronwyn. "Right?"

"You're awesome." Bronwyn's response was automatic.

"Good. As your friends, we can chase you down when you exhibit bizarre behavior," Landry said. "I'm relatively new to the girlfriend rulebook, but I'm confident it's in there. Somewhere."

Meredith nodded. "Oh, it's in there. We would be less awesome if we *didn't* chase you down."

Bronwyn gave them a slow clap. "You two should try stand-up. How much practice did that take?"

"None." Landry grinned. "Totally impromptu. Maybe we missed our callings and should consider a tour?"

Meredith patted Landry's baby bump. "Little miss might make road life difficult."

"True." Landry gave an exaggerated shrug of dismay. "I guess since we're staying here, we should find out what has crawled up Bronwyn's butt."

"Language." Meredith tapped her ears.

"Sorry," Landry stage-whispered. "But don't you think it's getting ridiculous?"

"Yes, but we discussed this. She has to tell us what's going on. We can't force it."

"I think we might need to try."

"You could be right."

Both women turned to Bronwyn and waited for her reaction.

"Again, how long did you practice?"

Neither of them spoke. And neither of them smiled. Playtime was over.

"I appreciate your concern, but I'm fine," Bronwyn said, not even believing herself. "I needed a moment. It's a big deal, having y'all here, what I'm about to do. If I'm wrong, it could cost me my job."

They continued to stare at her.

"What?"

"We're patiently waiting for you to talk yourself around to the truth." Landry managed to deliver that line with no judgment.

Bronwyn fell back on her bed and covered her eyes. "What do you want from me?"

"We want you to be happy." The bed dipped, first on her left, then on her right. She peeked through her fingers. They were now sitting on either side of her. She was trapped.

Meredith tapped her arm. "We want you to give yourself permission to live."

"I *am* living."

"You're hiding from life." Landry's eyes shone. "I've been there. I understand. The hurt, the pain, you want to avoid it. But you're too young to assume you can't have more than what you have now."

"What are you talking about?" Bronwyn didn't understand where this was coming from.

Meredith patted her knee. "You forget. I was there the first time you fell for him. I know the signs."

Cal joined Mo and Eliza in the kitchen a few seconds after Bronwyn left. "What's wrong with Beep?" he asked.

Mo opened the box of cookies on the counter. "You're married. You tell me."

"I'm not married to *her*. And what does being married have to do with anything?"

Mo glanced at Cal and got the nod before he offered a cookie to Eliza. "Only one before dinner, yeah?"

"Yes! Thanks!" She climbed onto a stool and munched away.

Mo took a cookie for himself. "You want one?" he asked Cal.

"Why not? There's no telling when we'll eat."

They took their cookies into Bronwyn's living room, and Mo walked around, looking at the pictures and art on her walls. He felt like a voyeur, wandering around her home, looking for the things that made her, her. What did adult Bronwyn like? He'd guessed right earlier today with the coffee. But what changes had the past seventeen years brought?

If her home was any indication, she liked to decorate with photographs, but very few of them were of people. She favored mountains and beaches, with a few random shots of wildlife and flowers. He paused at a photograph of Catherine's Falls. It was taken in winter. Snow was on the ground, and part of the falls was covered in ice.

And that tree . . . he reached toward the picture before he realized what he was doing.

Cal joined him. "That's a great shot. I wonder if she took it?"

Mo moved to a different picture, but his mind stayed frozen on the image. The tree that was down in that photo had fallen this past winter, sometime between Christmas and mid-January. It wasn't there now. Hadn't been since early February.

Bronwyn had been at Catherine's Falls in the past six months.

Why?

"Hey." Cal pointed to the photo. "Is that the tree that's in my shop now?"

"Yep." The Quinns preferred to let the forest take care of the forest, but in this case, the tree had been perched precariously against another. Mo had taken one look and made the call that it was too risky to leave it there. He'd been right in his guess that Cal would do just about anything to have that trunk for his woodwork.

"I'll have to ask her for a copy. I'd love to have it to go with the pieces I make from the wood."

Mo didn't want to talk about Catherine's Falls. He didn't want to talk about things that had been strong and beautiful and had fallen for no obvious reason. Not that he needed to be present for this conversation. Cal was carrying it all on his own.

"I can't decide what to make. Landry says I should chill and let the wood speak to me."

"Did you tell her the tree is dead and can't talk?"

Cal chortled. "What does it matter if it's alive or dead? It's a tree. It can't talk regardless."

"You know what I mean." Mo continued to walk around the room, but his eyes were unfocused. He needed to get out of here. Being in Bronwyn's space was messing with him. He'd spent too many years of his life falling out of love with her. Staying away from her as much as possible was best for everyone.

So why couldn't he stop thinking about her? Why was the thought of her being in danger bringing out every protective feeling he'd ever felt toward her?

He'd assumed she hated him. She'd acted like she did. But if she hated him so much, why had she kept the rock?

A door down the hall opened, and Meredith emerged. Her smile was bright and as fake as a three-dollar bill. She needed to up her game if she wanted to convince him everything was fine.

She laced her arm through his. "Gray's on his way, so let's take the food out."

So, she wanted to play. Fine. He could keep up. He followed her into the kitchen.

"Eliza, can you help me with these rolls?" Meredith handed a basket to Eliza, and she carried the bread to the dining room.

As soon as they were alone, Mo stepped in front of his sister. "Mer—"

"Not now, Mo. Please." Her voice was firm. "We'll talk later. I promise."

"I'll hold you to it."

"I know, but, Mo?"

"What?"

"I won't be able to give you all the answers."

"Because she didn't share?"

Meredith pinched her lips together. "It's need to know."

"You cannot be serious right now."

"I can be, and I am. I love you. Always have. Always will. You're going to have to trust me."

Eliza ran back into the room. "What's next, Aunt Meredith?"

Meredith handed her a stack of napkins, and she disappeared again. "Have you noticed how she says Aunt Meredith and Uncle Mo and Aunt Bronwyn more than anyone else does?"

Bronwyn chose that moment to enter the kitchen. "What do you mean?"

"None of our other nieces and nephews use our names that much."

"Ah." Bronwyn's smile was forced. "She's the only person who calls me Aunt Bronwyn, so I hadn't noticed. My guess is that she loves her new family so much that she's staking her claim. You're her aunt and uncle. Every time she says it out loud, and you acknowledge the relationship, you further cement your place in her world and her place in yours."

"You think?" Meredith pursed her lips. "It makes sense. Wait, no one else calls you Aunt Bronwyn?"

Bronwyn pointed to herself. "Only child. Dysfunctional family."

Meredith acknowledged the truth of Bronwyn's words with a slight shrug. "Well, you'll have another niece soon. But you'll have to wait a couple of years before she starts butchering your name. I bet she calls you Bobbin. That might be cute."

Bronwyn's laugh had a brittle edge that sliced against Mo's nerves. He loved his sister, but right now he wanted to strangle her. The forced cheer was making him twitchy.

"And you'll be Aunt Bronwyn to my kids too." Meredith's eyes widened, then she rushed to add, "Although, not anytime soon. I'm not sure I'm ready for motherhood. I'm afraid I might mess it all up."

In his surprise, Mo accidentally made eye contact with Bronwyn.

Her eyes reflected his own shock. She gave him a look and a little wave of the hand that he took to mean, "You take this one. I've got nothing."

Okay then. "You're going to be the most amazing mom ever," Mo said, meeting Meredith's eye. "You're fun personified. You love everybody. You take care of everybody. Your kids will be some of the most loved children in the universe."

Bronwyn chimed in. "And don't forget, you have your own parents as examples of how to do it right. You guys turned out pretty awesome."

Meredith bumped Mo's arm. "We did, didn't we?"

Bronwyn wasn't done. "And, unlike me, you don't have to worry about turning your children into narcissists or psychopaths. So—"

"That's not true," Meredith spoke at the same time he did. It was the closest he'd come to speaking directly to Bronwyn in years, but for her to think that? He couldn't keep his mouth shut.

They were interrupted again by Eliza. "Aunt Bronwyn, Daddy says we need to eat because his girls need their rest."

"He's right about that."

"See," Meredith whispered. "Mom fail on my end. I didn't even think of that."

"You would think about it if you had your own kids," Bronwyn whispered back. "That's how it works."

Mo stayed in the kitchen as the others walked into the dining room. For a moment, it had felt like . . . like old times. Like Bronwyn didn't hate him. Like they were a team and they didn't need to talk to communicate. They could speak volumes with a look.

He hadn't forgotten what that was like, but he'd been sure he'd never experience it again.

If he'd dared to hope for it, he would have expected it to be more satisfying. Not like the thrill that he experienced when he uncovered a crime. More like the sense of rightness that came over him when he proved someone's innocence.

This was neither of those things.

This was walking on fire barefoot while wearing a jacket made of glass shards. Every breath was agony. Every motion was excruciating.

He forced himself to move to the dining room. He ate. He smiled at Eliza. He avoided eye contact with Bronwyn and counted the minutes until they would go to her office.

At some point, the pain lessened enough for him to breathe through it and wonder what had happened. Why now? She'd mostly ignored him for years, and then when she finally deigned to stay in his presence for more than a few seconds, they'd found some kind of weird equilibrium.

It was uncomfortable to be around her at times, but not painful.

Why did this hurt so much?

"Mo?"

Mo focused on Cal, then on the rest of the room. Everyone was staring at him. Everyone except Eliza was frowning.

Eliza giggled. "Uncle Mo! Daddy had to call you five times!"

He cleared his throat. "Sorry, doodlebug. I was lost in my thoughts." He sent a quick wink at Eliza before he focused on Cal. "What did I miss?"

Cal gave him a look that said, "You and I are going to talk later." But what came out of his mouth was, "Are you ready to head over to Beep's office?"

"Meredith and I will stay here and clean up," Landry offered. "Eliza too. Y'all go on and do what you need to do." She gave Eliza a bright smile. "Come on, sweetheart. Let's clean Aunt Bronwyn's kitchen before we go home."

Bronwyn immediately protested, but Meredith and Landry put up a united front.

As their discussion continued, Mo caught Cal's eye, and he stepped closer to him. "She doesn't want Eliza over there. Neither do I. If Meredith goes, Eliza will want to go. Gray and Donovan will meet us over there. That's going to be too many people in the office." He dropped his voice to a bare whisper. "Also, I think Landry and Meredith want to talk about Bronwyn."

"They need to back off." Mo was tired of people messing with his life. And Bronwyn was probably tired of it too.

"They can't. And they won't."

"They could."

"They aren't wired that way. They show their love by fixing things."

"Some things don't need to be fixed."

Bronwyn stalked toward them, shaking her head in clear frustration. "Let's go before Landry goes into labor while doing my dishes. Wouldn't that be awesome."

TEN

TWENTY YEARS EARLIER

Bronwyn checked her watch.

Mo was late.

She scanned the trail that led into the forest, then turned back to the book she was pretending to read. She was on The Haven property, but since Mo had shown her how to get to her house from Catherine's Falls, they'd figured out a way for Mo to sneak onto her family property, then skirt the side and into The Haven grounds.

It was a security failure, to be sure. But she wasn't about to say anything. And it wasn't like anyone from the public could access the path from Quinn land. Quinn land was almost as protected as Pierce land.

Except, apparently, at the border.

"Excuse me, miss."

Bronwyn dropped her book as the voice pulled her from her thoughts. She looked up into a face that was . . . interesting. And one she recognized immediately. Corbin Driscoll.

Her parents had been giddy when he'd first come to The Haven a few years ago. He was a regular now, and while every guest at

The Haven was a VIP, something about this man put everyone on their best behavior.

He knelt and picked up her book. “My apologies, Bronwyn.”

“You know my name?” The question popped out before she could stop it.

He winked. “I make it a point to know all the important people wherever I go.”

“I’m not important.”

He glanced over her shoulder, then leaned closer. “Something tells me you’re important to that young man lingering in the trees.” Another wink, and he walked away without a backward glance.

Bronwyn clutched her book to her chest as he left, and when Mo joined her a minute later, her mind was still reeling.

“Who was that?”

“You know I can’t talk about the guests, Mo.”

“I can figure it out.”

He could. Mo could figure out anything. But, “No. Don’t ask me. You know I can’t.”

Mo glared in the direction Mr. Driscoll had gone. “Why was he talking to you out here?”

“How should I know? He’s a guest. He goes where he wants to go. He walks a lot. I heard him tell someone that walking gives him ideas.”

Mo’s stomach growled loud enough to wake the dead, and Bronwyn tucked her arm through his. “I guess your walk gave your stomach ideas. Let’s go hit up the kitchen.”

“You promised me a waterfall.”

“Food first. Then the waterfall.”

“How are you going to get me to the kitchen without being seen? If your uncles see me, we’re toast.” Mo glanced around. Was he nervous?

Not that she blamed him. She was nervous too. “We’ll go into the small kitchen. It's on the edge of the property. No one will be in there right now."

"Bronwyn—"

"Come on. This is our opportunity. My parents are out of town and my uncles are in a board meeting. We won't have another day to do this until next month. Or maybe even the month after that."

"Good point." Mo grinned at her, and whatever had been bothering him when he walked up seemed to fade away. "And it's not like arguing with you would make any difference."

"What's that supposed to mean?"

Mo's smile deepened. "Once you decide to do something, you're going to do it. Even if it's risky."

He wasn't wrong.

They raided the kitchen and packed snacks into a small bag before slipping back into the forest. The walk to the waterfall was clearly marked for guests, but they had to be on alert in case any guests decided today was the day they were going to visit as well.

The thought had Bronwyn stopping to turn in a circle before continuing on.

"You have a weird look on your face." Mo took a bite of an apple.

"No I don't."

"One hundred percent weird."

Bronwyn rolled her eyes. "Whatever."

"What's going on?"

Bronwyn shrugged. "I was thinking about what you said, about me being determined to do something even if it's risky. If we get caught . . ."

"If we get caught, your parents will probably have me arrested for trespassing." Mo took another bite.

"That's my point! The risk is for you, not me."

He grinned. "My parents would be so ticked. But Granny . . ." He chuckled. "I think Granny would bail me out. She'd be furious with me, but I think she'd do it just to frustrate your parents. She does not like them."

"No one who really knows my parents likes them."

"True."

They talked about everything and nothing until they came to the waterfall. A small sign declared it to be the Emerald Cascade. Mo studied it with a small smile on his lips. "This is beautiful. I can see why your family wanted to make it accessible to the guests. Do many come see it?"

"A good many during the summer and fall. Not as many in the winter. But I think winter is the prettiest time for any waterfall."

"We'll have to come back in the winter, then."

They stayed at the base of the falls for an hour. Mo pulled their travel Chinese checkers from the backpack he carried, and before long, they each won a game. They tried to find a way to climb to the top of the waterfall but gave up when Mo slipped on a rock and slid ten feet before catching himself.

Getting hurt was a one-way ticket to getting caught. And neither of them wanted that.

The trip back took longer than the trip there, with neither of them in a hurry to say goodbye. At some point, Mo took her hand, and they walked with their fingers entwined.

"Do you think our families will ever get along?" Bronwyn leaned her head on Mo's shoulder and felt him shrug.

"Does it matter?"

"Of course it matters!"

He stopped and looked at her. "Why? I'm not, um, I mean, they aren't the ones I . . ." Mo dropped her hand and took a step away from her. "I don't care if they get along. I just care if you and I get along."

Bronwyn felt heat flooding through her skin. "We're forever. That isn't the issue."

"Then why does it matter what our families think of each other?"

"Don't you think it would be easier if we didn't have to hide?"

Mo turned back to the path, and she jogged a couple of steps to stay with him. It was a full minute before he said, "It's okay now, but, eventually, we won't hide. We won't let them do that to us."

Bronwyn wanted to believe him, but she'd known him too long.

She heard the doubt.

Her family was a problem. They would always be a problem.

ELEVEN

PRESENT DAY

Bronwyn hadn't expected to be escorted into her office by four large and, it was finally dawning on her, very angry men. When they walked over to her office, she'd been surprised to find Gray and Donovan leaning against Gray's Explorer, which was parked in her space.

They'd smiled and laughed and put on a good show for anyone watching. They claimed that Gray was dropping off Donovan because the newlywed wanted to spend the evening close to Cassie. They pretended to be interested in what Bronwyn wanted to do with her office, and since Cassie was in the middle of the dinner rush, Donovan wasn't in a hurry. They'd just come along to see.

The story worked because it wasn't unusual for Gray to drop Donovan off at The Haven. But that wasn't why either of them were here tonight.

Bronwyn had always been sensitive to the emotions of others, and even though she couldn't explain how she knew, she was certain that none of the anger she was picking up on was directed at her.

No. These men, Mo included, were angry on her behalf.

But they kept up the lighthearted charade as they filed into her office and even after they were inside. Donovan and Cal chatted about her desk while Mo and Gray walked around the perimeter of the room in a way that might have passed for casual and relaxed if someone had managed to plant surveillance cameras and was watching a live feed.

"Cal," Mo said in a relaxed voice that set every one of Bronwyn's nerves on edge, "have you ever made a desk before?"

"No, but I don't think it would be too difficult."

"I'll tell you one thing I'd be sure of." He pushed her chair away from the desk and knelt in the space behind it. "I'd make the leg space bigger than the standard."

"Bronwyn's not a giant, Mo. She doesn't need extra legroom." Cal's voice held a hint of amusement that Bronwyn might have believed had she not been looking at his face.

"Everyone needs extra legroom. And Bronwyn likes to sit cross-legged in her chair. She needs a desk that can accommodate that." To emphasize his point, Mo sat in her chair, then pulled his legs into the position that, in fact, she did enjoy sitting in. "Look. There's not enough room for her knees."

Cal groaned. "Mo, the desk is for Beep. Not you. She can decide what she wants or doesn't want."

"Actually, he's right." Bronwyn almost laughed at the shocked expressions on every face in the room. Even Gray turned around to look at her. "What? I do like to sit that way, but I don't do it because I can't with this desk setup. And because it would look very unprofessional. But in my off hours, I would love to be able to sit cross-legged."

Mo didn't make eye contact with her, but his smile was smug when he stood from the chair. Bronwyn tried to smile, but she couldn't. They'd agreed before they left that they would hold to the plan and keep up the story until Mo and Gray gave the all clear. She'd kept waiting for them to tell her everything was fine.

But neither had.

Cal glanced at his watch, then pulled his phone from his pocket. "Sorry. Hang on." He tapped his screen for a few seconds before turning to her with an apologetic slump of his shoulders. "I'm so sorry to do this, but Landry isn't feeling well. I think she's tired. She hasn't been sleeping much." He waved a hand around the room. "I've seen the space. Would it be okay if I come back later to take measurements? I can work up some ideas for you and then we can decide exactly what you want."

"Of course." Bronwyn had to work to swallow, her mouth so dry it felt like her tongue was coated in sandpaper. Mo hadn't even glanced in the direction of her computer, and it didn't look like he planned to. "Let's go back to my place so you can take her home." She tucked her hand in Cal's arm. "I'm so glad she has you. I love how you love her." Words she didn't have to fake. Thank goodness for that, because she'd lost the ability to pretend.

"She's easy to love." Cal's words were soft, his smile real. "She makes every day beautiful."

Gray and Donovan coughed and pretended to gag. Bronwyn turned on them. "Excuse you? Should I tell your beloveds that you mocked Cal for expressing his devotion to Landry?"

They chortled. Gray recovered first. "I'm all for talking like that to Meredith. But I'm certainly not going to say anything that mushy in front of these yahoos."

"Exactly." Donovan gave Gray a fist bump. "Keep the mushy stuff at home. Please."

Cal shook his head. "Ignore them. I've seen and heard them. Gray is so disgustingly in love with Meredith, I can barely stand to be in the same space with them sometimes. And Donovan? Why is this man even here right now? It's so he can make goo-goo eyes at his wife while she's cooking for the celebrities, and then he can drive her home. Because she'll be so tired." His voice kicked up an octave as he teased Donovan. "And he wants to spend every possible moment with her."

Cal patted her hand. "But that's okay. Words are great, but actions are even more important. And their actions say everything. Which is good because I'd take both of them down in a heartbeat if they didn't love my cousins the way they deserve to be loved."

"Hear, hear," Mo chimed in.

The four men teased each other until they were back at Bronwyn's house and safely inside. That's when the mood shifted. Mo and Gray checked her living area and seemed satisfied that it was clear, but no one spoke until Meredith and Landry joined them.

"I've set Eliza up in the other room with a movie." Landry tucked herself against Cal. "She has on headphones. We can talk."

Mo seemed to be ignoring everyone in favor of sketching something on a notepad he must have found in her kitchen.

"What did you find?" Bronwyn directed her question toward anyone who would answer.

Gray huffed out a breath. "There are three listening devices in your office, Bronwyn. And I think there's a small camera."

"There is." Mo turned the notepad over, revealing a sketch of Bronwyn's office. "Here." He pointed to the bookshelf. "In the lamp here." He tapped a rough depiction of a small table. "And here." He used the end of his pencil to indicate the space under her desk. "The camera is on the picture of The Haven while it was under construction. It's tiny. High end. Probably not on all the time to save battery. I'm confident we found everything in the office, but there could be other devices throughout The Haven."

Bronwyn sank into a chair. "I wasn't imagining it."

"Not even a little bit." Cal knelt beside her. "I'm not okay with this, Beep. You're out here alone, and someone's gone to a lot of trouble to spy on you in your office. It makes me wonder if you're safe anywhere on the property."

"Agreed." It was one word, but Gray's low rumble, combined with the set of his jaw, sent a chill racing through her. The police chief took the safety of everyone in Gossamer Falls seriously.

"You can't live like this, Bronwyn." Donovan leaned against the doorjamb, crossed his arms over his chest, and managed to convey menace with every breath.

"No. She can't." Mo's demeanor hadn't altered, but she'd known him most of her life. She sensed the burning fury that she couldn't see. Felt the heat of it, even though to anyone else, he looked and sounded cold.

Once upon a time, she'd taken her broken and battered heart and hidden it away. She convinced herself that needing people was a weakness she could no longer afford. And for many years, she'd clung to her independence. She'd pulled herself out of the hole she'd dug, stood on her own two feet, and had proven her worth and value. She'd done it all by herself.

She'd made a name for herself and a lot of money for her family.

She'd helped others.

She'd been generous with her time and resources.

But she'd locked away her heart, and only in the last few years had she allowed that poor, fragile part of herself out. And even then, with boundaries.

And in some cases, with silence.

But her heart was out of its cage, and in this moment, she allowed herself to absorb the protective anger surrounding her. These men weren't toxic, but they were dangerous to anyone who thought to harm those they loved.

And somehow, that included her.

She looked around the room and for the second time in less than twenty-four hours, she asked for help. "I'm not leaving my home.

I'm not leaving The Haven. I'm going to fight for this place, for my future here, and for the future of Gossamer Falls. But I can't do it alone."

Was it Mo's imagination or did Bronwyn look at him a second longer than anyone else as she scanned the room?

Her gaze landed on him again.

Was she going to say something? Her mouth opened.

"We need to focus on keeping you safe. That has to be our top priority." Gray's pronouncement cut off any words she might have been about to say.

So close.

"And the second priority needs to be finding out who is behind this and why." Mo patted his chest. "I'll start my dive through the computer system as soon as we figure out how to do it without anyone watching."

"That's simple enough." Donovan smirked. "Cassie can come by tomorrow and accidentally-on-purpose knock that picture off the wall. Problem solved."

"How's she going to do that?" Cal asked.

"The same way she knocked a picture off the wall in my office last week. She leaned against it and *voila*." He made a flashing gesture with his hand. "Broken glass. Shattered frame. No more camera."

"Is the photo one of a kind?" Landry asked.

Bronwyn shrugged. "I don't know, and I don't care. I'm not going to be able to be in that room for even a second if I'm being watched. What if someone saw me last night? Could they have seen the email I sent to you?"

The question was directed at Cal, but Gray answered. "No.

It's pointed straight at your desk. No line of sight to the screen. My guess is they wanted to combine the visual with the audio. Maybe they plan to record a meeting in your office in the future. They could be trying to set you up. Get you to say something incriminating so they can oust you."

"If they showed up to a board meeting with illegally recorded video from my office, I can assure you that would not go over well."

"Blackmail." Mo's statement dropped like a bomb in the room. He waited until things calmed down before he continued. "We all know Bronwyn isn't doing anything illegal, immoral, or against the best interests of The Haven or the community. But I'm not sure her family realizes she isn't like them. They may think they can catch her in the act of doing something, then blackmail her into supporting what they want done at The Haven."

Somber nods in the room showed everyone's agreement, except Bronwyn. She looked gobsmacked.

He didn't have time to process why that might be. "I'm not convinced they want Bronwyn out of office. She's done amazing things for The Haven. It's more profitable than ever. And she works more than any Pierce has ever worked, and that includes her grandfather and great-uncles, who, despite the family feud, worked hard to make The Haven what it is today."

"He has a point," Meredith spoke to Bronwyn. "Your cousins are lazy bums. Nathan's the only one with any gumption, and he's still not much to talk about. A few may want you gone, but it's more likely they want you to stay in your position but be under their control."

Bronwyn still looked like she couldn't comprehend what they were saying. "What could they think they'll catch me doing?"

"Not to bring up old wounds, but my guess is they'd love to catch you doing drugs, drinking on the job, or hooking up with a guest." Landry's words were soft but cut Mo like a torch slicing through metal. "As Mo has already stated, we"—she waved her hands to indicate all the people present—"know none of that's possible, but I'm not sure your family understands grace or redemption."

If her first statement had the power to cut through metal, her second statement was a blowtorch to Mo's soul. Had he treated Bronwyn the same way her family had? Always assuming the worst? Always believing she would fall, fail, or flee?

He'd been behaving like a Pierce. If Granny found out, she'd string him up by his ankles and beat him with a broom.

And he'd let her because he deserved it.

"True that." Meredith held out her hand and bumped Landry's fist. "Let's switch gears though. I have a better way to remove the devices. One that doesn't involve sending Cassie in there to wreak havoc."

Gray squeezed her close to him. "Let's hear it."

Meredith grinned. "I do believe it's time to redecorate."

Her declaration was met with a collective groan, then laughter, then nods.

"It's brilliant, Mer." Mo gave her a thumbs-up.

"I know, right?" Meredith bounced on her toes and turned to Bronwyn. "Your office needs a fresh coat of paint. That will require us to take everything off the walls. And while we're at it, we might need to remove everything from the office. As soon as we take the offending picture off the wall, Mo can work his magic on the computer, and we can take the rest of the devices out by removing everything and putting it all in storage. You, of course, will have to work from home for a few days. So sorry."

"It's not a bad idea." Cal looked at Mo, and Mo gave him a nod.

"I'm sure Meredith can find a reason for me to be there while she's doing her thing," Mo added. "She and Bronwyn can talk while I clone the hard drive."

Meredith clapped her hands. "We have a plan. No, wait. We don't have a plan. When are we doing this? I have patients tomorrow. But I'm done by early afternoon. Can we empty the office tomorrow?"

Bronwyn shook her head. "I want the office cleared out as soon as possible, but how will we justify it? We aren't ready for that stage. We have no idea what we're doing. We haven't picked out paint or anything!"

"Sure we have." Meredith smirked. "I have a Pinterest board already done for you. I'm thinking we go with this gorgeous pale blue for the walls, ceiling, and trim. There's something very luxe about having everything the same color, just using different finishes. So a flat on the ceiling, a gloss on the trim, and then maybe an eggshell on the walls?"

"You . . . what?"

"Your office is too masculine. You inherited it, and you've improved it, but it's time for a total refresh. I've been considering it for a while. We can use the paint as an excuse to take the unwanted items out. Then we'll go shopping. Once the painting is finished, we can tackle the rest of it a few pieces at a time."

Bronwyn shook her head. Mo pulled Meredith away from Gray and gave her a hug. "Brilliant. I love it."

The room filled with chatter until Cal let out a sharp whistle. "Okay. Here's the plan. Meredith drags Mo back to the office tomorrow afternoon. She has paint samples for Bronwyn to see. They remove everything from the walls and paint some swatches in places where we can cover them up with paintings that are safe. While they're doing that, Mo gets the hard drive and Bronwyn gets to have some say in her office renovation. I don't know if I can have a crew available this week, but we should be able to start next Monday."

"How?" Bronwyn asked.

"I have a crew that's supposed to be on another job. But it won't take long to paint your office. I'll pull a couple of guys, and they can knock it out in a few hours. But that means we need to take everything out of your office and store it somewhere. To be clear, we don't actually need everything moved out. We could shove it all to the middle and cover it up. But since we're trying to get it all jostled and moved and switched around, we'll say we need it out."

"It does need to go." Meredith gave Bronwyn a somewhat apologetic smile. "It's bad, sweetie. It's time to say hello to new and fresh and modern. We'll give you a space that's all yours, free of bugs and cameras, and put some new locks on those doors."

"That sounds wonderful, actually." Bronwyn's eyes had a suspicious shimmer, but it disappeared after a few rapid blinks. "I think this is all a great idea."

Cal looked at Mo. "You have other jobs in the works. How does this fit into your schedule?"

Why was Cal asking him such a stupid question? "I'll make it fit." He turned his focus to Gray. "How are we going to protect her? I'm not comfortable leaving her here alone."

"We worked that out already." Meredith gave him a beatific smile. "I'm going to spend the night tonight."

"You are?" Bronwyn and Gray asked at the same time with almost identical levels of incredulity.

"Yes, I am. This is, of course, how we're going to sell the quick nature of the office renovation. I was here, we started talking, and let's face it, everyone knows how much I like to decorate. It will be completely believable. I'll run to the hardware store in the morning and order the paint. I'm done with patients by two p.m. So that's when Mo and I will come back over, take pictures off the walls, and remove the creepy camera, then Mo will copy the hard drive."

"Thanks for letting me in on the plan." Mo wasn't angry. It

was a solid plan. But Meredith did have a tendency to run off and expect everyone to jump on board.

"I just did. And you're welcome."

"It sounds to me like you've covered tonight and tomorrow afternoon. What about tomorrow morning?" Gray asked.

Meredith held out her hand toward Landry. "I'll let Landry do the honors on that one."

"Why, thank you." Landry gave a slight bow. "Bronwyn, the silly goose, failed to put it on her calendar, but she has a planning session with me tomorrow morning. We will discuss my plans for new workshops, and she will be my guinea pig for a new class. If she likes it, we may add it to the list of options for our guests in the fall."

It was Bronwyn's turn to say, "Thanks for letting me in on the plan." And she said it with the same sarcasm Mo had.

"You're so welcome," Landry continued in mock sincerity. "I knew you'd want to drop everything for me, what with me being with child and all."

Bronwyn's eye roll was spectacular.

Everyone in the room laughed, but the laughter held the tension of what they'd learned tonight.

"I don't love the idea of either of you staying here, but I doubt anyone will try anything unless Bronwyn is alone," Gray said. "I'll have extra patrols nearby overnight."

Meredith gave a theatrical sigh. "You're such a romantic. Some men send flowers. My man sends extra patrols."

"And some men do both." Gray pulled her against his chest and returned his attention to Mo. "Maybe you can prioritize checking out the security guards here. Let's see if we have any bad apples. I want to secure Bronwyn here before we rock the boat too hard."

"I can do that. It would help if I had a list of names and basic contact info."

"I'll make one and send it over tonight," Bronwyn said, her voice thick with emotion. "Thank you all. I'm still frustrated, but I'm not scared anymore."

Mo was glad she wasn't afraid.

He was afraid enough for both of them.

TWELVE

TWENTY YEARS EARLIER

Fourteen-year-old Mo Quinn stood beside Meredith, Cal, and Bronwyn. They held bags of rice at the ready. Cal had suggested that they throw the whole bag at Chad, but Meredith and Bronwyn had insisted they only throw the rice.

Rice was stupid.

In fact, this entire concept was questionable. Standing around in the dark waiting for the bride and groom to run the gauntlet on their way to their getaway vehicle. Why? What was the point?

He had enjoyed decorating the car. Connor, Cal's oldest brother, had let them help. The back seat was filled with balloons and the windows had all kinds of random comments on them. They'd tied old cans and shoes to the back bumper. It would make a terrible racket as they drove away.

He leaned toward Bronwyn. "Do you want all this stuff when you get married?" He pointed at the crowd, the chaos, the mess.

Her eyes glowed. "It's traditional and fun for everyone. Why? Don't you?"

He shrugged. "I would think when you get married, the part

that matters is the getting married part. Not the reception. And definitely not all this stuff. I don't think I'd want all this."

Bronwyn rolled her eyes. Funny, but when she did that, he thought it was cute.

When Meredith did it, it ticked him off.

"What?"

"When you get married, you'll go along with whatever your bride wants. You'll want her to be happy. And you won't care if there are shoes tied to the bumper and whipped cream on the windshield."

At that moment, Naomi and Chad appeared at the end of the line. Chad was laughing. And Naomi was smiling at Chad in a way that made Mo think they had some private joke going between them.

Bronwyn leaned in and whispered, "All this stuff won't matter, but the smile on her face will be all you need. And you'll do anything you have to, to put it there."

Maybe she was right.

He turned so their faces were inches apart.

"You think so?"

"I know you. And I know so."

THIRTEEN

PRESENT DAY

As soon as the plans were finalized, Donovan left to hang out with Cassie. Cal, Landry, and Eliza said their good nights soon after. But Gray and Mo continued to hash out details for another twenty minutes. Bronwyn wanted to stay up and talk to Meredith long into the night the way they'd done a hundred times as teenagers. But the lack of sleep from the night before and the stress of the day hit her almost as soon as the doors closed on Mo and Gray. She made her apologies to Meredith, settled her in the guest room, and was in bed well before ten.

Despite her worries about what they'd found tonight, fatigue won, and she had no memory of tossing or turning. But now she sat in bed, panting for breath, convinced that something had awakened her—a quick glance at her nightstand, and she understood.

It wasn't that she'd heard something.

It was that she'd heard nothing.

She looked to her bedside clock, but the familiar red glow was absent.

The power was out.

Wait.

If her power was out . . .

She jumped from her bed and scrambled into the clothes she always left prepped in her bathroom. In her job, middle-of-the-night emergencies required her to look at least somewhat presentable. It didn't happen often, but occasionally, a guest flipped out, received traumatic news, or—once—became convinced they'd seen a ghost and demanded to see her.

She grabbed her phone from beside the sink and checked the time.

3:57 a.m.

She called the reception desk.

No response. That was weird. That desk was supposed to be staffed 24/7.

"Bronwyn?" Meredith's voice floated down the hall. "Are you okay?"

"I'm fine. Just need to run to the office."

"Why?"

"The power's out."

"Yes, I noticed that when my fan cut off. But why do you need to go to the office?"

"No one's answering the phone."

Meredith grumbled something unintelligible, then, "I'm getting dressed. Don't leave without me."

"This isn't your problem. Go back to bed."

"Like I would do that." Her voice was closer now, the light from her phone a glowing orb bouncing along the wall. Meredith pointed the light at Bronwyn. "There's a zero percent chance of you walking out the door alone. Also, where's your gun?"

That's when Bronwyn noticed the small pistol in Meredith's other hand. "Why are you walking around the house with a gun?"

"Hold that thought." Meredith disappeared into her room and emerged thirty seconds later with her shoes on and her hair up in a clip. "I think under the circumstances, the more important question is why aren't you carrying yours? We're in the middle of a situation here."

"Just because I can doesn't mean I make a habit out of walking around armed! And I don't want to make it a habit. Since when do you carry a gun everywhere you go, anyway?"

"Since I got myself engaged to the chief of police and he decided I should become even more proficient with firearms than I was before. And I don't always carry it. I'm not walking around like half the old ladies in town with a pistol in my purse."

"That's a relief." Bronwyn headed to the door, but Meredith held up a hand. "What now?"

"Now we tell Mo, Cal, and Gray what we're doing. And we do that before we go running off into the night. If"—Meredith pecked away at her phone—"I wanted to grab you, this is the kind of thing I'd do. I'd create a situation that forced you out of your house. Anyone could snatch you and have you in the woods in seconds."

Bronwyn waited until Meredith was done. "Would this be a good time to point out that this property is fenced? Even if they drag me into the woods, they can't get far."

Meredith nodded. "True. But it only takes a few seconds to kill you and leave your body behind. So let's not tempt fate. Okay?"

On that cheery thought, they jogged to her car and drove to the main reception area.

The night desk clerk, a bubbly and beautiful young woman named Miller, threw up her hands when she saw them. "Oh, Ms. Pierce. Thank goodness you're here! I was sitting at the desk and pop! Everything went dark. The emergency lights are on, of course, but still! Some of our guests will flip right on out when they realize there's no power!"

"There will be power," Bronwyn said. "We have generators. We'll need the maintenance crew to get them fired up, but it won't take long."

"How did I not know that?" Miller's eyes were wide. "That's something I should have known."

She was right. It was. But, unlike many of her coworkers, most of whom shared Bronwyn's last name, Miller genuinely seemed to want to learn and do her very best. Bronwyn couldn't fault her work ethic.

"We haven't needed to use them since you've been here. Don't worry about it. We'll get things sorted. The first step is to find out what happened and when we can expect to regain power. There's an emergency protocol in your desk drawer."

"Yes, ma'am."

"Find it and bring that and your phone to me."

"Yes, ma'am." Miller dashed away. She returned a minute later, huffing but with a beaming smile. "Got it!"

"Excellent."

Moments later, Bronwyn was on the phone with their local electric company, Miller was on the phone with their lead maintenance engineer, and Meredith was on the phone with someone she'd decided needed to be awake at 4:00 a.m.

A few guests wandered over, but no one was upset or frustrated. They were curious and returned to bed once their questions were answered. Fifteen minutes after she'd arrived on the scene, the maintenance crews were preparing the generators, the electric company was trying to hunt down the source of the outage, and Miller was proving to be an even better employee than Bronwyn had realized. She'd taken it upon herself to call their twenty-four-hour room service and ask them to deliver coffee, hot chocolate, and any available pastries to the lobby.

Bronwyn munched on a doughnut and stared at her phone, willing it to ring with good news.

"It's so weird." Meredith took a sip of hot chocolate. "I mean, it's summertime. It's not like we've had snow or ice. The last time it rained was three days ago. There've been no thunderstorms lately. I wonder what would have caused the power to go out."

"That's what I'd like to know as well." Bronwyn's uncle William came around the corner. He looked like he'd just left a business meeting. His pants had a crisp crease, his button-down shirt was wrinkle-free, and his shoes gleamed when hit by cell phone flashlights. "Bronwyn." He stepped into her line of sight.

She didn't respond. Her mother would have a hissy fit over what she would perceive as rudeness. But Uncle William had pushed every button Bronwyn had for so long, she simply didn't care anymore. This was a power play, and he was about to find out who held the reins.

"I'm speaking to you, young lady." His voice was low, his tone aggressive and hostile, and his breath reeked.

"Uncle William, before you come out in the middle of the night again in a situation that might involve interacting with our guests, do us all a favor and brush your teeth. Or, at the very least, grab a mint." And with that, she walked away.

Meredith slid into step beside her a moment later. "You're a rock star."

"I'm done, is what I am."

"Well, he isn't. Round two incoming."

"Bronwyn!" Uncle William's voice boomed out. She continued on her path. She could hear him getting closer, his feet pounding as he ran up to her. She expected him to step in front of her again. She wasn't prepared for him to grab her arm above the elbow and yank. Hard.

She stumbled back a step and then caught her balance. Before she could react further, a large body slid between her and Uncle William. One masculine hand wrapped around her waist. The other gripped Uncle William's arm above the wrist.

In a tone that she'd never heard and hoped she would never

hear directed at her, Mo said, “If you want to maintain the use of that hand, I strongly suggest you let her go.”

Uncle William’s fingers immediately relaxed their grip on her arm. “I’m not sure what business it is of yours, Mr. Quinn. I need a word with my niece, and she is treating me with disrespect.” Despite his big words, he stepped back . . . or tried to.

Mo didn’t release his arm, and he leaned into Uncle William’s personal space. “She’s been my business since we were five years old. And you can sell that spiel to someone who might believe it. I saw and heard the entire interaction. You don’t get to demand respect just because she has the misfortune of sharing DNA with you. Respect is earned, and you haven’t earned it.”

Bronwyn experienced a flicker of fear when Uncle William looked at Mo. Her uncle generally regarded her with disgust, but the look he gave Mo was one of full-blown hatred. “You’ll regret this, Quinn. I’ll see to it that you never step foot on this property again.”

Mo’s smile was so cold, it could have frozen the Amazon solid. “Another suggestion for you tonight. This one’s for free. Before you threaten me or anyone I care about, you might want to do a better job of covering your tracks.”

Bronwyn had no idea what Mo was talking about, but based on Uncle William’s expression, he did. It didn’t help that he spluttered and tripped over his words in a pitiful attempt at a comeback. He eventually landed on, “I have no idea what you mean.”

Mo turned and walked away from him, and in the process, Bronwyn went with him. After they took a few steps, Mo called over his shoulder, “Make sure you don’t try to claim that little trip to Greenville as a business expense.”

Mo kept his hand at her waist until they were back to the spot where Meredith stood, cell phone out and pointed in their direction. “I got the whole thing on video.” Her grin was a little scary.

"I'd like to see him try anything like that again." She pursed her lips. "I'm not sure what your dad would say, but your grandmother would lose her mind if she saw this."

"We can't show that to Grandmother."

"Duh. I would never. But that doesn't mean we can't use it for leverage. What's his problem, anyway?"

"He hates me. He always has."

"Bronwyn!" The call came from Emory, The Haven's maintenance engineer who kept everything running.

"Excuse me." She stepped away from Mo and Meredith. Or she planned to. Mo was no longer touching her, but he stayed beside her.

Emory didn't speak until they were standing in front of him. He threw an unmistakable look at Mo. "You sure he needs to be here for this?"

"Whatever this is, he can hear it."

"Okay, but you aren't going to like it."

"What happened?"

"Got a call from the power company. They know what the problem is."

"And?"

"Someone took out a transformer." Emory made eye contact with Mo.

"Can that actually happen?" Bronwyn asked.

"Yes, ma'am. It's not a common occurrence, but it has happened."

"How'd they do it?" Mo asked.

"Rifle." Emory mimicked shooting a gun. "The transformer is fenced in, and there are security cameras. It's not impossible with a high-powered hunting rifle, a good scope, and some knowledge of where to aim. Whoever did this didn't have to risk being caught on video, and they could have been long gone before anyone responded."

"Does Gray know?" Mo ran a hand through his hair, and the motion left it standing up in ways Bronwyn itched to fix.

"He's on his way there now." Emory turned back to Bronwyn. "The good news for us is that the transformer was old and was already slated for replacement. They have what they need to do the work. The current estimate is four hours. Maybe less."

"That's not bad at all." Bronwyn almost sagged into Mo but caught herself. What was wrong with her?

"No, ma'am, it isn't. My crew will have us running on generators in the next ten minutes. We'll have a few blips in service when they put us back on the grid but nothing that should cause anyone too much drama today." Emory looked at his watch. "Not that it's any of my business, ma'am, but you should go back to your place and get some more sleep. There's not a thing you can do out here."

"She micromanaging you, Emory?" Mo's voice held nothing but gentle teasing.

Emory grinned. "Not usually. She just takes good care of her people. She can't help it. But she's dead on her feet. Anyone with eyes can see it."

"I guess you told me." Bronwyn couldn't argue. She *was* dead on her feet. And frustrated. And scared again. Because there was no way this was a fluke.

FOURTEEN

EIGHTEEN YEARS EARLIER

"Bronwyn!" A pause. "Bronwyn! Are you here?"

Bronwyn watched from her hiding spot behind a mountain laurel. Mo would find her soon enough, but it was fun to play with him. At fifteen, hide-and-seek hadn't been part of their time together in a long while. But they hadn't seen each other in a week.

They met at Catherine's Falls whenever they could, and she usually waited for him on their favorite rock. But sometimes they played this game because she liked watching him. Liked hearing him call for her. There was hope and longing and maybe something that someday might be love in the way he said her name. So she held perfectly still and waited.

"Bronwyn Elena Elizabeth Pierce! I know you're here." Mo was laughing as he walked past her hiding spot. She let him get two feet away, then she moved. She'd planned to jump on his back, but he turned and she wound up in his arms instead, their faces centimeters apart.

Their eyes met.

Held.

"Hi." His voice had deepened and sometimes, like now, when he spoke, it was more rumble than word.

She didn't mind.

"Hi." She brushed her nose against his and tried not to let her disappointment show when he bent down until her feet hit the earth. She expected him to release her. Maybe he'd keep her hand. But he didn't move.

"I missed you." The words were a gift. The tone, a promise.

"I missed you too." Why was she struggling to catch her breath?

His hand came up and cradled her cheek. "Bronwyn?"

"Mm?"

"Could I, I mean, would you mind . . ." His voice faltered, and a hint of red stole up his neck. He cleared his throat. "I'd really like to kiss you."

"Okay."

He caught his breath. "Are you sure? You only get one first kiss."

"So do you."

They stared at each other, the crashing of the waterfall drowning out all other sounds. Standing this close to him, she could feel his heartbeat.

His thumb brushed her cheek, and she rose onto her toes. "I'm sure, Mo."

It was soft, sweet, and entirely without finesse. Neither of them had any idea what they were doing.

And it didn't matter.

He pulled away after far too short a time. "Can we do that again?"

She lifted her hands and wrapped them around his neck. "Yes."

This kiss was as tender as the first but more confident. "Bronwyn?" Mo whispered when he pulled away. "I know we can't tell anyone 'cause your parents would flip out. So in public, we'll just be friends. But when it's just you and me, will you be my girlfriend?"

She didn't tell him that she'd already thought she was. Maybe he'd thought so too but wanted to make it official.

Either way, her answer was easy. "Yes."

His smile was a little bit triumphant. "Does this mean you're mine?"

"I've always been yours."

FIFTEEN

PRESENT DAY

Mo walked Meredith and Bronwyn to Bronwyn's car, then followed them back to her home.

When they arrived, he climbed from the Jeep, flashlight and laptop in hand. "Stay put. I'm going to make sure everything's clear inside."

Neither of them argued, which was good because there was no way he would stand by and watch them go inside until he was sure this hadn't been an elaborate scheme to lure Bronwyn out of her home.

He set his laptop on the entryway table and scanned each room with his flashlight. The generators were running almost everything else on the property, but Bronwyn had told them her home was on a separate system and she'd wait to see if they needed to turn it on.

He did his best not to snoop, but when his light landed on the magnetic Chinese checkers board on Bronwyn's home office wall, he did a double take. It was all he could do to keep himself moving.

The rock on her mantel had surprised him. But this? He pulled his mind away from rainy days and nights by the fire and a game he'd played many times as a kid but never since she left.

He kept moving and checked in the bathrooms, behind shower curtains, and in closets. He was quick but thorough.

Five minutes later, he held the door for Meredith and Bronwyn to enter. "It's clear."

They walked inside, and he followed them in and locked the door.

"Um, Mo?"

He tilted the light to where the two women stood. They wore matching confused expressions.

"Yes."

"Whatcha doing, bro?"

Mo pointed to Bronwyn's sofa. "I'm staying right here until the power comes on."

Meredith narrowed her eyes at him. "Is Gray behind this?"

"No, but he agreed with me. I didn't like that whole situation with William. And the timing of that text Bronwyn received the other night with this outage? I don't believe in coincidences. It's unlikely that anyone would attempt to do anything now, but it's not worth the risk. I'll stay here and make sure you both make it to where you need to be in the morning. Assuming the power is back on and everything is working, Bronwyn and Landry should be safe in a public space with security cameras. And you"—he pointed to Meredith—"will be as safe as you ever are in town."

He held up a hand as both women tried to talk. "As much as I would love to hear your objections, I think if you went to bed now instead of arguing with me, you'd get a solid ninety minutes in before the day begins."

Bronwyn turned to Meredith. "Huh, I wasn't going to object. I was going to say thank you."

Meredith laced her arm through Bronwyn's and turned them toward the hallway. "I say we leave him out here without blankets as penance for assuming the worst." She lowered her voice. "Although, to be fair, I was going to share that I have a gun and don't need any protection, so I don't have an excuse for righteous indignation."

Mo couldn't help it. He laughed. Then yelled down the hall, "I knew it. Go to bed. Sleep."

He waited to retrieve his laptop until he heard both bedroom doors close. Then he settled on the sofa. He hadn't mentioned his own weapon, but it was in easy reach. Three minutes later, a door opened, and the sound of footsteps coming down the hall reached his ears.

He didn't look up from his screen. "Mer, seriously, get some sleep."

A fleece blanket dropped onto the sofa beside him, and he looked up in time to catch Bronwyn's smile before she all but ran from the room.

He didn't need a blanket. It was July. It wasn't cold. But he picked it up and draped it over his lap anyway. It would have been rude not to. That was all.

Bronwyn slipped back into her room and forced her heart to slow down.

Mo Quinn was in her house, sitting in her living room and staying awake to protect her.

No big deal. Right?

She lay in bed and stared at the ceiling. Her room was too dark. The house was too quiet. And . . . was that Mo tapping away at a keyboard?

How was she supposed to fall asleep?

But as she lay there, she found something soothing in the rhythmic sounds coming from her living room. Little reminders that she wasn't alone.

That for tonight anyway, she was safe.

And she slept.

When her phone alarm went off at 7:00 a.m., Bronwyn lay in bed for a full minute, mentally reviewing her bank balance and investments. If she bought a ticket and moved to Spain, would anyone miss her? How long would it take to find work?

She spoke minimal Spanish, so that was a potential flaw in the plan. But the temptation was real.

How many days did she go through this ritual? The country changed. Sometimes it was Italy. Sometimes Chile. The British Isles were top contenders. But what would it be like to run away?

Her eyes filled with tears because she'd done that once.

And it had ruined everything.

Her running days were over. She was here. Was she trapped? Maybe. But was she making the best of it? In some ways, yes. In others? So much no.

With that warm and fuzzy thought, she climbed from bed and walked into her bathroom. It was only when she flipped the switch and nothing happened that memories from the night flooded back through her.

The cameras and listening devices in her office. The power outage. Meredith.

Mo.

Was he still here? Had he left when the sun came up?

She used her phone flashlight to see as she brushed her teeth, dressed, put her hair up in a messy bun, and slapped on some mascara and lip gloss. Mostly au naturel was the name of the game today.

She took several deep breaths and walked out of her room.

Meredith sat on the sofa beside Mo. Her hair stuck out in a million directions, she still had her pajamas on, and she was sipping coffee with her eyes closed. "Morning," she mumbled. "When did

I get too old to pull an all-nighter?" She spoke without opening her eyes. "I think my eyelids are broken."

Mo closed his eyes. "Do you need me to drive you home?"

"You're going to have to. I don't have a car."

"You don't?"

"No. Landry took it last night."

"How were you planning to get to work this morning?"

Meredith yawned. "Landry was going to drive it in on her way to work, but Cal texted and said he's driving her in today and he's going to hang out with her. We're supposed to make sure Bronwyn makes it to Landry's studio safely, then you can take me home."

"Sounds like a plan."

Meredith dropped her head to Mo's shoulder. "Wake me up when it's time to go."

He shoved her off of him. "Go get ready. Bronwyn's ready. You're the holdup here."

She grumbled unintelligibly as she staggered to her feet. But she held out her coffee cup in a toast. "Thank you for the coffee."

He reached for the cup as he got off the couch. "I'll pour you some more. You're going to need it."

He made the barest hint of eye contact with Bronwyn, but she was sure she saw a smile before he escaped to the kitchen.

"Is it ridiculous that I'm already dreaming about going to bed tonight?" Meredith asked as she walked past Bronwyn. "You know what, I don't even care. My bed is calling me, and I must go." She paused in the hallway and turned back. "Are you really ready to go?"

"I'm as ready as I can be with no power." She turned to the kitchen. "Wait. How did he make coffee? We still don't have power."

Before she could say more, a cup of coffee was placed in her hand. The coffee was the exact shade of brown she preferred.

Meredith made grabby hands as Mo handed her a fresh cup as well. "Mo can do anything when he sets his mind to it."

Bronwyn took a sip. The coffee was piping hot. Lightly sweetened. How?

"Mo," Mo said, "had the good sense to have the room service staff bring him several carafes of coffee as soon as they had generator power in the kitchen."

"Like I said." Meredith yawned so big it almost split her face. "You can do anything. Give me five minutes."

Mo went to the sofa and packed his computer. Bronwyn had no idea how long she stood there, staring at him. When she realized what she was doing, she followed Meredith down the hall. But instead of going to her room, she escaped into her office. Once she was in there, she took a seat at her desk and sipped her coffee. The sun was coming up, and she could see around her office a little bit.

Enough to see that something had changed.

There, across from her desk, on the magnetic Chinese checkers board she looked at every single day, someone had moved a blue marble.

No. Not someone.

Mo.

She stood and walked to the board. Her free hand hovered over the red. Should she do it?

"Beep?" Meredith's voice came from the hallway.

"Coming." Bronwyn clutched her coffee and studied the board a few seconds longer before she hurried from the room and ran into Mo.

Literally.

His arms braced her and kept her from falling, but in the process, he twisted around, slammed his back into the wall, and pulled her against him.

The hallway was too dark to make out anything but the rise and fall of his chest and the sound of his breathing.

And the racing of her heart.

"What's going on?" Meredith yelled.

"Nothing," Bronwyn called out.

"Bronwyn's trying to kill me." Mo's voice came over the top of hers.

A light shone down the hall. "Huh." Her light disappeared. "I hate to be disagreeable, but from the looks of things, I'd say you're both lying."

At her words, Bronwyn took a step back, but Mo didn't release her arms.

"Flirt later." Meredith sounded exasperated and delighted at the same time. "I have patients. Let's move."

Mo's hands dropped away, and Bronwyn could swear she still felt their warmth the entire way out of the house, as she'd settled into the back seat of Mo's Jeep, and when she climbed out of the vehicle at Landry's studio.

Cal stood at the door and looked them all over. "I'm jealous you didn't invite me to the slumber party." Landry stepped outside and leaned against him.

Mo's humorless smile sent a chill down Bronwyn's spine. "You can come tonight if you want. I wouldn't mind the company."

"What?" Cal, Landry, and Meredith spoke in unison.

Bronwyn was too stunned to say anything.

"We can discuss it later." Mo was all business, and his tone brooked no argument. "I have to take Meredith to her office. Cal, you've got Bronwyn?"

"You know I do." The response was more serious than Bronwyn had expected.

"Thank you." Mo nodded at Cal, then nudged Meredith. "You're the one in a hurry."

He stepped forward and kissed Landry's cheek. "Sorry we can't stay to chat."

She smiled at him and placed a hand on his heart. "Do what you need to do. We've got her."

Bronwyn looked between Mo, Landry, and Cal, and the pain that slid through her didn't have a name. Was she jealous? Or was it that she felt left out of their relationship?

She considered her reaction as Meredith and Mo drove away and she followed Cal and Landry inside The Haven's art studio.

Landry had told her, more than once, how much she adored Mo. She'd always wanted a brother and loved how he treated her much like he treated Meredith.

Bronwyn didn't think she was jealous of that. She was happy for Landry and for Mo. For all his efforts to appear taciturn and aloof, Mo had a deep well of love and affection, and he needed people to love.

But maybe she was jealous of the ease, the tenderness, the certainty that all was well between them.

She'd felt that way once. And what did it mean that she wanted to feel that way again?

SIXTEEN

EIGHTEEN YEARS EARLIER

Bronwyn stood on the edge of The Haven Christmas party and pretended to be interested in the people around her. Thirty more minutes and she could escape. Her parents had been so excited to get her out of their hair, they'd agreed to a sleepover at Meredith's tonight.

"Bored?" Corbin Driscoll stood a few feet away, sipping on some kind of amber drink in a glass. He didn't look at her, but there was no one else around so he must be talking to her.

Bronwyn called on every moment of etiquette and manners her grandmother had ever attempted to instill in her. "Of course not, Mr. Driscoll. I'm having a lovely evening. I hope you are?"

A large round ice cube sloshed in his glass as Corbin Driscoll snorted a laugh. When he regained control of himself, he took another sip and leaned toward her. "Bronwyn, darling, you're already excellent at schmoozing the guests. You'd make an excellent producer. But do us both a favor and don't go into acting."

She lifted her chin ever so slightly.

"And please, for the love of all that's holy, I'm not *that* old. Call me Corbin."

A thrill shot through her. Corbin Driscoll—the producer everyone wanted on their project, the mind behind some of the biggest movies of the past five years—just told her to call him by his first name. "I couldn't—"

"Nonsense. You aren't a child. Anyone with half a brain can see that. You're smarter than almost everyone in the room. Those who claim anything different are just trying to bring you down to their level."

Corbin believed in her. The idea settled into the spot that had been ripped open earlier when her mother had told her that, at the rate she was going, they'd be lucky if they could marry her off to a B-movie director, as if she was breeding stock instead of their flesh-and-blood daughter.

She couldn't wait to tell Meredith and Mo what Corbin had said.

But an hour later, when she curled into the cozy sofa in the Quinns' living room and Meredith asked her about the party, she kept that tidbit to herself. It would have sounded haughty to say that one of the brightest minds in Hollywood thought she was a shining star.

Right?

A month later, when the email hit her inbox, Bronwyn could hardly believe it. Corbin had sent her a list of articles about movie production. She read everything he sent and then, with trembling fingers, hit reply.

SEVENTEEN

PRESENT DAY

Mo drove in silence for five minutes.

Meredith wasn't asleep. She just wasn't talking.

That was okay. He could wait.

Five more minutes passed before the dam broke.

"Are you going to explain why you plan to spend the night at Bronwyn's again?" she asked. "Or are you going to leave me in suspense?"

Mo considered leaving her in suspense, but he was too tired to mess with her. "After what happened in the last six hours, do you think she should stay alone?"

"Do you plan to answer every question with a question?"

"Do you?"

She huffed, then leaned toward him. "You're in big trouble, bro."

Didn't he know it.

"I don't disagree that she needs someone around, but there has to be more."

"Why do you say that?" Mo asked.

"Because if it was just about keeping her safe, you could move her into Cal's tiny house. Or into my house with me. I would think that would be your first choice. So, why stay at her place?"

"I had time to think while sitting there last night. This morning. Whenever. And I remembered something that's come up a few times in my work."

Meredith looked at her watch. "You're going to need to give me the fast version."

"Bronwyn has hired me. Sort of. But not really. There's no contract. And as CEO of The Haven she can't enter into a contract with me without making it clear to everyone there that I'm working on the systems."

"Which we don't want to do. At least, not yet." Meredith twisted in her seat to face him. "Why is the contract important?"

"Because one thing The Haven prides itself on is the privacy and security of its guests and their personal information. Even though I would never do anything with that data, if I remove it from the premises, even if it's later proven that I did it for the benefit of The Haven, the board could use it to force her out."

"How?"

"It could be considered a breach of her contract. I'll confirm it this afternoon when I look. This isn't about whether or not she would do anything inappropriate with the data, or even if I would. This is about the letter of the law or, in this case, the letter of the contract. If she's in breach, they could remove her. I won't save her job for her to lose it over a technicality."

"So what's the solution?"

"The solution is for me to use only computers that are the property of The Haven and that are located on-site. I can duplicate her hard drive in her office, then work from her laptop in her home."

"Would that be sufficient?"

"I think so."

Meredith was quiet for a few moments, then she squeezed his

arm. "Is it possible you're making this up so you have an excuse to stay with her?"

Yes? No? He had no idea. No. Definitely not. "Does it matter?"

Meredith sighed. "I don't guess it does."

"The alternative is to see if she can come up with a reason for me to work from her office. But, given the current climate, I don't think that's wise. Not yet."

"I agree."

"So you'll explain it to her?" Mo asked.

"No."

"What?"

"You heard me. I'm tired of playing the go-between. Talk to her yourself."

"You know I can't." The words were gritted out. "I'm not the problem here."

"I'm not sure I'd go that far." Meredith made a sound in the back of her throat that was disturbingly growl-like. "Fine. I'll talk to her. But, Mo—"

"The ball's in her court. It's her move. I've opened the door. I've cleared the decks. If you can think of a way to describe it, I've done it."

"I wonder what her problem is?"

"She's scared." Mo hadn't realized that truth until he said it out loud. But with the verbalization came a sense of rightness. Before he could elaborate, Meredith's phone rang, and she answered it on speaker.

"Hey, babe." Gray's voice came through loud and clear.

Mo pretended to gag.

Meredith took the phone off speaker and put it to her ear. "Yeah. Almost to the office." A pause. "I have a change of clothes." Another pause. "Okay. See you soon." A longer pause. And then a breathy, "I love you too."

She placed her phone in her lap. "I won't apologize for telling my fiancé I love him."

"Could you be less gross about it?"

"Nope."

He parked in front of her dental office, where Gray was waiting by the front door. "See you in a little while."

She leaned over and kissed his cheek. "Love you too."

"Yeah, yeah."

She climbed down from the Jeep and closed the door. She took two steps before he called out, "I love you too."

She turned and beamed at him. "I know you do." She blew him a kiss and then squealed when Gray pulled her into his arms.

She was laughing when Mo drove away.

He was so thankful for the women in his life who loved him and whom he loved in return. But somehow, platonic sibling love left him feeling more hollow than he'd been in a long time.

He shook himself from his melancholy thoughts and called Cal to fill him in on his new plans.

Twenty minutes later, he was at his desk. It was time to do a deeper dive into William Pierce.

He hadn't shared what he knew about the man before because he'd been undecided about what he should or shouldn't say. He was sure William would assume Mo had somehow hacked into his finances, but the truth was that the tidbit of information he had on William had come about the old-fashioned way. He'd seen him, followed him, and documented what he saw.

Last winter, Mo had watched as William Pierce sat at a hotel bar with a much younger woman, who was not his wife, and after several drinks, the two headed up to a room.

He had no proof that anything inappropriate had happened. He didn't know who the woman was or why William had met her there. His dig at the man when they met at The Haven this morning had been a risk, but based on William's reaction, he was guilty of something.

And Mo was about to find out what.

It didn't take long, and as had happened far too many times in the past, he wished he hadn't.

The woman was the daughter of another resort manager, which begged the question, Was it a sordid affair? Business espionage on his part or hers or both? Something else entirely?

Mo hadn't found anything conclusive when Meredith called him at lunchtime. Her last patient of the day had a stomach bug and had cancelled, so she was headed back to The Haven earlier than planned.

"I'll be there by one."

"Great. See you then."

He grabbed a protein shake, took a five-minute cold shower, dressed, and was parked outside Bronwyn's office at 12:55 p.m. He sat in his Jeep and waited for Meredith. There was no point in going inside. It wasn't like Bronwyn would talk to him.

And he didn't blame her. Not with listening devices in the office. Now wasn't the time.

But soon. She was going to cave soon.

Meredith arrived two minutes later, and they walked inside together.

"Mr. Quinn. Dr. Quinn." Bronwyn's assistant, June, gave them a cheery smile. "Ms. Pierce mentioned that you were coming by this afternoon. She's in a meeting at the moment. Could I bring you some water? Coffee? Tea?"

"No, thank you." Mo smiled at her, then took a seat on the small sofa. Meredith joined him. They didn't speak, but Mo knew what his sister was thinking.

Bronwyn hadn't had a meeting on her calendar. She was supposed to be with Landry all morning.

So who was in her office now?

The answer came ten minutes later. The office door opened and out walked a curvy brunette who spent so much time in the spotlight that even someone as intentionally out of touch as Mo recognized her. "Darling, you're the best. The absolute best." She and Bronwyn did that hug-and-kiss thing where they kissed the air on either side of their faces. He'd never understood the point of it.

Bronwyn's smile was . . . off. On the one hand, Mo was sure she genuinely liked the woman who sashayed by him. On the other hand, she wasn't happy that this person had been in her office.

Bronwyn waved them in and closed the door behind her. She pulled out her phone. "Excuse me for a moment. I need to send this and then we can start talking."

Meredith didn't miss a beat. "Mo, why don't you help me move a few of these pictures? I told Beep we'd paint some swatches on the walls where we can cover them easily."

Mo removed several photographs before reaching the frame he most wanted out of the room. "Where should we put this one?"

Meredith made quite a show of hemming and hawing before she said, "I think we should stack all of them in the conference room. That way, we won't risk knocking anything over."

The story was flimsy, but Meredith had a reputation for being a force of nature. She'd decided the police station needed to be redone and had it finished in less than a month. It was town lore, so no one would find this suspicious. At least, he hoped they wouldn't.

He and Meredith took the framed prints and photos to the conference room.

When they returned to the office, it took Meredith less than thirty seconds to devise a reason to remove a lamp that held one of the listening devices. The other two would be harder to clear out, given that one was on a bookshelf and the other under Bronwyn's desk. But they'd find a way.

For now, Mo sat down at the computer and did what he needed to do to clone the hard drive while Meredith and Bronwyn chatted about paint colors, the power outage, how the guests had reacted this morning, and the surprising news that one of them thought Bronwyn should offer an unplugged experience—tent camping, not glamping.

Mo kept one ear on their conversation while he searched the computer system for hidden files and malware.

It took him almost thirty minutes to be satisfied that he had everything he needed. By then, the new paint color had been chosen, and plans had been made to remove everything from the office because Meredith had walked around the room a few times and said, "Bronwyn, don't hate me, but what's under this carpet?"

It turned out to be a hardwood floor.

Meredith and Bronwyn stared at each other in delight and then talked over each other in a swirl of wonder.

"These floors—"

"Could be gorgeous."

"We have to pull up all the carpet—"

"We need Cal . . ."

"Mo will help us." That last came from Meredith, and it was those words that finally forced Mo to spin around in the chair he'd commandeered.

He leaned back, laced his fingers across his chest, and tapped his thumbs together. "What's in it for me?"

"The delight of knowing you've brought beauty to Bronwyn's office."

"What if the floors were covered up for a reason? They might be ugly. Stained. Beyond redemption."

"What if they just need a little TLC to be glorious?" Meredith countered.

Mo rose from the chair. "Show me."

"We need to move this bookcase to get a good pull on the carpet." Meredith patted the sturdy piece of furniture like it was a pet. "This right here is gorgeous. I hate to move him out of his home, but he will have to go for us to get to the floors. He will come back." She pointed to a small table that held a barely alive plant. "That, however, is gone. Forever. And good riddance."

Bronwyn coughed a little. "Um, my grandmother . . ."

"Your grandmother would be horrified that you've kept such a gaudy piece here. You're the CEO of The Haven, Bronwyn. Your office should reflect that. I can't believe I haven't thought of this sooner. But now that I have, consider it done. Your space will be your own private haven at The Haven."

She grinned at them, gave a small bow, and patted herself on the back. "Thank you. Thank you."

Bronwyn made the briefest eye contact with Mo before she offered up a pitiful golf clap. Mo joined in.

Meredith lifted her nose into the air. "Mock me if you will. I'm not wrong. That actress who was in here earlier? She was probably horrified by the condition of this room."

Mo ignored Meredith's dramatics and pulled books off the shelf. "We need to empty this before we try to move it or none of us will be doing anything for the next month after we throw out our backs."

Bronwyn didn't respond but joined Mo in the effort while Meredith, now in full character, continued to discuss the horrors of the office.

She'd loved drama in school, while Bronwyn had avoided anything theater related.

She'd always said that was a world she had no interest in becoming part of—until she left town for Hollywood. Supposedly to learn the ins and outs of the business and become a producer.

Mo had never bought it. Still didn't. But he'd lost the right to ask her about it years ago.

"Mo?" Meredith's question pulled him out of the dark hole he'd fallen into.

"Yeah?"

"You okay?"

"Fine." He smiled. Or tried to, anyway. Based on her reaction and Bronwyn's grimace, he must not have pulled it off. "Let's empty this thing so we can move it out of the way."

Bronwyn and Meredith were whispering about him, but he ignored them. He took a few moments to focus his mind on the present. To take in the beauty of the furniture, the texture of the books in his hands, and the smell of paper mixed with a faint trace of lemon polish.

"How often is this room cleaned?"

Meredith snorted. "Are you implying Bronwyn's office is dirty?"

"Not at all. I can smell the furniture polish and there's almost no dust. Bookshelves are hard to clean."

Bronwyn took a stack of books and moved them to her desk. "Our housekeeping staff is exceptional, and the standards for my office are the same as those for each cabin. This space is cleaned three times a week."

Mo tucked that tidbit away. The "exceptional" housekeepers had access to Bronwyn's office in a way few others did. He needed to get their names and check the security footage. They could have been bribed to set the bugs. Or leave the room long enough for someone else to do it.

Or they could be completely innocent of everything except an overuse of lemon oil.

Once the shelf was empty, he took one end, Meredith took the other, and Bronwyn took the middle.

"Good grief," Meredith grunted as they slid it across the carpet. "Are the shelves lined with lead?"

Despite her grousing, with the three of them working, moving the shelf to the opposite wall took only a minute.

Then all three of them hit their knees and pulled the carpet back.

Once they got it started, it came up with relative ease. Bronwyn's small cry stopped Mo from his efforts.

A dark stain covered a space the size of a laptop. Splatters of a similar shade flecked the area around it.

It probably wasn't blood. But . . . it sure looked like it.

Bronwyn could feel Meredith and Mo standing close to her, staring at the stained floor.

"Do you think it's blood?" Meredith asked.

"It could be." Mo's answer was thoughtful. "But it could also be from wine or water. Look at the floor around it. There's almost no finish or protection on the wood. Any liquid could have left that stain. And let's think this through. If it was a bloodstain, covering it up with carpet isn't a solid way to hide your sins. The stain is still there. If I were trying to hide a stain, I'd sand it or cut it out if necessary."

"Which leads back to the theory that there's a perfectly reasonable explanation for this." Meredith leaned closer. "Who in your family might know?"

Bronwyn reached down and grabbed the edge of the carpet. "My dad might." She tugged. "Or my grandmother." Mo and Meredith both returned to their spots and pulled as well. "I'll ask.

This carpet isn't new, but it was when I returned to town. When I moved into the office, I saw no reason to replace it."

Meredith tsked. "Well, it's time now."

They continued pulling the carpet up, sliding furniture, desks, and chairs off the carpet and onto the now-revealed hardwood floor. They ended up removing the bookshelf from the room entirely.

Except for that dark stain, the floor had real potential. "I'll call Cal." Mo had his phone in his hand. "If you're going to redo the floor, that will alter the plans for the paint. These floors need work." He tapped the screen and held the phone out. "Cal, you've got me, Meredith, and Bronwyn."

Bronwyn fought the little zing at the sound of her name. She'd always rather liked her name. But no one had ever said it quite the way Mo did.

She turned away and took a deep breath. She was well and truly losing it. *Pull it together, Beep.*

Behind her, Mo filled Cal in on their discovery. Cal's groan filled the space. "Seriously? It was a paint job, Meredith. A paint job. Now we're sanding and refinishing floors?"

"But they're gorgeous. Or, they will be. I think. Maybe you should look at them first and tell us."

"Send me a picture. You do realize if we're doing the floors, we'll have to take everything out of the space, and no one will be able to go in for several days?"

"Yes."

"But does Bronwyn?"

Bronwyn turned then and walked to where Mo stood with his phone. "I know, Cal. But now that Meredith's caught the scent, she's gotten me excited about the possibilities. I'll have to work from home more. Or from the conference room. It will be worth it. Besides, we've already removed a lot of things while pulling up the carpet. There isn't *too* much left."

Cal's sigh was loud and long. "Send me a picture of the floor and a close-up of the stain. I'll have to see it in person, but a picture will give me a clue about what we're dealing with. And send the picture to Gray. He might be able to tell you if it's blood or not. He's seen some . . . stuff."

Meredith's eyes were wide, and she nodded in agreement. "True enough."

"And, Beep?"

"Yeah, Cal?"

"This also means you'll have to pick out a wood stain. I have samples at my office. Come by anytime. I'm in the office this week."

"I can do that."

"Okay. Later."

The call disconnected, and Mo slid the phone into his pocket. "I guess the best thing for me to do is hightail it out of here before you put me to work on the rest of this 'not too much' that needs to go." He gazed around the office, lingering on the small sofa, the table, the chairs, the desk, and a few other cabinets that they'd moved around but hadn't taken out of the room.

Bronwyn couldn't help but laugh. But instead of talking to Mo, she focused on Meredith. "I'll talk to Emory. He's still busy with the electrical stuff, but we can probably have a crew here tomorrow to haul everything out. We'll store some of it in the conference room. Whatever won't fit we can put in a storage building."

"I'm proud of you." Meredith slid her arm through Bronwyn's. "It's not like you to be so spontaneous. I promise we'll make it awesome."

Bronwyn met Mo's eyes. He reached into his opposite pocket and handed her something black and heavy for its size. The cloned hard drive. She took it and slid it into her purse.

While her back was turned, Mo spoke. "I'm out. Be careful. Be good. I'll be back later. Don't spend all of Bronwyn's money on a new office chair."

Meredith swatted her brother's arm as he walked out the door laughing. "You love that chair!" she called after him. "You said it was worth every penny."

Mo's laughter was his only response.

"He does love it." Meredith flopped into Bronwyn's chair as she spoke, then jumped to her feet. "And you are totally getting one just like it. How do you sit in this? It's awful."

Bronwyn looked around the office. The place was trashed. There was still one active bug. Meredith's drama had gotten rid of the one on the bookshelf. Or moved it anyway. And the one under her desk would be gone by tomorrow.

The next time she used this office, it would be clean of whatever filth had infiltrated her space.

And that stain. Which she really, really hoped wasn't blood.

But for now she caught Meredith's eye and nodded for her to follow. She grabbed her purse and they walked out together. When they were in the parking lot, she said, "I can't have Mo stay with me tonight."

She'd been thinking about it since Meredith called her in between patients this morning. And while there was a lot to be said for having Mo all to herself and being able to talk things out, she wasn't ready.

"I'm a chicken, I admit it. But—"

"It's okay. I talked to Cal. We have a plan that will work."

"Then let's hear it."

"For tonight and tomorrow, I'll spend the night. We'll say we need to discuss the renovation. Gray's working—he has people out of town doing some training, so he's pulling doubles."

"Mer—"

"No arguing. All of us, including Mo, will be going to bed early tonight. He can't work on no sleep, despite what he thinks. Tomorrow, you and I are going out with Landry. Cal says she needs a girls' night. We'll leave Mo at your house to work. That gets us through two nights. After that? We'll see how it's going."

"I don't like this."

Meredith cocked her head. "Do you think any of us do? We don't have to like it, but we all have to deal with it." Before Bronwyn could respond, Meredith kept going. "Let's go see Cassie and you can tell me what that starlet in your office wanted."

Bronwyn had little choice but to follow along. All the while, Meredith's words rang in her soul. Her actions. Mo's actions. They hadn't happened in a vacuum, and their impact reached everyone they knew and loved.

EIGHTEEN

SEVENTEEN YEARS EARLIER

"Mother, Father, I'd like to ask you a question." Bronwyn stood with perfect posture and did everything in her power to keep emotion out of her voice. If her parents had a clue how desperately she wanted this, they'd never go for it.

Her father glanced at his watch. "You have five minutes, Bronwyn. Your mother and I have a dinner engagement."

"Yes, sir. I wanted to ask if you'd be agreeable to me going on a trip with Meredith and her family this summer."

At the mention of the Quinns, her mother's already stiff posture grew impossibly more rigid. "No."

"Mother, it's not a regular vacation."

"No."

"It's going to be educational. They're visiting national parks all over the western US. I've never been to any of those places. You want me to expand my horizons and be well-traveled. This would be a way for you to make that happen. And I'd be busy all summer. It's perfect."

Her parents exchanged a look. At her mother's nod, her father gestured toward a chair. "Bronwyn, please have a seat. We had planned to discuss this with you later, but now's as good a time as any."

Bronwyn braced herself for the lecture she knew was coming. All about how she needed to find friends more in keeping with her social standing. How she should spend less time with the Quinns. How her future depended on her focusing more on her studies and learning the family business.

"You can't travel this summer because you'll be leaving for Switzerland in early July."

Bronwyn's thoughts screeched to a halt, then raced away in fifty different directions. Switzerland? July? Leaving? What? But what she said was, "I'm sorry. I don't think I understand."

Her mother picked up the conversational baton. "We've enrolled you in a prestigious finishing school in Switzerland. It's all very hush-hush. Your father and I have been working on this for a couple of years. It's very exclusive, and we didn't want to get your hopes up if it didn't work out. We have a backup plan, of course. You have a place at the same school I attended in Massachusetts. But we had hoped for even more for you, and we've succeeded."

Her parents shared an exultant smile.

They were happy. They had worked hard to . . . ruin her life. How could they not know her at all?

"She's stunned," her father said. Was he . . . proud? He smiled at Bronwyn. "You'll need all of June to pack and prepare. Once you leave here, you'll be in year-round classes and sessions for the next two years. So, you see, there's simply no way you can go gallivanting all over with the Quinn girl and her family. Let them have their big adventure. You'll be heading off on one of your own. One they could never even dream of."

Bronwyn forced herself to speak slowly. "I can't go to Switzerland."

Her parents frowned.

"Or Massachusetts. Or anywhere. I want to stay here. I want to graduate with my class. I'm junior class president! I have obligations and plans here."

Her mother waved all of that away with one elegant gesture. "Please. No one expects you to do all of that when you have an opportunity like this!"

Bronwyn fought her rising panic. "Mother, I'm sure this is a lovely opportunity, but it should be for someone else. I have no interest in—"

"Young lady." Her father's voice had lost all its pride and pleasure and was now hardened. "You seem to think this is optional for you. It is not. You will be going. You will succeed. You will make us proud. Have I made myself clear?"

"I can't go." Bronwyn tried one more time. "I can't. It would kill me. I would hate every moment."

Her mother said, again with the dismissive wave, "I felt the same way before I left for my junior year. And the young women I met there are now my best friends in the world, all of them in highly influential positions. You don't want to leave now, but you'll grow to love it. Someday, you'll thank us for this."

"I can't go."

Her father looked at his watch, then at his wife. "We're late." They both stood and walked to the door, as if they hadn't shattered her world with their words and plans. "Bronwyn, you need to understand that we won't entertain any nonsense from you about this. You will do this. Your grandmother has already given her seal of approval. The deposits have been processed. I expect you to get over this little tantrum by the time we return."

They walked out the door, and Bronwyn heard her mother say, "That went about as expected. I don't know how we managed to raise such an ungrateful child."

Bronwyn refused to cry. She wouldn't give them the satisfaction.

They would get nothing more from her. Not her emotions. Not her conversation.

Not her obedience.

They could keep her from going with Meredith and Mo.

But they couldn't make her go to Switzerland.

Two months later, Mo held Bronwyn close and tried, so hard, not to cry as hard as she was. "It's not forever. It's two months. I'll be home before you know it."

She continued to sob like her heart was broken. Bronwyn was many things, but a crier wasn't one of them.

He tried to pull away so he could see her face, but she clung to him. He held on another minute but then pushed her back until she finally released him enough for him to tilt her chin up. "Bronwyn? What's going on? Why are you like this? What aren't you telling me?"

She shook her head, tears spilling over faster than he could wipe them away. "I'm going to miss you so much. You have no idea."

"I won't go." The words flew out of his mouth, but as soon as he said them, they felt right. "I'll tell Mom and Dad . . . something. I'll figure it out. Please don't cry. I'll stay here this summer. I can stay with Papa and Granny."

"They'll never let you do that, Mo." Was that a hint of desperate hope in her words?

"I'll make something up. I'll . . . I don't know what I'll do. I'll get sick. Or hurt. I'll fake it until they leave me."

"You can't lie to your family!" Bronwyn shoved away from him. "What are you saying?"

"I'm saying you're the most important thing in my life and they all know it." Mo's eyes gleamed with intensity and a hint of desperation. "They think we're too young, but I know, Bronwyn. You and me are forever." He reached for her arms and gently squeezed them as he spoke. "I won't leave you."

"You have to." Bronwyn swiped at the tears. "You have to go."

"Do you really think I would leave with you crying like this? How could I?"

"I'm sorry." She shook her head and swallowed. "I'm just . . . I'm going to miss you so much, Mo. So much. But you can't skip this trip."

"They'll forgive me. They forgave Connor and Carla when they ran off and got married."

"Are we getting married?" Bronwyn ran her hand under her nose.

"Well . . ." Mo hesitated. Of course they weren't getting married now. But, "I mean, someday."

Bronwyn leaned toward him and rested her forehead on his chest. "You have to go, Mo. You can't stay here. Your mom and Aunt Carol have been planning this trip for two years. I'll be okay."

They argued for another twenty minutes, but as usual, Bronwyn won.

Mo watched her walk back down the trail toward The Haven and fought the clawing need in his chest to run after her.

Bronwyn walked half a mile before her legs gave out and she crumpled to the forest floor. She'd done it. She'd let him go. It had been a close call and she'd almost given in. He would have run away with her. She knew he would. If she told him everything that was happening, he'd sneak her out of town, marry her, and deal with the consequences. He was only sixteen, but already, she could see that about him.

When faced with a threat to someone he loved, Mo Quinn would always come through. No matter what it cost him personally.

And this would cost him everything. His plans for college, the Army, the computers he planned to know better than anyone. She couldn't do it. She loved him too much.

She would always love him.

But now, she had to figure out how to get out of this mess. Maybe there was a way. Maybe when he got home, this would all be a bad dream. There had to be a way.

NINETEEN

PRESENT DAY

Mo had gone home and slept for two hours. He needed eight, but he wanted to be able to sleep tonight. He showered, ate a sandwich, and settled in to work on what he could from his home office since he wouldn't get access to Bronwyn's computer until later.

His first order of business, after his deep dive into William Pierce, was to dig into the background info for Bronwyn's security team. He was an hour into the work when Meredith came in without knocking.

When he, Cal, and Meredith had moved back to Gossamer Falls, they'd built what soon became known as the tiny house compound on the edge of their property. Last year, Cal had moved out of his place and into his forever home with Landry. Meredith still lived in her house, but she'd be gone soon. But she'd be back. Her land was beside his, and when she and Gray nailed down what they wanted for their forever house, she'd be next door once more.

But until then? The compound would be lonely.

Meredith came up behind him and draped her arms around his neck. "Hey."

He patted her hand, then went back to work. "Hey."

She was quiet for maybe ten seconds before she said, "We went to see Cassie and then I helped Bronwyn pack up her desk. We took everything back to her place."

"Good."

"She told me what that movie star wanted."

"Yeah?" He was listening. But he could listen and, at the same time, scan files for the telltale signs he was particularly good at finding.

"She wants to get married at The Haven."

"Have they ever done a wedding?"

"No. They've allowed people to book out the whole place before, but there's never been a wedding."

"Did Bronwyn say yes?"

"She told her she'd see if she could devise a plan to satisfy all parties. But she's not sure the wedding will happen. That woman's been engaged to at least three different men."

Mo snorted. "She'd hate to do all that work for nothing."

"That's what she said!" Meredith straightened behind him and rested her hands on his shoulders. "Are you okay, Mo?"

"Why wouldn't I be?"

"Oh, I don't know. You've had a lot of Bronwyn time lately. And sometimes, after you're around her, you get sulky."

"I do no such thing."

Meredith's silence was her response.

He knew this tactic. It didn't matter if he didn't want to discuss it. Meredith would wait him out. He gave in. "I keep thinking she'll speak to me. And she continues not to. It's ridiculous."

"I think she keeps thinking it needs to mean something."

Mo stopped and turned so he could see Meredith. "What does that even mean?"

"It's a big deal, Mo. She's frozen you out for years, and now, I think she feels like just talking to you, without a big production of some sort, would somehow cheapen all of it."

Mo turned back to his computer. "I'd rather she just said, 'Hey, Mo' so we can move on. There are no words for how much I do not want to rehash the past. Not now. Not ever."

"I don't know." Meredith's words held a musing quality. "Sometimes you have to put the past to rest and only then can you move forward."

"Our past is nuclear."

"Not all of it."

A chime sounded and Mo clicked over to a program he'd had running in the background. "Wait a minute." He studied the screen.

Meredith leaned over his shoulder again. "What is it?"

"I'm not sure yet."

"I don't see anything."

Mo ignored her and continued to analyze the report.

"What does this mean?" Meredith pointed to a red highlighted area on his screen. "Has someone done something bad?"

Mo tried to shoo her away, but she leaned closer. "I wish this made more sense to me."

"You can't read forensic accounting reports. I can't read dental X-rays."

"True. But the red is bad, right?"

"The red is bad," Mo confirmed. "The tricky part will be figuring out who, what, when, where, and why."

"So I should leave you to it?" Meredith moved away, but he grabbed her hand.

"Thanks for all your help the past few days." He needed to say this as carefully as possible. He would never hurt his baby sister if he could help it. "You want a fairy tale ending for us, but I think you should prepare yourself that we're more Romeo and Juliet than Anne and Gilbert."

Meredith's eyes glistened with unshed tears. "Not so long ago, you thought we might be destined to live out our lives like Matthew and Marilla Cuthbert, but now look at us."

Mo huffed. "In this version, Marilla gets her man and leaves Matthew all alone."

A tear slipped down her cheek. "I don't want to leave you all alone."

Mo stood and pulled her into his arms. "Mer, please. Don't cry. We've discussed this. I'm so happy for you. I love Gray. I love how he treats you. I love how you are with him. I want you to marry him and give me nieces and nephews. I want you to hurry up and build your house so we'll all be close forever. You aren't leaving me. You've given me a new brother. I'm not complaining."

She snuffled and wiped away a few tears. "You were kind of complaining."

"What do you want me to say? Am I lonely? Sometimes. Yes. But not always. And I wouldn't ask you or Cal to return to how you were two years ago. Not for anything."

"But . . ."

"But I do think that you and Cal have gotten all loved up and now you want that for me—"

"And Bronwyn."

He nodded. "And Bronwyn. But me and Bronwyn? It isn't going to happen."

"It might."

"It was always a long shot, Mer. From the first time I held her hand, the odds were against us. Right now, I'd be happy to be able to have a conversation with her. I want to apologize. I want to set the record straight on some things that are still out there between us. I think we both need it. But I can't do anything until she moves first. And I'm not sure if you've picked up on this, but Bronwyn Elizabeth Elena Pierce is one of the most stubborn women in the universe."

Meredith grabbed a tissue from the small box on his desk. "She's worth the wait. I know she is."

Mo couldn't keep having this conversation. "Meredith, I promise that I've given all of this to God. I've asked him to fix it. I'm trying to let him lead and handle it. And I'm trying to be okay with whatever his answer is. If I can do that, then so can you. You need to let it go."

"I can't. I want her for my sister. I want you to be happy. I want to see the two of you together again, and I want to be able to say I told you so." She swallowed. "But I can stop badgering you. That I can do. Or, at least, I can try. I might slip up."

"That's okay. Thank you."

He squeezed her close for a second before releasing her and stepping back behind his desk.

"So, the red thing on the screen?" she said.

"Talk about stubborn."

"Quinn women are always stubborn. This is a documented fact."

"Fine. That red thing, as you put it, tells me that money is moving in a way that is not normal. There are algorithms that can predict this stuff. Sometimes they're wrong. But when there's more uncertainty, the feedback is in orange or yellow. I've never seen a red report that didn't indicate some form of tampering. Now, I need you to go home and let me find out what it is." He pointed to the chair. "Or you can stay here. But if you stay, you have to stop looking over my shoulder and commenting on everything."

She gave him a watery smile. "I'll go home, but only if you promise to tell me if you find something big."

"I promise."

He watched until Meredith walked into her tiny house. She blew him a kiss from her window, then let the curtain fall. She would probably call Gray and talk to him for the next hour. He didn't mind. He liked living close enough that he could hear her when Gray said something that made her laugh.

He hadn't lied. Much. He liked Gray. And Meredith was one of those people who was meant to be married, have several kids, probably foster a few more, then adopt them and need to build onto her house. She would have dogs, cats, and maybe a ferret because she wouldn't be able to say no. Her life would be chaotic and happy, and he couldn't wait to see it play out. She deserved every bit of it.

But he was lonelier than he'd fessed up to. And sometimes, when she was with Gray, and Cal and Landry were at their house, and he was alone by the firepit? Yeah.

He wished things were different.

But for now, he had a trail to follow that would keep his mind too occupied to dwell on what could have been.

He sat back down at the computer and dove in.

But before he did, he considered Meredith's words.

Then he remembered Meredith and Landry having a chat with Bronwyn in the bedroom. A chat that Meredith had yet to share with him. And he remembered how Bronwyn had looked at him today.

And he wondered if there was a way he could win his friend back after all.

At 7:30 p.m., Bronwyn looked up to see June standing in the doorway of the small conference room. They'd managed to move most of her things in and turn it into a functional office during the remodel of her old, and forever in her mind contaminated, office.

"Ms. Pierce?"

"Yes?"

"This was delivered for you." June stepped inside and placed a room service tray in front of her. "I received a call from Chef Cassie. She told me it was coming and that I should bring it to you and tell you that her cousin said for you to eat it because you haven't eaten anything all day."

Bronwyn lifted the lid and found a bowl of decadently creamy pasta. She could tell from the scent of garlic and rosemary that it would be heavenly. "Which one?"

"Which one what?"

"Which of Cassie's cousins?"

"She didn't say, ma'am. I'd be happy to call her back an—"

"No." Bronwyn waved a hand. "It doesn't matter."

It does so matter.

That annoying inner voice was getting louder by the minute. It didn't help that the inner voice was currently behaving like a toddler.

Possibly because she, the adult-Bronwyn in charge of her own self, thank you very much, was starving, hangry, emotional, and wanted nothing more than to crawl into something fluffy and go to sleep.

She unrolled the silverware that rested on the tray as fast as she could. She hadn't realized how hungry she was. But now, she was fighting the temptation to go for it face-first.

"If you don't need anything else . . ." June's voice trailed off as Bronwyn crammed a bite into her mouth and moaned.

She held her free hand over her face and spoke around the food. "Sorry."

June smiled.

"I was hungrier than I realized. Of course, go home. You stayed way too late as it is. Take your time coming in tomorrow."

"I'm fine, ma'am." June pinched her lips together, clearly

fighting a smile. "Enjoy your dinner. And you should take your own advice. Go home and get some sleep. You've had a long day."

Bronwyn chewed, swallowed, and waited before she took the next bite. "I will. Meredith's coming in a few minutes, then we'll head to my house to talk all things decorating."

"That sounds fun, but don't stay up too late."

"Yes, Mom."

June made a face, then laughed. "See you tomorrow." She closed the door behind her, and Bronwyn took five more bites before she slowed enough to truly taste the food. The ache in her stomach eased, but with the surcease came awareness of other small miseries. Her head hurt. Her eyes burned.

Exhaustion was winning.

And if the unknown Quinn cousin hadn't sent her food, she would have settled for some yogurt and a few berries before she crashed.

This had been the longest week ever. How was it only Tuesday night? She took another bite. The pasta deserved to be savored, but right now, her body refused to do anything more than consume the needed calories. She ate with single-minded focus for several minutes, and the bowl still looked full. Cassie must have assumed she hadn't eaten for three days, not just one. She'd sent enough to feed her for a week.

Her phone buzzed. She glanced at it and saw a text from Meredith.

I'm inside the gates. Sorry I'm so late.

Bronwyn gathered her things, including the pasta bowl because she wasn't done and there was no way she was leaving it behind, and walked outside to meet Meredith.

What she found was Meredith parked behind her car, with Mo idling in his Jeep behind her.

Meredith lowered her window and waved. "I guess when you run the joint, you can walk off with the dishes."

"You know it."

"We'll follow you home." Meredith rolled her window up, and they waited for Bronwyn to climb into her car. She'd had Cal give her a ride home after she was done at Landry's this morning, and she'd driven back to her office. She'd hoped Meredith and Mo would give up on the whole "let's have a sleepover at Bronwyn's" idea, meaning she would need her own car to get home.

But here they were.

They all parked at Bronwyn's home. Once again, Mo cleared her house before they entered. He caught her eye as he returned to the door, but she had no idea what the look he gave her meant.

Bronwyn went straight to the kitchen and called over her shoulder, "I have this pasta from Cassie. It's possibly the best thing I've ever eaten."

"That's because she isn't eating enough to remember what food tastes like." Mo's low grumble wasn't directed at her, but also . . . it was.

"We already ate," Meredith said. "Besides, Mo will strangle me if I eat your food. He took the time to check your fridge and decided it was alarmingly empty. And yes, that is an exact quote. He's worried you're losing weight from stress and general neglect."

Bronwyn had returned to the living room during Meredith's speech, and Mo's eyes didn't waver from hers. He'd said all of that. And right now, he was daring her to say something about it.

She dragged her focus to Meredith. "So he decided to send creamy pasta to my office."

"No. He called Cassie and asked her for the most decadent thing she had on the menu tonight."

Bronwyn looked between the siblings. "That would be the lobster."

"Yeah, but you don't eat lobster. At least, that's what Mo said. And it doesn't reheat well, anyway."

She couldn't stop her eyes from returning to Mo. Again, he was looking at her. No hesitation. No shying away. What was happening?

"Bronwyn?" Meredith waved a hand in front of her. "Hon, you need sleep. Go to bed. We've got this." She made shooing motions with her hands. "Seriously. I'll prep your coffeepot, hassle my annoying brother for a few minutes, and then be right behind you."

"It's only eight o'clock."

"We got up at four."

"We went back to sleep."

"For what? An hour? Two?" Meredith grabbed Bronwyn's arm and pulled her toward the hall. "No. We're in a sleep deficit. It's time for rest."

"Who put you in charge?" Bronwyn complained, but she let Meredith push her toward her room.

"Self-appointed role. You're welcome." Meredith paused at her door and gave her a quick hug. "Go to bed."

Bronwyn paused in the doorway. "Will Mo sleep? Because he shouldn't stay up all night again. He's running on fumes too."

"He's going to work for a little while and then he'll sleep on the couch."

Bronwyn pinched the bridge of her nose. "That couch isn't very comfortable. He should go home."

"Don't argue, Beep. There's no point in it. If you push him too hard, he'll sleep in his car out front."

"No I won't!" Mo yelled from the living room.

Bronwyn hadn't realized he could hear them.

"If you kick me out, I'll grab a lawn chair and sleep by the front door," he continued.

"See what I mean?" Meredith patted her arm. "Go to bed. Sleep. Wake up tomorrow with new hope."

"Mer, if something happened to him . . ." She couldn't even finish the thought.

"Nothing's going to happen. First of all, if either he or Gray, or Cal for that matter, thought something was going down, neither of us would be here. This is about *not* giving them an opportunity."

"I'm not sure if that's as encouraging as you seem to think it is."

Meredith waved away her snide remark. "He's already vetted your security. He knows who we can trust, and he has them on speed dial. He's in touch with Gray and the officers, who will be nearby. We have extra cars parked out front. If anyone was thinking of trying anything, tonight is not the night."

Bronwyn leaned against the doorframe. She had a sneaky feeling that there was something faulty in Meredith's logic, but she didn't have the mental capacity to suss it out. "If anything happens to him . . ." she said again.

"He feels the same way about you. That's why he's here." Meredith squeezed her temples between her palms. "You two are giving me a headache. Go to bed." And, with a lot of love but also a look that said she was done with the conversation, Meredith shoved Bronwyn into her room and closed the door.

Bronwyn stared at the door but when it moved . . . wait. No. The door hadn't moved. She was swaying. Maybe sleep would be the best option.

But . . . Mo was on her couch again.

She went back into the hall and to the linen closet. She grabbed a set of sheets, a pillow, and a blanket, and walked back to the living room.

Mo sat on the sofa, again, computer in his lap. When she placed the linens on the sofa, he gave her a chin lift.

It wasn't words.

But it was communication.

She swallowed hard, then nodded at him in acknowledgment before turning and running to her room like the big chicken she was.

TWENTY

Once again, despite her churned-up emotions, Bronwyn fell asleep and slept hard. When her alarm went off at seven, she rolled over and stared at the clock she kept on her bedside table.

She'd slept ten hours. Ten. She couldn't remember the last time she'd done that, and she refused to dwell on the reason why. Especially because she was sure her sleep had been peaceful—not as much because of her exhaustion but because she hadn't been alone.

She pulled on a robe and went to the kitchen for coffee. Meredith blew her a kiss from the front door. "Gotta run. I'll check in later."

Mo sat in the same spot he'd been in when she left him last night. But the sheets had been used, refolded, and now sat on the opposite end of the sofa.

Something about the way he'd positioned them made her think he expected to need them again soon.

Was he planning to stay again tonight? What if he was? Would that be such a bad thing?

Mo jumped to his feet and stalked to her front door. As he reached it, the doorbell chimed.

She moved toward him, but he caught her eye and shook his head.

She froze.

Mo glanced at the camera and opened the door but left the storm door closed. "Good morning." There was no hostility in his words. If she hadn't seen the intense look of warning on his face seconds before, she would have thought he was chilling on a beach somewhere.

"Um, hi. Good morning, sir. I'm sorry." The young voice on the other side of the door was familiar. "Mrs. Pierce sent a message for Ms. Pierce."

"I'll take it."

Bronwyn finally placed the voice, and when she did, she moved to the door. Sure enough, a wide-eyed bellhop stood on the other side.

"Good morning, Sebastian."

"Ms. Pierce." He looked relieved and also shocked to see her. Or maybe the shock was at seeing Mo.

Mo opened the door, took the envelope Sebastian held out, closed the storm door, and handed it to Bronwyn.

She took the envelope.

"Mrs. Pierce asked me to wait for a reply." There was no need to ask which Mrs. Pierce Sebastian was referring to. The heavy paper and formal lettering answered that.

"I'll just be a moment," Bronwyn told him.

"Yes, ma'am." He had a definite gray cast to his skin. Poor kid. He looked like a man who'd seen some stuff this morning. If he'd been anywhere near her grandmother, he probably had.

She stepped away and opened the envelope. "I would be pleased if you would join me for an early luncheon. Eleven a.m. My home." She read the words aloud, almost to herself, but also so Mo would, maybe, stop hovering and glowering.

She read the words again. Her grandmother was dying, and she was still scheduling brunch. Of course she was. And heaven forbid she do anything so bourgeois as to send an email or a text. No. It had to be a written invitation.

Bronwyn ran to her office and grabbed a correspondence card from her stash—a gift from her grandmother several years ago that she rarely used—and dashed off an acceptance.

Mo hadn't followed her into the room, but he stood in the hallway. When she emerged from the office, he held out his hand.

She could argue, but it wasn't worth it. She handed the envelope to Mo and followed him to the door.

Mo kept his body mostly in front of hers, like Sebastian was a threat, and again handed off the envelope with quick efficiency. The storm door closed, and Bronwyn spoke to Sebastian through the glass. "Thank you for running her errands." It was part of his job description, but still.

"I don't mind, Ms. Pierce. Mrs. Pierce is a nice lady."

Bronwyn didn't try to hide her surprise, and Sebastian grinned, finally relaxing in Mo's presence. "She *is* nice," he said. "She tries to come across as grumpy. But she just likes things the way she likes them. She's lived long enough to earn that, I think."

Maybe. Maybe not. But at least she wasn't terrifying the kid on a regular basis.

"We'll see how nice she is to me later this morning." She winked and sent Sebastian on his way.

Mo closed the door, locked it, and reset the alarm, all without looking at her.

That had been . . . weirdly intense.

She should head in to the office, but her office was chaos. What she needed most was to breathe some fresh air. She glanced at her watch. If she put some speed on, she had time for a walk.

Her phone rang and she put it on speaker. "Cal, good morning."

"Morning." He yawned. "Listen, if you're going to your grandmother's later, I think you should be reasonably safe, but you need to understand that someone will be hanging close. Either Mo or Donovan will be nearby. And Randall will be on-site."

She sent Mo what she hoped was a laser beam of annoyance, but apparently she got it wrong because he smirked at her. Smirked! His eyebrows raised, his head cocked, his look said, "What are you going to do about it?"

Who needed words when they could communicate with body language?

"Cal—"

"Not optional, Beep. Mo has more digging to do. We have to get this sorted. Deal with it. Go about your business. Do what you need to do. But don't be surprised when you have company."

"My grandmother won't accept that."

"She can't stop Randall from being nearby. He works security. You can sell that."

"Is there any point in arguing?" She spoke to Cal, but her eyes were fixed on Mo as she said the words.

His response was to turn back to his computer.

"Not really." Cal's response was gentle but firm. "Beep, you've stepped in yellow jackets, and those buggers are mean. Give us a few days of paranoia. If Mo can sort it out and we're sure you're secure, we'll let it go."

His voice dropped into a low whisper. "We aren't taking chances. There've been too many close calls the last couple of years. Give us this. Please."

He had a point. Landry and Eliza, Cal, Cassie, Meredith . . . there'd been too much drama for anyone to press on naively believing everything would work out.

"Fine."

Mo's shoulders dropped in relief. Cal's relief was audible. "Thank you."

"But I'm not sitting around like some kind of princess in a tower being guarded by a dragon."

And why did the image of Mo as a dragon fit so well?

"No one expects you to. That would be suspicious, and we don't want anyone more on alert than they already are."

"Fine. I'm going for a walk. I need to breathe. I need some sunshine and fresh air. Then I'm going to come home, then go to Grandmother's for brunch."

"Fun."

"Yeah. Fun."

"What's after brunch?"

"I don't know." She closed her eyes and blew out a slow breath. She was the one who'd called in reinforcements. She'd asked for help. For a moment, she let the terror from a few nights ago sweep over her and appreciation swamped her irritation. "I'll let you know. Okay? I do have work to do." She always had work to do. "I'll probably be in my office."

"Okay. Sounds good. Enjoy your walk. And brunch. Tell Grandmother hello from me."

"Sure."

"She likes me."

"Since when?"

"Since I married Landry." That was probably true. "She thinks bringing Landry to The Haven is the best thing you've ever done. We have that in common."

"Huh. Well, okay. I'll tell her."

Cal's humor faded away. "Beep, maybe don't tell her that."

"Why not?"

"She's tried to get Landry to tell her how y'all met several times, but Landry always deflects. So if that isn't a conversation you want to have, maybe don't go there. I'm sorry I brought it up."

Bronwyn had never talked to her grandmother or her parents about the rehab facility where she'd met Landry. They knew she'd been in rehab, but they'd assumed it was for alcohol or drug dependence.

They had no idea of the battle she'd almost lost. Landry and Meredith knew, so she had to assume that Cal, Gray, and Mo did as well. But no one in her family had a clue that when control had been stripped away, she'd sought to control the one thing she could, and in the process had nearly starved herself to death.

Cal's tone was so contrite that Bronwyn wished they were talking in person so she could hug him. "Thanks for the heads-up, Cal. Maybe it's time to have that conversation. I'll play it by ear."

"I'm sorry, Beep."

"Don't be. It all worked for the good. Remember that. I got what I needed, and I met Landry and then I was able to help her when she needed it. And now we're both safe and whole." Well, Landry was. Bronwyn wasn't sure if she'd ever been safe or ever would be.

"Alrighty," Cal said. "Stay sharp. Keep your eyes and ears open. Pay attention to weirdness. Don't let pride keep you from reacting. We'd rather you cry wolf a hundred times than stay quiet and be eaten."

Mo grunted and shook his head at Cal's words.

"Thank you for that vivid imagery."

"You're welcome." Either Cal didn't pick up on her sarcasm or he didn't care. Probably the latter. "Later."

"Later." She disconnected the call and tried to put Cal's dire warnings out of her mind as she changed.

Ten minutes later, she walked out of her house. She had her

phone in the pocket of her hiking leggings, and that was it. The door to her home had a keypad, so she didn't need anything else.

She'd nodded at Mo as she walked out. He'd acknowledged her but hadn't moved to get up. Maybe he assumed she was safe on the property? No. That didn't match his current level of paranoia. But *she* was pretty sure she was safe in broad daylight. So she headed out and focused on breathing and being where she was.

It took her five minutes to reach the private walking trail that was her favorite place to walk when she didn't have time to hike to Catherine's Falls. The trail followed a small stream and wound through mountain laurel and pine trees that hid the rest of the resort from view. It was open to all the guests, but only a few ever used it.

Bronwyn set a brisk but maintainable pace. She wasn't big into cardio. Or sweating. And she didn't have Meredith's sense of direction. She'd never go wandering around in the forest. She needed a trail, and the flatter, the better.

Even though she wasn't a speedy hiker, she loved to be in nature. Despite the hours she put in at the office, she made time for a walk almost every day. The trail wasn't long. The loop from her house to the path and back was about a mile. But that mile was a lifesaver.

She was crossing the bridge that marked the halfway point when she heard . . . something.

Then she heard it again. A rustle that didn't sound natural. Was someone on the trail with her? Her heart rate increased and her breathing quickened. Was she being ridiculous? She was. Wasn't she?

A moment later, what had been a faint noise turned into heavy footfalls behind her. Should she run? No. This was her trail. She was on her property. The only people here were guests and . . . staff.

A staff she no longer trusted.

But running . . . well . . . that wasn't exactly her strong suit. She'd never outrun whoever was coming up behind her.

Instead, she got her phone out of her pocket and pulled up Landry's contact info. She sent a text.

Please call me in 30 seconds. I'm walking the trail.

She maintained her pace and kept moving, even as the footsteps neared.

She stepped to the far side of the trail, came to a stop, and turned to face the newcomer.

The man behind her slowed, then smiled, then came to a complete stop when he reached her. "Good morning."

"Morning."

She recognized him. He'd come with a politician who was here for the week. He was probably in his early forties. Good looking. The little bit of hair he had was salt-and-pepper, leaning toward salt. His muscles had muscles. He hadn't gotten that body by running a one-mile walking path in the forest.

"You didn't have to stop." His smile was blindingly white and a shade too far on the side of predatory to calm her skittering nerves.

"I didn't want to mess up your time. It sounded like you were on a quick pace."

"I was. But I never pass up the opportunity to speak to a lovely woman."

Did he think that made him sound charming? Because . . . ew. "Well, if you'll excuse me . . ." She made it a point to walk away from him.

He jogged a few steps, then settled in beside her, which would have been annoying under any circumstances but was particularly off-putting because this trail was barely wide enough for two. It was best walked single file.

"I'm Bob."

"Yes. I know who you are." She knew the names and faces of every guest on the premises.

"Then you have me at a disadvantage because I don't know you."

Should she call him on the obvious lie? She decided to let it slide. "Bronwyn Pierce."

"As in the Ms. Pierce who runs this place?"

"That would be me."

"How do you like it?"

"Like what?"

"Running a resort for people who think they're better than everyone else."

What was this guy's deal? She had no doubt that he was well compensated in his position. If he didn't like working for snooty people, he could leave. No one was forcing him to stay in the job.

"I oversee an exclusive mountain getaway. In my experience, most of the guests who choose to come here don't want anything more than to be left alone for a few days so they can recharge. I'm happy to give them the space to do that."

"A very smooth answer."

"Not my first rodeo, Bob."

"I'm not trying to get you to gossip. I signed an NDA. I know the drill."

Everyone who worked for a celebrity, athlete, politician, or as it so happened, The Haven signed a nondisclosure agreement. The NDAs varied in their specifics, but all of them were designed to keep people from blabbing about their employers.

For the most part, they worked well. There was always a risk that someone would be coerced into sharing things they shouldn't, but given that the cost for breaking an NDA was exorbitant, most people behaved themselves.

"I'm just curious," Bob said. "Seems like an isolated life here. I'm wondering why you stay."

"It's my home." It was that simple and that profound.

"Huh." She couldn't tell if his response indicated doubt or surprise. She didn't have long to consider it because he kept talking. "Do you have rules about dating guests?"

"Excuse me?" He couldn't be serious. Could he?

"Are you allowed to date your guests?" He looked her straight in the eye and enunciated. "Because I'd love to get to know you better."

While a part of her appreciated the blunt way he stated what he wanted, nothing about this man appealed to her. "Thank you, but I'm not interested."

He cocked his head at her. "Not interested? Or not allowed?"

"Both."

"Ouch."

"I don't play games."

"Clearly you don't." He heaved a sigh. "Can't blame a guy for trying. Guess I'll see you around." He gave her a big smile and jogged away. His jog turned into a full run as he moved out of sight.

"That was weird," she muttered as she resumed her original pace. She couldn't shake the feeling that there was something more to the interaction than what had been said on the surface. She made a mental note to check up on Bob. There had been something smarmy about him, and it left a bad taste in her mouth.

The annoyance at having her walk interrupted followed her home. So much for spending some time in nature to settle her mind and heart.

She was a hundred yards from her house when footsteps sounded on the path behind her.

Really? Again? Had Bob lapped her?

She turned and stopped in the middle of the path.

Mo gave her a salute as he ran past her and went to her front door, opened it, went inside for a few minutes, then returned and held the door for her as she jogged up the stairs of her porch.

He'd followed her. He'd probably been out there behind Bob. But, unlike Bob, he hadn't interrupted her time. He hadn't revealed his presence until she was home.

He'd protected her *and* given her the space she needed.

And . . . she didn't know what she thought about that.

She didn't have time to think more about it though. She received four texts while she was in the shower, two calls while she was getting dressed, including a frantic one from Landry who had apparently just seen her earlier text, and an email with twenty—she counted them—exclamation marks while she did her hair and makeup.

She called her assistant as she walked into her kitchen to fill her water bottle. "June, I'm headed to Grandmother's. Please hold all my calls unless it's a true emergency."

"Yes, ma'am. Good luck!" The last words had been whispered. June and Grandmother had a somewhat adversarial relationship. Grandmother thought June was too big for her britches. June thought Grandmother was a bully.

Both were wrong, and weirdly both were right.

Mo gave her that same salute but made no move to get up as she went to her garage.

She wasn't surprised when she looked in her rearview mirror and saw a security car that followed her until she parked in the circular drive.

Grandmother's home wasn't technically on The Haven property, but it could be accessed through a private gated entrance. Since the first visitor stayed on the premises, Grandmother had benefited from room service, housekeeping, security, and pretty much every perk of being a guest at The Haven.

And she took full advantage.

Bronwyn smiled at the maid who held the door for her. "Ms. Pierce, your grandmother is sitting by the fireplace. She asked for you to join her there."

"Thank you."

She walked in to find her grandmother dressed like she was headed out for a business meeting, hair and makeup perfect, sitting by the fire with a blanket over her lap. A tray of tiny sandwiches rested on the table in front of her.

"Good morning, Grandmother."

"Your father told me you destroyed your office yesterday."

Bronwyn ignored the disapproving tone and kissed the papery skin of her grandmother's cheek.

"Yes. Can you tell me about the stain on the floor? We pulled the carpet up. It looks like a bloodstain, but surely that's not what it is."

Before Grandmother could respond, a different maid entered the room. "Would you care for a beverage, Ms. Pierce?"

"Tea would be lovely. Thank you." The maid nodded and left as quietly as she'd come.

"We had that room carpeted for a reason, young lady." Grandmother's hand moved restlessly on the arm of the chair.

"Was it blood?"

"Of course not."

"Then—"

"It's red wine."

Bronwyn waited, but Grandmother didn't elaborate. "We're going to sand it out or maybe replace that part of the floor if necessary. And I'm going to have gorgeous hardwoods instead of carpet."

"Mistake."

Bronwyn pointed to the rich, gleaming floors around them. "How so?"

"Hardwood floors are lovely, but you want the padding and sound dampening of a carpet for your office. You'll hear every sound. It will echo around the room. Like I said, a mistake."

"Sorry, Grandmother. It's too late to put the carpet back. We've moved everything out of the room except my desk. Cal Shaw is going to build me a new desk. He's sending me a few sketches this weekend."

At the mention of Cal, her grandmother's expression went from displeased to angry.

"I told you not to associate with the Quinns."

"Technically, Cal—"

"Don't try that with me. He's a Shaw and a Quinn."

Bronwyn made a mental note to tell Cal that her grandmother didn't like him, after all.

"Grandmother, the Quinns are lovely people." It was an old argument, but one she would keep having. "They've never been anything but kind to me." Far kinder than her own blood.

"Kindness? Is that what you want out of life? For people to be kind to you? Granddaughter, I hate to point this out, but the real world doesn't run on kindness."

Bronwyn selected a sandwich and studied the filling. Chicken salad. Her favorite. She took a bite and swallowed.

"Grandmother, I hate to point this out, but I learned about the real world a long time ago." Before her grandmother could speak, she added, "Thank you for the chicken salad. It's delicious."

Grandmother waved away her thanks. "You're the only one of my grandchildren who will have anything to do with me. I think you only come around for the food."

"Now, Grandmother, is it possible you've failed to invite your other grandchildren for luncheon?"

"No, it is not. I invited Nathan last week. He declined—declined!—without any explanation at all."

That was . . . not normal. Nathan had a black belt in brown-nosing. Grandmother's will was going to make things interesting for everyone. No way Nathan would pass up an opportunity to schmooze Grandmother.

"I asked William if there was a problem, and he told me Nathan has been swamped at work." At this, her grandmother cut her eyes to Bronwyn and shook her head. "You and I both know that isn't true."

Bronwyn held her grandmother's gaze but didn't flinch.

Grandmother sipped her tea.

"Are you going to eat?" Bronwyn asked.

"No." Simple. To the point. "I'm dying, Bronwyn. The doctor says I only have a couple of weeks to live." She stared at her teacup. "I don't have time to squander. I won't let anyone destroy what we built here." She waved a hand around the room, but Bronwyn knew she meant The Haven. "My own children and grandchildren have done their best to make a mess of things, but here it stands. And it will continue. It must."

She focused on Bronwyn, and just like that, Bronwyn was ten again, sitting at the dining room table getting an etiquette lesson. "Yes, ma'am."

"I've done all I can do on my end. It's up to you now." She sniffed. "But I don't like having the Quinns involved in our personal matters."

"Grandmother—"

"Enough of that. Finish your lunch. You need to get back to work."

Bronwyn dutifully took another bite. And then another. By the third bite, her grandmother was asleep.

What had she meant by done all she could?

Knowing her grandmother, it would look pretty, but it would be deadly.

TWENTY-ONE

SEVENTEEN YEARS EARLIER

Corbin was the only person Bronwyn had been able to talk to about boarding school. She could trust him not to say anything, and he understood her frustration with her family the way very few people did. Over the past year, their emails had become more and more frequent. She'd never tell him this, but in many ways, he'd become the big brother she'd never had but always wanted.

But never in a million years had she expected him to show up at The Haven in person so she wouldn't be alone. Now, Bronwyn stared at the man sitting on the porch swing across from her. "You're serious?" she asked.

"Of course I am."

"You'd take me with you? Why?"

He cut his eyes to her. "Bronwyn, I'm not an altruistic person. I'm a businessman. And you, my dear, would be excellent for my business. We could help each other out. I need an assistant who isn't an idiot. I've fired the last three for incompetence. You don't have an incompetent bone in your body. And you're loyal. You're loyal to your family even though they treat you like gum on the bottom of their shoes. I don't have to worry about you jumping ship and running to another boss as soon as I get you trained up."

"I would never."

"And in return, I would teach you about the industry. Introduce you to the big players."

"Why would you do this for me?" Bronwyn was desperate for a way out, but as Corbin said, she wasn't an idiot.

He winked at her. "Look, I got my big break at twenty-two. A producer took a chance on me. It worked out great for both of us. He got an assistant who wanted to learn. I got a mentor who smoothed the way for me. We still have lunch three or four times a year. In this business, it's all about who you know. And now that I'm in a position to give back, I want to leave a legacy." He reached over and tugged a strand of her hair. "You caught my eye several years ago. You're a diamond in the rough. And as much as I love this place"—he waved a hand to encompass the mountains around them—"I've come to realize that your family is rotten. You need to get out of here, and you need to do it on your own terms."

He shrugged. "It's up to you. I want to help. And there's no pressure. The door's always open. But I have to tell you, I'm afraid if you don't take it now, you'll be stuck forever under the thumb of your controlling family. I'm offering you the chance to make something of yourself without them. Then you can come back here as a guest and rub it in their faces."

Bronwyn didn't want to rub anything in anyone's face. Not really. But what could she do when she had only bad options? She could agree to their wishes and go to finishing school.

She would hate it. And when she told Mo she was miserable, he'd come help her escape and then run away with her. But if he did that, the future he wanted for himself would be over. He wasn't like Cal. He didn't want to work in construction. He wanted computers to be his life, and that meant that he'd be leaving Gossamer Falls, probably for good.

Or she could go with Corbin. Mo would lose his mind when he found out. But by the time he got back to Gossamer Falls, she'd have an apartment and a job. She'd be working. She'd let him know not to worry. She'd be in control of what she did, where she went, who her friends were, and how she spent her time.

Mo would forgive her. He'd understand. She'd make him understand. A long-distance relationship was better than no relationship. And it wouldn't be forever.

Two months later, Bronwyn sat on the edge of a thin mattress in a seedy part of town. A girl she'd met on the street last night slept on the other mattress in the corner of the room. A needle lay beside her.

Mo would be getting home today. He would come looking for her. But he wouldn't find her. He might never find her again.

Nothing, absolutely nothing, had gone the way she thought it would. There'd been no apartment. No job. No introductions to people in the industry. There was no money. No future.

Corbin had lied. Every conversation, every email, every compliment, every wink—all lies. What he'd seen in her had never been "producer" potential. She'd landed in California, and the man had turned into nothing he'd ever been before. It wasn't an assistant that he'd really wanted.

She'd thought her options were bad before she left Gossamer Falls, but they became monumentally worse within hours of leaving home.

Corbin had lied *to* her, but later he'd lied *about* her. Manipulated photos. Curated messages she'd never seen or sent. None of it was real—not that anyone would believe her. He thought he could force her to do things she didn't want to do.

So she ran. And kept running.

She was on her own now.

If Mo did find her . . . she stopped herself from following that train of thought.

She couldn't go home. Not now. She'd refused to stay with Corbin. Refused to return to parents who didn't understand her. But survival on her own terms hadn't turned out the way she'd hoped.

She wasn't the girl Mo had left in the forest two months ago. She'd never be that girl again.

If there was one thing she could be sure of, it was this—Mo could never know.

Mo stared at the waterfall, but he'd stopped seeing it hours ago. He'd said all he had to say. He'd screamed. He'd yelled. He'd used vocabulary his parents would be shocked he knew.

It hadn't helped.

Nothing helped.

Bronwyn was gone, and there was an empty space inside of him that he didn't think would ever be full again.

He'd heard Cal and Meredith approach earlier, but they'd stayed out of his line of sight. He should let them say what they needed to say so they'd leave him in peace. "You might as well come out. I know you're there."

Tentative footsteps, a few sniffles, and then Meredith's head dropped onto Mo's shoulder. Cal's hand landed on the other. They sat there, the three of them, for several quiet minutes.

"I'm praying she'll be okay." Meredith's words came out on a sob. "I don't understand why she left, why she stayed away, why she didn't tell us . . . but I'm going to pray for her every day."

Cal's grip tightened. "Same."

Mo couldn't tell them that he agreed. Or that he appreciated it. A few months ago, he would have been the first to start the prayer chain. But now?

What was the point?

He'd prayed for Bronwyn Pierce since he'd been old enough to realize she was something special in his life. He'd prayed for her parents. He'd prayed for her family. He'd even prayed for The Haven to be successful because that was good for her.

He'd prayed for her every day while they were away.

Every day.

Maybe Cal's and Meredith's prayers would work, but it was clear his didn't.

"She'll come home." Cal probably thought he sounded confident, but Mo heard the uncertainty.

"Are you kidding? She found a way out, and she took it. She won't be back." Mo's words were right but also completely wrong. Bronwyn was tough and stubborn and sometimes headstrong. But she wasn't an idiot. Ultimately, she'd come around to the right decision.

At least, he hoped she would.

Cal and Meredith spent the next ten minutes trying to convince him everything would be okay. In the end, Mo knew he had only one option. He would have to pretend to be okay or his family would never let him hear the end of it.

He had to go through the motions and keep up appearances, but he could never let on that something inside of him had died.

TWENTY-TWO

PRESENT DAY

Mo didn't like sitting in Bronwyn's house when she wasn't home. Even though she knew he was there, he couldn't shake the sense that he was an unwanted intruder.

His phone rang and he picked up with a grumbled, "What do you want, Cal?"

"What's your plan for the day?"

"My plan is to go to Bronwyn's office and work on her computer."

He'd done all he could do from his laptop. There was nothing more to be done until he had access to The Haven's internal network.

Bronwyn had been correct that the computer in her office was one of only a handful that could be used to access their server. And she'd also been correct that it was hardwired.

Where she'd been wrong was in believing that all the information Mo would need could be found on the hard drive of her computer.

Somewhere at The Haven, there was a network server. She probably didn't realize that it would be possible for people to save data there and not keep it on their hard drives.

He wanted to have things locked down better before he shared details with her. And to do that, he was going to have to find a way to work at The Haven on her computer. Mo stood and looked out the window. "I don't suppose you have any ideas how we can make that happen?"

"Yep."

"Really?"

"Why did you ask me if you didn't think I could come up with something?" Cal laughed. "Where's the trust, man?"

"I didn't expect you to have an immediate answer."

"As it so happens, I'm heading to her office this afternoon. You can come with."

"Why?" Mo asked.

"So you can work on her computer." The implied duh rang through the phone loud and clear.

"I mean, why are you going to her office?"

"The desk. I want her to look at some prototypes. Eliza helped me yesterday. We made a couple of models for her to look at. Different wood, different stains. Eliza thinks she should have a waterfall in her office."

"Please tell me you told her no." The last time Cal and his brothers created a waterfall, Mo thought they would need to be in family counseling for an eternity.

"First, we're more mature than we were then. Second, we know what we're doing. And third—"

"Third, you don't like to disappoint Eliza."

Cal laughed again. "True, but no. Third, Bronwyn doesn't want a waterfall. She wants the desktop to resemble the reception desk and the conference room table."

"She has good taste."

"The question is more about dimensions and cabinets—that kind of thing. We need to stand in her office and put tape down with the exact dimensions of the desk to be sure it's what she wants. I want to do that before the crew starts working on the floor."

"When do they start?"

"Hopefully on Friday. We need to sand that stain out. I may work on it tonight. Eliza thinks helping me with work is fun. That won't last, but I'm going to enjoy it for as long as it does."

"It might last. Meredith likes helping Dad on cars."

"No she doesn't. Meredith likes hanging out with Uncle Doug. She works on cars so she can do that."

An astute observation.

"Has it occurred to you that maybe Eliza likes to hang out with *her* dad? Which is why she likes helping you work?" Mo had seen Eliza "help" Cal, and he was pretty sure he was dead-on about this.

Cal was quiet for a few seconds. "If that's why, I'll take it." Cal cleared his throat. "Anyway, we'll be there this afternoon. And Cassie promised dinner for all of us."

"Does Bronwyn know about this?"

"Not yet. She's still at her grandmother's. Landry texted her, but I doubt she's seen it. You could always tell her when she gets there."

"I'm at her house. Not her office. You'll see her before I do."

"Fine. I'll talk to her. Want me to call you when I get there?"

"That would be great."

"Later."

At 1:30, Mo walked into Bronwyn's office carrying four to-go cups and a bag of treats. He found everyone in the conference room. Cal took a coffee and riffled through the bag until he found a blueberry scone. "Which ones are Bronwyn's?"

"The mocha and the lemon doughnut."

Cal took them to where Bronwyn sat, reverently holding one of several scale model desks.

She glanced up, and he saw the wonder in her eyes before she spoke. "Thank you. These are amazing, Cal."

Had she been thanking him? Cal? Both of them? It didn't matter. Until she looked him square in the eye and said something, it didn't count.

"They were fun to make. Eliza has some strong opinions about your desk."

"I'm sure she does. Which one is her favorite?"

Cal pointed to the one on the far right of the group. "She likes this one."

The desk surface was oval-shaped and had four beautifully designed legs. But it wasn't a particularly practical desk.

"Oof. I hate disappointing her, but that oval top would drive me bonkers." Bronwyn grimaced. "I want it to be a piece of art but also functional."

"You don't have to decide now. Think about it. I have some sketches of a few others that might be better than these models." He handed her a stack of paper. On the top was a note.

Mo read it upside down, a peculiar but handy little skill he'd picked up somewhere along the way.

PLAY ALONG. MO NEEDS MORE ACCESS TO THE COMPUTER.

Bronwyn took the stack and shuffled the top page to the bottom, then continued to look through the sketches.

"You know, while Mo's here, you should get him to take a look at your computer."

"What's wrong with it?" Mo asked.

Cal shrugged. "How should I know?"

"You're the one who said I should take a look at it."

Bronwyn finally got with the program. "Cal, I can't bother Mo with this. I'm sure it's just a glitch."

"It's no trouble." Mo jumped in. "I can take a look." He wasted no time sitting down behind Bronwyn's computer, which was now plugged in and hooked up in the back of the conference room. He tuned out most of the conversation happening behind him. Cal and Bronwyn returned to discussing her desk. Good call, given that they were both such horrible actors. No one who overheard their stilted conversation would have believed it for long.

After a few minutes of work, he took advantage of a lull in their chatter. "I think this is fixable, but I'll need some time."

He twisted in the chair and made eye contact with both of them before turning back to the screen. "I think a day or two should cover it. I can always bill Bronwyn. But, of course, if she needs this device to get any work done, that will be a problem."

Cal jumped in. "What do you think, Beep?"

"I'm sure I could work on my laptop. If I need that computer, I can let him know."

And how, exactly, would she do that when she refused to speak to him? Morse code?

An hour later, Bronwyn sat at one end of the conference table. Mo continued to peck away at the computer in the corner. She had no idea what he was doing or how he was doing it. He stared at the screen for so long after Cal left, she was afraid he would burn out his retinas.

A soft tap on the door pulled her attention away from Mo. "Ms. Pierce?" June poked her head in. "Your lunch is here."

"My . . . what?"

"Your lunch." June pushed a room service tray inside the room. "I think you'll like it." She set several plates on the table, silver covers hiding the contents from view.

"Mr. Quinn, some of this is yours," June added, turning to Mo. "Would you like to eat now?"

Mo stopped what he was doing, twisted in the seat, and made eye contact with her. "Thank you, June." Did her assistant blush? Yes, she did. Bronwyn couldn't blame her. When Mo Quinn gave you his full attention, it made an impression. "You can leave it down there," Mo said. "I'll grab what I want in a few minutes."

"Yes, sir." June gave him a warm smile. "And thank you for taking care of Ms. Pierce. She forgets to eat."

Wait. What?

"I've noticed that." He'd . . . what? "Between the two of us, we'll keep her fortified."

June giggled.

Giggled.

Did Mo even realize the effect he was having on the poor woman?

Probably not.

"Sounds like a plan." June's smile was radiant. She was too young for Mo. Well, okay. No, she wasn't. But . . .

Bronwyn gave herself a mental shake.

She lifted a lid. A huge sandwich, cut in fourths, all diagonals, rested on the plate. "How am I supposed to eat this? I've already had brunch with Grandmother and a doughnut today. And apparently, Cassie is providing my supper."

"Ms. Pierce, most people eat more than twice a day," June told her. "I've seen the sandwiches your grandmother makes for brunch. Unless you ate a dozen, they barely counted as a snack. One doughnut? Also a snack. So you've had two snacks today."

June lifted another lid and revealed a salad. "Besides, this isn't all yours. Mr. Quinn said you would split it." Another lid. Another salad. "I had them put the salads on separate plates." She turned to Mo. "And they cut the sandwich for you like you asked."

"I can see why Bronwyn loves you, June."

Bronwyn sat down. Even when it wasn't directed at her, Mo's voice was . . . *phew*. If he ever started talking *to* her? She might pass out. Or throw herself at him.

She swallowed and asked, "Since the two of you are managing me, what did you decide we're having for lunch?"

"The sandwich is a club with avocado. The salad is the house salad." June glanced at Mo again. "They put the dressing on the side, but they may not have sent enough. Should I—"

Mo held up a hand. "I'm sure it will be fine. You've done more than enough. Thank you."

June pinched her lips together, then turned to Bronwyn. "I'll, um, leave the cart here. You can pile the dishes on there when you're done. I'll have housekeeping come clear it whenever you're ready."

"Thank you."

June winked at her and walked to the door. And she . . . did she fan herself as she left?

Bronwyn stared at the food in front of her. Despite what June and Mo seemed to think, she didn't forget to eat. She'd just learned to deal with being hungry. She was careful to never skip meals entirely. But sometimes, she didn't have time to stop for lunch, so she munched and nibbled throughout the day.

But this was so much better. She took a triangle of the club sandwich and bowed her head. *Lord, I'm in a mess here. Thank you for the food and for the man who provided it. Please show me what to do . . .*

Five minutes later, the clacking of computer keys stopped, and Mo stood, stretched, and approached the table. He grabbed half of the sandwich and his salad and sat at the end of the conference table. His phone rang and he answered it. "Yo."

"How's it going?" Meredith's voice came through the phone.

"Good. You're on speaker. Bronwyn's here."

The zing that went through her when he said her name almost distracted her from Meredith's greeting.

"Bronwyn?" Meredith said her name again.

"Yeah, I'm here."

"I have more thoughts about your office. Could I swing by tonight?"

"I wish you could, but I have plans."

"Tomorrow?"

"Sure."

"What kind of plans?" Meredith asked, nosy as ever.

"If you must know, I have a massage tonight."

"Ooh. Nice."

"Perks of being the boss."

Meredith scoffed. "More like perks of having Landry make you take care of yourself. Have you noticed that if the people who love you didn't insist on it, you would never eat a real meal, get any rest, or have that fabulous masseuse work the stress out of your neck and shoulders?"

Before Bronwyn could say anything, Meredith continued, "Don't let her fool you, Mo. Landry sets up the appointments and guilt-trips Bronwyn into going. And even then, she only agrees because Katrina, the massage therapist, uses her as a guinea pig for new techniques."

"That doesn't surprise me," Mo said. "I've only been here for a few hours, and I've already had to order her lunch because apparently *someone* doesn't stop to eat."

"How did you learn that?" Was there a hint of eagerness in Meredith's voice?

"June and I had a lovely chat."

"I see." Definite disappointment.

"June needs to be careful who she spills my secrets to," Bronwyn grumbled.

"Whatever. The Haven would fall apart without you, and you would fall apart without June," Meredith added.

"She runs a tight ship." Mo's tone was approving. "I like her."

"What?" Meredith sounded as surprised as Bronwyn was. "Did you say you like her?"

"I do. Like I said, we had a chat. She's Team Bronwyn all the way."

"Oh good. I was wondering."

"Bronwyn knows how to put good people around her when she has control of the situation," Mo said. "We just need to sort this mess so she can put the people she wants in positions of authority across The Haven. If she could put good people in a few key positions, she wouldn't need to work eighty hours a week."

"Well, then get on with it and get this mess sorted." Meredith's voice faded out and Bronwyn thought she heard her say something like, "Okay, just a sec." Then her voice came back through the line. "I have to dash. My afternoon looks like two root canals. What do you have on your agenda?"

Mo didn't say anything, so Bronwyn assumed he assumed the question was directed at her. "After I eat this lunch, I have rounds to make."

"You need a little face time with the guests and staff." Meredith didn't make it a question.

"Exactly. I'll deal with whatever drama unfolds from that. Then I have an interview with a reporter."

"What?"

"It's for a travel magazine that caters to a European market. I forgot I'd said I could squeeze it in today. We've had a few new guests in the past couple of months that have convinced me there's a market there."

“How does this help you stay under the radar?”

“It doesn’t. But I’m not trying to stay under the radar of those who want to be here. I’m just trying to be sure Gossamer Falls doesn’t wind up overrun with paparazzi desperate to sneak a peek at the guests here. Plus, my father asked me to take the interview.” Bronwyn sighed. “But I think Uncle William is the one behind it.”

Mo sat straighter in the chair.

“Is this an in-person interview?” Meredith asked.

“It is. The journalist should arrive in the next hour. We’re supposed to talk around four thirty. Then he’ll be staying here for the next two nights. We’re supposed to meet again before he leaves.”

“I don’t like the sound of this.” Meredith’s voice was laced with worry.

“I don’t like it either,” Mo said. “That’s why I’ll be going to the interview with her.”

“You’ll what?” Meredith shrieked.

“You took the words right out of my mouth,” Bronwyn added.

“I have concerns. This guy could be who he claims, or he could have nefarious motives. Either way, I don’t think it would be prudent for Bronwyn to be alone with him. And since I’m sitting right here, there’s no reason for her to take that risk. I’ll go with her and help judge the situation.”

“Good plan. I like it. Bronwyn, what do you think?” Meredith asked.

“I think it’s overkill, but I won’t argue about it.” Bronwyn stared straight at Mo as she spoke.

“Good.” His eyes held hers.

“I wish I could be there. Sometimes being an adult is so annoying. Responsibilities and all that stuff. Why did we grow up again?” Meredith’s plaintive voice almost made Bronwyn smile.

“No choice in the matter, Mer Bear.” Mo held up three fingers. Then two. Then one.

"Mo! No! We removed that nickname from usage years ago."

Mo shook with silent laughter. "Did we? Sorry about that."

"Payback, brother dearest. Prepare thyself."

Mo's laughter was no longer silent. He continued to look at Bronwyn. She was laughing now too.

Meredith sounded like she was trying not to laugh as she said, "I have to go. One of you text me when you're done and give me an update."

"*I'll* call," Mo said, not dropping his gaze. "Bronwyn has a massage."

Bronwyn couldn't look away.

"Oh, right. Okay. Talk soon. Love you both."

"Love you," Bronwyn replied the same way she always did. And Mo also replied with the same words.

And for the split second before he returned his focus to his computer, Bronwyn wasn't sure if he'd been talking to Meredith.

Or to her.

TWENTY-THREE

Mo kept his hands on the keyboard and his face pointed at the monitor. But he wasn't seeing anything except Bronwyn's face. She was so expressive. Or was she? Maybe it was that, even after all these years, he could read her emotions. At least, he could when she wasn't trying to keep them from him.

When June had brought in the lunch, Bronwyn's expression had morphed from confusion to delight and then consternation, landing on what he decided was confused delight when she realized what was happening.

She was softening up. Hopefully she appreciated his efforts on her behalf.

He would have liked to spend the afternoon thinking of more ways to remind her he could be a good guy. Unfortunately, the look on her face when she talked about the interview this afternoon didn't give him warm and fuzzy feelings. He could focus on being charming later. For now, his priority was to keep her safe.

There was something . . . off about the whole thing. Had she ever granted a reporter an interview before?

A quick web search gave him the answer. Surprisingly enough, yes. There were quite a few interviews about The Haven. But they were presented in a way that protected the resort and the town from scrutiny. He read through an interview she had done last year and tried to read it as if he'd never heard of The Haven before. Based on the information provided, he drew two conclusions. One, the place was far out of his price range. And two, it was somewhere in the mountains of either North Carolina or Tennessee, maybe even Georgia, but he wasn't sure exactly where.

In this day and age, keeping The Haven off the map would prove difficult, if not futile. Maybe Bronwyn's goal wasn't to keep it hidden but to minimize the impact on the community. That would make sense.

Mo shot June a text.

What is the name of the reporter B has an interview with?

Seconds later, she replied.

Peter Brown

Mo snorted. Fake name. Had to be. Peter Brown? The only way it could have been worse was if it had been John Smith.

What's the name of his media outlet?

June's reply took a bit longer this time. He continued to work while he waited. His phone pinged.

Obscure Opulence

A few more minutes of digging and he was unsurprised by what he saw. The magazine was real enough, but they didn't have anyone named Peter Brown listed as writing for them.

Did he send you authentication for who he is and what he's up to?

The request came from William Pierce. I assumed he was legit. Do you think he isn't? I could ask for more info. I could say I'm helping Ms. Pierce prepare for the interview.

Mo considered the risks and decided they were minimal.

Go ahead. Let me know what you learn. Thank you.

Not a problem.

Bronwyn stood and let out a small groan as she patted her stomach. She piled her empty dishes onto the cart and wheeled it into the hall. "I shouldn't have eaten so much, but it was delicious."

Mo heard the words coming from the front desk but knew they weren't directed at him.

"I'm glad you enjoyed it," June said. "But Mr. Quinn gets the credit."

"I'll have to thank him too."

"Yes, ma'am. He was very specific. It's so sweet the way he's looking out for you."

Bronwyn's reply was too low for him to hear. But then she said, "I'm going to freshen up. I'll be out of here in the next ten minutes or so. Please make sure the interview space is ready for our guest by three. I'd like to get this over with as soon as possible."

"Of course."

Mo waited two minutes before he shut down the computer, grabbed his iPad, and walked into the reception area of the office. June quirked an eyebrow at him.

"I'm going with her," he said.

"Does she know that?"

"Yes."

"Seems like she might be giving you the slip."

"She can try."

June rolled her eyes. "She usually gets her way."

"Who gets her way?" Bronwyn paused at June's desk. Mo wasn't sure what she'd freshened up. Maybe her lips? They were glossy, and . . . he was going to stop looking at them.

"You do," June answered.

"She's always been that way." Mo winked at June. "Remind me to tell you about the time she talked me into—"

"Whatever he was about to say, it isn't true."

Mo looked at Bronwyn, then back to June. He stage-whispered, "We'll talk later."

June looked between Mo and Bronwyn and then grinned. "You two are a trip. Mr. Quinn, I hope you'll be around more often."

"I'll be here tomorrow as well. After that, we'll have to see. At some point, she's going to kick me out."

June shook her head. "Not if I can stop her." She gave Bronwyn a sassy grin. "Ms. Pierce, I got word from hospitality that the interview room is ready for you. I'll message you when Mr. Brown arrives."

"Thank you." Bronwyn checked her watch. "I'm going to head to Hideaway and check in with Cassie. Then I'll visit the front desk. Depending on how long that takes, I may or may not make it to housekeeping before the interview."

"Yes, ma'am."

Did she need to give June the play-by-play? Or was that for his benefit? Either way, he was glad to know the plan.

Bronwyn grabbed her iPad from the conference room table, took a deep breath, and walked down the hall. Mo took a position slightly to her left and stayed there until they walked into Hideaway's kitchen.

"Mo!" Cassie's smile had been infectious since she was a baby. "What's my favorite cousin doing here?"

"I came to see you, of course."

"Yeah, right. You saw me yesterday."

"It's already been too long."

Cassie removed her apron and spoke to Bronwyn. "It's the quiet ones you have to look out for." She walked to him, and Mo opened his arms. Cassie snuggled in, and he pressed a kiss to her forehead.

"How's married life?" Mo asked.

The answer was obvious. Her glow was enough to brighten any room, but he wanted to hear her answer anyway. He wasn't supposed to have favorites, but aside from Cal, Cassie really was his favorite Quinn cousin.

"Amazing! As you already know since you asked me yesterday." Cassie looked toward the ceiling. "Save me from overprotective cousins." Then she looked at Bronwyn. Mo didn't know what she saw, but Cassie's eyes widened. "Okay, okay. I know. I'm the luckiest girl in the world."

"And I will continue to point that out anytime you start acting put upon when you're so loved, you bump into it everywhere you go." Bronwyn's reply made Mo think this was an ongoing conversation between the two of them.

"You're loved too, Bronwyn."

Bronwyn's response wasn't a grin or a joke. She changed the subject entirely. "How's everything here today? Anything I need to know about?"

Mo tuned out most of the conversation after that. Did Bronwyn not believe she was loved?

To be fair, there were few people on earth as loved as a Quinn. The family was loving, affectionate, and not shy about it. But Bronwyn was . . .

Bronwyn was . . . what?

Her grandmother loved her. But that lady had spent her lifetime manipulating everyone and everything around her to the point that it was hard to tell if her motivations were pure or not.

Her parents loved her but not the way parents should. Mo had disappointed his mom and dad on more than one occasion. He'd had a multi-year run of disappointments after Bronwyn left. And then, when she came back, they were disappointed in him again.

Not that they'd ever said that. They loved him through all his faults and foibles. They loved him when he made them proud and when he made them despair. He'd grown up certain of that.

Bronwyn had not.

Her extended family didn't love her. They loved that she could bring in money. They loved that she ran The Haven so well they could go on vacations and live their lives without worry. But Bronwyn herself? No. They didn't love Bronwyn for who she was.

Her friends . . . well, Cal and Landry and Meredith loved her. And had never wavered in that love.

The kids adored her. Eliza's "Aunt Bronwyn" had nearly killed him from a cuteness overload.

She was loved. And loved deeply.

But that didn't mean she felt loved.

Mo couldn't shake the way that saddened him. He followed her from Hideaway's kitchen to the front desk to housekeeping, watching how she interacted with the staff.

They adored her.

But did she see it?

Somehow, he didn't think she did.

Bronwyn had been speaking to the surprisingly young head housekeeper, Adeline, for five minutes when her phone rang. She glanced at it, then at Mo, and her entire body deflated. She turned back to Adeline. "Well, it's time for me to go be charming."

"You're always charming." Adeline's grin was cheeky.

"Hah." She pointed at Mo. "He could tell you stories."

Interest lit Adeline's face. "Do tell."

Mo went with an innocent look. "I have no idea what she's talking about. Bronwyn Pierce is always the epitome of grace and beauty. Well, she is now. But I've known her since we were five, and we all go through an awkward phase."

"My awkward phase included braces and truly bad hair decisions." Bronwyn laughed.

"Your hair is phenomenal," Adeline said. "I can't imagine—"

"Pixie cut." Bronwyn grimaced, and Adeline couldn't hide her shock.

"No way."

"It was cute." Mo spoke before he could stop himself.

Bronwyn shook her head. "Nightmare."

Adeline turned to Mo. "I bet it *was* cute."

"It was." Mo was firm in his response. "But I wasn't sad when she let it grow out."

"It was the growing out that was the worst!" Bronwyn shuddered. "Okay. On that dreadful thought, I'm out of here."

Bronwyn walked into the press room with Mo on her heels. She'd been dreading having him along today, but he'd somehow managed to turn what could have been a stilted and challenging afternoon into one filled with laughter and mostly good memories.

The smile on her face was genuine as she greeted her interviewer. "Mr. Brown, it's a pleasure to meet you."

He took her hand and, instead of shaking it, lifted it to his lips and kissed it. "The pleasure is mine, I'm sure."

Bronwyn kept her smile but extricated her hand. Beyond the outdated and cringey hand kiss, there was something she did not like about this man, but she couldn't quite figure out what it was.

She kept her face calm while her brain worked to nail down the cause of her discomfort.

Something about this man set off alarm bells. It was only years of etiquette training and experience that kept her from walking out the door. "Won't you sit down?"

Peter Brown gestured toward a chair. "After you."

She didn't argue and took a seat. When she did, she spotted Mo standing in the doorway in an "at ease" position. His Army days were showing, and she didn't mind at all.

Then she remembered the weapon tucked into his pants at his back. Standing the way he was, with his hands behind him, he could pull it out in the blink of an eye.

She didn't mind that either.

She focused on Peter Brown and gave him her most professional smile. "How was your trip?"

They made small talk for longer than she wanted, and when the opportunity presented itself, she redirected the conversation to the interview. "I'm sure you're eager to settle in and explore the property."

"Well, I was," he said, "but now that I've met you, I'm finding that I don't feel any need to rush."

Was it possible for words to make her want to take a shower? She fought to keep her tone even. "I happen to know that you have a dinner reservation at five thirty and, believe me, Mr. Brown, you don't want to miss it. I'd say we need to move this along."

"I'll only agree if you promise to call me Peter."

This guy got slimier every time he opened his mouth.

"I appreciate that, but we have a policy that requires a certain level of formality with our guests."

"I won't tell if you won't." She could tell he meant to pass it off like a joke, but something in his eyes told her he wasn't kidding.

"We have exceedingly high standards at The Haven. Those standards apply to all staff at all levels of guest interaction. I would suggest you ask me the questions you have prepared so that we can both go on with our day."

"What if you join me for dinner tonight? That would be a far more enjoyable way for us to get to know each other." His smile was movie-star white and as fake as a flea market Rolex.

Bronwyn could sense Mo's frustration. She didn't think he'd moved a muscle, and she was very careful not to draw any attention to him, but knowing he was there helped her maintain her professionalism. "I'm afraid my schedule is packed this week, so if you want to interview me, this is your time. I have a prior engagement tonight." She tried to keep her voice conciliatory.

"Tomorrow? I mean, you have to eat, right?" He leaned forward in his chair. "I'd really like to spend more time with you."

There was something about his eyes. She almost had it, but the connection slipped away. "While I appreciate the flattery, I'm afraid I'm not available for anything more than a professional conversation."

"Are you in a relationship?"

"Excuse me?"

"That's a no." His grin was smug. "Okay, I can see you're playing hard to get. I respect it. I can play too." He pulled out a notebook and a recorder and before she had a chance to respond to his remark, he hit the record button. "Peter Brown interviewing Bronwyn Pierce at The Haven." He consulted his notes. "How long have you been the CEO of The Haven?"

What kind of question was that? She wasn't the one being interviewed here. Well, she was, but the interview was supposed to be about The Haven. Not her. "A few years now."

"You're young for a role like this, aren't you?"

"Not really. I grew up here. I know this business better than anyone. I was the perfect candidate for the job."

He winked at her. "Confident. I like that in a woman."

Mo was growing increasingly tense in her periphery. She didn't think her interviewer was aware of the predator watching him.

"You've had some family issues in the past few years. Some drugs. Attempted murder. That kind of thing?" He asked the question with a look that said, "You poor thing."

"Mr. Brow—"

"Peter."

"Mr. Brown," she said with more force, "my family is like any other in America. We aren't perfect. But we ensure that personal drama doesn't affect the running of The Haven."

"And how do you do that?"

"We have strict rules for everyone on staff, including family members. This ensures that everyone who interacts with our guests is above reproach."

"I see. So how long did Steven—"

She let her exasperation bleed into her voice. "I'm sorry to disappoint you, but I won't be taking any questions regarding specific family members or staff, past or present. If you'd like to ask questions about The Haven, our facilities, and our amenities, I'm happy to talk to you about that. If you want to talk about legal matters, I'll gladly direct you to our attorneys."

Peter Brown leaned back in his seat. "Okay, how about this. Why do you feel the need to have an armed bodyguard with you?" He pointed his thumb toward Mo. "I interview a lot of folks and usually the armed guard stuff is for the celebrities, not the hotel managers."

She didn't bother to correct him about her position or Mo's role. "Again, these are inappropriate questions not germane to our discussion today." She stood. "I think it would be best if you and I table this interview. You can enjoy your time here for the next two days, and if you have further questions, I'm sure our marketing and publicity department will be able to answer them."

He stood and slid his notebook into the satchel he'd brought with him. "I'm sure I'll see you around, Bronwyn."

"I'll see you out, Mr. Brown." Mo's tone didn't give the man any wiggle room. Peter walked out the door Mo held open for him. She watched until they were both out of sight, then let her legs give out as she collapsed into her chair.

June walked in. "Is everything okay? Mr. Quinn looked ready to strangle that guy."

Bronwyn shook her head. "That was the weirdest thing that's happened to me in a long time."

"Can I bring you anything?"

"No. Thanks," she said as Mo returned.

"She needs some water, June. Would you mind?" Mo had his phone to his ear, and as soon as he'd spoken, he went back to his call. "Yes. That's correct. Everything, and I mean everything. Thanks."

He disconnected that call and dialed another number.

June returned with an unopened water bottle and handed it to her, eyes wide. "Ms. Pierce?"

Mo spoke into his phone again. "Hey, I'm going to escort Bronwyn home so she can go to her massage, which she needed before, and now she *really* needs. What kind of security do we have in the spa?"

He listened, and Bronwyn motioned for June to sit. She sipped her water and fought to keep from trembling as the adrenaline left her system.

It hadn't been her imagination. That whole situation had been beyond weird. Mo was clearly cool and calm as he gave orders, but she knew he was masking his fury. He was probably fighting the need to run Peter Brown out of town.

And what was with her reaction to the man? She was in the hospitality industry. She handled come-ons and put-downs without giving them a second thought. But Peter Brown's very presence made her skin crawl.

"Okay." A pause. "Good." A longer pause. "Well, that's the problem, isn't it?"

Bronwyn took another drink. Mo looked at her, then at June. He put his hand over the phone. "Do you have anything sweet around here? A candy bar? A Coke? Something with a little sugar?"

June jumped to her feet. "On it." Mo returned to his phone call and when June came back thirty seconds later with a tub of salted caramels and two Cokes, he gave her a thumbs-up.

Bronwyn didn't bother to argue. She had no idea if chocolate and Coke would settle her nerves, but they couldn't make things worse.

Mo continued to talk to someone, but his side of the conversation was mostly grunts and *hmms* and, once, a "we have to do better than that." Then he looked at his watch. "Gotta go. Yeah. Thanks."

He turned to June. "Thank you for getting those things for Bronwyn. I apologize if I was abrupt."

"No, sir. You weren't."

"I don't want to overstep, but you need to be on your guard around that man," he said, his eyes on June. "He'll be on-site for the next two days. I don't know what his game is, but I'd bet a year's salary that he's not who he claims to be. I suggest you wrap up and go home. Marcus will follow you to your car and make sure you make it out of the gates. Then he's coming back to escort us to Bronwyn's house and then to the spa."

Marcus had been part of the security team here for most of Bronwyn's life. She trusted him. Apparently Mo did too.

"June, there's a chance Bronwyn won't be in the office at all tomorrow. Can you hold down the fort if she's not in?"

"What?" Bronwyn tried to protest but June and Mo ignored her.

"Of course."

"Marcus will be here, and he'll have everything locked down. But if I can figure out how to keep Bronwyn off-site the entire time Peter Brown is here, I will."

"I think that would be a good idea." June would agree with anything Mo said. That was plain to see.

"Maybe you can talk her into it for me?" Mo held his hands in a praying position.

"Ms. Pierce is too smart to be manipulated."

Bronwyn wished that were true.

"She has incredibly good instincts." Mo seemed to be agreeing with June. What? "Which is what had me on alert. She didn't like that guy from the moment she laid eyes on him. If she ever reacts that way to someone, pay attention. She's almost never wrong. And that"—Mo pinched his lips together—"is why I think we'll be able to convince her to stay off-site. Maybe by the time her massage is over, she'll come around."

June didn't look convinced. "Good luck with that."

"Oh, I've stacked the deck in my favor. She might be able to ignore me, but when her favorite niece asks her to come spend the night tonight—"

"That's brilliantly diabolical."

Marcus knocked on the door. "Ms. June, you almost ready?"

"Do you need me for anything else?"

Bronwyn noted that June's question was directed at her but also at Mo. When Mo didn't answer, she said, "No, thank you. I'll touch base tomorrow."

Before Marcus followed June, he looked from Bronwyn to Mo. "Don't like this, ma'am. Don't like it one bit."

"I don't either. I still can't figure out what happened. It was so . . . odd."

"We'll get to the bottom of it. You gather your things while I see Ms. June out. Then I'll be back."

"Marcus—"

"Bronwyn." Marcus said her name in the same whiny tone she'd used. He almost never called her Bronwyn anymore. He must be really worried.

She gave up the argument before it even began. "Fine."

"I'll be back in ten minutes."

When Marcus and June left, she stared at Mo for a long moment. Then she got up and went to her temporary office. She packed her laptop, a few files, and her planner. Her phone rang and she answered it while she worked. "Hey, Landry."

"Hey, Eliza wants to ask you something."

Before she could respond, Eliza's little voice came through the phone. "Aunt Bronwyn, could you come do a firepit tonight? Please? Uncle Mo always has stuff for s'mores, and Aunt Meredith said she also had stuff for mountain pies. Please? Can you come?"

As if she could say no to that. "Of course, sweetie. It will probably be a little while before I can be there."

"That's okay. Mom says I can eat before you get here, but there will be plenty left over for you and Uncle Mo."

"Okay. Will you let me talk to your mom again?"

"See you soon!" Eliza's cheery voice disappeared, followed by Landry's cool, "Hey."

"What has the world come to when you use your child to do your dirty work?" Bronwyn asked.

"She wasn't doing *my* dirty work." Landry laughed as she protested, making Bronwyn think she wasn't taking this nearly as seriously as she should have. "She's doing *Mo's* dirty work."

"You're going to blame this on Mo?"

"Oh yeah," Landry continued, "he cleared it with us first, of course, but then he talked to her and said something about how it'd be nice to have Aunt Bronwyn over for a firepit tonight. And then he said he might have a hard time convincing you, but that she would be able to do it for sure. And here we are."

"I'm surrounded by conspirators." Bronwyn shook her head.

"We love you. Go get relaxed and then come eat campfire food. You know you'll feel better if you do."

TWENTY-FOUR

ELEVEN YEARS EARLIER

"Hi, Mo."

Lieutenant Montgomery Quinn closed his eyes and, for a sliver of time, accepted that the emotional breakdown he'd been putting off for six years had picked the worst possible time to manifest.

"Hey there, gorgeous." The New Jersey accent and flirting tone made it clear that Lieutenant Carpenter had inserted himself into the situation and was talking to the woman who'd walked out of his nightmares and stopped him on a sidewalk.

What was she doing here? Why was she here?

Mo executed a crisp about-face and slapped Carpenter on the back. "I do believe the lady spoke to me. Why don't you go on and find us a seat?"

"I'd rather stay here and talk to . . ." Carpenter paused and looked over Mo's shoulder. "What's your name?"

"Bronwyn Pierce. And I'd rather you left so I can talk to Mo."

Mo had to fight to stay standing. Why was it hard to breathe? What was this?

"Now you don't want to do that." Carpenter leered at Bronwyn. "This fool's shipping out tomorrow, but I'll be in town for the next four months." The idiot waggled his eyebrows in some kind of villainous move that was so over-the-top, Mo half expected Bronwyn to laugh.

Mo still hadn't faced her, but he could imagine the look on her face when she replied with a heavier-than-usual Southern accent that somehow coated the blade of her words in silk. "I don't take kindly to men telling me what I do or don't want to do. Why don't you run on now?"

Carpenter laughed and mock punched Mo's arm. "Good luck, brother. Call me if plans change." He winked at Bronwyn and disappeared from Mo's line of sight.

A long beat later, Bronwyn cleared her throat. "You have interesting friends."

Translation: What are you doing hanging around with a moron like that?

Mo turned the final few degrees required to see her, and an emotional tsunami crashed over him. He had never been a fan of drowning. And the last time he'd felt this way was the day he got home from a two-month summer trip out West to find that the most important person in his world had run away from home with a Hollywood producer who was twenty years, two divorces, and a million light years away from the innocence that was Bronwyn's sixteen-year-old self.

He'd been so in love with her it hurt.

She'd been in love too. Just not enough.

He'd dreamed of this moment for six long years. Imagined every possible scenario. And never, not in one of them, had it taken place on a busy street. It also hadn't included her acting like she had the right to speak to him as if they were still friends.

Because they most definitely were not.

"Ms. Pierce." The spark in her eyes dimmed at his formal response. "I'd appreciate it if you wouldn't disparage my friends.

Carpenter's a good man." A man Mo frequently wanted to strangle, but he had no plans to share that with Bronwyn. "He's just trying to take me out before I leave the country, and I can assure you, he didn't need to be hassled by someone who wouldn't understand loyalty if it slapped her upside the head with a frying pan."

Bronwyn took a step back. She dropped her gaze to the ground, and a pang of guilt zinged through Mo's gut. He shoved it aside. Because, really? Six years pass and she shows up like this? No phone call. No warning. Just ambushing him on the sidewalk?

"I'm sorry, Mo." She audibly gulped in a lungful of air. "I should have started with that. I'm so very sorry."

Mo crossed his arms and waited.

"I should have called. But I found out you were here and that you're leaving. And . . . I had to see you."

Bronwyn tightened her hand on her purse strap. "I had hoped we could maybe get coffee and talk, but"—she gestured toward the restaurant Carpenter had entered—"I don't want to take time away from your friends."

"I appreciate that." The edge in his voice could have sliced a redwood to ribbons, but he couldn't find the strength to be gracious.

She closed her eyes. "You aren't going to make this easy on me."

He didn't respond.

She opened her eyes, caught his, and gave him a grim nod. "I know I don't deserve easy." She looked at the restaurant again. "But I had hoped."

"Yeah. My easy button broke a long time ago. I don't put up with anything from anyone anymore. And right now, I'm going to need you to hurry this along. We have reservations, but I don't know how long they'll hold them if the entire party isn't present."

Bronwyn's spine went straight. "Right. Okay. Look, I screwed up."

Mo doubted anything could top that for understatement.

"I hurt you and I'm so very sorry."

His brain swirled with years of pain, hurt, confusion, and yes, righteous anger. He fought to keep his response measured and to hide the turmoil her appearance had caused. He wasn't going to tell her he forgave her, because he didn't, and he wasn't sure that he ever would.

His mouth formed the only words his brain could come up with. "I appreciate you telling me."

Bronwyn gaped at him. "You *appreciate* it? That's . . . that's your response? I hunted you down, hopped on a plane, and walked three miles to be able to tell you in person—"

"None of which I asked for." Mo lost the battle with his temper. "It's always about you, isn't it? Let me guess, you're in a twelve-step program or whatever there is for someone like you?"

Her eyes widened and filled with tears. She dropped her gaze to the pavement.

But he wasn't done.

"You're on whichever step it is that has you making amends, and you decided today was the day you'd mark this one off your list. And to make it even more impressive, you jumped through a bunch of unnecessary hoops. I'm sure you could have found my phone number—"

"You would have hung up on me."

He ignored her interruption and continued, "My parents still live in the same house, so you could have sent me a note. But you had to make a production out of your apology. Were you thinking I'd feel extra sorry for you, or was this some kind of penance for what you did?"

Bronwyn shook her head but didn't speak.

"Look, you've done your part. You apologized. And I heard the words. I even believe that you think you mean them. But here's the thing—I don't care. You walked out of my life, and you stayed out of it. That was your choice. I had no way to contact you for months, and when we finally found an address, I sent you so many letters, my mom made me switch to postcards to save on postage."

"I never got them."

"Maybe you did, maybe you didn't. But you know what I got? I got smart. I realized one day that even if you weren't getting my letters, you had no excuse not to write to me. I'm not the one who left without saying goodbye. And that's when I accepted that you cut me out of your life on purpose. That you didn't want to hear from me. You didn't want to see me. You didn't want to know me."

Tears streamed down her face, and her entire body shook.

"I have no idea whether you're really sorry or not," he went on, "but the truth is that it doesn't matter one way or the other. We're no longer part of each other's lives. That's what you wanted, and that's what you got."

"That isn't what I wanted, Mo."

He didn't know what his face looked like, but when Bronwyn looked up at him, she immediately took a step back.

"Spare me the lies, okay?" He pointed to his chest. "*I* didn't go anywhere. You could have found me anytime you *wanted* to, but now you show up the day before I deploy so you can, what? Ease your conscience? Are you worried that I'll die and you won't have a chance to finish all your steps?"

"I wanted to . . . explain."

"You explained plenty. I have six years of empty mailboxes to prove it. I don't need an explanation. You're sorry? Good. You should be. Now go back to wherever you came from, and I'll go on living my life the way I want to—without you in it."

He turned on his heel and walked into the restaurant. Once inside, he paused and looked down the sidewalk. Bronwyn wiped her eyes and took a few steps in his direction. Then she dropped her head, turned, and walked away.

He watched her until she was out of sight, then he found his friends.

He needed the chaos of a night out to get his mind off what had just happened.

But what he needed most was to forget the pain in the eyes of the only woman he'd ever loved.

Five days later, Bronwyn grabbed her mail and walked upstairs to her third-floor apartment. She had an exam tomorrow and another on Friday. She needed to study. Her flight to see Mo had messed up her schedule and she . . . oh, who was she kidding? The flight wasn't the problem. The emotional atomic bomb that Mo had detonated was the problem.

She'd spent more time than was healthy over the past few days rehashing every second of their encounter. She'd been sure he would respect her for showing up in person rather than writing a letter.

She couldn't have been more wrong.

She wasn't sure what she'd expected him to say, but she hadn't been prepared for the anger.

Which was stupid on her part. She should have been. Her mistake had been thinking he was still the gentle soul she'd left behind.

Mo had been her person. Her playmate, her confidante, her best friend, her crush, and her first and only love. And that's how she still thought of him. She'd been unprepared for the reality that the boy who'd loved her had grown into a man who hated her—and had some serious anger issues.

She tossed her backpack into a chair and sorted through the mail.

Her hand froze as her mind registered the distinctive handwriting.

Her breathing came fast and hard as she ripped open Mo's letter. It took several rounds of intentional breath work to avoid hyperventilating before she could read his words.

Dear Bronwyn,

It's my turn to apologize. I'm sorry for what I said, for the way I said it, and for the anger that I allowed to take over.

You were trying to do the right thing. I can see that now—and I can respect it—because I would much rather be having this conversation in person, and if it were possible, I would have gotten on a plane and come to do just that.

To top it all off, after going on and on about how my address didn't change, I find myself in the awkward position of having to say that I can't tell you where I am or how long I'll be here or when I'll be home.

But if I do make it home, I would like to apologize in person, and I would like to hear the explanation you wanted to give.

I'm not rational when it comes to you. Never have been. Never will be.

I don't expect you to believe this, but I regretted everything I said almost as soon as I said it. I went inside the restaurant, fully intending to enjoy the evening as planned, but five minutes in, I bailed on my buddies and took off in the direction you'd gone.

I've missed you. And I've missed our friendship. I'm glad you're getting your life sorted out. So glad.

Anyway, I'll find you when I get home. And if you're up for it, we'll talk.

Mo

Bronwyn stared at the letter.

She reread it ten times over the next two days.

She knew she should forgive him.

But she wouldn't.

She pulled a pen out and wrote over the top of his last words.

No thanks.

Then, under that, she wrote,

You aren't who I remembered either. I guess we've both changed, and not for the best. Live your life without me, Mo. I'll happily live mine without you.

She took the letter, folded it, and placed it in an envelope. She mailed it to his parents' house. He'd get it eventually.

And it didn't matter to her anymore, anyway.

She was done.

THREE YEARS EARLIER

Mo took the stairs from the hospital parking lot three at a time. All he wanted was to get inside and see his mom. It had gutted him to be so far away from her while she was sick.

People her age weren't supposed to get pneumonia and almost die from an allergic reaction to the antibiotics, especially while their sons were twenty hours away.

Aunt Carol had called him while he was en route and promised that his mom was stable. But that call couldn't erase the terror that had invaded his soul when Meredith called to tell him that their mom was being rushed to the ICU because she couldn't breathe.

He'd gotten an emergency medical leave, but it still took more time than he wanted to make the arrangements and get home.

He paced by the elevator and tried to slow his breathing. His dad and Meredith were here. So were Cal and Aunt Carol. He didn't need to come busting out of the elevator like that great big Kool-Aid man.

When the elevator chimed, he dashed inside and paced the small space until the doors opened again. He half walked, half jogged to the room. The door was open and when he heard the voice inside, he froze.

Why was Bronwyn in his mom's hospital room?

"When you make it home, call me," he heard her say. "I'll bring you some of Chef Louis's finest creations. And we can watch old movies together."

Why was Bronwyn offering to hang out with his mom?

"Okay. See you soon."

Bronwyn stepped into the hall and straight into Mo. Her eyes went huge as he stepped back, then around her. "Excuse me."

He rushed into the room and promptly forgot about the interaction. Or tried to. After he'd talked to his mom for fifteen minutes, he could tell she was worn out. He wouldn't do anything to jeopardize her recovery.

"I'll go for now, Mom. You get some rest. I'm home for the next two weeks."

"Oh, that's lovely. I'm so glad."

He bent down to hug her, and she grabbed his hand and held on. He didn't try to pull away.

His mom's voice was weak, but her joy was strong. "Maybe you and Bronwyn can find some time to chat while you're here."

"Mom, you don't need to have anything to do with Bronwyn Pierce."

"What?"

"Seriously? You can't trust her. What was she even doing here?"

"She came to see me. She's back in Gossamer Falls permanently now."

Mo scowled. "She cut ties with us. She's a Pierce. I would prefer it if you didn't let her too close."

"Sweetheart—"

"Son, let your mom rest," his father said, stepping in. "We'll talk later." Mo's father was a quiet man who had always had his children's respect. When he spoke in that tone, the subject was closed.

"Sure. Love you both. I'll see you in the morning."

He squeezed his mom's hand one more time before heading to the door. When he stepped into the hallway, it was to see the furious face of Bronwyn Pierce staring back at him.

He stalked past her.

She followed but didn't speak until they were in front of the elevators.

"She can't trust me?" Bronwyn sucked in a breath. "I'm a *Pierce*?"

"You *are* a Pierce."

"You know what I mean. What is wrong with you? Are you truly that filled with hate that you would speak to your own mother that way when she almost died?"

"I don't want to see her hurt. She loved you like a second daughter. When you pulled your little disappearing act, it nearly broke her! Can you blame me for wanting to spare her that kind of heartache?" The remembered pain of those days sharpened his words. "You won't stay. You'll find a new sugar daddy and take off for California. And where will that leave everyone here? Oh, wait, we know, because we've already been there."

Bronwyn's lip trembled, but when she spoke, her words were as cold as a mountain pass in January. "You haven't changed a bit, have you? You're still looking for every opportunity to hurt me." She shook her head and her lip curled in obvious disgust. "I feel sorry for you. I truly do. But don't worry. You win. I won't speak to you ever again."

With that, she raised her chin, turned, and walked away without another word.

It wasn't until two days later that Mo confessed to Meredith about his altercation with Bronwyn.

"Oh, Mo. What's wrong with you? Why did you do that?"

He dropped his head into his hands. "I'm an idiot. I wasn't prepared to see her. I hadn't slept in thirty-six hours. I was stressed to the max. And it all just came out of me. I can't ever get things right with her."

"You could start by apologizing."

"She made it clear that she won't talk to me."

"Then you'll have to write her a letter."

"I tried that once before. As you may recall, it didn't work."

Meredith grimaced. "I think you have to do it anyway."

So he did.

Bronwyn,

I did it again. I don't know why. I have reasons. Lack of sleep. Fear. Emotional turmoil. But they're all just lame excuses for my incredibly bad behavior. I'm a jerk. An imbecile. A moron. I'm a worm. I'm the absolute worst. You don't deserve to be subjected to me and my sharp mouth.

This letter is an apology, but it's also my way of acknowledging that you win. I won't speak to you until you speak to me first. It's the least I can do.

Sincerely,
Mo

TWENTY-FIVE

PRESENT DAY

Thirty minutes later, Mo sat in the spa lobby while Bronwyn, as Meredith would say, got her zen on.

Mo hoped it helped. He'd been anti-massage for anything other than injury purposes until Meredith had ambushed him last year. He'd found himself getting a cut, a shave, and a massage, followed by some time in the sauna.

He'd walked out calmer and more relaxed than he'd been in months.

And he'd gone back twice since.

He should probably schedule another one.

When they left Bronwyn's office, they'd made a quick run to her home before heading to the spa. As he'd done for the past couple of days, he cleared the house before letting her enter. When he walked into her office, he'd nearly come unglued.

She'd moved her piece on the Chinese checkers board. It was right there, plain as day. She hadn't made a move the last time he looked. But now, her red marble was on the board.

He needed to finish clearing the house. Leaving her outside

while he stared at a Chinese checkers board was . . . ridiculous. But before he left her office, he made another move of his own. Maybe this time it wouldn't take so long for her to respond.

Not that she would be home. He was keeping her on Quinn land tonight. And maybe tomorrow night. And maybe the night after that.

He'd keep her there forever if he could get away with it.

His phone vibrated in his hand. He kept his voice low and answered. "What do you have for me?"

"Nothing that makes sense." The female voice on the other end of the line was clipped and didn't pause for him to respond. "Your Peter Brown is running through my facial rec software now. It picked him up at the Charlotte airport yesterday as he got off a flight from DC. We have another capture at a rental counter. He's driving a black Suburban. He flew in and rented the vehicle under the name Peter Brown, so he has photo identification and credit cards in that name, but that's an alias."

Mo wasn't surprised. But he was impressed with how fast Sabrina found the information he requested.

"Peter Brown goes by several other names," she went on. "Three so far. And the system hasn't checked all the databases I have access to. Two of them are as obviously fake as the one he's using now."

"John Smith?"

"No, but they might as well be. David Black and Robert White. Someone needs to tell him to step away from colors. The other name is Kevin Glen Masters, and that's the one you need to spend some time on. I know there's something there. I just don't have it yet."

"I'm not in front of a computer. Won't be for a while."

"Not a problem. I'll send you what I have. It doesn't make sense to me. Why would a man with a criminal record for assault be posing as a reporter?"

Mo jumped to his feet and paced the room. He wanted to grab

Bronwyn and take her far, far away from here. But he couldn't. Not yet.

"I assume from your silence that you have an idea of why he might be doing that?"

"Yes," he answered. "And no."

"Explain, please."

"We're having some trouble here. Suspicious activity. Weird behavior. Possible threats. Having someone pose as a reporter when he intends to do harm doesn't come as too much of a shock. Especially after the way this guy harassed Bronwyn during their so-called interview today."

"I see." A pause. "Is she safe?"

"I'll make her safe."

Another pause. "I'm sure you will. I'll send you what I have. And if anything new turns up, I'll let you know."

"Thank you for this. I owe you. I certainly didn't expect you to drop everything and run with it. Were you sitting at home with nothing to do?"

"I've made a few mods to my algorithm. I've played with it a few times, but this is allowing me to put it to a real-world test. I've been itching to play with it, and your timing was perfect. Adam's working late, and the baby is spending the evening with her grandparents."

"Uh-oh."

"Why uh-oh?"

"If you have a sitter, I assume you and Adam had plans, and he's working late."

"We did. But his parents watch the baby anytime we ask. We aren't hurting for opportunities. Adam rarely works like this, and when he does, it matters. I'm the one more likely to be tied up at work, so I don't complain when it happens to him."

"You're a remarkable woman, Dr. Fleming-Campbell."

"That's a nice way of saying I'm weird." Sabrina's laughter confirmed that she wasn't angry. "Which is true. But I'm good— Oh. Adam's calling. Keep me in the loop."

"Will do."

The line disconnected.

Kevin Glen Masters, I'm coming for you.

There wasn't much he could do until he was at his computer. He checked his watch. Made a few phone calls. Checked his watch again.

Thirty-seven minutes later, Bronwyn emerged with hair mussed, makeup gone, and eyes heavy-lidded in a way that told him Katrina, the massage therapist, had worked a miracle.

Her smile was soft, and she blinked at him several times.

Katrina followed her out and laughed. "Mo, you're going to need to keep an eye on her. She's so relaxed I'm not sure if she can walk straight. I wish I could use before and after videos for endorsements."

"No doubt." He agreed. "She walked in there strung tight. And now?" He pointed toward her.

"Right?"

Bronwyn made a production out of tapping her ear. "I can hear you, you know."

Was she slurring her words?

"Not that I care. I'm not sure if I care about anything right now." Bronwyn took in a deep breath and closed her eyes as she exhaled. "Katrina, whatever you plan to charge, I suggest you double it."

Katrina turned off a few lights and walked with them to the door. "Mo, she told me she's headed back to your place for some firepit action and to spend the night with Meredith. Or maybe with Landry?" She waved a hand. "Anyway, she mentioned that the only thing that could make her feel better was some ice cream. Something with cornflakes in it? Do you know it?"

Mo groaned. "I know it. Meredith, Landry, and Bronwyn are singlehandedly responsible for Lionel carrying it at the grocery store now. Never seen anything like it."

"Is it good? Because it sounds a little sketchy." Katrina wrinkled her nose. "Cornflakes?"

"You owe it to yourself to try it. I hate to admit it, but it is quite possibly the best thing you'll ever eat." He looked at Bronwyn. "I guess we'll swing by the store and grab some on the way to the house."

"I might follow you," Katrina said. "You've intrigued me."

"Good. We'll see you there."

Mo watched as Bronwyn hugged Katrina and whispered something that made her laugh.

If you could be drunk on relaxation, Bronwyn was.

"Are you sure she's safe to drive?" Mo asked Katrina.

"She'll be fine. She's just trying to hold on to the feeling as long as possible."

"Fair enough. I'll follow you both out."

He was unsurprised when both women pulled into the Gossamer Grocers parking lot. Bronwyn appeared to be less spacey than she'd been earlier, but she also looked a little bit like she might have been crying in the car.

Mo followed them inside but hung back near the doors. The store was small, and it wasn't hard for him to keep an eye on them as they went straight to the ice cream case. They didn't dawdle. They were in line two minutes later. Mo stepped outside and waited for them by his Jeep.

The sun was still up, but it had dropped behind the mountains, and the air was cooling off ever so slightly. It was more ice cream weather than it was firepit weather, but he wouldn't argue with Eliza, especially when she was doing such a good job of giving Bronwyn the excuse she needed to leave The Haven property.

Maybe if he could keep her on Quinn land for a few days, he could keep her safe *and* get some sleep. He rubbed his hand over his face.

The crunch of tires on the pavement behind him caught his attention and he turned to see who else was doing some evening shopping.

Lionel, the store owner, walked by as the cashier scanned Bronwyn's ice cream. "You'd better be getting that for Landry." He winked at her.

"It's for me, but I'm planning to share." Bronwyn took her receipt and the bag of frozen goodness. "But unless you have some in the back, you'd better order more. I convinced Katrina here to try it, and we took the last two pints."

"Good to know," Lionel said, scanning Katrina's purchases. "I'll get some more in. I still haven't tried it."

"Don't." She held up a hand and walked backward, toward the door. "This is dangerous stuff. One taste and you'll be ordering it by the truckload."

Lionel's laughter followed her out the door.

She turned and froze.

Mo was pacing outside the store. His eyes weren't on her. They were on the parking lot.

He looked so tired. His shoulders were slumped. His eyes, those bright blue Quinn eyes, were shadowed. And his face somehow looked older than she'd ever seen it.

Her heart hurt.

This probably wasn't the time. It definitely wasn't the place. But maybe she could say "Hi." Or "Thank you." Or "Mo, I really appreciate your help." And then, like the cowardly lion, she could hop in her car and drive away before he had a chance to reply. And she would have spoken to him and opened that door, and he could walk through it or not. But at least if she ran away, he wouldn't have a chance to slam it in her face immediately.

But she couldn't do that. Not now. She wasn't going home. She was going to his home. Or, beside it. His property. Sort of. If she ran away, he would follow her. He had to follow her. And the level of awkward would be . . . She cringed at the thought.

Ugh. She was such a coward. She waited near the door for Katrina to complete her purchase, then walked with her to the parking lot.

A truck pulled up behind Mo's Jeep, and the passenger window slid down. She expected someone to call out to Mo. The occupants were probably Quinns.

But instead of a friendly face, the unmistakable end of a rifle appeared. And pointed straight at—

"Mo!" she screamed as she ran straight for him.

He looked up and caught her reflexively as she barreled into him. The crack of the shot came a split second before Mo's body jerked, and they fell to the ground.

Bronwyn heard the thunk as his head made contact with the asphalt. But they didn't stay where they landed. His arms wrapped around her, and then he rolled until his body covered hers.

"I've got you," his low voice whispered into her ear. "Don't move."

Bronwyn hissed, "Get off me. They could shoot you."

"Does everything have to be an argument with you?"

Before she could tell him that arguing was a defense mechanism and she was only doing it because she was terrified, more shots were fired.

Somewhere behind them, Katrina screamed. Bronwyn might have screamed too. She wasn't sure. All she knew was that Mo covered her completely and then his body jolted again, and he let out a grunt.

The next sound she registered was the unmistakable squeal of tires as someone peeled out of the parking lot. Mo lumbered to his feet and did a weird shuffling run toward the fleeing vehicle. What was wrong with him? Did he want to get shot?

She turned her head enough to watch him, and that's when she saw the bloodstain spreading across his left shoulder.

He'd already been shot.

Katrina's low "Oh my word. Oh my word. Oh my word" registered in her senses, and she rolled to her feet.

"Get down!" Mo yelled at her. But she ignored him. If Mo could run after the shooters, she could at least get vertical. She turned to her friend and found her curled in a near-fetal position on the ground a few feet away.

Bronwyn stumbled toward her as Lionel ran out of the building and joined her. "Katrina? Are you hurt?" Had she been shot?

Katrina shook her head and wiped a hand over her face. "No." It sounded like she'd been swallowing gravel.

Lionel helped Bronwyn pull Katrina to her feet, then he put his arm around her and led her back into the store.

Bronwyn watched her. She was moving, and there were no obvious wounds. Hopefully, she'd been on the ground because she'd dropped and made herself as small a target as possible, not because of any external force.

A strong body leaned into hers. Mo put his arm around her and hustled her inside before she could get a good look at him.

The cashier was on the phone. Lionel guided Katrina to a bench by the office door.

Bronwyn stopped and turned to Mo. "You—"

He placed his hand over her lips. "Bronwyn." Her name was a growl. "Turn around."

Turn around. Why? When she didn't move, his hands landed on her shoulders, and he spun her, eyes on her body. "What are you doing? You're the one who's bleeding."

Mo ignored her complaint. He pulled in a shaky breath as she faced him again. "You're not hit."

She wasn't sure if it was a question or a statement, but she answered him anyway. "No."

He swallowed hard, his hands still on her shoulders. His breathing accelerated, and he pulled her against his chest. His hands slid down her arms and then around her. His breath tickled her ear when he spoke. "You saved my life."

"I don't think so. You saved mine. You've been shot. And I'm pretty sure those bullets were meant for me." She tried to pull away. "We need to stop the bleeding."

Mo's arms tightened around her. "It's just a graze. Please. Just . . . give me this." His voice was rough. "I need to hold you."

The desperation in his voice nearly broke her, and she answered with the full truth. "I'm not going anywhere, and . . ." Could she say it? Yes. She could. "I don't want you to let go."

He shuddered at her words and pulled her closer. She desperately wanted to sink into his embrace, but the horror of the past few minutes refused to give her any peace.

She wasn't sure how long they stood there, but she couldn't take it any longer. She was certain he'd been shot at least once. He might be running on adrenaline, but at some point, that would disappear and pain would kick in. "Mo, I need to check your injuries."

He didn't release her, but he loosened his hold enough for her to lean back and look into his eyes. His pupils were . . . were they dilated? What size were they supposed to be? Why hadn't she taken more first-aid courses? Or, well, any first-aid courses?

What were the signs of a concussion? What about blood loss?

Shock? She had no idea. She should know these things. But if he was walking around after being shot, it couldn't be too bad. Right?

But then she remembered the way it sounded when his head hit the ground.

What if he had internal bleeding? Brain swelling?

"Chief Ward is on the way. So is Dr. Shaw." The cashier, a lovely girl whose name Bronwyn couldn't recall, spoke from the office. "She's on the phone with me and wants to know if anyone was hit."

"Yes!" Bronwyn tried to keep the panic out of her voice, but it wasn't working. "Mo's been shot. Tell her to hurry."

"Bronwyn, I'm fine."

She ignored his words. "I think you should at least sit down." Should he lie flat? No. That would hurt his arm. Should she do something with a rolled towel? Put it under his knees? His head? Feet? That was it. Right? Elevate his feet?

She walked around him and stifled a gasp when she realized he was bleeding from more than one place. "There's blood on your shirt and your pants. Please sit down." She couldn't stop herself from pleading with him.

"It's just a scratch."

"It's a bullet wound. That's not a scratch!"

"Sometimes it is."

"Argh!" She threw up her hands in frustration and turned to the cashier. "I don't know what to do with him!"

"Dr. Shaw says she's two minutes out. Hang tight."

Bronwyn closed her eyes and inhaled. *The Lord is my Shepherd.*

Exhale. *I have everything I need.*

It was the first breath prayer she'd learned and now it was the only one she could remember. She didn't feel like she had everything she needed. She needed medical knowledge, which she didn't have. She needed safety, which she didn't have. She needed Mo to be okay and she needed him to hold her again. But now was not the time because he was bleeding.

Her mind skittered again.

So this was it. She could handle anything at work. Snooty actors, entitled billionaires, even corrupt politicians. But Mo bleeding? Nope. She couldn't do this.

Inhale. *The Lord is my Shepherd.*

Exhale. *I have everything I need.*

Two more breaths and her panic began to ease. It wasn't gone, but she could think more rationally.

She didn't have any skills that would help this situation, but she did know the Great Physician. So maybe she did have everything she needed?

Inhale. *Jesus, please don't let him have a brain injury.*

Exhale. *Jesus, please don't let him lose too much blood.*

She didn't try to change the prayer. She continued until Gray and Cal ran into the grocery store with Dr. Carol Shaw on their heels.

Gray was all business.

But Cal came to a stop beside her and reached a trembling hand toward Mo. "What happened?"

Bronwyn answered the question without hesitation. "He's been shot. And he hit his head hard. But he's been talking."

Dr. Shaw—or Aunt Carol, as Bronwyn had known her for most of her life—set a bag beside Mo. "Cal, out of the way. Bronwyn, darling, I need you to move back so I can figure out where this blood is coming from."

"His shoulder, I think." Bronwyn dropped her head. "I could have put pressure on it. That's what I should have done."

Aunt Carol ran her hands over her nephew's scalp. "Mo, do you have anything to add to the conversation?"

Was she . . . amused? Her tone made it seem like something was hilarious. But Bronwyn couldn't think of what that might be.

"Let's take this shirt off."

Mo tried to move his arm but winced and hissed. Aunt Carol held his wrist. "Stop that. Don't make it worse. I didn't mean for you to pull it over your head. This shirt is destined for the burn pile now. I hope you weren't particularly close to it."

Cal snorted.

Mo chuckled. "No, ma'am."

"Good." She took scissors from her bag and cut Mo's shirt off. Then she studied the wound on his arm. She didn't seem to be in any hurry. Why wasn't she more . . . frantic? Aunt Carol reached over and patted Bronwyn's hand where Mo still hung on to her. "It's hard to put pressure on a wound like this, darling. You did fine."

She looked down and saw the blood oozing from what looked like a five-inch gouge on Mo's arm. It wasn't spurting. That had to be good.

"That's going to need some stitches. But we'll fix you up so you won't have a bad scar." She winked at Mo, who grinned at her.

Grinned!

Bronwyn was very close to screaming at the top of her lungs. Why wasn't anyone taking this seriously? Aunt Carol looked at Cal. "Hand me that dressing from my bag." Cal did as requested, and she applied it to the wound with practiced precision. "Now, let's take a look at this leg."

She made small talk as she cut Mo's pants off at the knee. Bronwyn bit back a cry when she saw the hole in his calf. "Is there a bullet in him?"

"Probably." Aunt Carol was matter-of-fact, as if she saw her nephew riddled with bullet holes on a daily basis. She looked over her shoulder, then back to her son. "Cal, can you check to see where the ambulance is?"

"Ambulance?" Bronwyn's voice shook.

"Mmhmm." Aunt Carol had her flashlight in hand and was looking in Mo's eyes. "He needs to go to the hospital."

"You can't take care of him here?"

Aunt Carol reached out and took Bronwyn's hand. "Darling, he's going to be fine. And yes, I could take care of him here. But I want him to have a CT scan. He may have a concussion. And while I could stitch him up just fine, if he's going anyway, there's a plastic surgeon in Asheville who will do a much better job with his arm and leg. He can minimize the scarring better than I can."

"I don't care about a stupid scar. Who cares about a scar?" Bronwyn bit down on her bottom lip. "I'm sorry, Aunt Carol. It's just that . . . they won't let me stay with him if you take him to the hospital." The words were a whispered cry. She couldn't bear for him to be out of her sight. Not now.

Mo squeezed her hand.

"I don't expect them to keep him, Bronwyn."

She shook her head. "I can't . . ." She swiped at her eyes. What was wrong with her?

Mo leaned his head against her side.

Aunt Carol pulled her into a hug. An awkward hug because Mo refused to let go of her hand. "The hospital is the best choice. If it were just the bullet wounds, I'd take care of it here. But we want to check his head. It's hard. Goodness knows it is. Most stubborn child I've ever known, this one." Aunt Carol released her and smiled at Bronwyn. "Well, look who I'm talking to. Maybe he's the second-most stubborn. You take the prize."

The ambulance pulled into the parking lot and stopped by the door. The EMTs hopped out but didn't pull the gurney out. Mo was able to step inside and lie down without any fanfare.

He continued to hold Bronwyn's hand, and she followed him inside the vehicle.

Cal spoke to one of the paramedics, but Bronwyn couldn't hear what he was saying. She didn't care. She would stay with Mo as long as she could. Then she'd follow them to the hospital.

The paramedics were talking to Aunt Carol when Meredith's 4Runner came to a screeching halt in the parking lot.

"Mo!" Her panic mirrored Bronwyn's own. "Mo!" Meredith ran straight to the back of the ambulance.

"He's been shot and he might have a concussion. But he's walking and talking," Bronwyn told her, trying to stay calm for Meredith's sake. "Aunt Carol wants him checked out to be safe."

"Shot?" Meredith's skin paled and she clambered into the ambulance. "Montgomery Douglas Quinn. What on earth do you mean, going and getting shot? That's on the list."

Bronwyn didn't know what list Meredith was referring to, but Mo must have. He pulled his sister down to hug her. Meredith's eyes zeroed in on his other hand. The one still holding onto Bronwyn. And her eyes, which had been filled with fear, shifted to confusion and then a wary happiness. Cal leaned into the back of the ambulance. "Mo, man, I'm just going to say it since no one else has."

"What?"

"If I'd known getting shot was what it would take to get Bronwyn to start talking to you again, I'd have shot you myself."

"Cal!" Meredith and Bronwyn both yelled at him, but he was laughing so hard, he had to hold on to the side of the ambulance.

"Come on, Meredith. He's tough. He'll be okay."

"I'm going."

"Not alone, you're not." Gray appeared behind Meredith and pulled her into his arms.

"Gray!"

Gray leaned toward Meredith and whispered something in her ear. She relaxed into him and nodded.

Cal had gotten himself together enough to speak. “Come on, I got it cleared for Beep to ride in the ambulance. Although if you ever tell anyone, we’ll have to deny it. Let her go with him, Mer. Gray has to stay here, but you can ride with me. We’ll follow them to the hospital and then drive them home. How about that?”

Meredith conceded. She gave Mo another hug and sent Bronwyn a wide-eyed look that said, “Girl, you have some explaining to do.”

“Thank you, Cal.” Bronwyn didn’t know how he’d done it, but she wouldn’t complain.

He gave her a small salute, and he and Meredith hurried to his truck.

A paramedic climbed in on the other side of Mo. And then they were headed to the hospital.

Mo still hadn’t let go of her hand.

TWENTY-SIX

For the first few minutes of the trip to the hospital, Mo cooperated with everything the paramedic asked him to do. He'd known Kyle for years, and he didn't want to keep the guy from doing his job. But when there was a pause in the action, he finally asked, "Did I need to take the ambulance? Couldn't we have driven ourselves?"

Kyle smirked. "You could have. But if you drove to the ER, you'd be put in line with everyone else and you'd have to wait. Possibly a long time. When you arrive via ambulance, you get first-class treatment." He seemed to think better of what he'd said. "Not that you don't receive excellent care normally. But you go to the front of the line when you roll in with us. And Dr. Shaw will have already called ahead and talked to the docs. They know her. And better, they like her. My guess is they'll have you scanned, stitched, and on your way home before dawn."

"Assuming he doesn't have a concussion, right?" Bronwyn's voice was husky, and Mo wanted to close his eyes and soak in the sound. But if he closed his eyes, she would freak out. On another day that might be funny. But today was not that day.

"Eh." Kyle wrapped a blood pressure cuff around Mo's arm.

"Even if he does have a concussion, they'll probably send him home." He smiled at Bronwyn and there was something in that smile that Mo did not like at all. "Don't worry."

"I'll worry until he's fine, thank you very much."

Mo squeezed her hand. "I *am* fine."

She breathed in through her nose. "No. Nope. Not listening to that. You have bullet wounds and a possible head injury. Bullet wounds, Mo. That is the very definition of not fine."

"Okay." He squeezed her hand again. "I'm not fine at the moment, but I will be fine."

She blinked rapidly. Was she about to cry? He wished Kyle wasn't here. He wanted to talk to her and tell her he really was fine and that he'd missed her and . . .

He reined in those thoughts. Talk about an overreaction.

She was speaking to him again. She was worried about him. But that didn't mean anything more. Not to her. And it shouldn't mean more to him either.

They didn't really know each other anymore.

And he couldn't assume anything.

But she wasn't even trying to remove her hand from his. So for now, he'd take that.

They rode the entire way to the hospital with nothing more than a few comments from Kyle as he checked Mo's vitals.

When they arrived at the emergency room, he was pulled away from Bronwyn with no ceremony. Before they rolled him down the hall, he called out to her. "Bronwyn?"

"Yeah?"

"If I'd known, I'd have let Cal shoot me a long time ago."

She half laughed, half sobbed. "You're an idiot." They wheeled him away before she could say more. He hoped Cal and Meredith weren't far behind and would wait with her. The thought of her alone in the waiting area did something unpleasant to his insides.

Not that his insides were particularly happy. He felt a little queasy, and his head was pounding.

He hoped he didn't have a concussion. He'd had one before, and it made it hard to do his job.

And now, more than ever, he needed to be able to do his job.

As the doctor scanned his head, stitched up his wounds, and then left him to wait for the results of the tests, Mo considered the list of possible suspects and targets.

He couldn't come up with a solid reason for anyone to target him. Even if they were afraid he would find something in The Haven's accounts that would expose their crimes—and that was a valid concern—it wasn't as if he was the only forensic accountant in the world. He could think of at least five others who could do the job. Taking him out of the picture wouldn't prevent the discrepancies from being uncovered. But it would delay them, and maybe the delay would be reason enough.

Maybe.

It seemed far more likely to him that Bronwyn had been the target.

Take Bronwyn out of the picture, and Nathan would be CEO. And he would be far less likely to dig too deep. Nathan struck Mo as the kind of man who wouldn't rock the boat.

He might even be the one responsible for the discrepancies. If that were the case, he would carry on as before, with no one to stop him.

Mo shifted on the hospital bed. His head ached. His arm and leg throbbed. He wanted to go to sleep.

But he also wanted to get to the bottom of this whole mess.

An interminable hour later, the doctor came back into his room. "Well, Mr. Quinn, I'm going to discharge you. There's no sign of concussion, although I have no doubt your head will talk to you for the next little while."

He dispensed his medical wisdom, told Mo to follow up with his family doctor, and laughed when Mo pointed out that his family doctor would chase him down if he didn't.

When he walked out with his discharge papers in hand, he found Meredith and Bronwyn huddled together on the plastic seats of the waiting room. They jumped to their feet, but Meredith was the only one who came to him.

Bronwyn hung back and looked like she didn't know what to do with herself.

"Well?" Meredith asked after she gave him a gentle hug.

"All clear." He spoke loud enough for Bronwyn to hear. "No concussion. Minimal scarring expected."

"Thank goodness." Meredith led him toward Bronwyn, and when they reached her, she gave him an awkward smile, then bolted for the door.

Meredith sighed.

He pointed toward Bronwyn's retreating back. "What's that about?"

Meredith shrugged. "She's embarrassed."

"Why?"

"Oh, I don't know," Meredith said airily. "Maybe because she refused to speak to you for a few years, then when you got shot, she came unglued and, in her words, 'Made a fool out of herself.' And now she's not sure how to act around you."

Mo waited for Meredith to laugh. She didn't. "Wait. You're serious? You aren't guessing? She said those exact words?"

"She did."

They didn't speak again as they walked to Cal's truck. Cal waited in the patient pickup area. Bronwyn had already climbed into the back. His King Cab had plenty of room for all of them, but the back seat was a little tight.

Meredith squeezed his good arm. "You'll figure it out. I have no doubt. For now, I'll climb in the back with Bronwyn."

He should let her. It would be more comfortable to ride in the front. But . . . "That's okay. I'd rather have the back."

She didn't stop walking or even look at him, but he sensed her surprise and something else. Approval?

He opened the door and then climbed into the back. Cal quirked an eyebrow but didn't say anything. Meredith made sure he was settled, then climbed into the front seat beside Cal. "We're ready to roll."

Bless her for keeping things as normal as possible.

He shifted in his seat, and despite his best efforts, a grunt of pain escaped through his teeth.

Bronwyn's hand shot toward him, then froze in midair. She pulled it back, but he caught it. He leaned back in the seat, closed his eyes, and laced his fingers through hers. "Thanks. That helps."

Again, she didn't pull away.

He'd count it as a win.

Bronwyn could barely keep her eyes open. She didn't think she'd been this tired in a decade. All things considered, they'd gotten in and out of the hospital in record time. But it would be 3:00 a.m. before she could crawl into bed, and she wasn't sure she'd be functional tomorrow. Today. Whenever.

She shifted in her seat. How was it possible to be this exhausted and this edgy at the same time? Mo wouldn't let go of her hand, and she wasn't about to tell him to.

He wasn't drugged. He wasn't concussed. But was he truly lucid? What would happen tomorrow? Or the next day?

His thumb made slow sweeping motions across her hand. Then

he leaned toward her and whispered, "I'm going to beat you at Chinese checkers."

It was the last thing she'd expected him to say. And somehow, it was perfect. "In your dreams."

They continued to sit in silence, lulled by the sway of the truck as it wound its way up the mountain.

A random thought popped into her brain. "I hope Lionel put the ice cream back in the freezer."

Mo's body shook with silent laughter.

"I'm serious," she said.

"I know you are. That's what makes it so funny." He yawned. "Is Katrina okay?"

"She is. She made it home. With her ice cream, I might add."

"How do you know that?" Meredith asked, turning toward the back seat.

"Because she texted that it was the best thing she'd ever eaten and that it was exactly what she'd needed to help her decompress. Gray let her go after he questioned her, but he said she may need to come in tomorrow. Or today? Or is it tomorrow?" It was her turn to yawn. "I guess Gray needs to talk to us too."

"No one is doing any talking until you sleep." Cal was in Papa Bear mode. "Dad got all the cars back to our place. I'm going to drive you straight home. Mo, you can sleep in your own bed. Bronwyn, you can either stay with Meredith or you can stay in our guest room, or you can have the tiny house."

Cal's tiny house was empty now that Cassie was married and she and Donovan had moved into their own place, but Cal kept it guest ready.

"I think someone should stay with Mo," Bronwyn said.

At her words, Mo, eyebrows raised, turned his body toward Bronwyn. "The doctor cleared me."

"The doctor wasn't there when you were shot. He's allowed to be objective." She didn't say that her objectivity had disappeared and she couldn't find it. That would be too revealing. Of what, she wasn't sure. But she wasn't mentally competent at the moment.

"I have to be in the office at seven." Meredith yawned.

Bronwyn yawned in response.

"I'm driving Landry to work and then I'm meeting some new clients on their property at eight." Cal tapped the steering wheel with his thumbs. "Congratulations, Bronwyn, you're on Mo babysitting duty."

Bronwyn wasn't sure if she should thank him or strangle him. Maybe both.

Mo leaned toward her again. "I don't need a babysitter. But I don't want you going anywhere alone."

There was an intensity in his words that did something to her on the inside.

"Bronwyn? You good with that?" Cal asked.

"Of course. I was already planning to work from home today. No one's expecting me in the office."

"Great. The problem is that you can't stay at Mo's. He has a twin bed in his bedroom with a sofa so small, even Eliza couldn't sleep on it. Oh, and a single chair in his living room. It's like he doesn't want company."

Meredith chimed in. "I have a solution. You two go to my place. I'm the only one who had the good sense to put two beds in my house. Yes, you can all tell me I was right. Go ahead."

No one spoke.

"I get no credit." Meredith put on a lofty air. "But we all know it's true. Anyway, I'll sleep at Mo's. Bronwyn can have my bed. Mo can take the guest bed. I'll come back over in the morning and get ready."

"Can't you take your stuff and get ready at my place?" Mo asked, his eyes still closed.

"I could. But I'm not going to. I'll grab my clothes, but I won't need anything else from upstairs. You'll sleep right through it."

Both Cal and Mo laughed.

"What's so funny?" Bronwyn asked.

Meredith answered. "These two chuckleheads claim that they can hear me getting ready from their places."

Bronwyn considered it. "The houses are very close together. I can see how that's a possibility."

Mo groaned. "You don't understand. She is the loudest person in the universe. She grinds coffee beans. She makes smoothies. She blends things. I don't know what she's doing over there. I swear she's making fresh almond butter or something. Whatever it is, it's loud. If we're trying to sleep right above her, I guarantee she'll wake us up."

Meredith's affronted huff made Cal and Mo laugh more. "It's true," Cal added. "Sometimes I think I can still hear you from my house."

"You cannot."

"Mo and Bronwyn, make a note. When you build a house, be sure you go heavy on the soundproofing."

Mo's thumb didn't pause at Cal's words. But his hand did squeeze hers a fraction. "You'll be building the house, so why don't you make the note?"

"Consider it done."

What . . . what had just happened?

"I'm just teasing you, Meredith." Mo's words were a little slurred. "You can come wake me up. I have work to do."

"Sure you do, big guy." Cal sounded exasperated. "It's like trying to convince Eliza to go to bed when she's so tired she can barely walk."

"What's that supposed to mean?" Mo's words really did sound wrong. Was this a problem? Could he be having some issues from hitting his head?

"It means you need sleep. Stop being so argumentative. Hush. We'll be home in twenty. I don't want to hear another word out of you."

Mo leaned toward Bronwyn. "He's really embraced the whole dad thing, don't you think?"

Bronwyn tried not to laugh but couldn't stifle her giggles. "I don't think he had far to go, but yes."

"I can hear you, you know." Cal's mock stern tone set her off again and Bronwyn's laughter broke free. If it had a bit of a hysterical edge, that was okay, right?

"I'm not taking either of you seriously until you get sleep." Cal caught Bronwyn's eye in the rearview mirror and winked. "We'll discuss your behavior tonight. Eliza was too worried about both of you to be upset about missing the firepit, but Landry promised her we'd do it tonight to make up for it."

"What does Eliza know?" Mo asked, his voice a low hum.

"Not that you were shot. We told her that there was a situation at the grocery store, that you were hurt, and that we had to go to the hospital with you. But she knows you're fine now."

"Do you think she believed that?" Bronwyn didn't know how much Eliza remembered about her life before Gossamer Falls, but her memories of her more recent abduction were fresh. She was doing well, but everyone knew that traumatic experiences could hit her extra hard.

"She believed me when I told her you were fine, but she doesn't believe that she's been told the whole story."

"You need to tell her." Mo's voice was hard. Not without compassion, but firm. "I bet it's all over town by now. If you don't tell her, someone else will, and then you'll be the bad guy for not being honest with her."

Cal sighed. "I know. But I didn't want Landry to deal with it alone. I'll talk to her before I leave for work."

Meredith leaned her head against the glass and blew out a huge sigh. "I want our town to be back to normal. Where no one gets shot at in the grocery store parking lot or snatched by stalkers or chased down by drug dealers."

Bronwyn didn't respond, but all she could think was, *Same, girl. Same.*

TWENTY-SEVEN

Mo had to turn Bronwyn loose when Cal parked in his driveway. He hated to let her go, but really, he had no right to keep hanging on to her.

They had been friends.

More than friends.

Then enemies.

Then nothing.

Then something weird that no one could figure out.

And now they were . . . something different. Friends? Maybe. People who'd been through a traumatic experience and who were experiencing heightened emotions? Definitely.

Was this one of those times when eight hours of sleep would return them to the status quo?

He hoped not.

But what would their new normal be?

Not that they'd ever been normal.

He stumbled into his house to brush his teeth and change into pajamas. Thanks to Aunt Carol, he'd had to leave the hospital in borrowed scrubs. He took the time to clean as much of his skin as he could with a washcloth. He didn't want to get any blood in Meredith's guest bed. But mostly he didn't want Bronwyn to see it. She got a funny look on her face when she focused on his injured arm, and he didn't want her dwelling on the thoughts behind that look.

By the time he made it the thirty feet from his tiny house to Meredith's, Bronwyn was upstairs and in Meredith's bed.

Meredith waited for him in the kitchen. She had her work clothes draped over the sofa. "I promise to be quiet when I get ready. I'll drink coffee when I get to work."

He grinned at her. "I was messing with you."

She tried to smile, but her face went through some bizarre contortions before tears filled her eyes and she threw herself into his arms.

"Shh, shh. It's okay. I'm okay." He muttered the words over and over until her quiet sobs eased and she relaxed in his arms.

"You . . . almost—"

"I'm okay." He leaned down and whispered in her ear, "And if Bronwyn keeps talking to me, it was worth it."

She pulled back a little. "Look at you, finding the silver lining. Bronwyn's already been good for you and it's only been a few hours."

He didn't disagree, but he didn't have the mental capacity to do anything more than shrug. "Are we surprised by that?"

Meredith gave him a watery smile. "Not even a little. Now, go to sleep. And don't be mad at me when I come up and check on you before I go to work."

He gave her another quick hug. "Go. Sleep. Let tomorrow take care of itself."

She chuckled at one of Granny Quinn's famous sayings. The fact that it came straight out of Scripture made it hard to argue with. Not that he hadn't tried a few times.

"Back at ya." She left her house and jogged over to his. Mo waited until she was safely inside before he turned out the lights and headed up to bed.

They'd built Meredith's home with a double staircase. One side went to the small loft where she'd made a guest room. The other went to her bedroom, which was a cozy nook that suited her personality. The stairs met on a small, raised landing a few feet from the main floor. Mo had one foot on the landing when he heard Bronwyn's voice.

"Mo?" she whispered the word into the near darkness.

He turned on his cell phone light and found her. Bronwyn sat at the top of the stairs to Meredith's bedroom, leaning against the wall. Her hair was a mess. No makeup. Eyes down.

Mo considered joining her, but instead, he climbed the stairs on his side and took a position mirroring hers. Then he turned off the light on his phone.

"Hi there. What are you doing, sitting in the dark?"

"I should have spoken to you sooner."

"Bronwyn—"

"No. I need to say this now. I won't keep you. You need to sleep. So do I. But if I don't say it now—" Her voice broke and Mo realized she'd been crying.

Bronwyn took a deep breath. "I never apologized. Not really."

"You tried."

"I made a mess out of that one, didn't I? You were right. I was still working through a lot of stuff, and I'd deluded myself into thinking you would welcome me back with open arms. It was selfish and small of me."

"We were young, Bronwyn."

She made a scoffing sound. "Young enough to be stupid, old enough to regret it."

"We've both made mistakes. If I could go back to that day,

I'd stand there and listen. I'd take you out for dinner and coffee and I'd let you tell me everything. And I would have told you everything. How it felt when I came home and you were"—Mo cleared his throat and fought against the sudden moisture in his eyes—"gone. How furious I was with your family for not making you come back. And how I wanted you to be okay. I wanted you to be happy. And if that was far away from here, then that would be okay. But not with *him*."

"Yes. Him." Bronwyn's voice quavered. "We can't have this conversation now, but I wanted you to know that I'm sorry. I'm sorry for leaving without saying goodbye. I'm sorry for hurting you. I'm sorry for treating you like someone who would always come to my beck and call."

Mo didn't know what to say. What could he say?

Bronwyn continued, "But I'm not sorry for going no contact after that last episode. I was not okay, and I couldn't be around you for a while. I needed the distance."

"Can I say that I'm so sorry for that?" Mo shook his head. "I have no excuse. But again, I wish I'd listened to you. I wish I'd asked you why you were at the hospital and what was going on in your life. I didn't. And I deserved your wrath."

"Well, you sure got it. And for a little while, maybe you deserved it. But not for the past year or so. I should have shown up here one day and said, 'Mo, we need to talk.' But I didn't. I was . . . embarrassed? Afraid? Stubborn?"

"Waiting for me to do something else to prove that you'd made the right choice the first time?" Mo suggested.

He couldn't see her face in the darkness, but he heard what might have been a shrug. "Maybe. But mostly it was stubborn pride. You hurt me and you were sorry. But I wanted to punish you for it, anyway. And that was where I went too far."

"I think it's safe to say we both screwed up. Big time and on repeat."

They sat in silence for so long, Mo wondered if she'd fallen asleep on the stairs.

"Mo?"

"Yeah?"

"What happens when we wake up?"

That was the million-dollar question. "What do you want to happen?"

"I don't know." He didn't think she was lying. But maybe she wasn't being entirely truthful either. "I don't want to go back to the way it was."

"Agreed." With his whole heart.

"But I'm not sure how to move on from here."

He didn't respond immediately. "I think we have to take it as it comes, Bronwyn. We have so much history and so much still in common that finding our way might not be as hard as we think."

"Or it could blow up in our faces." She sounded so sad. "We don't have a great track record."

"You mean I don't have a great track record." He would own his part in the debacle they'd turned into.

"No—"

"I'm not blaming. It's true. How about this? Let's say we don't know where we're going, but let's agree that we're going somewhere good. We aren't going backward. We aren't devolving into mistrust and anger. We're moving forward. Taking the next step. We don't have to be able to see the whole path to know that's the right move, do we?"

"I think," she said the words slowly, like she was being very careful to get them right, "that sounds like a good idea."

"Good." Mo sounded relieved. Had he really thought she would reject his proposal? Taking it a step at a time was as much as she could have possibly hoped for.

"Go get in bed, Bronwyn. You're tired. I think we'll both feel better tomorrow."

She stood and took one step up the stairs, but then, "Mo?"

"Yeah?"

She wanted to tell him she'd missed him and that she was so thankful they were talking. But what she said was, "Don't think I'll be throwing the game. I play to win."

His low chuckle warmed her to her toes. "As long as you understand that the same holds true for me."

With that, she slid into Meredith's bed. Her first thought was that she needed to find out where Meredith had gotten the sheets because they were divine. Her last conscious thought was that she should be afraid—someone had tried to kill her today, after all. But she wasn't.

She was . . . almost . . . maybe . . . happy.

She woke to silence. No. Not silence. There was a sound. What was it? It took her still sleepy brain a moment to make the connection.

A computer. Someone was typing on a computer. Another sound. Someone—no, not someone. Mo. Mo was typing on a computer while she slept the day away!

She bolted out of the bed and down the stairs, thankful that the comfy pajamas she'd thrown into her bag before she left home yesterday could pass for leisurewear.

Mo sat on the sofa in Meredith's living room. His laptop was on his lap. One leg was elevated on an ottoman. He looked up as she descended the stairs, and his smile froze her on the spot.

"What happened to your face?" She blurted out the question before she could think it through.

His smile turned into a laugh. "Good morning to you, Nurse Bronwyn. You might want to work on your bedside manner. A guy could get a complex from a question like that."

She ignored him and walked closer. "Seriously, Mo." She reached out to touch his face before she got ahold of herself and jerked her hand back. "Those weren't there yesterday." His cheek and jaw sported a purple-and-black bruise under his scruff. And he had the makings of a doozy of a shiner around his right eye.

"They were there. They hadn't developed yet. Bruises don't appear instantaneously."

"When did y—?"

"I don't remember the specifics. I think I ducked at one point when we were on the ground and hit my face on the pavement." He shrugged it off. "Aunt Carol has already texted." He looked at his watch. "We'll see her in about an hour. I'll have her take a look."

"You won't be able to stop her." Bronwyn forced herself to step back. "They'll get worse before they get better." She went into the kitchen in search of coffee. "Please tell me you used Meredith's coffee and not your own."

She'd heard horror stories about Mo's coffee.

He put a hand to his chest, clutching imaginary pearls. "I'm hurt. But yes, I used Meredith's coffee. And her eighteen million creamer options are in the fridge. I checked. There's a mocha and a peppermint mocha." He went back to tapping on the computer. "I don't understand why she has so many creamers. She enjoys coffee, but how does she keep them from going bad?"

"She takes them to work." Bronwyn selected the peppermint mocha. "They never go to waste that way."

"Huh." Mo's typing continued.

"How's your head?" she asked into what was right on the edge of becoming an awkward silence.

"Hurts like a son of a gun." Mo yawned and looked up at her. "But I'm not seeing double, I'm not dizzy, I'm not nauseated, and I remember everything that happened yesterday."

"Oh, well, that's good, then." It was good. She was relieved. And relieved that what they'd said to each other hadn't been a wasted conversation because she wasn't sure she had the emotional fortitude to put herself out there again anytime soon. "But I'm sorry your head hurts. Did you take anything?"

"I did, but I took it on an empty stomach. That was a mistake. I need real food."

"Does Meredith have anything in her fridge?"

"Next to nothing. She eats with Gray a lot now. But it doesn't matter." Mo shoved the laptop to the side and levered himself up to standing with only a small groan. "Because we've been invited to brunch."

Bronwyn blinked a few times, then looked at the microwave clock. It read 9:05. She looked at it again. "Did I really sleep until nine?"

"You did."

She'd been asking herself, not Mo. She never slept this late. Ever. It was rare for her to still be in bed at seven. Yesterday had been truly awful, but with everything that had happened, sleeping in a different bed, Mo . . . she couldn't believe it was this late already.

"I'm a horrible nurse."

"No you aren't."

"You just told me my bedside manner needs work. And I didn't check on you even once during the night. I just . . . slept."

"Bronwyn, so did I. I didn't move until fifteen minutes before you did. Don't worry about it. We needed the sleep."

She took a sip of her coffee. "Where are we going for brunch?"

"Granny Quinn wants to see us."

She set the coffee down.

"Why?"

"Apparently, she, Papa, and the entire family were getting blow-by-blow reports from Cal and Meredith last night." Mo rolled his head in one direction, then the other. "She informed me that if I was going to get shot in town, the least I could do was come see her so she could confirm with her own eyes that her prayers were working."

That sounded like Granny Quinn.

She caught the furtive look Mo shot her way and braced herself for what was coming. "They may have mentioned that we're talking now."

"May have?" she asked.

"One hundred percent did. She told me she wants to see and hear it with her own eyes and ears before she dies."

"Is she dying now?" Had she missed something?

"Not to my knowledge, nor anyone else's. She was just being dramatic."

"I'll say."

"You don't have to go, but I do. And since I don't want you to be alone, you . . . okay, so yeah, you do have to go. Sorry about that."

"Don't be. I love Papa and Granny Quinn. If I had been lucky enough to be a grandmother, I would have wanted to be like yours." Oh sweet mercy, had she said that out loud? What was wrong with her? Maybe Mo wouldn't catch the implications. No. He was frowning. She was doomed.

"Given up on being a grandmother, have you?" The question was far too casual for her to believe he was as disinterested as he sounded.

She took several sips of coffee to give herself time to answer.

His response was to raise his eyebrows and hold eye contact until she broke.

"I wouldn't say I've given up on it, but I have to become a mother before I get to be the cool granny. And I'm not getting any younger. I have to find a man, date him, fall in love with him, and have him fall in love with me, get engaged, get married, and then get pregnant. And realistically, I need to do all those things in the next five years. So, again, I wouldn't say it's impossible, but the odds aren't in my favor."

Mo muttered something under his breath. It sounded almost like "screw the odds," but she wasn't sure. Out loud, he said, "Been on any dates recently?"

Again, his delivery was so close to casual that she almost believed he didn't care about her answer. Maybe if she'd met him in college and they'd gone their separate ways, it would be different. But they'd grown up together. She knew his tells. Why did he care so much about her answer? Because, she knew, he did care.

It didn't matter. The answer was simple. "Nope."

"You've been asked out though. That guy asked you out yesterday. Or was it the day before? Whenever. The one on the walking path. Bob."

"I'm asked out a lot by people who know nothing about me and are interested in me for what they perceive are my connections, which is laughable because I don't have the connections they think I do. Or they're interested in my looks, which is flattering but shallow. It's not that I don't care about my appearance or put effort into it." She paused and ran a hand through her hair, belatedly realizing she was giving off scarecrow vibes at the moment. "Well, normally I do."

Mo nodded. "Of course. But, please, continue."

"But appearance is fleeting and mostly out of our control. We can have proper hygiene, stylish haircuts, trendy clothing, and make the most of what the good Lord gave us, but that isn't much of a reflection of who we are. In my case, I have an image to maintain, and I guess you could argue my efforts in maintaining my image is indicative of who I am as a person, but it's still only a tiny fragment of who I am."

Mo nodded in apparent agreement.

"So when someone who doesn't know anything about me expresses their burning need to get to know me, I generally assume that it's based only on outward things. And it's okay if that's the starting point, I guess. But I don't have the time or energy for casual flings with people who are more interested in the exterior. Not that my interior isn't banged up. But that's what makes me who I am. That's the part that's truly interesting. That's the part that I want someone to see and know."

She hadn't meant to say all of that.

Mo pinched his lips together before smiling at her with the radiance of an entire galaxy. He let out a deep, contented sigh. "I have missed you, Bronwyn. Truly missed talking to you."

"I would think after that monologue you'd be regretting it."

"Not a chance." He winked at her. "Come on, then. Let's get ready. Aunt Carol says you have to drive."

Bronwyn frowned at that. "Why? I mean, that's fine, but I thought you were given the all clear."

"I was. She's being overprotective."

"Ah. Makes sense. That's where Cal gets it."

"Right?"

"I'm surprised he hasn't been over."

"Oh, he has been. Meredith chased him off earlier. I had four text messages when I woke up. Check your phone. You probably do too."

Bronwyn went to Meredith's room to grab her bag and her phone.

And when she checked the latter, she wished she hadn't.

TWENTY-EIGHT

Mo was having about as much fun as possible for a man with a headache threatening to take him to his knees.

Talking to Bronwyn almost made him forget that he hurt from head to toe.

He'd expected her to look at her phone and roll her eyes in amusement at the texts he knew Cal had sent her.

He had not expected her mouth to tighten as she sank into the chair across from his spot on the sofa.

"Bronwyn?"

No response.

"What is it?" he asked.

She continued to scroll. "I . . ."

He counted to thirty before he tried again. "Bronwyn?"

She looked at him. "I didn't text my family yesterday and they are . . . displeased."

She handed him the phone, and he scrolled through a series of texts.

Mom **6:15 AM**
Bronwyn Elena Elizabeth Pierce! Call me right now.

Dad 6:22 AM
Call your mother.

Grandmother 6:30 AM
Your parents say you were shot at last night. Do me the courtesy of letting me know you're alive, won't you?

Dad 6:46 AM
This is childish. Where are you? The police chief assures me that you were alive and well when you left the scene. He claims to have no knowledge of your current whereabouts. He's lying, and I'll have him fired.

Mom 7:02 AM
How could you do this to your own parents? Just up and disappear? And June says you aren't coming in today. Have you abandoned all your responsibilities?

Marcus 7:13 AM
Ms. Pierce, your family is quite anxious about your whereabouts. I have declined to break into your house. They are threatening to fire me. I pointed out that your home is a private residence and it is illegal for me to enter it. They called the police chief. He backed me up and reiterated that you were fine twelve hours ago and as such, he has no cause to enter your home, nor do I.

Nathan 7:29 AM
I admire the way you've done a runner, but the least you could have done was leave your office intact. What on earth is going on?

That was a joke, by the way. Seriously. What is going on? Your parents are acting like you've disappeared. I get why. You have a track record. But there's no way you left without telling Grandmother. They're driving me crazy. Do something.

Dad 7:44 AM
When you come up for air, wherever you are, we're putting GPS trackers on your devices.

At that last text, Mo looked at Bronwyn. "Meredith can track you. So can Landry." He knew Bronwyn had given them access to her whereabouts as a general safety precaution.

"Yes, but apparently, my parents didn't want to talk to my best friends. Or maybe they didn't think about it. Or maybe they really do think so little of me as to assume that, at thirty-three, I still might disappear without a trace."

He'd picked up on the "you have a track record" remark. These people were . . . was there a word? Narcissists? Maybe. Unfeeling. Not one mention of worry. Not one concern for her well-being. It was all about them.

He scanned the remaining texts, finding them to be all the same until the last one, sent a half hour earlier.

Meredith 8:41
Your parents are not my favorite people. They came barging into my office and demanded to know where you are. I asked them to leave. I told them you had a late night, were probably still asleep, and would call when you woke up. They went on and on. No matter what they tell you, I promise, I did not call Gray.

But that doesn't mean that no one called him. Because Gray showed up and escorted them out of my office and gave them a strictly worded reprimand that involved words like "trespassing" and "invasion" and one "will not hesitate to put you in jail" . . . so, I'm pretty sure they won't be sending a wedding gift.

He couldn't stop the chuckle at that last comment and returned the phone to Bronwyn. "Remind me to buy my future brother-in-law a steak."

"I think I owe Cal, Landry, Gray, Meredith, and the entire Haven security team a meal at Hideaway. Do you think Cassie could be hired for a group apology dinner?"

He pointed to her phone. "Might as well call them quick and get it over with. Granny won't be happy with us if her biscuits are cold when we get there."

"Mo, I can't . . ." She looked at the phone, then looked at him. And grinned. "Yes. Yes, I can. One moment."

She dialed a number and put it on speaker. Mo wouldn't have asked, but he was delighted that she'd done it.

A gruff voice answered with an expletive followed by, "Where are you?"

She stared at it for a moment. "Dad, if you ever answer a phone call from me like that again, it will be the last time you receive a phone call from me."

"Bronw—"

"Not that you asked, but I'm fine. I had a very long day. In fact, I've had several long days in a row, and I was asleep when you reached out. You, Mother, Grandmother, and everyone else with the last name of Pierce needs to cool it. I am working off-site today. The Haven will manage fine, and if it doesn't, I'll fire the people who failed and replace them. Consider it a trial by fire. Please pass this information along to Mom. I'll call Grandmother." She took a deep breath. "And by the way, if anyone, Pierce or employee of The Haven, steps foot in my house while I'm away, I will press charges. Is that clear?"

There was a response all right. Lots of heavy breathing and spluttering, and eventually a few words. "What has gotten into you?"

Bronwyn paced as much as she could in the small space. "I'll tell you what's gotten into me, Dad. Someone shot at me yesterday. Real bullets. It's an absolute miracle that I'm still alive. And not a single person who blew up my phone this morning cares about anything other than *their* reputation and whether *they* might have to get off *their* rear and pull *their* own weight. I learned a lot in the past twelve hours. I learned even more in the last five minutes as I've read these messages."

"We are your parents!" Mr. Pierce roared into the phone. "We deserv—"

"You deserve nothing. Not one thing. You lost that privilege when you didn't drag my sixteen-year-old self back from California. You let me stay out there. You let me rot. You claimed it was because I was old enough and I knew my own mind when, in reality, you didn't want to offend the pervert who groomed me, lured me, took me, and then deserted me."

Bronwyn shook with rage.

Mo shook with an emotion he couldn't quite put his finger on, but it wasn't rage. It was more.

"You care about your reputation, and you need The Haven to be successful to keep it. So when I came home and it turned out I actually knew how to run a resort, you were more than happy to let me have at it. Less work for you. More certainty that everything would be done correctly."

"Now—"

"But never, not once, did it occur to you that you should let me come home because of the example of the prodigal's father. You know who filled that role in my life? Douglas and Jacqueline Quinn."

Mo's non-rage turned to confusion. *Wait. What?*

"They loved me. They welcomed me. They didn't hold my past against me. They acknowledged the pain I'd caused their son, their daughter, and their entire family, but they rejoiced that I was home. They never made me feel like anything other than a beloved daughter and a precious member of their family."

Mo's world shifted on its axis.

"They aren't your family!" Mr. Pierce's shrill voice screeched through the line.

"They're the only family I have." Bronwyn's tone held a finality that shocked him. "Take it to the board. Fire me. I don't care. I won't be in the office today. If you want to see me, you can make an appointment with my assistant."

Bronwyn hit the end button with so much force, Mo half expected the screen to shatter.

She dropped the phone and fell to her knees sobbing.

Bronwyn couldn't stop crying. Her entire body shook as decades of hurt spilled out of her.

Mo knelt beside her and brushed her hair back from her face until it wasn't in her eyes and no longer hid her agony.

"Shh." He soothed and whispered and rubbed her back, and all she knew for several minutes was that her world was shattered but that Mo was there.

"Come here." Mo stood, pulled her to her feet, and then immediately tucked her into his side before resettling on Meredith's sofa.

She cried.

"Get it all out."

At some point, she tried to process what had happened, but then the reality that she'd done something that needed to be done but she'd done it in the worst possible way flooded through her, and she shook with horror and grief for another indeterminate time.

Mo's arms were warm. His chest was solid. His low, rumbling words, which she was pretty sure were vocalizations, not even words, filtered through the pain and slowly settled her mind and heart.

"I think I've made a terrible mistake." The words came from her, but the voice was all wrong. Scraped and raw and hoarse, she sounded like she had a three-pack-a-day habit.

"I don't think so." He shook his head. "Your parents are horrible people, Bronwyn. I wish they weren't, but they are. I know there's a branch of the Pierces that are good, but I have to wonder if that's because they got out of town and away from the others."

"Probably." Bronwyn sniffled.

"The people you've grown up with and around aren't good, but they aren't stupid either. Even Nathan texted you this morning. He claims to want your job, but he doesn't. Not really. They need you. And people who need you will put up with an awful lot they don't like."

"I screamed at them. I told them they weren't my family."

"Yeah. They didn't like that, but was that really new information to them?" Mo asked the question gently.

Bronwyn shrugged and when she did, the motion must have hit Mo's arm because he released a little gasp of pain. "I'm hurting you!" She tried to sit up, but his arm wouldn't budge. "Mo."

"I'll make a deal with you." His lips were near her ear. "I will let you get up on one condition."

"What's the condition?" She had to move. His arm had to be throbbing by now.

"That you immediately resume this position on my other side. I'm not ready to let you go, but you won't relax until you're convinced I'm not in pain. Plus, my shirt is soaked on this side, so your face is in that wetness, and I don't want that for you either."

Now that he'd mentioned it, she realized that his shirt was drenched. And it didn't feel good on her skin. Not at all. "You drive a hard bargain."

"Don't you forget it." His arms loosened and he gave her a little boost to help her to her feet, but he kept hold of one hand and as soon as she crossed to the other side, he pulled her back down and scooched them around until she was tucked against him again.

Once she was there, she lay silent, breathing slowly until even the random aftershock shudders ended.

"I need to say something to you." Mo squeezed her hand. "I didn't know, but that's not an excuse."

What was he talking about?

"That day when I made such a jerk out of myself when you were visiting with Mom and Dad at the hospital, I didn't know how important they were to you. I didn't know they'd spent so much time with you and that your relationship was solid. I didn't realize what I was asking them to do to you, or how important it was. To you or to them."

"I know."

"Dad ripped me a new one after you left. It was the only time in my life when I thought he might want to hit me. I've never seen him that angry. He had to leave the room. And Mom"—Mo shuddered beside her—"let's say that I understand how my parents treated you because they've often had to treat me the same way. Meredith gets herself in trouble by being too good. I get myself in trouble by being a jerk. She's much easier to love than I am."

"But they do love you." Bronwyn knew that to her core.

"Oh, they do. Dad came to me later and apologized for his anger. Not for what he said, mind you. But for the way he reacted. He also told me in no uncertain terms that they would back you—

whatever you decided—unless you decided to stay away from them, in which case they would fight for you."

Bronwyn sat up and looked at him. "Are you serious?"

"As a heart attack." Mo looked like the act of telling the story was aging him. "Mom cried a lot. Meredith was mad at me for making them mad at me and for hurting you. It was bad. I deserved it. But still. It was bad."

"I bet you had dinner with them within a few days."

"Next day," Mo confirmed with a grunt. "It was awkward. I apologized to everyone over dessert. They forgave me. And they meant it. But I have to tell you, I'm not sure the breach will ever be truly healed until they see that you and I are speaking to each other again. They've been waiting for us to find some resolution. When they get home from their trip, they're going to yell at all of us. Especially Aunt Carol. But when they're done yelling, they'll be thrilled."

"Why will they yell at Aunt Carol?"

"She agreed with Meredith and didn't call them yesterday. They're flying home as we speak. We'll tell them everything after they get home."

"Bad idea. Bad, bad idea. Your mom is going to . . ." Bronwyn didn't want to think about it.

"To be fair, the original plan was to make sure I didn't have a concussion before calling, but then we realized they were on a plane. Their first flight was delayed due to weather, and the trickle effect has them hopping all over the place to get back home. There's nothing they can do, so there's no need to worry them."

"Call them." Bronwyn sat up and reached for the phone on the coffee table. "Call them right now. Leave them a message if they're in the air."

"Bron—"

"Mo, please. Lead with the fact that you're okay, but don't keep this from them."

"They can't do anything about it. They couldn't have gotten home any earlier."

"It doesn't matter. Please, Mo. Please." She couldn't explain why it was so important. Her own family was in shambles. Not that it had ever been whole. But his? She hadn't been joking when she said they were the only family she had. She wouldn't be party to any breach of trust with Doug and Jacque. She couldn't.

Mo took the phone and said, "Hey, Siri. Call Dad."

The phone rang four times before Doug Quinn's voice came through the line. "Mo! You just caught us. We're boarding in ten minutes. Can't wait to see everyone."

"Hi, Dad. And Mom, if you're sitting there."

"Mo. Oh baby, it's so good to hear your voice. We've missed you." Jacque's soft Southern voice turned each one-syllable word into at least two, and an argument could be made for three.

"Mom, Dad, listen. I need to tell you something." The silence on the line was ominous.

Bronwyn pinched him, and he yelped. "Ow!"

"Don't leave them hanging. What is wrong with you? I had no idea you'd be so terrible at this." She directed her voice to his phone. "He's fine. He meant to lead with that."

"Why is he fine?" Doug asked.

"Bronwyn?" Jacque asked.

"Bronwyn?" Doug repeated.

"Yes, that's not why he's calling." Bronwyn pinched him again. "Talk to your parents."

"I will if you'll stop pinching me."

"Why are you—?"

"What's going on?"

Doug and Jacque were firing questions at them so fast, she couldn't tell who was talking or what they were asking.

"Mom, Dad, I love you, and I need to tell you something before your flight takes off."

"Okay. We're listening."

"Last night, when we were headed back to my house. Long story. Bronwyn's got a creep at The Haven, and we agreed she should not be on the premises. Anyway, we stopped at the grocery store for ice cream. And while I was waiting, there was a drive-by shooting, and I was shot." A long pause.

Bronwyn didn't pinch him this time, but she did nudge him.

"Twice. Technically."

"Son, there's really no other way to get shot. You get shot or you don't. How did you *technically* get shot?" Doug Quinn was clearly holding on by the narrowest of margins.

"He took the bullets for me." Bronwyn cleared her throat. She would not start crying again. "One hit his arm and made a little ditch in it. The other went through his calf. And he hit his head pretty hard, and his face is bruised up pretty bad. But Aunt Carol sent us to Asheville, and her plastic surgeon friend did all the stitches and says there will be very little scarring. And they did a CT scan, and he doesn't have a concussion."

"So *now* we're heavy on the no scarring?" Mo asked her in a whisper.

She whispered back. "I had to say something. I was afraid they might pass out in the airport if I didn't give them some good news."

"It's okay, sweetheart. He's okay." Doug's voice came through the phone, but it was clear he was comforting Jacque. "And it sounds like some good came out of it." A pause. "Oh." Then his voice was louder. "Your mother says she's not crying because you got shot. She's crying because Bronwyn is with you and you're talking to each other."

TWENTY-NINE

Mo's phone beeped with an incoming text. He stared at it in shock.

Bronwyn, eyes puffy and bloodshot, blinked a few times. Then his mom's voice came through the phone. "I did not say that. I mean, I did. Look, I'm tired, and this has made me very emotional, because it's not every day your son calls to say he's been shot."

"Thank goodness for that," his dad said in the background.

"But I've been praying for so long for the two of you to have some kind of reconciliation, and listening to you over the phone . . ."

"She's crying again." Dad blew out a breath and was back to business. "I assume Gray is all over this."

"As far as I know. It was a long night. We got up a few minutes ago and there's been some drama with Bron—" He stopped himself. He'd almost said Bronwyn's family, but they didn't deserve that title right now. "With the Pierces, so we haven't talked to him yet. We're supposed to have brunch with Papa and Granny in a little while."

"Your granny will want to see you for herself," his father said. "Just like your mother will be banging on your door as soon as we roll into town tomorrow." A loud airport announcement paused all conversation. "We need to board. We don't want to miss our flight. They've changed our itinerary again." He sighed heavily. "I'll forward you the new flight schedule when we settle. And we'll call when we reach our next stop. And, Mo?"

"Yes, sir?"

"Good job, son. Couldn't be prouder."

And now Bronwyn was crying again. Shoot. He might join her if his dad didn't hang up soon. "Thank you, sir."

"We love you both so much," his mom said. "Please be safe. Be careful. And, Bronwyn, I need to see you with my own eyes too."

"Yes, ma'am." Bronwyn's response overlaid his.

"Love you, Bronwyn." His dad's response caught Mo off guard, although he wasn't sure why. Especially after what he'd learned this morning.

"Love you too. Both of you." Bronwyn swallowed hard and swiped at a tear. "Be safe. We'll see you soon."

They disconnected the call, and Mo turned to her. "That was . . ."

"Yeah." Bronwyn looked around the room for a tissue. "Um, are we in trouble with Granny now?"

"No." Mo rubbed a hand over his stubble. He needed to shave. "I texted them and Aunt Carol while you were, um, indisposed." He'd hoped she hadn't noticed and apparently she hadn't.

"Oh good. What's the new plan?"

"The new plan is that you take a quick shower here. I'll run to my place and shower and shave." And find some dry clothes because his tear-soaked shirt was starting to annoy him. "I'll let Aunt Carol know she can come on over. When she's done with us, we'll let Granny know. She said she'd hold off on the biscuits until we were en route."

"Do you want to let Meredith and Aunt Carol know that your parents know? Or should I do that?"

"I'll do it. Won't take but a second." He looked around the room. "Are you okay for me to go? I can wait."

She swiped a tissue and blew her nose. "No, go on. I'm okay. You have this place locked down like Fort Knox. We're safe here. And if we get ready at the same time, we can go to Granny's and then move on with the day."

"Okay." He hated to walk away from her. But she was right. And the sooner he got himself pulled together, the sooner he could be back with her.

And, yeah, he knew how bad that sounded, even in his own head. He knew that he and Bronwyn should take things slow, but he didn't seem to be capable of that. He was in big, big trouble.

Bronwyn kept both hands on the steering wheel of Mo's Jeep as they drove to Papa and Granny Quinn's. Her head hurt. Her heart hurt. Her eyes—there was no hope for them. They looked like blistered tomatoes.

Mo pecked away on his phone as she drove. "Okay, everyone's been notified. Gray says for us to come to the police station after brunch. Meredith says we took one for the team and she's proud of us. Cal says Landry needs to see you so we're to let them know when we're done at Gray's."

"Why does Landry need to see me?"

"I would assume for the same reason everyone in my family needs to see you. To confirm that you're alive and unharmed. Or, well, uninjured. Wrong words. Not shot."

"I wasn't harmed or injured. Why didn't those words work?"

"I'm sorry. I . . . you have been harmed. Maybe not physically. But emotionally. I didn't want to gloss over that."

She blinked a few times. "Do you suppose Granny has any eye drops?"

"Probably."

"I should have asked Aunt Carol if she had any in her Mary Poppins medical bag. I think she could do surgery out of that thing."

Mo chuckled. "I'm just glad she didn't try to make us stay home today."

They drove in silence for a few more minutes. "Mo?"

"Yeah?"

"Never mind."

"What?"

"Nothing. I mean, this isn't the time and place."

Mo tapped the armrest, then twisted in the seat. "No. I don't like this. We need to not do this. If you have something to say, say it. And I'll do the same. We can't move forward into . . . eh . . . anything good if we don't communicate."

"It's not anything bad. I started to say it and then thought it would be better to say it when I'm not driving. You know, face to face."

"Maybe it would be, but now that you've started . . ." He let the sentence hang, and she caved.

"Fine. I wanted to say thank you for taking those bullets for me, and for calling your parents, and for . . . letting me cry on you. You've been very kind to me. Thank you."

In her periphery, she could see Mo relax in his seat. "I'm not sure what to say to that. 'You're welcome' seems a bit out of place. 'My pleasure' makes it sound like I jump in front of bullets on the regular or that I think crying women are fun." He held up a hand. "To be clear, you can cry on me anytime. In fact, if you're going to cry, I think it *should* be on me. No one should cry alone."

If he didn't stop being so sweet, Bronwyn was going to be in serious trouble. They were friends. Good friends. Right? Or, whatever.

They were becoming something. But . . . she realized he was waiting on her to respond. What had he said? "I can't promise that, but I'll do my best."

"Fair enough." Mo fiddled with his phone. "While we're saying thank yous, we need to discuss how you tried to take a bullet for me first. Don't think I've forgotten that you ran *at* me when what you should have done was hit the ground immediately."

He glanced over in time to see Bronwyn narrow her eyes at him. He kept going before she could respond. "Thank you for trying to protect me. For talking to me and for trusting me to protect you. I'm even feeling glad that you made me call Mom and Dad, because you were right. If they'd come home and then Mom saw me like this?" He pointed to his face and grimaced. "I might not survive the tongue-lashing that would surely be coming my way."

They continued the ride in silence. Bronwyn didn't think it was awkward, but what if Mo thought it was? How did anyone know if a silence was truly awkward, anyway? What were the rules? At what point did it go from comfortable to awkward?

She was happy to simply be with him. Despite the chaos and turmoil in her life, she felt safe and . . . complete. Yes, it was a corny sentiment, but it wasn't like she was going to tell him he completed her. He didn't. It was more that this resolution of their drama felt like a decades-long wrong had finally been righted.

Which was good. Because she didn't think she could manage multiple dramas at once, and her family would be a nightmare.

She pulled into the driveway and turned to Mo. "Are you okay? How's your head?"

He tapped it. "Hard as usual. Don't move." He hopped out of his side of the Jeep, then walked to her side, opened the door, and extended his hand. She took it.

"Thank you, kind sir."

"You're welcome, good lady."

They were both snickering like children when they walked into the house.

Papa and Granny were in the kitchen, and they turned when they entered. "Lawd have mercy." Granny flew at Mo and hugged him tight, then turned to Bronwyn and pulled her close. "Oh, my precious girl. I'm so glad you're home safe."

Home safe.

Bronwyn considered that phrase as they ate. Granny had fried pork tenderloin and eggs, sliced tomatoes that had to have come from her garden, gravy, biscuits, and homemade muscadine jelly.

Home safe.

Had she ever been safe?

Had she ever been home?

She didn't have answers to those questions. Or maybe it was that she refused to acknowledge the ones flittering around on the edge of her consciousness. Regardless, she set it aside for now.

This was her favorite meal. Did Granny know that? It seemed like the kind of thing Granny would have tucked away in her memory banks and pulled out now, when Bronwyn needed comfort in the worst way.

Food hadn't always been her friend, but in Granny's kitchen, even the food felt safe. She had seconds of everything as they caught up on all the family news, which some might wrongly call gossip, but she wasn't one to judge.

Aunt Minnie blew through at one point with a big smile for Bronwyn and a long hug for Mo before she left to watch a show. She hadn't understood the delay and had eaten before they arrived. As she watched a prince get tossed into the water on TV, her laughter made for a fun backdrop to their conversation—a conversation that painstakingly ignored several elephants in the room.

"We have to head into town." Mo pushed back from the table and rubbed his stomach. "Gray wants to talk to us."

"Dare say he does." Papa Quinn took a sip of his coffee. "You got any ideas on who shot at you?"

"Got plenty of ideas, Papa," Mo said. "The problem is figuring out which ones are the real problems and which ones Bronwyn can fix by firing their sorry selves."

Papa winked at her. "Take it from an old man, sweetheart. Fire the ones that won't work or make mistakes and pass the blame. Promote the ones that work hard as long as when they make mistakes, they own them."

"I'd like to fire the lot of them." Bronwyn refused to think about the possibility that her family was even now removing her from her position.

"Why don't you?"

"I've been trying not to alienate my family."

"How's that been working for you?" Papa Quinn had never been one to miss an opportunity for a pointed discussion.

"Not well, sir."

He leaned toward her and patted her hand. "That's okay. You're young. Plenty of time to get it sorted."

"I hope you're right."

But she feared time had run out.

THIRTY

Mo sat in the passenger seat of the Jeep and texted Aunt Carol.

How long until I can drive?

It wasn't that he cared if Bronwyn drove his Jeep. Much. It was that he wanted to be the one behind the wheel in case some fool tried to run them off the road. Now that they were off Quinn land, his protective instincts were coming in rapid-fire, and he was not enjoying the experience.

They made it to the police station without any issues, and when they walked inside, Mo took Bronwyn's hand. "You okay?"

She looked at the new arrangement of wooden flowers Meredith had made for the front office area. "Am I supposed to be okay?"

Fair enough. "I don't guess so."

Gray called them back then. He took one look at Mo and his eyes widened. "Whoa. I wasn't expecting that, man." He pulled him into a bro hug that carefully avoided putting any pressure on his stitches. Then he tugged on Bronwyn, and she went into his arms. He squeezed her close. "Meredith made me promise to give you a good hug. She's up to her eyeballs in some kind of dental emergency, but she says we'll be at the firepit tonight and she'll see you then."

They both sat at the small table in Gray's office. He joined them with a stack of files. "I've already spoken to Katrina this morning. She's at work and says she's okay but will be taking advantage of the spa's hot tub and sauna this afternoon."

"She gets massages from a good friend of hers in Asheville. I'll schedule her an appointment." Bronwyn rubbed her temples. "I should have already done that."

"No, you shouldn't have." Gray's tone was kind but exasperated. "You were shot at. You went to the hospital with Mo. You're already in a sleep deficit. You aren't behind. You haven't dropped the ball. Got it?"

Bronwyn sat straighter in her chair. "Yes, Chief."

He gave her a sour look. "I do not understand women. Why do you assume you have to do everything? No one else expects you to do it all." He gestured toward Mo. "He doesn't expect you to. I don't. Katrina doesn't. She was worried about you and told me that I'd better not wake you up or call you in before you got the rest you needed. She also said that you need another massage because you undid all her hard work."

Bronwyn dropped her head. "Okay, okay. I get it."

Gray patted the files on the table and looked between the two of them, then focused on Mo. "Why don't you start by telling me why Bronwyn's been crying. You're still speaking to each other, so I'm hopeful the answer won't include anything about you being a moron. I've been given instructions from my beloved to kick your rear if you've done anything to, and I quote, 'mess things up.' And here you walk in together, but she's been crying. I realize I haven't lived here as long as most, but I've never seen her cry or even appear teary-eyed."

Mo wanted to tell Gray to mind his own business, but Bronwyn spoke before he had a chance. "Gray, you're awesome." She sounded amused and maybe a little bit touched by his words. "Thank you for the concern. But between you and me"—and at this her tone changed—"I'm going to have a chat with your beloved. We're done with assuming that Mo has done something wrong. If he does something, that will be between us, and we'll deal with it."

Gray sat back in his chair. "Acknowledged."

"This"—she pointed at her face—"is the result of a conversation I had with my parents this morning."

Gray leaned toward her. "What happened?"

"Words were exchanged."

Mo couldn't let it stand at that. "She said some things she probably should have said a decade ago, and they didn't like it."

She cut her eyes at him. "As I said, words were exchanged. And I may or may not have a job anymore. Too soon to tell."

Gray seemed to absorb that. Then he opened the top file in front of him. "Okay. Let's talk bullets. We sent the bullet casing from Mo's wound to forensics, but this isn't a TV show and there's no telling when we'll learn anything useful. We have a BOLO out on the vehicle, but it didn't show up on any cameras going in or out of town."

"Is that normal?" Bronwyn asked.

"Around here? Yes and no. If they were from out of town, I would expect them to show up on the traffic cams we have set up on the edges of the county. But if they're local, that truck could be in any of a hundred barns, sheds, or outbuildings by now. It could be parked in the woods somewhere. If they're willing not to drive it, we might never find it."

"It was a nice truck. No way they won't drive it." Mo pulled the file toward him. "Anything on the plate?" He'd seen the license plate and had given that info to Gray yesterday.

"Stolen off a Toyota Camry in Charlotte."

"Awesome."

"Mo, is there anything you've found in The Haven files that would account for this?"

"Maybe. There's some hinky stuff going on. I can almost taste it. It's right there. I have some searches running. What I need is time to work on it."

"He has a headache and isn't supposed to be looking at screens." Bronwyn gave the phone in his hand a pointed look. "Not that he's obeying that guidance."

"If you can't keep him in line, I imagine no one can." Gray made the comment in such a matter-of-fact way, it almost slipped past Mo. But based on Bronwyn's expression, it didn't slip past her.

She frowned and looked from Mo to Gray. "Why would you think I could keep him in line?"

Gray looked between them and grinned. "Oh, this is going to be too much fun. I do believe I'll let you figure that one out for yourself, Ms. Pierce."

He opened another file. "Until we receive forensic results on the bullets or find the truck, there's not much we can do. I'm sorry about that. However, I do need you to sign these statements." He slid the papers to them. "This is what you told me yesterday. Please read it, make any corrections, then sign."

Mo took his. It was significantly shorter than Bronwyn's. Probably because he'd been bleeding at the time. When he handed his signed statement to Gray, he asked about the grocery store. "Was there any damage?" He couldn't remember.

"Just to you. I've stationed an officer there today. Lionel's been busy. He sold a lot of pizza at lunch. I think he's relieved. He was worried people would be scared off, which wouldn't be good for business. But he's fine. The employees are fine. No one quit. So yeah, he's good."

That was a relief. Lionel was a good man. Mo hated for any of the Pierce family drama to have a negative impact on him or his business.

Bronwyn's phone buzzed, and she glanced at it. Then she handed it to him.

The text was from Marcus.

> Ms. Pierce, William and Nathan are having it out in Nathan's office. Lots of yelling. I specifically heard William say he was going to call the board to an emergency meeting. I thought you should know.

Bronwyn sagged. "I guess I should go find out what's happening."

Mo didn't think she should, but he wouldn't argue with her in front of Gray.

She slid her statement back to Gray. "Are we done?"

"We are. I'll keep you both informed of any developments." He glanced at the phone as Mo handed it back to Bronwyn. "Everything okay?"

"Lots of yelling between my uncle and cousin. That doesn't bode well." Bronwyn stood. "I'll also keep you informed."

Mo followed her as they walked out. When they reached the Jeep, he touched her arm. "May I make a suggestion?"

"Sure."

"Don't bust up the argument."

"Mo—"

"Hear me out. If you really want to head to the office, then let's go back to your house first. Do your hair, makeup, put on a power suit, then walk in there like the CEO you are. I'll support you all the way."

"But you don't think I should go at all?"

"I think it would be more prudent to carry on with your day the way you planned. Show no weakness. Don't let on that you care what they're up to."

He hoped he wasn't wrong, but he didn't think he was.

"I do, however, think you should pay a visit to your grandmother. She was worried about you. She should see you. Face to face."

Bronwyn climbed into the Jeep and waited for Mo to get in on the other side. "You have a devious streak."

"I'm sure I don't know what you mean." He batted his eyelashes at her.

She cranked the engine. "I can't go to my grandmother's like this though."

"What's wrong with what you have on?" Mo waved a hand in her direction. "You look great."

She didn't believe him. No, that wasn't right. She believed that *he* thought she looked great. *She* didn't think she looked great. "I lost my temper with my parents, but they're a different situation. I won't go so far as to say they don't deserve anything from me, but they have actively worked against me for too long for me to owe them any loyalty."

And didn't those words cut to the quick? "But Grandmother?" she continued. "She has expectations. Meeting those expectations is more about respect. She's not perfect, but at least she loves me . . . in her own way." She didn't say that she didn't think her parents loved her at all. She wasn't quite ready to go that far.

Mo rubbed the back of his head and winced. "I hear you, but do you think you should go alone?"

"I wasn't planning on going alone." She gave him what she

hoped was a confident smile. "Since I'm being all kinds of bold and brash today, I thought I'd see if you'd care to join me."

The words surprised her, but hearing them, she knew it was the right call. "There's so much going on, I don't feel safe . . ." She stopped herself before she finished the thought with "unless I'm with you."

She waited for him to say something, but he looked like she'd surprised him. She lost her patience and asked him flat-out, "Will you come with me?"

That knocked him out of whatever mindspace he'd been in, and he waggled his eyebrows. "I wouldn't miss it for the world. But I guess I should change too?"

Thirty minutes later, they parked in Grandmother's driveway. Both of them were dressed in what most people would call business casual but what Grandmother would consider to be right on the edge of loungewear.

To Bronwyn's surprise, Grandmother wasn't in the house. She sat in a wheelchair beside her flower garden. Sebastian, poor kid, stood guard a few feet away.

After Mo helped her from the Jeep, Sebastian acknowledged her presence but didn't move from his post.

Mo scanned the surroundings, then nudged her toward her grandmother. "I'll stay back. I won't listen in. If you need me, give me a signal."

Bronwyn didn't argue. Mo's presence on the property might be enough to send her grandmother to her not-so-early grave.

It wasn't until she knelt beside her grandmother's wheelchair that she realized she had no idea what signal she would use if she needed Mo. Oh well. She'd wing it.

"Grandmother?"

Grandmother Pierce looked at her and nodded approval. "I knew you would come." Her voice had a gurgly quality to it that

Bronwyn suspected did not bode well for her continued presence with them. "Do you know who tried to kill you?"

"Not yet. We've barely had time to breathe since it happened. But we're working on it."

"By *we*, I assume you mean you and that Quinn boy?"

"Yes, ma'am." In for a penny, in for a pound. "He saved my life."

"I heard." She studied Mo where he now stood, beside Sebastian. "It looks like he took more than a bullet for you. What happened to his pretty face?"

"You think he's pretty?" And why was that the part of the observation she'd focused on?

"The Quinn men have always been attractive. Catherine Quinn says it has nothing to do with appearance and everything to do with the fact that for the most part, she raised good men."

"Do you agree?"

"Hard to disagree when my own sons have turned into lecherous pit vipers and few would call them handsome at this point."

Ouch.

"The board plans to try to fire you."

Leave it to Grandmother to get right back to business. She'd probably be trying to run the show from her funeral. "They will do what they will do. I will do what I must." The words were true enough, but Bronwyn hoped she sounded more confident than she felt.

Grandmother nodded a few times, and Bronwyn wondered if she'd fallen asleep. But then a bony hand reached out and grabbed her arm. "Get the bylaws. Study them. Be prepared. This isn't over. I've made provisions."

"Grandmother, what provisions have you made?" This cloak-and-dagger stuff was more than she had the patience for. She needed answers, not vague assurances.

But she wasn't going to get them today. Grandmother's cough

started suddenly and continued so long that Bronwyn feared she might pass out.

She looked at Mo and with one glance, he turned to Sebastian, spoke a few words, and ran to the door of the house. When it opened, he spoke to the butler on duty, then returned to his spot by Sebastian.

Moments later, the day nurse dashed out the door and into the garden. "Good afternoon, Ms. Pierce. I'm Janelle." She carried a mask attached to a small oxygen tank. "Now, Mrs. Pierce, when you talk too much, you start coughing." Janelle settled the mask over her grandmother's face. "Let's take you back inside."

She unlocked the wheelchair and pushed it toward the back door where a newly constructed ramp allowed easier access to the home.

"Do you need any help, Janelle?" Bronwyn asked.

"No, ma'am. Will you be coming inside?"

"No. I need to go. A moment, please." She stepped in front of the wheelchair and leaned toward her grandmother. "I'll do what you said. You rest."

She didn't tell her she loved her. She didn't touch her. They weren't a touchy-feely family. That was okay. Although, now that she thought about it, she craved a certain amount of physical contact. Maybe it was because she'd had so little of it growing up.

Mo joined her then, and they stood side-by-side as Janelle pushed Grandmother into the house. When they were back in the Jeep, she didn't say anything. She drove back to Mo's place and parked the car. Even though he must have been curious about what was said, Mo didn't pry.

She appreciated that more than she could articulate.

By mutual consent, they walked to the firepit and sat in their chairs. It was warm but not miserable, a perk of living in the mountains in the summer. They had scorching days, but this wasn't one of them.

Bronwyn finally steeled herself enough to speak. "My grandmother told me she'd made provisions."

"Provisions?"

"Yep." She kicked her feet up on the firepit rim. "Oh, and that I need to study the bylaws."

"For The Haven?"

"Yes."

"Seems wise. She's not my favorite person, but no one could ever say she wasn't a sly fox."

Bronwyn stared across the firepit toward the property she owned on the other side of the river, and memories flooded through her. They'd played here as children. Splashed in the river. Played hide-and-seek in the trees. Their land wasn't heavily forested, but there were more trees than bare patches. Cal and Landry's house was so deliciously nestled into the trees that it felt like someone had planted a house seed and it had grown up right along with the woods.

"Did I tell you Landry tried to sell me the land back?"

If Mo found her abrupt change of subject surprising, he didn't let on.

"I told her I'd buy it back from her if she needed the money, but otherwise that she should keep it and sell it back to me when Eliza's ready to go to college. It will be worth a lot more then. It's not like I need it."

Mo eased his wounded leg up to the firepit rim beside hers. "Cal told me. He thought it was brilliant. Landry was offended that you would think she would take advantage of you that way."

"Landry is an incredible artist, but her business sense is nonexistent. She'd give everything away if she could."

Mo nodded in agreement. "I'll be right back." He disappeared into his house for a few minutes. When he emerged, he carried a laptop and two bottles of water. "Here." He handed her a water.

"Aunt Carol texted me and told me I needed to hydrate. Something about blood loss. I don't know. I don't care. But if I have to, you have to."

He resumed his seat and opened his laptop. "Please keep talking. I'm listening. I'm running down a hunch."

She didn't say anything. Not out of any spite or grouchiness. Not even because she doubted that Aunt Carol would approve. It was simply that she didn't want to disturb him. If he had a hunch, she wanted him to chase that thing down and beat it into submission.

And my, my, hadn't her thoughts turned vicious today.

She sipped her water, studied her land, and listened to Mo do whatever he was doing on the computer. After a few minutes, he tapped her arm. "You're being awfully quiet. Everything okay?"

She gave him a look.

He held up his hands. "Okay, okay. I get it. No. Everything is not okay. Your family is imploding, your grandmother is scheming from her deathbed, and don't think I've forgotten about Bob the super-friendly bodyguard who wants to date you. Or Peter Brown who is a lying scumbag if ever I saw one."

She had to laugh at his concise recitation of the facts. "Precisely."

"But, given the amount of consternation that level of chaos should be contributing to your mental clutter, one would conclude you would have plenty to converse about." Mo grinned at her. "And yes, I did include all that alliteration on purpose. I couldn't help it."

She tilted her water bottle toward him. "Well played, sir."

He gave her an expectant look.

"You're working. I'm processing. I'm . . ." She dropped her head and confessed, "I'm enjoying that we're sitting here together, and we don't need anyone to help us communicate."

Mo's grin was straight out of her childhood. Rare, mischievous, and devastating. "But we aren't communicating. I'm working, and you're not saying anything."

She took another sip of water. "I think we're communicating just fine." She wanted to slap her hand over her mouth. What was wrong with her? Was she flirting with him?

Based on the way his grin went from devastating to surprised, she thought maybe he'd taken it as flirty, regardless of how she meant it.

"I'll concede that nonverbal communication is something we excel at." He spoke the words without looking away from his computer, but then he turned those big blue eyes on her and winked. "But if we're going to share what we enjoy, then I should tell you that I'm enjoying hearing your voice. I've always loved the way your mind works. But I can't read it. You have to tell me what's going on in there."

Couldn't he?

As if in answer to her unspoken question, he continued. "Okay. Sometimes I can come close to reading your mind. And it's cool that we can still communicate without words."

She agreed.

"But it's been a long stretch without words, so for now at least, I prefer the words to the silence."

"Fair enough. I'm staring at my land, and I'm wondering why you haven't built on yours. Do you have plans? Ideas?"

THIRTY-ONE

Mo paused with his hands on his keyboard. "I could ask you the same question. Why do you live at The Haven? Why haven't you built a sprawling mansion? Why don't you have the photography studio you wanted? Or the deck with the view for miles?"

She fiddled with the wrapper on her water bottle. "I asked first."

He closed his laptop. "At first, I was afraid I'd be living here alone. I thought Cal and Meredith would find people to marry and then they'd live somewhere other than Gossamer Falls and the dream of living on this land and having our kids grow up together the way we did didn't seem likely."

"Were the tiny houses your idea?" Bronwyn looked at the three houses behind them.

"That is a matter of some debate. Meredith claims it was her idea. Cal and I both contend that she had nothing to do with it and that we came up with it one night while working in his dad's shop and moaning that grown men need to have their own place and not live with their parents."

"You did have your own place. So did Cal. And Meredith. You weren't freeloaders."

"True, but we didn't have a place here. When we came home to visit, we stayed with our parents, and that was fine. But when Cal and Meredith moved home, it made sense for us to each have a place of our own. But we didn't need or want to build our forever homes without our forever person."

Bronwyn absorbed that. "What if you didn't find your forever person?"

"We discussed that at length. We agreed if we weren't married by the time we turned forty, we'd build the big houses."

"So, do you have plans?" She was persistent. He'd always liked that about her.

"Not real ones. I have things I know I want. I usually walk through Cal's houses before he turns them over to their owners, so I've seen things I like and things I would never do."

"Oh, I have to know. Give me one must-have and one never-ever."

He drummed his fingers on the closed laptop. "Must-have . . . Master bedroom on the main floor. That's more because of what we've been through with Mom and Dad than anything I've seen. Mom could barely walk up and down the stairs for a while. Sickness and illness are part of life. I want my room on the same level as the living areas of the home."

"Good point. My home is all one level at the moment. I don't think I've considered what would happen if I broke my leg and my bedroom was upstairs."

"Exactly."

"Okay. What's a never-ever?"

"A single-car garage."

"Is there a story there?"

Mo nodded. "One of Cal's builds. The lot was fairly small and the guy wanted to maximize his house space. Understandable. But Cal told him not to skimp on the garage. He told him he would want more space, not less. The guy insisted. Said the house was great, decorated beautifully, all that good stuff. But that tiny garage was a mistake. A year later, the guy was back in Cal's office trying to figure out how to add on to it."

"Mo."

"Yeah?"

"I started talking, and you stopped working."

She was right, but he wouldn't tell her that. He opened his laptop. "Fine. I'll work. But that isn't getting you out of answering my questions."

She scrunched up her nose at him.

He laughed at her antics. "You didn't think I'd forget, did you?"

"I hoped."

"Come on. Let's hear it."

She blew out a dramatic sigh. "Fine. I live at The Haven for two reasons. One, I wanted to be closer to work. I'm a workaholic. And a control freak. I wanted to be sure everything was done and that I could be on-site whenever needed. I don't think it was a bad idea for a while, but that phase is over. If I don't lose my job, I'll make changes."

He didn't make eye contact but waited for her to continue.

"You already know the second reason. There was no way I could build a house here, right across from you, when we weren't speaking to each other."

She'd been brave enough to say it. He'd be brave enough to ask the next question. "And now?"

"Now? This has been the most intense week of my entire life, and it's only Thursday. I have a home. It's lovely and comfortable. So while I'll be moving off the property sooner rather than later, it's not a priority. My current future planning is limited to tomorrow."

"What's tomorrow?"

"Finding the bylaws and figuring out what Grandmother was talking about."

He gave himself an internal pat on the back. "Do you want to wait until tomorrow?"

"No, but . . ." She looked at the laptop. "Do you have them?"

"I do. I can print them now." A few keystrokes and a notification on his screen told him that the printer was at work. "I'll keep going through the files I downloaded. You can search the bylaws. And we'll enjoy the peace and quiet until Eliza arrives."

She only made it through half a page before she requested highlighters and Post-it flags so she could mark problematic areas. Every now and then, she'd mutter something about "control freaks" and "morons," and once she looked to the sky and said, "Lord, you are testing me." An hour later, Bronwyn was only halfway through the pages he'd printed for her.

For his part, Mo had brought out a second laptop and had moved away from the firepit to a shady area where he could see his screen.

And what he was seeing was not making him happy. He'd had a few programs running in the background since he first accessed the files. These programs were designed to look for anomalies indicating money laundering, embezzlement, or other forms of criminal financial conduct.

He hadn't been surprised that while a few red flags popped up immediately, they'd been nothing more than smoke screens. The best financial criminals knew how to hide the actions that could send them to prison behind sketchy behavior that was more likely to earn them nothing more than a slap on the wrist or maybe a note in their file, along with a reminder about professional ethics.

Catching those red flags left most accountants satisfied that the accounts were otherwise clean. Not that he was slamming accountants. It wasn't their job to dig deeper. They had their hands full and weren't equipped or expected to find the devious machinations a skilled and motivated individual could put in place to hide their thievery.

Mo had been careful not to do anything that could get Bronwyn in trouble. The programs running now were running in the background on The Haven's system.

But they were sending him reports, and those reports were problematic on many levels.

It would take him another day or two to hunt it all down, but if what he was seeing was correct, someone in the Pierce family had been blackmailing a politician and had used The Haven to launder the payments. Mo could track three payments a year going back at least four years. And another annual payment that went back a decade.

And there was one alarming payment from thirteen years ago that could be unrelated to anything else. Or it could be a sign of a very deep rot.

Based on the track record, the second payment due this year should have been made sometime in the last two weeks, but Mo couldn't find any record of it.

Had the politician decided they were done? Had the person behind the blackmail made a different financial arrangement?

Mo had suspicions, but before he could approach anyone with them, he had to resolve one glaring issue.

Everything in the records indicated that the Pierce family member behind the most recent blackmail scheme was Bronwyn.

Bronwyn stared at the stack of paper in front of her. She'd tabbed it, highlighted it, and considered burning it in the firepit to cleanse her brain from the gobbledygook she'd poured through.

"I want to find the lawyer who put this together and ask if they read any of this." Bronwyn expected Mo to laugh, chuckle, grunt . . . something . . . anything.

But she got no response. He was laser focused on the screens in front of him, and he did not look happy.

She stood, raised her hands above her head, touched her toes, repeated the process three times, and still, no reaction.

Maybe she'd been reading the situation wrong, but she'd rather gotten used to having Mo's undivided attention. Even when he was working, he was aware of her. She liked it.

But right now, he was in a land far, far away. And he wasn't having a good time.

She had good news to share. And she wanted to share it with him first. Should she interrupt him? Go inside and wait to see when he noticed she was gone?

She did neither. Instead, she set the bylaws on the rim of the firepit—where, if the wind blew them in and they burned, she would not be sad at all—and strolled down the path toward the river.

Fifteen minutes later, he joined her. He didn't say anything. He simply fell into step beside her as they followed the meandering path to a small bridge that crossed the river to the property Bronwyn had sold to Landry.

A bench that hadn't been there the last time she'd walked this path now graced the bank. "When did this happen?" She took a seat on one end. Mo took a seat as far away from her as possible.

The scene was peaceful. Idyllic. The river gurgled. The summer mountain air was warm but with a breeze that kept it from being oppressive. Everything was green, and there was the faintest hint of honeysuckle in the air.

But Mo keeping his distance left her cold and disturbed.

Maybe if she talked to him, he'd relax. "I found the clause in the bylaws that Grandmother wanted me to find."

No response.

"There's a provision for the CEO to no longer be subject to the whims of random family members on the board after a certain period. It's set up so the family gets a two-year window to be difficult, to essentially micromanage everything, and to insist on changes as they see fit. But after that, the CEO has sweeping powers. Too many powers if you ask me. I'll be making some modifications to that."

"So they can't fire you now?" he asked, finally breaking his silence.

"They could have done it with a simple majority vote during the probationary period. They wouldn't have needed any reason other than that they wanted someone else. It would have been legal to oust me. But now, they have to have cause. And the provisions are narrow. They have to prove I've done something illegal or that would fundamentally harm The Haven. Their hands are tied because I haven't done either of those things."

She'd expected a fist bump. A smile. A whoop. Okay, maybe not a whoop. Mo wasn't the whooping type. But what she got was brooding Mo. Brooding Mo did not bode well for . . . anything.

She waved a hand in front of him. "Hello?"

He turned toward her and rested a knee on the wood. He tapped the back of the bench and pinched his lips together. The fidgeting would drive her up the wall if he didn't explain himself.

He finally heaved a breath and said, "I need to tell you something. And it's important that you hear me out."

Bronwyn didn't want to hear him out. She didn't want him to say anything that came with that kind of warning. But she nodded.

"Tomorrow, we have to return to your office, regardless of who's there. If Peter Brown comes by, I'll have security remove him. If Bob shows up and asks you to lunch, I'll tell him you have plans into infinity and to shove off. But I need access to every file and every server."

She relaxed at his words. "No problem." That had been easy. "Maybe in the future you could be a little less dramatic. You had me scared there for a minute."

"I'm not done."

The fear came back with a fury.

"I'm sorry, Bronwyn, but you have to know. Someone's been playing a very long game. And right now, they're winning. I will get to the bottom of it. I will figure it out."

"What are you talking about?"

Mo reached for her hands and she placed them in his. He looked her dead in the eye and continued. "Right now, based on the information I currently have on the computer, if someone asked me under oath to tell them who was behind the misappropriation of funds at The Haven, I would have to tell them"—he cleared his throat—"that it was you."

Bronwyn tried to pull her hands free, but Mo held on. "I know it wasn't you."

His voice had no give. No hesitation. No doubt.

"Then, why—"

"I don't know why. Like I said, someone with way more intellectual savvy than I anticipated is behind this. That's fine. I've hunted down people far smarter than whoever this is. Right now, my money's on Nathan. Maybe Uncle William. The way they've slid the payments in under accounts you manage is . . . delicate. Honestly, if it wasn't for the fact that it's a total travesty, I would have to say that it's a diabolically elegant construction."

Bronwyn's brain was stuck on the "it looks like you did it" part of the conversation. "I would never—"

"I know."

"I didn't—"

"I know."

"How did they—"

"I'll find out."

"Mo?"

"Yes?"

"Why do you believe me?" That was the real question, wasn't it? "You just said everything points to me, but you don't believe it. Why?"

He couldn't have looked more shocked than if she'd slapped him upside the head with a dead fish. "I know you." He didn't release her hands but scooted closer to her on the bench. "I deserve the questions, I'm just not happy that you felt the need to ask them."

"I didn't mean—"

"I know you didn't. Listen. We have so much drama between us. So much hurt. So many times when one of us messed up and the other flamed out and refused to forgive, rinse and repeat, until we turned something beautiful that God gave us into something so toxic we couldn't even speak to each other."

He let go of her hand momentarily and tucked a wayward strand of hair behind her ear. "I acknowledge my role in that, but one of us has to stop the cycle. That's what I'm doing. I'm not looking at the numbers. I'm not looking at the supposed facts. I'm looking at you. I'm basing my decisions on who *you* are. On your character. On your dedication. On the way you love this place and the people who work here despite the way your family has treated you your entire life."

She'd dropped her gaze to where he clasped her hands. When he disentangled one hand, she didn't try to hold on. She didn't expect him to use that hand to lift her chin, but when he did, she forced herself to look into his eyes.

"I see you, Bronwyn. I haven't always. I was young and selfish, and I saw what I wanted to see and ignored the painful parts of your life to the point that I couldn't understand your choices. But

I'm grown up. We both are. And I choose you. I will keep choosing you. I will dig until I figure out who's behind this and what they've done and then I'll vindicate you in front of all the people who are too stupid to realize how amazing you are."

He slid his hand to cup her cheek. "I'll fight with you and for you. But I will not fight against you. Those days are over. You have my word."

She had no idea what to say. Or do. She probably should have said something profound.

Instead, she did what she'd wanted to do for . . . longer than she was willing to admit. She held his gaze while she leaned forward until her lips brushed against his.

His eyes widened, but his lips didn't move. She pulled back and whispered, "Thank you."

He still didn't move.

Well, that had not gone as—

His lips crashed down on hers. Hers responded eagerly. Both of his hands were in her hair. She slid her hands around his neck, and he pulled her closer. She never, ever wanted the kiss to end.

When he finally let her come up for air, he murmured against her lips. "You're mine. You've always been mine. I won't forget. Never again."

THIRTY-TWO

Later that evening, Mo sat beside the firepit and tried to focus on the conversation. Eliza was happy, per usual. Her cousin Abby was with her. They were having a sleepover, and Landry and Cal had made the bold decision to allow them to have both mountain pies *and* s'mores.

They were well away from the smoke, bouncing around the yard like blown-up balloons that had been released into the wild. Eliza's almost full-grown puppy, Pippi, chased after them.

Landry leaned against Cal, both their hands on her ever-growing belly. Meredith was building a new flavor of mountain pie that would either be delicious or an atrocity, and Gray stood by her, laughing as she debated which ingredient to add next.

Maisy couldn't seem to decide who needed the most attention. She was usually glued to Landry's side these days. But at the moment, she sat at Bronwyn's feet while Bronwyn petted her and scratched behind her ears in that spot she loved. It was hard to tell who was happier with the situation.

Bronwyn sat beside Mo, but she'd left room for the Holy Spirit and a few angels.

Mo understood. He even agreed. It was too soon for a public

declaration of . . . anything. And while the adults present knew, the kids didn't.

But his mind kept returning to her kisses by the river. The way everything in him—mind, soul, spirit, and body—was finally home. Those pleasant ruminations were battered by the ever-present fact that The Haven accounts told him the woman who'd kissed him senseless earlier today had blackmailed a state senator and embezzled enough money from The Haven that she could reasonably hop a plane for South America and disappear.

And she'd disappeared before.

He'd told her the truth today. He was choosing to believe in her. What he hadn't told her was that he was having to make that choice over and over again.

The facts in front of him were hard to ignore.

The facts from their past were hard to ignore.

But here he was, ignoring like he'd never ignored before.

She caught his eye and wrinkled her forehead. "What's wrong? Does your head still hurt?"

"It does, but it's not as bad as it was."

She twisted her lips. "It's me, isn't it?"

"No man in his right mind would ever say yes to that question."

She didn't smile at his lame joke. "What else did you find?"

He glanced at the others and shook his head.

She started to protest, but he raised his hand, and she paused on the inhale.

"Later." He looked at his watch and then at the girls. "It won't be long before they're tucked in at Cal's house with a movie."

She huffed but didn't argue. Another two minutes of silence went by before she scooted a fraction closer and leaned toward him. "If we aren't going to talk about that, let's talk about something else."

He twisted until he faced her. "What did you have in mind?"

"We could discuss your weird coffee issues."

That was not what he expected her to say.

"Or why a man who is practical about most things insists on driving a Jeep when it is not remotely practical or even comfortable to ride in."

He gasped but didn't try to hide his grin. Heavy conversations were coming, but she was clearly keeping it light. She wanted to play.

He could do that.

"Oh, I have another one. We could talk about how a manly man such as yourself has become, dare I say, addicted to that spa in Highlands?"

"Now you're being ridiculous. I'm not addicted to it. And as a woman who had a massage yesterday, you're in no position to throw stones."

"Hot stones?" She arched an eyebrow and laughed at her own lame joke. But the humor vanished almost as quickly as it came. "You should get a massage soon. Your body has to be a mess."

"It is, but I don't want to freak out the therapist when I roll up in there with bullet holes."

Bronwyn shuddered.

"Sorry." He reached for her hand and gave it a quick squeeze. "Let's move back to something light and fun. Let's talk about why you need to change the coffee at The Haven to something more—"

"Not happening. We order our coffee from a small co-op in Guatemala. The proceeds go to a mission there. The people who pick the beans and roast them are all paid a livable wage. And it's fresh and certified mold-free and all the other stuff coffee should be free of. We pay a fortune for it, and it's worth every penny because it is delicious." She pointed toward his home. "Unlike what I've heard about the stuff you keep over there."

"So, since I know the CEO—"

"For today."

"Fine, before you step down—"

"Or get fired."

"Would you stop? Can you get me a bag?"

"Of coffee?"

"No, of dirt from the outside of the cabin that the MLB pitcher likes to stay in. I want some of the ground he's walked on."

"You are so weird." She rolled her eyes at him, and it was . . . spectacular. For a split second, they were fifteen and bantering over brownies. She was team middle. He was team edge. He didn't realize they were leaning toward each other until Meredith interrupted them.

"Hey, you two! Stop flirting and come try this. It may be my best pie yet."

Bronwyn pinched her lips together and looked down at the increasingly shrinking space between them. "I don't suppose there's any point in ignoring her?"

"Sadly, no."

"I heard that." Meredith glared at them from the opposite edge of the firepit.

"I meant for you to hear me." Bronwyn blew her a kiss.

Meredith pretended to swat it away. "If you don't eat this while it's hot and melty, you won't experience the full effect of my culinary genius."

Mo stood and pulled Bronwyn to her feet.

"I didn't know she had any culinary genius."

Bronwyn's stage whisper had Meredith pointing tongs in her direction. "Watch it, Beep."

And for the next hour, Mo didn't worry about blackmailers or backstabbing. He didn't think about the future, and he definitely didn't think about the past.

He stayed in the present. And in the present, a beautiful woman who he knew better than most and simultaneously barely knew at all slowly but surely shortened the distance between them. When she stood on the opposite side of the fire with Meredith and Landry, she included him in their laughter. When she sat on the edge of the firepit and helped Eliza roast yet another marshmallow, her smile drew him into the moment. And when they settled back around the fire, and it was time to divulge what he suspected, he was surprised but pleased when she tucked herself against his good side and smirked at his sister and cousin with an expression that said, "Go ahead. Say it."

But they didn't say anything.

He put his arm around her shoulder and waited.

Gray and Meredith sat in their two-person chair, and he played with her engagement ring as it flickered in the firelight. "I guess I'll start."

"Please." Meredith gave him a light kiss. "If someone doesn't start, we'll all end up staring at each other all night. It could be weird and awkward, what with Mo and Bronwyn sitting over there like they've been dating for three years already and all of us wondering what happened but not wanting to ask because we're afraid we'll mess it up somehow."

Landry rubbed her stomach. "I don't think there's anything we could do to mess them up. They're pretty good at managing it all by themselves. Looking at them right now, I feel like I do when I'm working with a freshly thrown vase. If I put too much pressure on it, it will fold in on itself and I'll have to start all over."

Cal pressed a kiss to her temple. "Have faith." He looked from Mo to Bronwyn to Meredith. "This was always how it was supposed to be and we all know it. Let's be happy we're here now and figure out how to keep Bronwyn and Mo from getting shot."

"Again." Meredith glared at Mo.

"Why are you mad at me? It's not like I asked to be shot."

"No, but you need to figure this out faster."

"He's working as fast as he can." Bronwyn's response had an edge of . . . something. Protectiveness?

"I know, Beep." Meredith, to his surprise, backed way off. Her voice was gentle and even a little apologetic. "I didn't mean to imply anything else. I'm . . ." She blew out a breath and collapsed into Gray's side.

"We're all on edge." Cal tucked Landry closer to him. "We're exhausted and frustrated, and if we aren't careful, we'll start taking it out on each other. Let's not do that."

"Hear, hear." Gray raised his iced tea toward Cal. "It's like when Meredith drags me off on some twenty-seven-mile hike." That earned him a gentle swat. He caught her hand and kissed her fingers. "When I don't think I have it in me to walk another step, she tells me we're almost there and that it will be worth it."

Everyone laughed because they'd all heard Meredith say that.

"The thing is, that last push is usually brutal. Straight uphill on legs that are jelly, lungs burning for oxygen, and fatigue making me question all my life choices. And then we reach the top." He threw his hands in the air like he'd just won a race. "And it's all there. The money shot. The view. The payoff. The reason for the journey. And it's so worth it."

Landry leaned into Cal. "Did you know Gray had such a philosophical side?"

"I blame Meredith." Cal grinned at his friend. "But yeah, you're right. It does feel like that. Like we're close to something amazing . . . if we don't quit."

"Or turn on each other." Landry pointed at Meredith and Cal. "So, behave."

Both of them gave her wide-eyed, innocent looks that no one with three working brain cells would believe.

Gray cleared his throat. "It's like herding cats . . ." He shook his head. "Okay. Focus, everybody. We have real problems here."

"Yeah, like Mo getting shot," Cal said.

"And Bronwyn getting shot at," Landry added.

"And let's not forget about that creepy fake reporter." Meredith made a face like she'd taken a whiff of sour milk. "Him showing up now is too coincidental for me."

Mo almost mentioned Bob of the walking trail but held back. The guy had been over-the-top in his flirtation but hadn't done anything overtly dangerous. He'd been a bit pushy but not sleazy about it.

So he was a little surprised when Bronwyn chimed in with, "Don't forget Bob," and all three women shuddered.

What had he missed?

Bronwyn leaned harder into Mo's strong chest and forced herself to relax under his arm.

"Fill me in about Bob." Gray pulled a notebook and pen from a pocket. Did he keep one on him at all times?

Bronwyn told them about their encounter from the previous day. "I don't know how to explain it, but he was almost too nice, too polished."

Landry and Meredith nodded in understanding, but Cal and Gray looked confused. She turned to Mo, expecting him to back her up, but was met with the same confused expression. "You didn't think so?"

"I found him annoying and inappropriately assertive, but I . . ." He pinched his lips together and gave her a sheepish look. "I thought my opinion was based on my own jealousy. He could walk up to you, talk to you, flirt with you, ask you out, and all I could do was stand there. Mute. It was frustrating."

He'd been jealous? She shouldn't like that. But she kind of did.

Not kind of. She liked it a lot. And that was the problem, wasn't it? He'd told her flat-out that he was choosing to believe in her. Choosing to focus on the positive. Choosing not to suspect her of the worst.

But would he always? At what point would he stop choosing her? And could she survive it if he decided she was too much trouble?

"Earth to Bronwyn." Cal singsonged the words, then sighed in overdone despair. "Great. How long will we have to put up with these two being all goo-goo eyed?"

"Stop complaining." Landry swatted Cal.

Bronwyn heard them, but she didn't look away from Mo. "I was so glad you were there. The trail is open to anyone, but I've never had a guest approach me there. Not that way."

"That's because the kind of people who come to The Haven, for the most part, appreciate their privacy so they don't invade the privacy of others."

Bronwyn looked at Landry. "What about when Chantal and those strumpets made fools of themselves when Cal's crew was rebuilding Favors? As I recall, you were most displeased and let them know those men were off-limits."

Landry wrinkled her nose at the mention of one of their least favorite frequent guests. "Chantal is an exception to every rule."

Bronwyn agreed with Landry, but that wasn't the point. Although Cal was certainly taking an interest based on the way he was nuzzling Landry's neck and making her laugh.

"Get a room, people." Gray used his police chief voice, which, unfortunately, did not work on Cal. "Bronwyn, tell me more about this man."

"He's private security for one of the guests."

Gray's gaze landed on Mo first, then Cal. None of them looked happy. "I assume, given that he was on the trail with you, that his employer doesn't require his presence at all times."

"No. He doesn't," she said. "If he leaves to do anything outdoors—hiking, kayaking, et cetera—his security joins him. But he's stayed with us before, and he feels secure on the grounds. This is the first time he's brought private security, and my understanding is that there was a situation of some sort that made him feel it was necessary."

Bronwyn considered her words.

"What?" Meredith asked. "You look like you've had a revelation."

"Not a revelation," Bronwyn said. "More of a possibility."

"Care to share with the class?" Cal asked.

"When Bob's employer told me he was bringing security, he said he'd been asked to bring them. I assumed someone on his team had asked, or maybe his security staff at home. But now I'm wondering about that." She paused and tried to pin down exactly what was bothering her. "Like I said, he's stayed with us multiple times. In the past, he's had his team, which I always assumed included some security personnel, a private assistant, and one time, a personal trainer. They would come with him, help him settle, and then they would leave. I understood it to be a vacation for his staff as well. Once he was safe behind the gates, his team would leave for their own vacations. Then they would return the morning of checkout."

"I cannot fathom how these people live." Meredith took a sip of Gray's tea.

"In most cases, I agree that it's overkill. But with this guest, I can see it." If they knew the name and position of this man, they would understand. In fact, they'd be surprised he didn't always travel with security.

"Bronwyn"—Mo's low voice was a rumble in his chest—"are

you saying you don't think this guest brought security because he wanted to? But that someone made him bring dear old Bob?"

Bronwyn didn't want to believe it, but the press had been relentless over the past few months. This guest needed the respite, and it had surprised Bronwyn that his personal security was staying with him on this trip. Could someone have blackmailed him or influenced him to bring a security guard he didn't want or need? "It's possible."

"I know you don't like giving up info on your guests, but do you consider this Bob to be a guest?" Gray's tone was clear. He didn't want her to consider him as a guest.

"Yes." Bronwyn wouldn't budge on this. "My hands are tied."

"Mine aren't."

She looked up at Mo, and his smile was mischievous, but also a little bit predatory.

"As someone who has not yet signed any NDAs or received any compensation from The Haven, I am under no legal obligation to keep my observations to myself. In fact, out of the goodness of my heart, I'm willing to do the legwork on this individual and share my findings with the Gossamer Falls Police Department. Pro bono."

"That would be most magnanimous of you, Mr. Quinn." Gray was clearly trying for serious, but his grin ruined the solemnity of his words.

"Give me a few hours." Mo was confident, and he was right to be. She suspected he could hack into any system he wanted. It was good for all of them that he did his best to stay on the side of the angels.

Mo pulled his arm away from her shoulders and leaned forward, resting his elbows on his knees. "I need to fill you all in on what I found. Bronwyn already knows."

All silliness vanished from the atmosphere.

"Let me start by saying that I've only scratched the surface, and if I wasn't so tired, I would still be in my house working. But Aunt Carol threatened to put me under medical house arrest if I didn't stay off my computer until tomorrow. She indicated she would physically sit in my house to keep me away from screens. And she threatened to tell Mom and Dad that I'd been defying her orders."

Bronwyn loved Aunt Carol so much, and she understood why no one questioned Mo's decision to do as she said. They were all a little afraid of her. Not as Aunt Carol. Aunt Carol was warm and loving. But Dr. Shaw? Dr. Shaw took no prisoners.

Mo reached for her hand, and she slid hers into his. It felt like it had always belonged there.

Mo blew out a breath. "Someone with access to The Haven's accounts has been blackmailing a congress member and a state senator from North Carolina and possibly another one from Georgia. They've used The Haven to launder the money, and it's a real issue. But I suspect that money has become a smaller part of the blackmail."

"Doesn't it usually work the other way around?" Cal asked. "They ask for more and more?"

"Oh, they're asking. But now they're asking for something other than money. I think there may be judicial tampering at play." The words crept through their circle like a suffocating fog.

"Steven," Landry whispered the name.

"Yes."

Bronwyn was glad Cassie and Donovan weren't with them tonight. Steven Pierce, her own no-good criminal of a cousin, had tried to have Cassie killed. And he had succeeded in having one of his drug-dealing partners killed. It was a mess.

He was in jail in another city in North Carolina, still awaiting justice because his attorneys had somehow managed to get multiple delays. It hadn't made sense to her before. Why would they want to keep him in jail longer? Wouldn't his attorneys try to move the case through the courts faster?

The case was open and shut. It was hard to argue when the person who was kidnapped knew the kidnapper and the drug dealer and recognized them both. When Steven finally went to trial, he should be convicted, unless they found a way to rig the system.

Mo tapped the arm of his chair. "The payments became noticeably smaller after Steven's arrest."

"It has to be his mom then, right?" Meredith's comment started a stream of suggestions and theories, and Mo let them go for a few minutes.

Steven's mom had been convinced that her precious baby could never do anything so horrible as to deal drugs or kill people. Not her Stevie. She'd been a passionate mother in public and an unhinged shrew in private.

Then Mo blew out a sharp whistle, and everyone went quiet.

"There's more." He gave Bronwyn's hand a squeeze. "Again, I'm not done digging, but if I had to take what I currently have to court, I would have no choice but to testify that the person behind the blackmail and potential jury tampering was Bronwyn."

No one spoke for a long second. And then everyone spoke at once.

Mo leaned back and pulled Bronwyn with him. "I'm sorry," he murmured in her ear. "I wanted to get to the bottom of it before we had to tell them anything."

"It's okay." She rested her head on his chest and waited for the tumult to die down.

She couldn't make out much of what they were saying, but the general sense of outrage and disbelief comforted her battered spirit. As did the arm around her and the hand holding hers.

She wasn't alone. She didn't have to fight this alone.

And they believed in her.

THIRTY-THREE

Mo went to bed that night in his own house and without looking at a computer screen. As much as he was itching to dig deeper into Bob and Peter Brown and the corruption and blackmail at The Haven, his body screamed for sleep. His head hurt. His eyes hurt. His entire body ached.

His heart, however, was . . . not hurting, but it was not content either.

Bronwyn was staying with Meredith tonight. And they were close enough for him not to worry about her safety as they slept.

But he had so many other things to worry about.

He'd long ago given up on any true resolution with Bronwyn. On the rare occasions he allowed himself to think about it with any kind of hope, he assumed it would be months, maybe even years, before they found any kind of equilibrium. He'd been prepared for weeks of awkward interactions, stilted conversations, and ultimately, a lifetime of regret.

But she'd kissed him. And he'd kissed her.

Everyone was treating them like a couple.

But he had no idea what they were.

Before he went horizontal, he knelt by his bed. "Lord, I got nothing. No clue. Really?" He stayed there until he realized he'd nodded off. "Sorry about that, Lord. Where was I? Oh yeah. I can't do this. I want her. And I'm terrified of her. Or of what she could do to me."

He slid under the quilt without more words. His faith had taken a nosedive in the years after Bronwyn's departure. It wasn't that he didn't believe in God anymore. But he'd felt betrayed by both him and Bronwyn, and the journey back to a place where he could trust God with much of anything had been a long one.

Over the past few years, he'd seen things he simply couldn't attribute to anything other than God's hand. And now he had no trouble laying his burdens before God, leaving them there, and going to sleep. He and God both knew he'd do his best to pick them up and carry them for himself in the morning.

What he hadn't expected was for the morning not to come until 11:30 a.m.

He woke up slowly, and when he reached for the phone by his bedside and saw the time, he dropped it on his chest and groaned.

Then he took stock. His body still hurt, but the headache was gone. His mind was clearer than it had been in days. And once he got some coffee in him, he expected he'd be able to tackle the computer searches he desperately needed to finish.

His need to clear Bronwyn's name, protect her from her family, and stake some kind of claim that would let everyone know that she was his all swirled through him and drove him to roll out of bed and rush through his morning routine far faster than he normally would.

The sun was shining, the air was warm, and Bronwyn sat on Meredith's small front porch. She wore a tank top and shorts, her wet hair was twisted into a messy bun, and her bare feet were propped up on the railing. As he walked toward her, he could see that she had a coffee in hand, eyes closed, and a makeup-free face lifted to the sun.

She must have heard him when he walked outside, but she didn't so much as twitch when he stepped onto the porch. But when he stopped in front of her, blocking the sunshine from falling on her body, her eyebrows rose, even though her eyes stayed closed. "You're messing with my vitamin D absorption."

He couldn't stop himself from reaching for her. He cradled her face in his hand and brushed her bottom lip with his thumb. "You're so beautiful."

He didn't make any move to come closer. Would she pull away? Would she reject what was unquestionably an advance?

Her eyelids fluttered open, and her smile was soft. "I wasn't sure if you'd still think so today. Yesterday was . . . a lot."

"It was." She leaned into his hand, and he found a few more words. "What are *you* thinking today?"

She reached up and pressed her hand to his. "If you haven't booked a flight to Spitsbergen, then I'd say today has promise."

"Spitsbergen?"

"Norway."

He tilted her head up, and she let him.

She didn't break eye contact, but her breathing sped up. "It's a . . . small island."

He leaned toward her.

"Very cold." Her voice was barely a whisper.

"Bronwyn?"

"Hmm?"

"Can I kiss you?"

Her eyes flashed. "You'd better."

He rested his free hand on the arm of the chair and narrowed the distance between them without breaking eye contact. He paused a breath away from her mouth, giving her one more second to change her mind.

Her arms reached around his neck and pulled him to her. She started the kiss, and for a few seconds, his brain short-circuited in a heady mix of shock, awe, delight, and bone-deep certainty that he would never kiss anyone else.

She was it for him. She always had been. She always would be.

He adjusted his stance and pulled her to her feet and then he was kissing her with all the emotions and dreams and longings he'd kept buried deep inside.

When they broke apart, he held her in his arms and rested his forehead against hers, gratified that her breathing was as erratic as his.

"Mo?"

"Hmm?"

She didn't say anything, and he didn't press her. She'd talk when she was ready. And he'd listen. For now, he was content to listen to her heartbeat. Sometimes nonverbal communication did the job just fine.

At some point, she pulled in a deep breath, leaned back, and took his face in her hands. "Good morning."

He knew he had a goofy grin plastered on his face and he didn't care. "I think we should make it a point to say good morning like this every day."

She ducked her head and bit her bottom lip. "I'd like that."

"Then it's a deal."

She stepped back, but instead of pulling away from him, she slid her hand down his arm, then laced her fingers through his. "Come inside and have some decent coffee. Then let's talk about what we need to do today."

Bronwyn wasn't sure what had gotten into her. She'd spent most of the morning staring at Mo's house, wondering what would happen when he woke up and she had to face him. Instead of talking to him like a rational adult, she'd flirted shamelessly, kissed him, and clung to him after the kiss had made her too dizzy to stand on her own.

She didn't remember his kisses being quite so . . . potent. She grabbed a dish towel off Meredith's counter and fanned herself.

She needed to stop thinking about kissing Mo and focus on surviving the day. In her spare time, she needed to do all she could to keep everyone alive and not dwell on the fact that if Mo couldn't figure out who was behind the blackmail, she might not have a job anymore.

She poured a cup of coffee and added cream, then handed it to Mo. He took it with a quizzical look on his face.

"What?"

He took a sip. "This is perfect."

"Don't sound so surprised."

"How did you know how to make it?"

She refreshed her own mug. "Paying attention to what people like is kind of my job." She slid the carafe back onto its base. "Although I will admit that I don't generally remember how people like their coffee."

"So, what? I'm a special case?" He didn't sound like he minded that idea at all.

"Maybe." She was flirting again. This had to stop. She opened the fridge door and peered inside. "Meredith has no food. Do you think it's safe for us to go into town? Maybe grab a pizza from Lionel? Oh, and my ice cream. I need to pick up my ice cream. And—"

"Bronwyn?"

She closed the refrigerator a little harder than she'd intended and everything inside rattled. She leaned against it. "Oops."

Mo studied her. "Are you okay?"

"Of course I'm okay," she said in a voice a full octave higher than her usual pitch. She cleared her throat to try again. "Right as rain. Fit as a fiddle. Why do you ask?"

Mo shrugged. "No reason." A smile tugged at his lips.

He took her hand and pulled her along, out of Meredith's home and toward his. "What are you doing?"

"Fixing you lunch."

Mo opened the door to his house, and Bronwyn stepped in for the first time. His tiny home was laid out just like Cal's. There was a narrow staircase on one wall that led to a loft. His kitchen was small but functional. But where Cal's place had a sofa and a small but functional living space, Mo had . . . a desk.

A massive desk filled the space. Four computer monitors sat angled around a chair that looked like it had given inspiration to the designers of a space opera. A cozy chair with a soft blanket, a small ottoman, and a reading lamp were the only concession to comfort or relaxation.

The space was all Mo.

And it was all wrong.

He waved a hand around the room. "Make yourself at home. There's a chair." He opened his refrigerator and pulled out two glass casserole dishes. "We have options. Chicken supreme or lasagna. Which do you want?"

"Chicken supreme, please," she answered without looking. She was too busy studying his decor. Photos lined the wall. Each one had a modern feel, the subject matter was eclectic, and they were all in black and white.

The sound of spoons on glass filled the air as Mo filled plates and slid them into the microwave. "It would taste better if we heated it up in the oven, but I'm getting antsy."

So was she. But she'd bet it wasn't for the same reason. Everything she saw was monotone. Black, white, and every shade of gray.

Was this how Mo lived? All day long, in front of computer screens, in a tiny space devoid of anything bright?

And then, on the refrigerator, she saw a splash of color. Wild, vibrant, completely chaotic. She recognized the artist, and once she saw it, she noticed more evidence of the artist's touch. A potholder in a garish neon orange. A frame on the desk with pressed leaves inside. Another frame held a collage of photos with Mo and the artist. Their smiles lit the room and soothed the ache in her chest. A small vase with a few lumps, the hallmark of a novice potter, held a bold red poppy made with Meredith's signature style.

"You've been in the dark too long, Mo." The words were out before she could censor herself.

"Yeah. Eliza has made it her mission to add color to my house. I don't care, really. Or, I didn't care. I didn't notice. I was in a fog for a long time. But the first time Eliza was here, she told me it was scary and she didn't like black."

"So you told her she could redecorate." Bronwyn could imagine that conversation.

"Not exactly." Mo pointed to the pictures on his fridge. "I told her I'd put up anything as long as she made it. There was a stretch where she got a little aggressive with it. I had to put a limit on the number of drawings I could display. We agreed that the fridge could be a rotating installation. I have all previous drawings in a book in my room."

He pointed to the bathroom. "I did let her redecorate the bathroom. She's her mother's daughter. There's art in her soul."

Bronwyn peeked into the small room and laughed. "I'd spend all my time in here." The palette was gentle but masculine. Pale blue on the walls. A boldly patterned bath rug in front of the shower. Multihued towels on the racks. The space was cohesive and bright.

"She's trying to convince me to let her do the rest of the space. She and Abby are working on me."

"What are you waiting on?"

He grinned. "Their design portfolio. They've been working on it since school let out. I've not been allowed to look, but Cal says it's something."

"Is that a good something or a 'be afraid' something?"

"Probably both." Mo's laughter eased the final knot of tension from her chest. He pulled glasses from his small cupboard and poured iced tea for both of them. "But back to your point—yes, I was in the dark too long." His eyes held hers. "The light is a much better place to be."

She picked up the vase from the desk and held it. "I'm sorry, Mo. You were never broody and moody . . . before . . ."

He came around the counter, returned the vase to his desk, and put his hands around her waist. "Okay. Let's get it all out. I'm not saying we'll never talk about it again, but let's rip this Band-Aid off. I left town for the summer and when I came home, you were gone. And yes, it nearly destroyed me."

She refused to look away. She'd done this. She would own it. But she couldn't stop the tears burning at the backs of her eyes.

"You were manipulated and used, and it nearly destroyed you."

He wasn't wrong, but, "I have to take responsibility for what I did."

He brushed at a tear that broke loose. "Okay. Fine. You take responsibility for what you did at sixteen. I'll take responsibility for what I did on a busy city street before I was deployed and then what I did again when Mom was in the hospital a few years later."

"I don't blame you."

"You should." He pressed a finger to her lips when she tried to argue. "It isn't healthy to ignore the past. When you do that, it comes back to bite you." His hand fell to her arm. "But it isn't healthy to live in the past either. I spent too long dwelling there, stewing in the hurt and the anger. That's on me, Bronwyn. You didn't do that. We all choose how we want to handle the hard things. I chose to be a jerk. I chose to lash out at others. I became the poster child for 'hurt people hurt people' and I was miserable."

He pressed his forehead to hers. "And then one day, this little girl showed up. And my scraggly self scared her. She was five years old, and she didn't know me from before, the way my cousins did. My family saw me as my hair grew and my attitude darkened, and they accepted me. But this little sweetheart wasn't sure that I was safe."

"She didn't know—"

"She was five and she reacted to the external." Mo pointed to the pictures on his desk of him with Eliza. "It didn't take me long to win her over. But what she may never know is how much seeing myself through her eyes helped me realize how self-absorbed I'd become. I've done a lot of self-reflection, therapy, prayer, and hard conversations with Cal and Meredith. I'm not the same person I was. But the darkness isn't so far removed that it doesn't show up from time to time."

"I didn't know."

"I didn't tell you."

"I wouldn't let you."

"It wouldn't have mattered." Mo pressed a kiss to her forehead. "For whatever reason, our time wasn't then."

Bronwyn dared to look him in the eyes when she asked, "Do you think it's our time now?"

Mo didn't hesitate. "I want it to be."

"So do I."

"We'll mess up."

"Of course we will."

"But I won't shut you out when you try to talk to me about hard things." Mo crossed his heart, then reached down, took her hand, and pressed a kiss to one knuckle. "And I'll let you replace my coffee." A kiss to the next knuckle. "And I'll figure out who is behind the money mess at The Haven." Another knuckle, another kiss. "And I'll be nice to your parents." His face grew serious. "But I won't lie to you about the fact that I don't like them."

"Fair enough." She didn't like them much either.

He reached for her other hand and repeated the same procedure. "I will tell you you're beautiful every day. I'll continue to work with June to be sure you eat enough, and when this mess is resolved, I'll date you the way we should have dated in our teens. We'll go to the movies, and you can whisper all the secrets about the stars. I'll go for hikes with you so you can take photos of random tiny flowers on the trail, and every night, I'll tell you how lucky I am that you gave me another chance."

Mo's hands slid to her upper arms and squeezed. "I'm not telling you all this to try to force you to reciprocate. This isn't a 'define the relationship' conversation. Our relationship defies definition. It always has. What this is, is me giving you the good and the bad."

"I didn't hear any bad."

"That's because I'm not done."

"Oh."

"I won't lie to you. I won't pretend with you. I'll give you my authentic self, and as you may have noticed, that's no prize because my true self is messy and sometimes dark. Most importantly, I won't hide us from anyone."

Oh. Oh . . .

Mo tilted her chin so she was looking up at him. "You can have as long as you need to think about it. But if we're doing this, we're doing it in the open."

"Mo?"

"Yes?"

"Can I talk now?"

"Sorry. Of course."

"What exactly are we doing?"

He took a deep breath. "I'm not sure what you're doing, but I'm falling in love with you. Or maybe I'm remembering that I've always been in love with you and now I'm figuring out what that looks like."

She should have said something romantic and epic. What she said was, "Okay. Good."

"Good?" One eyebrow crept up. "All of that, and you say, 'Good'?"

"Well, yeah. It would have been awkward if you were thinking that we're starting from scratch and you didn't know where we might be headed when I'm over here thinking that we're . . . well . . ." She choked on the word. Her courage evaporated. Her skin heated. Her heart beat so fast, she was afraid she might look like one of those cartoon characters whose heart juts five feet out of their chest.

Mo's lips brushed her forehead. "Now that's cruel. Don't leave me standing here, desperate to know what you think we are." His lips danced across her ear. "You can tell me anything."

"You're a menace." Seriously. She could barely stand up.

His lips flitted over her cheekbones. "What are we, Bronwyn?"

There was no hesitation. "Forever."

Mo's arms wrapped around her and pulled her tight against him, and it was only then that she realized this man she'd loved her entire life was trembling against her. His reaction gave her the courage to rise on her tiptoes and press a series of kisses to his jaw. "Mine. Always. Forever." Then she gave him more of the truth. "Also, I'm terrified. I'm terrified of what I feel for you. Terrified of what it means to give in to this. Terrified that we'll mess it up and the pain will be a thousand times worse. But I'm choosing you, anyway. I'm choosing the person you are today. The person I know you to be. Your character. Your heart. Your determination. Your vulnerability. Your promise to tell me the truth. I'm choosing all of that. And I'm still afraid."

He held her for a long moment. She had no regrets about what she'd said. It was all true. But she did wish he'd say something.

He rubbed her back and spoke in a contemplative tone. "One thing I've learned about fear—you can't logic your way out of it, but sometimes you can experience your way out of it." He gave her a squeeze and stepped back. "I'm not sure when it will happen, but it will. One day, you'll wake up and realize you aren't afraid anymore."

THIRTY-FOUR

The sharp *rat-a-tat-tat* on the doorframe startled Mo, and he shoved Bronwyn behind him and pulled his weapon from his waistband in two frantic seconds.

"Yo, Mo! You in there?" Cal was at the door.

Bronwyn sagged against his back, and her arms snaked around his waist. "To be clear, that kind of experience is not helping my fears."

"Mo! Bronwyn!"

"What?" they both yelled back.

Cal knocked again. "I don't want to see anything that will make me need to bleach my eyes. Is it safe to enter?"

Mo slid his gun back into place and jerked the door open. "What are you doing here? Why aren't you at work?"

Cal stood there with his hands on his hips. "Why aren't you answering your phone?" He turned on Bronwyn. "Or you? What's wrong with you two? Everything has gone haywire, and you've fallen off the radar." He tapped on the phone in his hand, then made a phone call.

Mo slid an arm around Bronwyn. "We were busy. What's happened?"

Cal leaned a hand on the doorframe. "Give me a second. I raced over here." He'd put the phone on speaker, and the ringing came through loud and clear.

"Give me good news, Cal." Meredith's barely calm tone sent guilt spearing through Mo.

"Mer, we're fine," Mo said. "What's going on?"

A pause, then, "I'm going to superglue your phone to your hand, you moron. You're never out of touch. Never. And you pick today of all days? What were you doing?"

"I was kissing Bronwyn. A lot." Mo hoped the words would shock the fear out of Meredith.

Cal reached through the door and pulled Bronwyn away from Mo and into a hug.

Meredith, however, was not as easily appeased. "It's taken twenty years to reach this point," her voice came through the phone.

"Not quite that lo—"

"Do not interrupt me, Montgomery Quinn. I am on a very, very thin edge right now. Cassie called. Every Pierce she's ever seen has descended on The Haven. June called her and asked if there was any way she could spare a few of the Hideaway staff to help the breakfast kitchen for an hour or so because they've all settled into the large conference room and started ordering food and drinks."

Bronwyn pulled away from Cal, took the phone from his hand, and jogged toward Meredith's house, telling Meredith something he couldn't make out. Mo looked at Cal, and they took off after her.

"Meredith, I'm handing the phone back to Cal. And I'll call June as soon as I get my phone. Please call Gray and tell him what's happening. We might need law enforcement."

She paused on Meredith's porch, tossed Cal his phone, and focused on Mo. "Please call Cassie."

"On it."

Bronwyn ran inside.

Cal pointed toward his truck. "I'll drive." He sprinted to the driver's side.

Mo didn't argue. He was in no condition to drive. Bronwyn was too distracted to get behind the wheel. And there was no way to keep Cal from coming, regardless.

Bronwyn ran out the door, phone to her ear. Mo took her hand and led her to the passenger seat. As soon as she was in, he closed the door, then climbed in the back of the King Cab.

Cal drove with a focus that Mo appreciated.

Mo dialed Cassie's number, and she answered with a breathless, "Mo, where are you?"

"On my way, sweetheart. Hang in there. Fill me in. I heard that the family is causing a ruckus."

"I'll say. It's chaos over there. I don't know who they think they are!"

"Cassie, they own the place."

"Doesn't matter. The guests come first. Everyone knows that." The sound that came through next was a little bit terrifying given that it was coming from his usually bubbly cousin. "Here's what you need to know. If the food orders are any indication, they're settling in for a siege. Also, June has Marcus standing by, presumably to keep the family safe, but *we* all know it's so he can report back to Bronwyn."

"Smart. I'll tell her."

"Here's the other thing. There's a couple of people who've been here for dinner the past two nights that give me a bad vibe."

"The reporter?"

"Yes. He is creeptastic."

"Agreed. Who else?"

"Security for one of the guests. He says his name is Bob, but there's something off about him." She wasn't wrong about that. "You'll fix this, won't you, Mo?"

"You know it, sweetheart."

"You're the best. Oh . . . Donovan's calling."

"Answer it. Tell him what's going down. Bye."

Mo hung up and leaned over the seat so he could see the conversation Bronwyn was having with June via text.

I can do that.

Hang in there. We're ten minutes out.

Mo looked around. She was right. Cal clearly wasn't worried about getting a speeding ticket.

Bronwyn let the phone drop in her lap.

"What did June say?" he asked.

"William rolled in an hour ago, strolled into the large conference room, told her to prepare for a family meeting, then sat down." She twisted in her seat to face Mo. "She's not sure what's wrong but says he's in there cussing a blue streak."

Mo knew his face gave nothing away. He'd perfected the blank stare when he was in the Army.

But somehow Bronwyn saw through it. "What did you do?"

"What do you mean?"

She laughed. Amid all the chaos and turmoil, her laughter filled the cab of the truck. She reached for him and pulled him toward her. He went as far as the seat belt allowed. She managed to kiss his nose. "What did you do?"

"Both of you quit fooling around. With the way I'm driving, you need to stay in your own seats. It's dangerous to be twisted around like that."

Bronwyn turned around and crossed her hands in her lap. "Sorry, Cal."

Mo continued to lean forward. “I’m not.”

“Are you going to answer her question?” Cal asked. “Seems like she should know what’s up before she walks into chaos.”

“Whose side are you on, man?”

“I’m a neutral party. No. That’s not it.” Cal’s hands tightened on the wheel as he navigated through a tight turn. “I’m on both sides. Except in this. In this, I’m totally on her side.”

“Thanks, Cal.”

His response was a grunt. “He’s probably done something sketchy, and it’s better for him to tell us now so we don’t accidentally incriminate him.”

“Mo?” There was real concern in Bronwyn’s question.

“Hey! You said that to get me in trouble. I’m a white knight. I’m one of the good guys. I don’t do illegal hacks.”

Cal didn’t say anything.

“I did, however, block all access to most of The Haven’s files unless you have the new passcode.”

Bronwyn turned around again. “When?”

“Yesterday, before Aunt Carol threatened me. I wasn’t sure when I could log back into the system, and it seemed prudent.”

“You didn’t pick one of those passcodes my phone is always trying to convince me to use, did you?” Cal honked at a driver who was taking up their half of the middle.

“I did not.”

“Did it ever occur to you that Bronwyn might need to log into the system and, under the circumstances, you might not be around to give her the code? What then?”

“She could figure it out.” He looked at her. “I picked something she would expect.”

“Beep?” Cal asked.

“If it’s what I’m thinking, it’s not that obscure.”

“Not to you. But it would be to them.”

"Is it Catherine's Falls thirteen?" Bronwyn narrowed her eyes at Mo. "No spaces, with the apostrophe, and with the number not spelled out."

"Got it in one."

"How?" Cal's outrage would have been more believable if he hadn't been so obviously impressed.

"It's . . ." Bronwyn stopped. It wasn't a secret. It had been, at the time, but that was a long, long time ago.

Mo squeezed her shoulder. "It's up to you."

"You don't have to tell me. I can guess."

Bronwyn turned back around in time to catch Cal's grin. It could have lit an entire stadium. "You were thirteen when everything changed between you," he said. "And given the way Mo here reacted to that photo at your place, I'm going to go way out on a limb and say whatever changed happened at Catherine's Falls."

"It was innocent." Bronwyn didn't like the way he made it sound . . . scandalous. All they'd done was hold hands.

Cal reached out and patted her knee before returning his hand to the wheel. "I never thought anything else. And I agree with Mo. He chose a password you would come up with but one they never would. It's diabolically brilliant."

"I'm not sure if I should be offended or charmed," Mo said. "The more important issue is that they're trying to hack into the system. And they're doing it very much in the open. What's changed?"

Cal glanced at Bronwyn. "I know privacy is important to you, but there's no way I'm dropping you off and leaving you to your fate. So you might as well bring me up to speed. Are they going to try to vote you out?"

"They may try, but Grandmother, of all people, reminded me

to look at our bylaws, and unless they can prove I'm guilty, they can't get rid of me."

"I thought they could?" Cal took the final turn to The Haven at an alarming speed.

"So did I. And they could have until a few months ago. But I've been there long enough now that they have to have legitimate cause."

"Like tenure?"

"Sort of. It isn't that they can't get rid of me, but it's much, much harder. And I'm not sure they realize it. We could be facing two wildly different scenarios. One is that they think they have to schedule a vote, vote me out, and it's done."

"Is it bad that I'm hoping for that option? Because how fun would it be for you to swoop in there and wave the bylaws at them with a flourish and say, 'Think again.' It has a very superhero-like vibe to it. What's the second scenario?"

"The second is not as much fun. That one is that, regardless of whether they know they need legitimate cause or not, they think they have it. They plan to confront me with 'proof'"—Bronwyn made air quotes when she said the word—"and use that to either oust me or bring me to heel."

"I definitely like option one." Cal glanced at her. "Front entrance or employee?"

"Front. It's faster."

"On it."

Bronwyn turned in her seat. Mo had gone quiet while she talked. "You okay back there?"

His grunt wasn't particularly reassuring but interrupting whatever he was doing on his phone didn't seem like a good idea.

She leaned around Cal when he rolled to a stop at the gate. The security guard, Klaus, stepped forward. When he saw her, his eyes widened. "Ms. Pierce."

"Anything I need to know?"

"Security is on alert throughout the resort. Guests are unaware of anything unusual."

"Thank you."

He pressed the button that opened the gate and gave her a small salute.

"Klaus is a good one." The typing didn't stop, but Mo kept talking. "He has a solid background."

Was that information for her or Cal? Maybe both.

"Anyone I need to be wary of?" Cal pulled through the gate and floored it.

"Anyone with the last name Pierce." Mo reached forward and squeezed her shoulder. "Sorry, but it's true," he said. "I won't risk your life to spare your feelings."

"I know. And you're right."

Mo settled back in his seat. "Here's what I know for sure. William has committed some crimes. Nathan may or may not be complicit. Grandmother Pierce is on Bronwyn's side at the moment, but her loyalty is unpredictable. Bronwyn's parents are too weak to be counted on to do anything right, including standing up for their own child. It's possible there's blackmail involved, but I can't say for sure."

Mo's head appeared between Bronwyn and Cal as he leaned forward again. "Peter Brown is not a reporter for anyone, and if you see him, assume he's dangerous. As for Bob, he looks clean as far as I can tell. But I'm not sure enough of that to take any chance with him."

"What's our role here?" Cal pulled into a space and put the truck in park.

"We're Bronwyn's muscle. She can handle these people better than we ever could. We're just backup."

"You aren't *just* anything." Bronwyn corrected Mo. "Never *just*."

Mo's smile was a thing of galaxies and waterfalls. Wondrous to behold. Breathtaking to witness.

"Game faces." Cal barked the command in his most Marine voice.

To her surprise, Mo's face sharpened, and his salute was crisp. "Yes, sir. Let's go."

Bronwyn stared at the cars in the office parking area. "My parents are here. So is Uncle William. Uncle Ronald. Nathan. Beatrice. Candy. Oh good grief, Aunt Luna is here." She looked at Mo. "I honestly don't know if any of them are on my side."

"Well, we are." Mo grinned at her.

"Then let's go." Bronwyn waited for Mo and Cal to join her before she walked into the main office building.

June stood when Bronwyn walked in. She was usually pale, but today her cheeks and neck were flushed a bright pink. June was furious.

"Ms. Pierce." Her voice was calm. "Could I provide you and your guests a beverage?"

"No. But thank you."

"June." Mo's low voice wouldn't be picked up by anyone else in the building. "Perhaps you should go visit Cassie. I believe Donovan will be joining her soon."

"I can stay." Her eyes flicked to Bronwyn, confusion, and maybe even a little hurt, evident in her posture. Then she straightened and said, "I want to stay."

"You've done all you can." Mo's voice was gentle. "Above and beyond. Please do this. Go to Cassie. Text me when you're with her. Stay there until we give you the all clear. I don't want you out here alone. Anyone could come through those doors, and I can't leave you to face that. Please help us keep you safe for the next little while. I promise we'll fill you in on everything."

If he hadn't already held her heart, this act would have sealed the deal. How could Bronwyn have ever doubted this man? "He's right. You've done more than enough. Go to Cassie."

"Cal, why don't you go and stay with her and Cassie until Donovan takes over?" Mo suggested. "Then you can come back and stay close in case we need you."

"Sounds good." Cal turned to June. "Let's go."

June wavered for a moment, then grabbed her bag from behind her desk. She pointed to Mo but spoke to Bronwyn. "If he wasn't with you, I'd refuse to go. But I want him to focus on you, not anyone else. So I'll leave. But I'll be back in a heartbeat if you need me."

"Thank you." They waited until June and Cal were out of sight. Then Bronwyn opened the conference room door and entered into chaos.

Every family member who had anything to do with The Haven was present. Her parents sat at one end of the long table. Uncle William and Nathan were at the other. In between were a string of cousins, aunts, and uncles who held various positions from sales to marketing to interior design.

And at least one of them wanted her dead.

THIRTY-FIVE

Mo had never spent much time around the Pierces. But seeing them gathered together, with their faces masked in anger and hostility and their voices raised and furious, made him appreciate his own family more than ever before.

He didn't throw words like *evil* around lightly, but this gathering made his spirit protest. He'd seen stuff. He'd survived stuff. He didn't want to imagine what it would have been like to grow up in this family.

Mo schooled his expression. He wouldn't give away his reaction. But how was it possible that Bronwyn had turned out to be so very different? What was the key to her beauty, grace, and inner light?

And how could he ever hold it against her that she'd fled from these people at sixteen? Nothing and no one could have made him stay with them one second longer than necessary. Bronwyn released his hand but, instead of distancing herself, she leaned against his good side and watched the chaos with an air of nonchalance.

If things hadn't been so tense, it would have been amusing to watch the cascade of reactions as her family members realized

Bronwyn was there. That *he* was there. That they were there together.

Within thirty seconds of their arrival, all heated conversation trailed off and everyone stared at them.

"You should be ashamed of yourselves," Bronwyn started. "Grandmother is dying. The doctor gave her less than two weeks to live. And you're in here behaving like ill-bred toddlers. What is wrong with you? I've always known you to be heartless but not thoughtless. Why are you acting like fools?"

"Don't you—" William Pierce had stepped forward, but when he caught Mo's eye, he snapped his mouth closed and stepped back.

That's right, buddy. I've got your number, and I'm not afraid to share it with everyone from your wife to local law enforcement.

An aunt whose name he couldn't remember dove into the breach. "Bronwyn, this meeting doesn't involve you."

"Meeting?" Bronwyn made a show of looking from one face to another. "My, my, Aunt Beatrice, I realize it's been a while since you joined us for a board meeting, but this isn't how we do things. I can't speak for you, but the rest of these people were raised better."

Mo locked his jaw together to keep from snorting. Wow. Aunt Beatrice had not aged well. Everyone knew the woman came from a family of alcoholics and meth users, who were regular occupants of the local jail to this day.

"Enough." Bronwyn's dad, Darrell Pierce, stood. "Why don't we all take a seat and discuss things like the civilized individuals we are." He cocked his head toward Mo. "You can go. This is a family discussion."

"He stays, Father." Bronwyn's grip on his arm tightened.

Darrell narrowed his eyes but didn't dispute Bronwyn's decision.

When everyone except Mo and Bronwyn were seated, Bronwyn

broke the tense silence. "I have no idea what you are all doing here, or why you're behaving in such an unseemly manner. And to be honest, I don't care. I'm here for one reason and that is to discuss the future of The Haven. Since we have the board here, I'll call us to order."

The next few minutes were filled with boring procedural stuff. Mo didn't like how regimented it all felt. It gave off formal business vibes, not family business vibes. Maybe that mattered, maybe it didn't. But it struck him as odd that everything had to be just so before they could even have a conversation.

When the formalities had been observed, Bronwyn looked at the gathered board members. "Let me be clear about three things. First, I am the CEO. I was elected to this position by the members of this board, and in my role as CEO, I have done and will continue to do what is best for The Haven. It is not my job, nor do I have any interest in protecting members of the Pierce family when they act the fool, commit crimes, or generally behave like imbeciles. This family, and I use that word very loosely, is not my job. The Haven is my job."

She paused and looked at each person in turn. No one said anything.

"Second, in my role as CEO, I have put up with a lot of nonsense from members of the Pierce family. That ends today. If you want someone in this position to protect the family, then find someone else to do it. You can try to fire me if you want. I do not care. But know this. If you do manage to get rid of me, this"—she made a sweeping circle—"all goes away. The housekeeping, the laundry, the rubbing shoulders with influential people, the box seats, the private jets, the fancy houses at the beach, the days of doing whatever you want while money magically appears in your bank account? Gone. Done. Why? Because none of you can run this place. And that includes Nathan. He could do a halfway decent job for a while, but I'd give him a year, two tops, before he runs it into the ground."

Again, she looked at everyone. Again, no one spoke.

"Third, let me be clear that I do not care what you think of me. I do not care if you like me because, guess what? I don't like most of you, and I am not afraid of you." This Bronwyn was an avenging angel. A force for good. Wonder Woman, Samwise Gamgee, Lucy Pevensie, Captain America, and Anne Shirley—furious with Gil for calling her "Carrots"—all rolled into one.

"In keeping with my only mission, which is to secure the successful future of The Haven, I have hired Mo Quinn in his professional role as a forensic accountant. There are only a handful of people who could have used Haven funds in an illegal way, and most of them are in this room. Consider yourself on notice. When Mo finds you, and it's only a matter of time before he does, I will expose you. I will prosecute you. I will not hide your indiscretions or take it easy on you."

Bronwyn pressed both hands on the table. "This is not a threat. This is a statement of fact. Anyone found doing anything illegal will be fired, removed from the board, and prohibited from accessing The Haven's grounds. And before you say anything, I checked our bylaws. I am well within my rights as CEO."

"You won't be CEO for long." William's face was a shade of purple that couldn't possibly be healthy.

"Actually, I will." Bronwyn pulled the bylaws from the small file she'd carried in with her. "I'm not sure how many of you have read these lately, but according to recent changes, you can't fire me without cause. And you don't have it. The Haven is financially healthier than it's ever been, and when we root out the corruption, it will be stronger still. You cannot fire me for anything short of gross negligence or criminal conduct, and given that I haven't done anything illegal in a very long time, you have no choice but to get on board with the new way of doing things or find another way to spend your days, because you won't be at The Haven."

Was it possible that the temperature in the room had gone down? Or was it the malevolence emanating from the Pierces as a whole that made the room feel chilled?

Bronwyn waited for the shock to clear and the anger to surface. She expected the hostility to come from Uncle William, but it was Uncle Ronald who spoke up. "We never agreed to any changes to the bylaws. I'm not sure when you got so big for your britches, young lady, but my lawyers will have a field day with this stunt. You'll be removed from the premises by nightfall."

It was a bold statement, given that it was already Friday afternoon.

"Uncle Ronald, I'll be happy to show you the board meeting minutes where changes were made and instituted."

"There's no way I ever agreed to that." Uncle Ronald didn't back down.

"Funny enough, I believe you. However, you did approve the change to the bylaws, as did everyone on the board. The vote was unanimous."

"What?"

"Grandmother Pierce plays the long game."

She could almost see her uncle's brain working, and when his expression went from anger to horror, she smiled. "Yes. Grandmother Pierce has always been a bit of a wild card."

"Explain." Her father's voice cut through the tension. "Bronwyn, what are you talking about?"

"Eighteen months ago, we made a change to the bylaws to

allow for a charitable fund to be created. Grandmother specifically requested it."

Awareness slid through the room. "Yes. And that's the only change we made." Uncle Ronald didn't sound quite as sure as he had just minutes before.

"There was one other."

"No, I distinctly recall that we made changes to two sections to allow for the fund and to allow it to be managed by the CEO." Uncle William looked around the room as if waiting for everyone to agree with him.

"Actually, I have the audio recording of the meeting right here." Bronwyn scrolled to the file on her phone, then hit play.

Bronwyn's voice came through the speaker. "Motion made to change bylaws section four paragraph seven, section six paragraph twelve—"

"And section eight paragraph two," Grandmother Pierce interrupted. "I'll have to tweak that one as well. Any objections?"

Bronwyn hit pause and checked to be sure everyone was following along. Then she hit play again, and they all listened to the unanimous vote. "What's section eight?" Aunt Beatrice asked.

"That would be the section that puts a time limit on the probationary period."

Bronwyn wasn't proud of the fact that she'd failed to read the final section herself a year and a half ago. She'd never dreamed her grandmother would do something so . . . underhanded. But it was clear that no one, including herself, had thought to question it.

"The modifications to the bylaws were handled by the attorneys at Grandmother's direction. At the next board meeting, they were signed by everyone present."

Stunned silence greeted her pronouncement.

Bronwyn tapped her phone screen. "I can play the recording from that meeting if you'd like."

The words that flowed around the table next were less than complimentary.

Uncle William glared at her. "We'll change it. You won't be able to outvote us."

Bronwyn had considered that. "You may want to wait until the investigation into the financial discrepancies is completed, Uncle William."

Behind her, she heard Mo shift. He didn't say anything, but his presence seemed to shake her uncle's resolve.

"One other thing." Bronwyn paused and prepared for the fallout. "I spoke to Grandmother's attorney briefly, and he mentioned something else that has bearing on this matter."

"Let me guess, Grandmother made you queen while she was at it," Aunt Beatrice snarled. "You always were her favorite, even after you nearly took us down when you ran off with that senator's brother."

Bronwyn's body chilled. *Senator's brother? He . . . no . . . He hadn't? What?*

Aunt Beatrice pointed at Uncle William. "You said nothing would blow back on us." She pointed at Uncle Ronald. "And you said it would turn out to be a good thing for the family in the long run."

Bronwyn regretted the decision to stay standing for this meeting. She desperately wished for a chair to hold her up and a table to block her trembling hands from view.

Aunt Beatrice patted her chest. "I told you we should distance ourselves from everything associated with that family, but you said we couldn't afford to alienate them." She aimed her finger back at Uncle William.

She flung a hand at Bronwyn. "And now, this little strumpet has us all dancing to her tune. We're going to lose everything."

"Shut up, Beatrice." Uncle Ronald stood. "All of you, shut up." He turned to Bronwyn. "What, exactly, did the attorney tell you?"

Bronwyn struggled to remember what Uncle Ronald was referring to. Oh. Right. "Grandmother made changes to her will."

Uncle Ronald sat down. Hard.

Uncle William got to his feet. "I move to conclude this meeting and reconvene on Monday."

Her father stood. "I second the motion."

Bronwyn lifted her chin. "A motion to end the meeting and reconvene on Monday at one p.m. All in favor?"

Everyone said, "Aye."

But she still asked, "Anyone opposed?"

No one spoke.

"We'll reconvene on Monday at one."

Bronwyn turned and left the room. Mo was right behind her, and when his hand took hers, she laced her fingers through his and held on for dear life.

THIRTY-SIX

Bronwyn didn't speak until she and Mo were back in the small conference room. She leaned against the table and dropped her head.

Mo rubbed her back in slow circles. "That was amazing."

She couldn't speak.

"Hey." He pulled her arms from the table and wrapped them around his waist.

She sank into the hug. She needed this moment before she ripped the scab off their oldest and deepest wound.

"What's going on?" When she didn't move, his tone changed. "Hey, baby? What's this? What did I miss?" She tried to pull away, but he didn't release her. "Talk to me."

"I . . ." How could she do this? "Peter Brown and . . . the senator . . . I remember."

"Tell me when you're ready."

She didn't think she'd ever be ready. But once she started, the words tumbled out. "The senator's brother. I didn't know Corbin was the senator's brother."

"He can't hurt you anymore, Bronwyn. He's been dead for close to a decade."

"I know. But I didn't know he was the senator's brother. Peter

Brown. I knew I'd seen him before. He was younger, had different hair, and he was with the senator when he stayed here. He has to know, Mo. He knows about . . . everything."

She expected him to go quiet. Or to get angry.

"I gathered the lot of them knows more than they ever let on, the morons. It's a good thing you have a real family now. You won't ever be hung out to dry again."

She sagged against him. "I know you don't want to talk about . . ."

"I will never be able to think about that whole situation without having to fight down my rage. But don't ever, not for a second, think that even a drop of anger is directed at you." He pressed a kiss to her forehead. "Trust me."

Bronwyn took a deep breath and steeled herself for the coming confession. "When I saw him, he was going by the name Glen Masters, and he was the security chief for Senator Carlsman."

"Senator Clayton Carlsman who everyone thinks will run for president?"

"The same."

Mo swallowed hard. "And this Senator Carlsman was Corbin's brother, and you didn't know?"

"No clue." Her own fury raged. "My family knew Corbin was Senator Carlsman's brother and never told me so they could keep having him come and stay at The Haven. My own parents . . ."

A soft knock on the door pulled her back to the present.

"It's me." Cal's voice came through the door.

"Come in," Mo called, without turning her loose.

Cal slipped in and closed the door behind him. "Sorry to interrupt. It looked like your uncles and your dad were going to come to blows in the parking lot. I suggested they take it off the property."

Mo resumed rubbing small circles on her back. "Did they?"

"It took a little bit of encouragement." Cal gave Mo a look

that didn't show up on his face often. "I may have indicated that I have arrest authority."

"You do not."

"I didn't say I did." Cal shrugged. "It's not my fault if they made assumptions."

Bronwyn forced herself to step back from Mo. "Did they leave?"

"They did. And Brick happened to be parked outside the gate, and he followed them."

Bronwyn had a bad feeling about this. "Where did they go?"

"To your grandmother's."

Cal and Mo exchanged a look but neither said anything.

"Even on her deathbed, Grandmother can handle them. I've had all I can handle of the Pierces today." She turned to Mo. "Take me home?"

"Of course."

A few minutes later, Cal climbed behind the wheel, but Mo slid in beside her in the back of the cab. Cal turned around and asked, "Where to?"

Mo answered, "My house."

Cal started the truck and drove off The Haven grounds. No one spoke for the first several miles. "Mo?" Cal said.

"Yeah."

"What do you need?"

"I need you to stay in touch with Gray and Marcus. I'm going to be deep in the files, but I don't want to be out of the loop."

"You got it. Bronwyn, what about you?"

What did she need? There were too many things for her to narrow down.

Cal caught her eye in the rearview mirror. "Ice cream?"

"Ice cream would be great, but I can't take from a pregnant woman. That's criminal."

He laughed. "My beautiful wife made a run to the store while we were out. Lionel restocked. She bought five pints."

"I love your wife."

"So do I. If I haven't mentioned it lately, thanks for bringing her and my daughter to Gossamer Falls. I owe you."

"I'll take ice cream as payment."

"Excellent." Cal lapsed into silence, and Bronwyn dropped her head to Mo's shoulder.

They rode that way until Cal pulled to a stop beside Meredith's 4Runner and a 1965 Ford Mustang. Bronwyn knew next to nothing about cars. But she knew that Mustang.

Doug and Jacque sat with Meredith by the firepit.

Cal turned in the driver's seat. "Give them my love. I'm going home for a few minutes. I'll be back."

Mo climbed from the truck and Bronwyn followed him. He took her hand, and they walked toward the firepit.

It was awkward for all of three seconds. Then Jacque hopped to her feet and ran to them. Doug wasn't far behind. Soon Bronwyn was surrounded by hugs and kisses and warmth and concern.

At some point, they disentangled themselves for one-on-one hugs. Jacque pulled Bronwyn close and whispered, "I'm so happy to see you, sweetheart."

Then Doug pulled her away and pressed a kiss to her forehead. "Come here, darling girl." Everyone in the family talked about Mo's hugs. He'd learned his technique from his dad. Doug squeezed her tight, then stooped to look into her eyes. "I'm only going to say this one time, so I want you to listen good."

Bronwyn nodded.

"If things don't work out with you and Mo, that will be hard on all of us, but it will not mean you lose me or Jacque. You got that?"

The tears she'd fought for days streamed down her face. "Yes, sir."

He pulled her in for another hug. "But do give him a chance, okay?"

That made her laugh through the tears.

"Dad! What did you say to her?" Mo pulled her away from his dad and tucked her protectively under his arm. "You're supposed to be Team Bronwyn."

"I am, son." He winked at her. "All the way. Just making sure she knew that."

"Come over here and fill us in on what happened." Meredith waved at them from the firepit. "Gray won't tell me anything, but you can."

They spent the next thirty minutes filling in the two people who'd done the most to teach Bronwyn what parents were supposed to be. When Mo got to the part about Corbin and the senator, Jacque Quinn lost her cool. She stood up and stomped around the firepit for a full minute.

All Bronwyn could understand of her words were "can't believe" and "should have known," and "but who would ever?" and several occurrences of, "I'm going to give Lacey Pierce a piece of my mind."

"Mom, when you go talk to her, please, I beg of you, let me wire you with a camera. Please."

Jacque shook her head at her son. "Oh no, Mo. When I finally say what I need to say, it would be best if there's no documentation."

Bronwyn soaked up the love for the next ten minutes until Doug and Jacque left with promises of Sunday lunch and admonitions that they keep them informed, particularly if anyone got shot again.

Mo watched his parents drive away. Meredith tucked her arm in his. "We hit the jackpot in the parent lottery."

"We sure did."

"I'm going to change clothes." She was still in her work scrubs. "Holler if you need me."

After Meredith left, Mo studied Bronwyn as she sat by the firepit. She looked like someone who'd lost a puppy and had been given a new one on the same day. Grief and joy comingled.

Her eyes met his. He pointed to his house. "I'm going to do what I do."

"I'm going to sit by the river for a few minutes."

He didn't stop her when she walked away from him. He couldn't keep her tied to his side 24/7. Although the idea did have some merit.

He went inside and dove into the world of Senator Carlsman, his brother, and Glen Masters—aka Peter Brown.

Three hours later, he looked up to see Bronwyn asleep in his chair. He didn't remember her coming in. It was almost dark outside, and he was tempted to let her sleep.

But he had answers. Well, partial answers. The rest of what he needed was at The Haven. There'd be no sleep for him until he got what he needed.

He stood, stretched, and walked to her chair. "Bronwyn?"

She made a small sound, shifted, and went still again.

"Bronwyn, baby, we need to go back to your place."

She cracked an eye open. "Why?"

"Because I need access to the main server."

She opened both eyes. "You figured it out?"

"If you hadn't made the connection between Peter Brown and Senator Carlsman, I never would have known where to look. That was the missing piece. Once I had that, everything else fell into place."

She blinked several times. "Okay. Let's go."

It took thirty precious minutes to get everything he needed packed, the files saved, and details sent to Gray. He didn't tell Bronwyn that he was doing all this in case something happened to them before he could share his findings.

They got into his Jeep and drove toward The Haven. Mo kept his head on a swivel. They made it to the front gates without any issues. Klaus stepped out from the guard house with his business face on. Mo rolled down his window and Klaus peered inside. "Good to have you back, ma'am," he said to Bronwyn. "Should I arrange for a key card to be made for Mr. Quinn?"

"Yes." Bronwyn leaned over from the passenger side. "And program his vehicles into the system as well. Full access."

"I'll get right on that." Klaus stepped back inside, and the gates opened.

"Does this mean I can come into The Haven grounds anytime I want?" Mo asked as they drove through.

"It does."

Bronwyn might not have seen it, but for Mo, this was a big step of trust. "Thank you."

She sighed. "It's not much of a prize."

"Sure it is. This is some of the most beautiful acreage in North Carolina. To be able to come here whenever I want is a gift. Not to mention that you have a few waterfalls I haven't seen since you snuck me onto the grounds when we were fifteen."

Finally, a smile. "We had fun, didn't we?"

"We did. Bet we'll have even more fun now."

"Are you going to tell me what you found?"

"As soon as I have it. I'm so close."

"You told Gray."

"No, I sent Gray an encrypted file and instructions about who will be able to access it. He won't be able to make any sense out of it without Sabrina's help."

Beside him, Bronwyn sat straighter. "Sabrina?"

"You sound jealous." Mo took Bronwyn's hand and brought it to his lips. "To be clear, I like it."

She scoffed. "I'm not . . . okay. Maybe a little. Jealous sounds too vindictive though. Curious is a better word."

"Curious with a side of 'that girl better not have ever dated you' is what it sounds like to me."

She cut her eyes at him. "That sounds about right." Her tone was frosty.

"Sabrina Fleming-Campbell is one of the nation's leading computer forensic experts. She can also hack anything. She teaches at UNC–Carrington. Our paths have crossed quite a few times. I think the world of her."

"Huh."

Funny how one sound could hold so much hostility. Although maybe it was too soon to mess with Bronwyn this way. "She's happily married. With two kids and a husband who believes he's the luckiest man in the world."

"She sounds lovely." Bronwyn's tone had softened. A little.

"She is. And I trust her completely. She's the one who got me the facial recognition info about Peter Brown and told me that he also goes by Glen Masters. I had no idea you would recognize that name."

"Is that legal? Because we need everything to be legal, Mo."

He nodded. "She knows we're in the thick of a serious situation. She'll have everything documented."

"Wait a minute. Why would Gray need this stuff when you don't have it finalized? Do you think something's going to happen?"

"I think we're in the deep end, and we need to be sure we take all necessary precautions."

"Okay. I trust you. What's our next step?"

"I think it's time to check out your servers."

"Yeah, so . . . I don't know much about that."

"Do you know how to give me access?"

"Of course. I know where everything is. We paid a small fortune for a secure system." She made a sound in the back of her throat. "And my stupid relatives still managed to sneak in there and make a mess of it."

"We're going to fix it. And then we're going to set up a new system, and we're going to have it monitored so heavily that no one will dare play a game of solitaire unless they've been given written permission."

Bronwyn bit down on her lip. "I don't want to do that to my people."

"I'm kidding. Kind of." He hadn't been, really.

"No you weren't."

"Okay. Fine. They can play solitaire. But you'll know how much time they're spending on it." She didn't look convinced, so he added, "You don't really want to pay people to play games, do you?"

"It depends. My night desk clerk needs something to keep herself awake. I'd rather pay her to play solitaire than to sleep. Now, if we're talking about the security guards, they'd better not be playing solitaire. But if Juniper wants to play a game while she's waiting on me to finish a meeting, I don't care."

"Juniper?"

"June. Her full name is Juniper, but she thinks it sounds too hippie."

"I'm so glad I know this. Did they name her after the prickly bushes around here or the tree in the Bible?"

"I have no idea."

"I'm going to ask her."

"Mo, you can't. She'll strangle me for telling you."

He winked at her.

"You weren't serious?" she asked.

"Of course not."

She shook her head, a slight smile on her lips. "You're very good at distracting me."

"You were getting a little tense."

"I'm still tense."

"Yeah, but now it's about Juniper and not about your relatives."

She gave him a sour look. "And now I'm back to thinking about them."

He parked in front of her office. "They're going to be hard to avoid. We have to take breaks when we can."

He jogged to her side of the Jeep and opened the door. "Lead the way, my lady."

He followed her into the quiet office building. She scanned them in, then spoke to the security guard and told him where they were going so he wouldn't sound any alarms if he saw them on the cameras.

Bronwyn opened the door to the server room, but Mo didn't immediately walk inside. She stood slightly behind him. Then she leaned against him. "Mo, I'm not sure if you know this, but this equipment can't talk."

"That's what you think." Then he entered the room.

He studied the layout. He estimated it was 20'x20', which was larger than it needed to be, but he wasn't surprised. Bronwyn thought ahead, and this room had several rows of empty server cabinets that would be needed in the future.

The space was well designed, well ventilated, and well protected. Hardware wasn't his area of expertise, but he liked what he saw. There were cameras in the corners of the room, but based on what he knew about security at The Haven, he suspected that William, Ronald, Nathan, or—he truly hoped not—Bronwyn's father could have paid someone to look the other way while they removed files from the main server.

Mo took three minutes to walk around the space and orient himself. Each server was labeled. "Who did all this?"

Bronwyn named a company out of Charlotte. A good one. "Has anyone made changes in here since they set everything up?"

She bit her lip. "Not to my knowledge, but . . ."

Mo found the server he was looking for and plugged his laptop into it. It took him ten minutes to be sure the data he'd been looking for was downloading.

"Can you explain what you've found?"

Mo glanced at the cameras. "When we get back to your place."

"Okay."

It had to be infuriating for her not to have all the information, but he hoped and prayed that the data he was downloading would clear her father.

Her uncles were going to jail. Hopefully.

And possibly Senator Carlsman too. Although there was something about the senator that Mo still hadn't been able to sort out.

Carlsman had paid, and paid dearly, for almost fifteen years. Mo couldn't prove it yet, but he was almost certain that the senator was still paying, although in a different way. Once upon a time Carlsman had been a partner in the law firm representing Steven Pierce.

On paper, that affiliation no longer existed. But no senator running for president had ever let go of a potentially profitable alliance.

THIRTY-SEVEN

Mo checked the status of the download. "Almost there."

"Maybe this is my total lack of computer knowledge at work, but I thought this would go . . . faster."

Mo could tell Bronwyn was trying to be nice. And she had succeeded. For the most part.

"If I knew exactly what I was looking for, I could have downloaded less. Instead, I'm downloading a lot of information, most of which I don't need, but it's more efficient to do it this way. Tonight, my computer programs will filter it out. In the morning, we should have some shiny answers waiting for us."

He glanced at the computer. Another minute. "Almost there."

"Then what?"

"Then we go back to your house and pack your bags."

"I thought you had to stay on-site for this kind of work."

"I did while we were being covert," he said. "You've hired me. We're all out in the open now. Everyone knows what I'm doing, and I'm obligated to protect your interests."

"Mo?"

"Yeah."

"You haven't signed anything."

"Sure I have."

"When?"

"This afternoon. I printed out my standard contract. It's signed."

"Do you think of everything?" She sounded impressed.

"No. I don't. And I'm sure you'll figure that out soon enough." The laptop chimed, and he disconnected it from the server. "Got it. Let's—"

A piercing shriek filled the room. Light flashed all around them.

Bronwyn covered her ears and bent in half. "What's going on?"

He yelled into her ear, "Fire suppression system. Come on! We need to get out of here!"

If this system was like most, they had anywhere from fifteen to thirty seconds to vacate the room before it filled with a gas designed to extinguish fire without damaging electronics.

No one would put this much money and effort into their servers just to see them destroyed by sprinklers. He and Bronwyn weren't about to get wet. But they might be about to breathe in some very unpleasant chemicals. Some of the systems on the market were better than others. Some even claimed to be safe for humans, but Mo didn't care to test that theory. He'd had some experience with tear gas. This wasn't the same, but if he could spare Bronw—

"Mo!" She tugged on his arm. "There's no way this is an accident. Stop! If we run out that door, who knows what's waiting for us."

Mo froze. He'd been so focused on getting her out, he hadn't stopped to think about what had put them in this situation.

He pulled her to the far corner of the room and then draped his body over hers with no time to spare. The system activated, and the sound of high-pressure gas releasing filled the room for ten seconds.

When it was over, Mo had the disturbing sense that they were no longer alone. The room remained dimly lit from the emergency lights and, thankfully, the alarms had stopped shrieking. But had someone used the noise to break in? Mo held one finger to his lips, and Bronwyn nodded that she understood. He handed her the laptop and retrieved his weapon from his waist.

He took precious seconds to consider and discard options. He had no idea who was in the room with them. Was someone waiting outside? What were their motives? Were they here to destroy data or lives?

"This would have been so much easier if you'd just gone to dinner with me, Ms. Pierce."

The voice was familiar. Where did he know that voice?

Bronwyn pulled her phone from her back pocket and typed. She held the phone up so he could see the text she'd sent to Gray.

> Bob's at Haven. Armed. Server room. Mo's with me. Call me and I'll put you on speaker. Do not make any noise.

Bob had been interested in far more than dinner, after all.

A second passed, then a thumbs-up emoji flashed on the text thread. When the incoming call from Gray popped up, she answered it and put the audio on speaker. She held the phone, then closed her eyes. Her lips moved in what he assumed was a silent prayer. He was glad she'd come up with something because he didn't even know what to pray for.

He had few options for how to proceed, but none of them were great. He went with his best guess. "What's your end goal?" he called out into the now eerily silent room. Then he motioned for Bronwyn, and they moved as quietly as possible toward the opposite corner.

"Ah, Mr. Quinn, is it? Come now. I know you and Ms. Pierce

are in here. No reason to hide. I'm not here to kill you. I just want to chat."

Mo didn't need words to translate Bronwyn's look. Her face said "does he think we're stupid" loud and clear. He agreed.

They moved away from the voice.

"I know, I know. You don't believe me," Bob went on. "But I feel sure we can come to some sort of mutually beneficial arrangement. I have information you need. And you have something I want."

Mo and Bronwyn continued to move as quietly as possible. Based on his voice, Bob had almost reached the spot they'd been when this all started. They weren't far from the door. Did they dare exit the room?

Who was the greater enemy? Bob on the inside? Or whatever—or whoever—waited on the outside?

It was possible that Bob was alone and if they left the room, they could make a run for it.

Or they could run straight to their death.

"I can see you aren't the chatty type." Bob tsked in what sounded like fake disappointment. "Fine. I'll start. I'm here because my employer is convinced that the person blackmailing her father is none other than one Bronwyn Pierce." A pause. "Oops. Did I say that out loud? I guess I did. My bad."

Bronwyn looked as mystified as Mo felt.

Her father? Did that mean Bob was employed by Senator Carlsman's daughter? Why?

"Really, Ms. Pierce, you should have Mr. Quinn completely revamp your computer security. It wasn't difficult to pay off a few people to hack into your files. And, as I'm sure he has informed you, it does look like you've been milking the dear old senator out of large sums of cash for a very long time. My employer was convinced it was you, and she wanted you . . . well . . . let's say, out of the picture. I've always liked that phrase. I mean, it's not so bad, being out of the picture."

A scuffle of feet, and Mo and Bronwyn moved again.

The next time he spoke, Bob was in a different place in the room. "This is becoming tedious. Here's the problem. I'm not just hired muscle. I have a brain. And while it looked like you had been blackmailing Carlsman for a while, Ms. Pierce, this latest move just didn't make sense to me." Bob clearly had some things to get off his chest. "I mean, don't get me wrong. No one could blame you for wanting him to pay through the nose. Teenage pride is a fragile thing. I'm sure his brother made you think you were so special and then he left you to fend for yourself. And why? So he could do research for a film? He was a horrible person. A definite bad apple."

There was something very unhinged about this guy.

"But why would you try to protect your cousin? Talk about a bad apple. It doesn't fit your profile at all. And, believe me, you have a profile. I worked on it for a long time. And this play? It doesn't fit."

The next sound was unmistakable. He'd popped the clip out of a gun and then popped it back in.

"This clip holds fifteen rounds. There's no way you get out of here. I know it. You know it. But I can make sure you go fast. No pain. No drama. I swear. You won't even know it happened. All you have to do is tell me who is behind the blackmail. Because I promise you, they're going down too."

Mo didn't think Bob was joking around. If Mo started firing, he might be able to take Bob out. Or they could both die.

He looked to the exit.

"Oh, and don't bother trying to leave. I left a present on the door. The next person to open it will lose a hand, at the least. Maybe more."

Well, that certainly limited their options.

Bronwyn glanced at her watch, then showed it to Mo. There was a text from Gray.

Keep him talking. Marcus is outside the room.
I've told him not to open the door.

"You really aren't giving us much of an incentive to help you." Mo shoved Bronwyn down the row of servers and plastered them against the end of the row. Even if Bob started shooting, he wouldn't have the right angle to hit them. He'd have to come around the corner or down the aisle, and Mo would have a chance to take him out.

Bob chuckled. "Yeah. Stinks to be you. Look, I know it's cliche and all, but I really don't have anything against you personally. You seem like good people. But I have a job to do."

Bronwyn's body trembled against Mo, but when she spoke, her words were clear. "You said you know it isn't me. Why do you need to kill us? Why go through all this?"

"Ah, Bronwyn. Can I call you Bronwyn? The thing is, you know too much. Simple as that."

Mo had his body pressed against Bronwyn's. He covered as much of her as possible. When Bob made his move, Mo would open fire. He'd never shot a person before. Didn't want to do it now. But he'd die to protect Bronwyn.

He shifted his grip on his weapon, leaned toward Bronwyn, and breathed the words into her ear. "I love you. Forever."

Bronwyn looked into Mo's eyes and mouthed, "I love you."

Shots rang out. From where she stood, her back to the frame of the server, she couldn't tell where Bob was. Mo leaned toward her right and fired three times.

And then the ceiling collapsed all around them. Something hit her hard on the shoulder. Mo went down. She grabbed him around the waist and went down with him.

Another shot.

Then lots of yelling. "Clear! Clear!"

"Mo! Bronwyn!" Gray's voice came through the cacophony. She tried to move, but the motion jerked a scream from her throat as agony pulsed down her arm.

"Over here!" Gray stood over her. "Bronwyn. Let me have Mo. Come on. You need to turn him loose." Gray sounded . . . wrong.

"Mo?" The question rasped from her throat. Blood. So much blood. Was it his? Hers? "Mo!"

Then Cal was there and he was rolling Mo off her body. She fought through the pain in her arm and made it to her knees. Mo lay beside her.

Breathing. He was breathing. Oh, thank you, Jesus, he was breathing.

His eyes opened, wild with terror.

"I'm here. I'm here." She fell across his chest. "Mo?"

"Love you." The words were slurred.

"Love you more."

"You're bleeding." His eyes were on her arm.

"I'm sure it's just a scratch." Bronwyn ignored Mo's muttering and lay across his chest. She rode the steady rise and fall of his breathing until he started yelling for someone to come get her to a doctor.

"Calm down, man," Cal said. "I can see the cut. It's probably going to need stitches, but she's not going to die. Mom will be here in a few minutes."

Cal helped her to her feet and pressed what looked like someone's shirt to her arm. She hissed, and Mo nearly levitated off the floor as he tried to get to his feet.

"I'm fine." She bit back a cry when Cal shifted to help Mo up.

Mo put an arm around her, and Cal helped them both maneuver down the hall and eventually onto a small sofa outside the security office.

She snuggled against Mo, and he held her hand on her good arm while she tried very hard not to think about Bob's very dead body lying in the server room.

Cal stood sentry in front of her and Mo, and no one was allowed to approach until Doug and Jacque, both in pajamas, came through the door. They ran to where she and Mo rested and then knelt beside the sofa. Mo pulled his mom into a hug and held her close. When he released her, she went to Bronwyn's other side and settled in beside her, careful to avoid her wound.

Doug rested a hand on Bronwyn's knee. "Sweetheart, we need to tell you something."

Mo must have heard the same thing in his tone that she did because his hold on her tightened. "What is it?"

Doug looked at the floor, then back to Bronwyn. "I don't have all the details, but there was a confrontation at your grandmother's house tonight. Your dad's on his way to the hospital in Asheville. Your mother's with him. Your uncle Ronald didn't make it. Your uncle William and a reporter are en route to the police station for questioning."

Bronwyn heard the words, but they didn't make sense. Uncle Ronald was dead? Her dad was on his way to the hospital? That was all bad, but she got the feeling there was more. "What else happened?"

Jacque scooted closer and rested her hand on top of Doug's.

"Sebastian was injured, but he was able to tell Donovan that a reporter came in and made some accusations about blackmail and that your grandmother somehow got caught up in the fight. I'm sorry, but your grandmother didn't make it."

"Grandmother?" Bronwyn dropped her head to Mo's shoulder.

"I'm so sorry." Doug squeezed her knee. "You are not alone, darling. No matter what."

Jacque laced her fingers through Doug's. "You are so loved, sweet girl. So loved. We'll be here. We'll help you through this."

THIRTY-EIGHT

The next twenty-four hours went by in a blur. Mo's mom and dad went with him and Bronwyn to the hospital while Cal stayed in Gossamer Falls to support Gray. Meredith stayed at The Haven with Landry and Cassie to keep the guests as much in the dark as possible.

Bronwyn had eight stitches in her arm, and her shoulder had already turned a nice shade of "oh my word, what happened to you." Aunt Carol assured her it would get worse before it got better, but that it would get better.

Mo had just had the breath knocked out of him. No concussion or head injury. And nothing to keep him from digging into every piece of evidence he could get his hands on.

But he wasn't touching it. Sabrina was all over it and had decided to make the blackmail/money laundering hunt a "fun" project for her students at UNC–Carrington. She was grudgingly impressed by the way the Carlsmans had managed to hide their connection to Corbin and Glen Masters. She'd found the smoking gun they needed to prove everything in court. But she was upset that it had taken so long to find and that she hadn't been able to prevent the deaths of Bronwyn's grandmother and uncle. She'd be coming to The Haven in a few weeks to oversee the installation of new systems that would be secure and cutting edge.

A tiny part of Mo wanted to see the job through to the end, but Bronwyn didn't need him to be a forensic accountant. She needed him to be . . . hers. And while he was gutted that she was hurting the way she was, he was ecstatic to be with her.

Tonight, they'd gathered in his parents' living room. He and Bronwyn were in an oversized chair. Gray and Meredith were in the love seat. Landry was in his dad's recliner with her feet up. Cassie had moved dinner reservations around and then left her kitchen in the hands of her sous chef. She'd brought food for everyone and now she and Donovan sat in chairs they'd dragged from the dining room.

His mom was in her recliner, while his dad and Cal sat on the hearth of the fireplace.

The room was filled with people he loved. And filled with people who loved Bronwyn. And that's what she needed, because tonight's conversation was going to hurt.

Gray leaned forward. "I've already spoken to Bronwyn, and she agreed that it would be good for all of us to be on the same page so we can move forward without any confusion."

Meredith rolled her eyes. "What he means is he wants us all to know the facts so we can shut down the gossip."

Gray grinned at his fiancée. "That too." He turned to Bronwyn, and Mo felt more than saw her nod her head at him.

"It's okay, Gray. I want it all out. No secrets."

Gray rubbed his forehead. "Short and to the point, then."

Meredith squeezed his hand and Gray began. "When Corbin groomed and seduced Bronwyn years ago, no one here knew that he was the younger brother of an up-and-coming then-congressman from Illinois. Now senator, then-congressman Clayton Carlsman had distanced himself from his brother Corbin, but he kept tabs on him. When Corbin pulled that stunt with Bronwyn, the Pierce family did some digging, and as far as we can tell, Ronald Pierce made the connection to Carlsman. Ronald told William, but they agreed not to tell Bronwyn's father, Darrell." Gray glanced around the room. "It's too soon yet to say for sure, but there's no evidence at the moment that Bronwyn's parents knew about any of the blackmail."

"So, they're horrible people, but they didn't profit from what happened to Bronwyn. Does that sum it up?" Cal asked.

"Pretty much." Gray nodded. "As far as I can tell, Darrell and Lacey have always been about social climbing, status, and influence. They left Bronwyn on her own because it worked for their purposes. But Ronald and William kept them out of the blackmail scheme. From what we've been able to piece together, they didn't think Darrell and Lacey would be okay with taking blackmail money."

"I interviewed William," Donovan said, lacing his fingers through Cassie's. "That man is a piece of work. He claimed that Ronald was the one behind taking the blackmail to a new level. I'm not sure if I believe him. It's too soon to say. Either way, Corbin was a thorn in Clayton's side and his death was not an accident. Peter Brown killed him."

Bronwyn cuddled into Mo's side as the others in the room reacted to Donovan's revelation.

"Allegedly." Gray held up a hand. "He didn't confess to it."

"You didn't expect him to, did you?" Bronwyn asked.

"No. But it would have made things a lot easier. Anyway, now we're veering into a bit of speculation, but we think William took the news of Corbin's death, put two and two together, and came up with a way to make even more money. The blackmail cranked up after Corbin's death, and as far as we can tell, Nathan was brought into the scheme shortly after he returned from Europe. He's the one who started laundering the funds through The Haven's books, which is why there was no money trail until five years ago."

"Then Steven happened last year." Cassie's usually bubbly voice was sharp. "I hope this means he's going to serve the jail time he deserves."

Donovan pressed a kiss to his wife's head. "We would have made sure of that regardless, but yeah, baby. He's going down."

Gray pointed to Cassie. "When Steven was arrested, Steven and his mother pushed William and Ronald to use their influence with the senator. And yes, that means judicial tampering. But no, we don't have proof, and we might not ever have it. But the judicial tampering is over, and the money is no longer flowing, and I anticipate that Steven will be going to trial sooner rather than later."

"But what drove these men to come to The Haven and attack Bronwyn and the family?" Mo's mom asked.

"That's where it gets . . . extra interesting. Glen Masters, aka Peter Brown, aka a bunch of other names, has proven to be a wealth of information. He knows the Carlsmans will throw him under the bus, and he has information that he's convinced will help him cut a deal."

"Is he right? Will they cut him a deal?" Cassie asked.

"Probably." Gray sighed. "That man is so dirty, it's hard to be in the same room with him without feeling like you're being slimed. But, thanks to the involvement of a US Senator from a different state, the Feds have already taken over the entire case. I could have fought to keep it here," Gray said, giving Bronwyn an apologetic look, "but our force is small. We don't have the investigative power needed for a major case. And my entire department has a conflict of interest. We have friends and family who work at The Haven. And a bunch of us are related to you by marriage, or, well, we will be."

Cal and Donovan both let out whoops. "That's what I'm talking about." Meredith gave Gray a fist bump.

Mo squeezed Bronwyn closer and prayed they weren't wrong.

Bronwyn spoke once the laughter died down. "Gray, please tell me you don't feel conflicted about handing the case to the Feds. It was the right call. Your job is to take care of Gossamer Falls. Let the Feds deal with senators and creepy hitmen."

"I'm glad you feel that way because proving the facts of this case is going to be a headache." Gray shook his head. "From what Bob told you and Peter Brown told us, Senator Carlsman's daughter, Scarlett, learned about the blackmail. Then she took it upon herself to dig to the bottom of it."

"And when she went digging, she found everything that had been planted to make it look like Bronwyn was the blackmailer?" Meredith didn't wait for an answer. "And then she decided to get rid of her?"

"Pretty much. Scarlett Carlsman seems to be cut from the same cloth as her uncle, and she decided the best way to make it all go away was to take out Bronwyn."

Mo couldn't help the frustrated sound he made at Gray's words. "And that's where Bob comes into the picture."

"I thought he was some bigwig guest's security." Meredith shook her head. "This stuff is making my head hurt."

"Mine too." Gray rubbed his temples. "Bob claimed to be security, but that was an excuse to get onto The Haven's grounds. Bob had been digging into Bronwyn and the files from The Haven for a while. Scarlett wanted him to stop the blackmail by killing Bronwyn. But when Mo started poking around, things got too hot for Bob to take her out the way he'd planned. As far as we can tell, Bob's the one who took out the transformer. He's also the one who shot at Mo and Bronwyn in the parking lot."

"If Bob did all that, what was Peter Brown doing here?" Mo's dad asked.

"Excellent question," Gray said. "Please keep in mind that this is all from Peter's confession, so take it with a grain of salt. He claims he didn't know about Bob. He was here because Carlsman got tired of being extorted. Unlike Scarlett, the senator knew who was behind the blackmail. He wanted William dead, and if possible he wanted Ronald and Nathan gone as well.

"But he hadn't been working on it for six months like Scarlett had. Carlsman sent Brown in to get the lay of the land and to take out William if the opportunity presented itself. He was never a threat to Bronwyn directly. The threat to Bronwyn was Bob. But the threat to William, Nathan, and Ronald was always Peter Brown. Peter decided to use the hubbub to take all three out. And he almost succeeded."

Mo's dad turned to Donovan. "How did you know things were going down at Bronwyn's grandmother's house?"

"Brick had been stationed outside the grounds. He saw the Pierces leave and didn't like the look of things, so he followed them over there. When things got heated, he called me. We were a minute out when the knives came out and guns were drawn." Donovan turned to Bronwyn. "I wish we could have stopped it. I really do."

Mo would have given anything to spare Bronwyn this pain. Bronwyn's dad was in critical condition in the hospital and might lose the use of one eye. But all Mo could do was be by her side as she navigated everything coming her way.

"I know. I'm glad you got there when you did," Bronwyn said. "Not that I plan to have much to do with any of my relatives anyway, but it's good we have a better idea of what happened."

Mo spoke up then. "I still don't have a good handle on how you came through the ceiling, Gray. Bullets started flying and next thing I know, you and Cal were coming through like superheroes." Cal and Gray high-fived. "Seriously, though. I'm thankful. I don't know if I could have stopped him before he killed both of us. Your timing was impeccable."

"We were nearby." Cal shrugged. "When Bronwyn texted Gray, we came through the gates in a hurry. Marcus was all over it. He's a good man, Bronwyn."

She smiled. "He's about to receive a big promotion. He's always been the best, but he was out for over a year with cancer treatments and things really fell apart without him. I have no doubt he'll whip our security staff into shape in no time."

Cal grinned. "That's great news. He's the one who told us the ceiling was accessible. Said he'd pointed it out as a possible security issue when that room was installed, but his concern was overridden."

"It sure came in handy yesterday." Mo rubbed the back of his head. "Although getting flattened by that much ceiling definitely wasn't on my bingo card for this year."

"I'll take cuts and bruises from the ceiling over bullets any day." Bronwyn rested her head on his chest.

Gray clapped his hands. "That's pretty much the whole story. Greed, corruption, blackmail, money laundering, murder, attempted murder, judicial interference . . . it's a laundry list of crimes. But I do believe the guilty will be prosecuted and the innocent will finally be free to live their lives."

Mo's dad stood. "I couldn't be prouder of the whole bunch of you. I know only two of you are mine by birth and two of you are blood, but Jacque and I have claimed all of you. Sons, daughters, nieces and nephews, cousins, whatever. It doesn't matter. You're all Quinns at heart."

EPILOGUE

THREE MONTHS LATER

Mo took Bronwyn's hand as they hiked the last hundred feet to Catherine's Falls. The leaves had started to turn, and the early fall day was crisp and cool under the forest canopy. The ground was damp from last week's rain, and everything smelled earthy and clean.

They didn't speak as they scrambled onto their rock and sat.

Bronwyn pulled her camera out of her bag and took a few shots of the waterfall. She had photos of Catherine's Falls in every season, and she couldn't choose a favorite. Each one was unique.

Beside her, Mo pulled out a travel set of Chinese checkers and set it between them. Their game on her office wall had been moving forward, one play at a time, for months. Anytime he was at her house, he made one move. She always followed his moves with one of her own. She hadn't told him, but she was almost certain that she would win, mainly because she'd made it a point to distract him with kisses before he could take his turn. Her strategy was working.

Although now that she thought about it, she had to wonder if letting her seduce him was part of his strategy. It wasn't like he was suffering through it.

Today, they played on the tiny board while the waterfall crashed around them. She employed her kissing strategy and won three games straight before Mo conceded and packed the game away.

The light was fading, and they would need to go back soon. Back to The Haven where nothing was the same, which was a good thing for the most part. She'd made several strategic promotions, hires, and fires in the weeks after the attacks. Her staff had never been happier. Her guests had never been as well cared for.

And she had never had so much free time.

It was still a work in progress, but it was coming along.

She hadn't spoken to her parents in a month. Her dad lost his left eye, and somehow, her mom had blamed Bronwyn for it.

Her grandmother's will had been altered in one significant point, and it probably would have made everyone angry, except that with her father's injuries, William's and Nathan's arrests, and Ronald's death, no one had the heart to argue.

Grandmother had left The Haven to her.

The board was no more.

The Haven was hers to do with as she chose, and the responsibility was a heady one. She felt honored, humbled, and a little bit panicky about it. Still, she was determined to give it her all and move The Haven into the future in a way that protected Gossamer Falls, the rest of the Pierce family, the Quinn family, and the guests who loved to visit.

Mo pulled her close. "You're thinking deep thoughts. Everything okay?"

"Yeah." And it was. It wasn't perfect, but it was good.

"I've been thinking." Mo ran his hands over her arms.

"About?"

"You." He kissed her nose. "Us." He kissed her chin. "The

future." This time, his kiss stole her breath and left her a little dizzy. "Marry me, Bronwyn. Please."

She looked down and saw a diamond glittering in his palm. "On one condition."

He raised an eyebrow. "Let's hear it."

"I don't want a big wedding. I don't want anything fancy. And I do not want to wait."

"Deal."

Bronwyn practically crawled into his lap as he slid the ring on her finger. She kissed him with all the hope and joy and love in her heart, and there was a lot of it. When they came up for air, Mo tucked a strand of hair behind her ear. "I don't want to wait either, but we can't elope. Mom would strangle us."

"I don't want to elope. Uncle John can marry us. We need a license and we need family. That's it. That's all I want." She grinned. "Well, that and a honeymoon. I want you all to myself. No phones. No computers. No distractions."

"Give me two weeks."

TWO WEEKS LATER

Mo couldn't believe this day was here. Bronwyn stood beside him. A vision in white. Their family stood loosely around them in Papa and Granny Quinn's yard.

Uncle John, Cassie's dad, had given them a pass on his usual six-month premarital counseling requirements. "Known you two would be getting married since you were ten. Never dreamed it would take you this long. Honored to be the one to make it official."

The vows had been said.

The rings exchanged.

They faced each other and Bronwyn's smile told him he'd gotten it right. He'd do anything to keep that smile on her face.

Uncle John stepped to the side and grinned as he said, "Mo, you may finally kiss your bride."

And he did.

READ ON FOR A SNEAK PEEK
AT THE FIRST BOOK IN THE

EVERETT HOLLOW
SERIES

COMING SOON

The screen door entrance to the Laurel Trading Post needed another healthy dose of WD-40. The screech it made as Adeline Day pulled it open could have been heard all the way in Raleigh.

"Get that door closed, Daisy." Verna's voice had a raspy edge. "The bugs are feisty this morning."

"Good morning to you too." Adeline gave the door a little kick at the bottom. It took two more kicks, each harder than the last, before it was finally snug in the frame. "It's sticking again."

"Don't I know it." Verna Everett, the owner, operator, and opinion manager of the LTP came around the corner. Her long, graying hair was in its customary single braid. She peered at Adeline through her reading glasses, purple today, perched on the end of her nose. "Chief Delgado is on my case to get those infernal automatic glass doors. Says they'd be more secure."

Chief Delgado had to know he was fighting a losing battle there. And while Adeline agreed with him, she would probably cry if Verna ever replaced the creaky screen door.

Verna frowned and shook her head before she gave Adeline a shrug that said, "What can you do?" and returned to her spot behind the coffee bar. "You're out and about early today. I thought it was your day off."

"So did I." Adeline pointed to the display case. "I'll take an orange cranberry scone and an iced Americano. Large."

Verna sucked in a breath. "That's your third 'today is going to be rough' order this week."

Adeline perched on a stool as Verna got to work on her coffee. "It *has* been a rough week but today will be better."

"Hard to understand how it will be better when you're headed to work on your day off. What was it you said yesterday?" Verna tapped a finger to her chin. "Oh yes. I believe it was, 'The only thing that's going to get me through this day is knowing that tomorrow I can sleep late and stay in my pajamas.'"

Adeline couldn't stop the small groan of longing that escaped her. "I was looking forward to that, but two of my staff have a stomach bug. Dr. Shaw says it's going around."

Verna was right though. She wasn't nearly as annoyed about going into work today as she should have been. As the head housekeeper at The Haven, an exclusive mountain resort where the rich, famous, and influential came to unwind and relax away from the paparazzi and whirlwind of their normal lives, Adeline was responsible for the cleanliness of every cabin on the property, and her standards were high. Especially when there was a virus running amok.

"Hang on. I've got some muffins fresh out of the oven in back. They're better than the scones."

Verna disappeared through the swinging doors, and Adeline glanced at this morning's text thread with her best friend, June, the executive assistant to the CEO of The Haven.

You won't believe this. Two more are down for the count. Sick all night. Looks like I'll be working today after all.

I'm sorry. That really stinks. But I have some news that might make things a bit less painful.

Don't leave me in suspense.

Sorry. That blasted cat was squalling at the door. I had to feed her.

This would be the cat you claim not to own but that you've bought a small house for and placed on your back deck?

Do you want to know or not?

Sorry.

The Sterlings are checking in a week early. They'll be in Dogwood starting tonight. And they're booked for three weeks.

Seriously?

Seriously.

The Lord knew I needed that!

I thought you might see it that way.

The Sterlings would be a balm after the stress of the past week. Adeline wasn't the only one who loved it when they came, and it wasn't just because Nathaniel Sterling tipped better than most. It was because they were easy guests. Pleasant, undemanding, and genuinely kind.

"I know you can't give me details, but did you get everything sorted?" Verna set the muffin on a plate in front of Adeline, then returned to the counter for the iced coffee.

Adeline peeled the paper away from the muffin and took a bite. Verna had been right. It was better than a scone. She'd swallowed her second bite when Verna slid the coffee toward her. She took a sip as soon as it was in her hands and thought maybe she really could make it through the day. In anticipation of sleeping in and having a pajama day, she'd stayed up until two a.m. reading the final pages in a five-book series. Would she ever learn?

Probably not.

Verna stood waiting, her fingers tapping on her crossed arms.

"I'm not sure if it's resolved or not." Adeline couldn't tell Verna any of the details. She couldn't explain how Celeste Thorne, a name even Verna would recognize, had threatened her with lawsuits and jail time. But Bronwyn Pierce Quinn, the CEO of The Haven, had reminded her last night that while it was their job to keep guests happy, that didn't include putting up with abusive language and behaviors. "We had a very difficult guest." Adeline forced her hands to relax on the cup before she squeezed it too hard and made a mess everywhere. "They aren't my problem anymore."

But Celeste *was* Bronwyn's problem. Adeline would have felt worse about that a year ago, but these days Bronwyn smiled and laughed and glowed like the woman in love that she was. And her husband, Mo, wouldn't put up with anyone making Bronwyn's life difficult. They were so happy it almost hurt to see them together.

"That's great, but it doesn't explain why you seem almost excited to go to work." Verna narrowed her eyes and studied Adeline. "Your makeup game is strong today." She patted her own head. "And I like what you've done with your hair."

Adeline grinned. She'd piled her mass of often unruly red curls into a loose bun with a few tendrils left free to float around her face. She usually wore her hair down, but it was unseasonably warm this week. And today, instead of being in her office, inspecting the rooms, and handling concerns, she'd be actively cleaning.

"It suits you." Verna's grin was sly. "Makes you look more grown up, more like an Adeline and less like a Daisy." Verna had overheard June call her by her childhood nickname and had refused to call her anything else ever since. "But what I don't understand is why you've put in the effort. You don't usually doll up quite so much for work. Trying to impress someone?"

Verna was too observant for her own good. No one else would have noticed or paid any attention. "I just wanted to look my best." Which was true. "They say that when you're tired, it's even more important to appear put together. It tricks the brain into thinking you're good to go, even when all you want to do is go to sleep." Also true.

Adeline refused to say more. Verna was a great sounding board, even if she was a hopeless romantic. But Adeline's nondisclosure agreement prohibited her from confirming the presence of guests at The Haven. And even if she could talk about the Sterlings, she wouldn't. Not that there was even anything to tell. Nothing had ever happened. Nothing ever would. There were rules about fraternizing with the guests, and no man had ever been worth risking her job over.

Although . . . this one might be.

No. Her infatuation was entirely one-sided. He was kind to everyone. He had a way of charming people that she'd seen work on the grouchiest gardener and the most glamorous socialite. So when he turned that charismatic energy toward her, she knew it didn't mean she was anyone special. That's just how he was.

"Sure. Sure." Verna's agreement came with narrowed eyes and a speculative gaze.

Verna believed she had two callings in life. One was to keep the residents of their small town caffeinated, fed, and generally provided for. The LTP had everything from a real espresso machine to gas pumps. You could pop in for a muffin, a sandwich, or a dessert, and while you were there, you could grab some pain relievers and dog food.

In a town like Jamison Gap, tucked away in the mountains of North Carolina, a good general store was a gift. And Verna had made her store into a modern-day watering hole. This helped her to fulfill her second calling.

Verna was a relentless matchmaker.

And Adeline Day was her current project.

Verna sniffed. "That's fine. Don't tell me. But a word to the wise, young lady. Falling for one of those hoity-toity types at The Haven would be a bad idea."

Adeline was saved the need to respond by the arrival of Police Chief Carlos Delgado. He nodded in her direction, ordered his coffee, and chatted with Verna while Adeline finished her muffin.

They were still talking as Adeline stood, tossed her trash, and grabbed her coffee. "Sorry to interrupt, but I have to run. Put it on my tab, please. I'll pay up tomorrow."

"Adeline, before you go," Carlos held up a hand and she paused. "I came home later than usual last night and noticed a truck I didn't recognize driving up and down the road."

Carlos, like Adeline, lived on Everett Hollow Trail, a long, winding road that dead-ended at the old Everett homeplace.

The memory of Celeste Thorne, her face mottled in anger as she promised that she would prove Adeline had stolen from her, replayed in Adeline's mind. The memory brought with it a cold finger of anxiety that started somewhere around Adeline's ears and trickled down her neck and across her chest until it settled into an uncomfortable knot in her stomach.

Worry must have shown on her face because Carlos grimaced. "I'm not trying to scare you. It could be nothing. But I've learned to trust my gut, and I didn't like the way it looked. It's probably just some kids looking for a spot to get up to no good. But make sure your doors are locked and stay alert."

"I will. Thanks."

She nodded at Carlos and Verna.

Verna came around the counter and gave Adeline a quick hug. "Remember what I said, young lady."

"Yes, ma'am." Adeline remembered both Carlos and Verna's warnings all the way into Gossamer Falls, through the gates of The Haven, and all morning as she cleaned a few cabins and helped refresh a few others while guests were at meals or enjoying the amenities.

And then she walked into the Dogwood cabin and forgot, because in a few short hours, tech billionaire Nathaniel Sterling and his daughter, Piper, would arrive.

They thought she took such good care of them because she was good at her job, but she knew it was something more. What harm was there in having a secret crush? It hurt no one . . . except herself.

ACKNOWLEDGMENTS

No one ever writes a book on their own. My eternal gratitude to:

Brian, Emma, James, and Drew—for reminding me every day how wonderful families can be.

Jennifer—for being the gold standard for sisters everywhere.

Mom, Dad, and Sandra—for crushing it as grandparents and making so many things possible for our family.

Sara, Alison, Dianna, Brennan, Joelle, Erica, and Ginger—for friendship that makes my life so much better than if I tried to muddle through alone.

Deborah and Debb—for bringing the sweetness and the snark to every situation.

Lynette—for writing with me in all sorts of places and never failing to commiserate when I'm questioning all my life choices.

Kelsey Bowen and Robin VanderWall—for the extraordinary effort you put into Mo and Bronwyn's story. Truly, this one took all of us!

The entire team at Revell—for championing these stories. You're the best!

My agent, Tamela Hancock Murray—for always looking out for me!

Most of all, to my savior, the Ultimate Storyteller—for allowing me to write stories for you.

> Let the words of my mouth and the meditation of my heart
> be acceptable in your sight,
> O LORD, my rock and my redeemer.
>
> Psalm 19:14 ESV

LYNN H. BLACKBURN is the bestselling and award-winning author of *Never Fall Again* and *Break My Fall*, as well as the Dive Team Investigations and Defend and Protect series. She loves writing swoonworthy Southern suspense because her childhood fantasy was to become a spy, but her grown-up reality is that she's a huge chicken and would have been caught on her first mission. She prefers to live vicariously through her characters by putting them into terrifying situations while she sits at home in her pajamas. She lives in Simpsonville, South Carolina, with her true love, Brian, and their three children. Learn more at LynnHBlackburn.com.

MEET LYNN

LYNNHBLACKBURN.COM

 LynnHBlackburn  LynnHBlackburn  LynnHBlackburn

A Note from the Publisher

Dear Reader,

Thank you for selecting a Revell novel! We're so happy to be part of your reading life through this work. Our mission here at Revell is to publish stories that reach the heart. Through friendship, romance, suspense, or a travel back in time, we bring stories that will entertain, inspire, and encourage you. We believe in the power of stories to change our lives and are grateful for the privilege of sharing these stories with you.

We believe in building lasting relationships with readers, and we'd love to get to know you better. If you have any feedback, questions, or just want to chat about your experience reading this book, please email us directly at publisher@revellbooks.com. Your insights are incredibly important to us, and it would be our pleasure to hear how we can better serve you.

We look forward to hearing from you and having the chance to enhance your experience with Revell Books.

The Publishing Team at Revell Books
A Division of Baker Publishing Group
publisher@revellbooks.com